Junkland

The Hoarding
Book One

Patrick Johns

Junkland
Text copyright © 2017
Patrick Johns

All rights are reserved. This work may not be reproduced in whole or in part in any form without permission from the author.

This is a work of fiction. Names, characters, places, events and incidents are either the products of the author's imagination or used in a fictitious manner. Any resemblance to actual persons, living or dead, or actual events is purely coincidental.

Editing: Katie Herring
Cover Illustration: Nele Diel
Cover Design: Steph Wulz

Special Thanks

To Katie Herring: for her time and commitment in editing my novel. Thank you for making my story come to life.

To Nele Diel: for her beautiful job on the cover art, making my world come to life visually.

To Steph Wulz: for her help formatting my cover design.

To Brandon Brown and Jen Dul: my informative beta readers.

To Drew Jenkinson: for his media expertise.

To Jake Kennelly, Jason Kraft, and John Jenkins: for their support and help with my writing and the shaping of my world.

To Granny and MomMom: for being the strongest women I know and to PopPop, for being the best storyteller there is.

To Chris, Matt, and Kevin: for being the best squad a brother could ask for.

To Mom and Dad: for all the dinosaurs and toys you bought me when I was a little tyke. Thanks for allowing me to spend countless hours in the worlds I imagined.

And to all the people who dream, believe, and pursue, thanks for showing me anything is possible.

*Thank you for showing me the importance of enjoying the simple things in life,
especially the people who are there for you in the end.
I love and miss you every day.*

This one is for you, Poppy.

TRUST:
> A STRENGTH THAT IS BUILT WITH TIME,
>> BUT CAN BE TAKEN AWAY,
>>> IN A BLINK OF AN EYE.

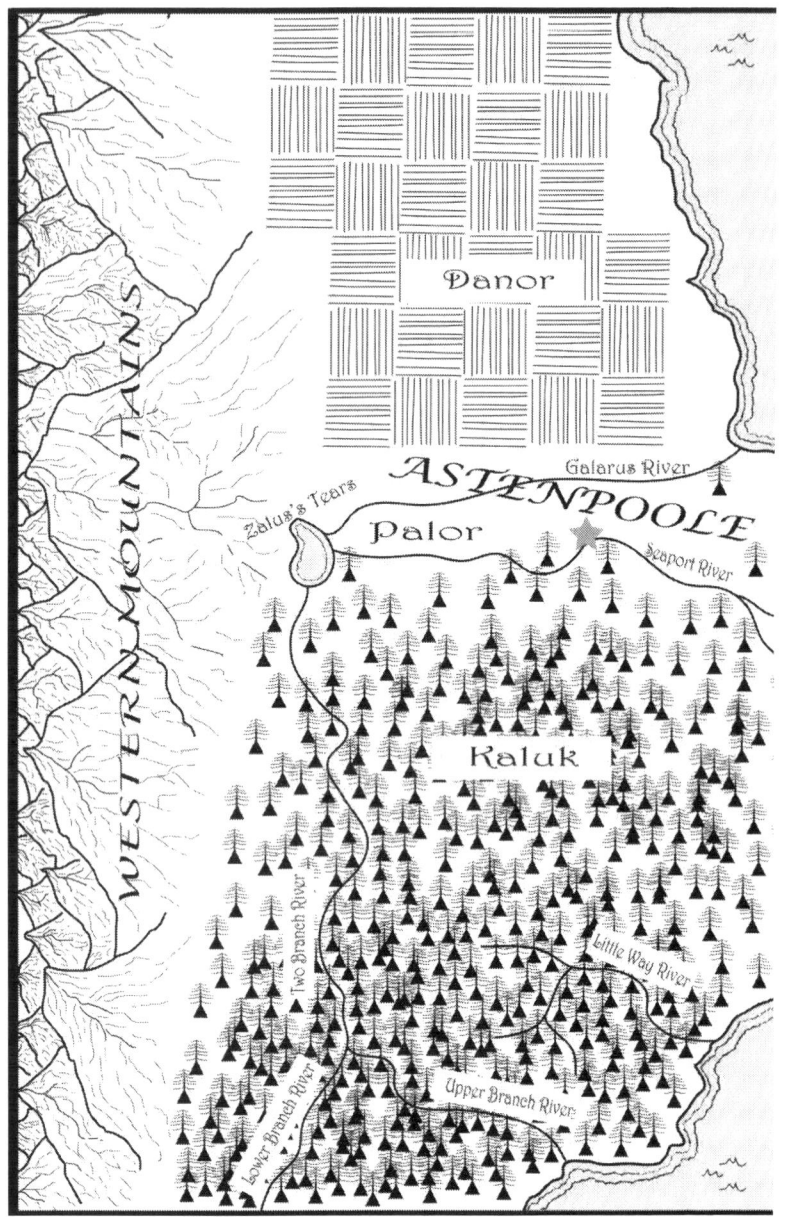

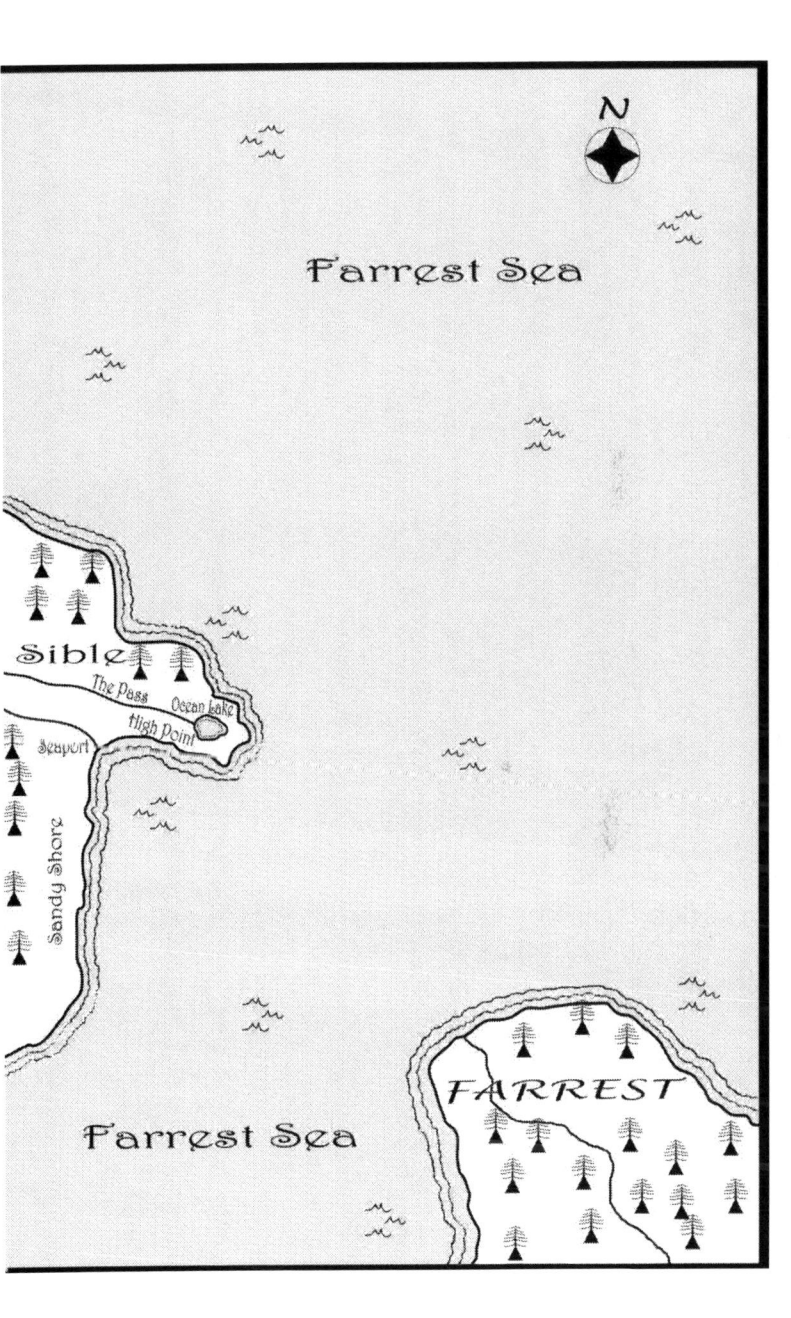

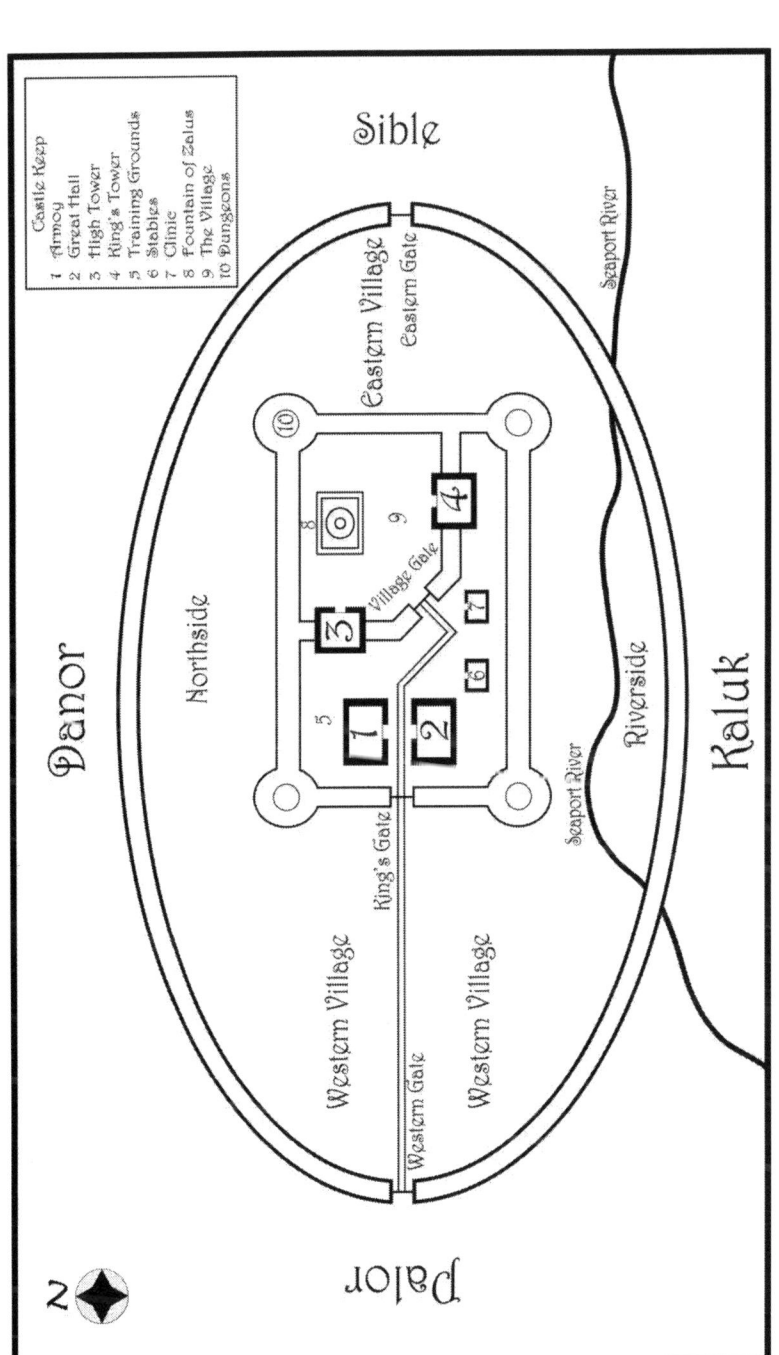

P r o l o g u e

THE SPHERE GLOWED a faint blue at the top of her staff; its energy was low, but she needed to keep running—she needed to make it to the mountains. The wind was howling in all directions and the trees danced and whistled in the night as if they were alive. The branches whipped violently through the thick, humid air. Thunder cracked above, releasing raindrops onto Partha's face.

She picked up her pace.

Partha's hair was blowing in a tangled mess, making it difficult to see in front of her. She didn't have a free hand to fix it, nor could she adjust the bag digging deep into her shoulders like razor sharp teeth. Her heart was racing in her chest as she moved one foot after the other; she had to keep moving.

Her baby was crying in her left arm, wrapped in a woolen blanket. She clutched him close to her chest as she clenched her staff tightly with her right hand.

She heard something whip past her on her right side, feeling the heat as it zipped by. A yellow blast collided into a tree five feet away, sending shards of wood dangerously close to her in the air. She ducked, pulling her cloak over her body to shield herself and her

Junkland

baby.

When the lightning lit up the sky, Partha took a quick glance over her shoulder. She saw the yellow glow from their suits among the dark green foliage. There were three of them chasing her.

She spun her head back around, wincing as a thin branch whipped across her cheek. She felt blood slide down her face—but she kept running. One foot after another, that was all that mattered; she couldn't be caught. Not until she knew her baby was safe, but in order to do that, she had to make it to the mountains.

Partha heard another blast echoing behind her. She covered her baby's head as she ducked behind a tree. The yellow blast blinded her as it exploded into the trunk of the tree, catching it on fire. The rain was falling harder now, but it wasn't enough to stop the quickly spreading fire throughout the forest.

A dense cloud of smoke covered her. Coughing profusely, she hunched over, staying as low to the forest floor as possible.

She saw a path through the smoke on her left and she decided to take it. It quickly became steep, and she had to hold her baby tighter so not to drop him. She ran down it and realized it opened up underneath a small cliff. She took cover underneath a rocky crevice. Leaning against the rock wall, she felt the scars on her back tug as she took deep breaths—in and out, in and out. The rain fell like a waterfall over the crevice making it hard to see, but she could hear the rustling of branches and heavy footsteps over her head.

Partha pulled her baby closer to her chest and glanced at the sphere at the top of her staff. She knew she could stop them in a heartbeat, but she had to save energy. She had to keep her promise to Ren. A tear rolled down her cheek as the horrible events flashed through her mind.

She had been lying in bed, worrying about her husband fighting in the war. Somehow, sleep had found her, but the crashing of a door woke her. Ren had been sprinting up the steps, yelling her name. Partha recalled the fear in his voice. Breathlessly, he had barged into their bedroom. He had tried to explain as best as he could: *she* was coming for their boy, and they had to get him far, far away. Ren had told her to run east, to the mountains, before…before…

The men's footsteps brought her back to reality. They were directly above her now, on top of the cliff, and the smoke was beginning to fade. If she stayed, they would soon discover her, but if she ran now…

She ran.

She kept her baby close to her chest as she sprinted out into the forest. Shouts from above told her they had spotted her. Partha heard the clicking of weapons and another blast zipped by her. The blast hit the ground by her feet. She went flying forward, crashing into a wet blanket of leaves on the forest floor. Her baby shrieked as he rolled out of her arms. Her staff was gone, too.

Her head was spinning from the explosion and her mind was going black. Her baby's cry sounded far and distant, almost hollow. She heard shouting from behind her, taking her out of the black fog surrounding her consciousness.

Thunder boomed over her head, and smoke and rain fogged her vision. A flash of lightning gave her enough light to locate her baby and her staff. They were both about ten feet away. Clawing at the loose dirt beneath her fingernails, she pushed herself forward with her legs. A root scraped her stomach, ripping her tunic. She stretched another hand forward and another, towards the cries of her baby and towards the blue sphere that was still glowing faintly through the smoke. She was almost there.

A blast hit the ground a foot away from her right hip.

Too close.

She picked up the pace. She recalled her husband's words as she pushed forward. *'Promise me you will save your energy. Promise me you will save it, Partha.'* Ren was right. She needed to save it for the long journey over the mountains. But what choice did she have? The men were almost on her, and she would soon be caught. She had to use it—only a little.

"I'm sorry, Ren," Partha whispered.

She dove forward, covering her baby from the blasts that stormed around her. She desperately reached her right hand out in front of her, towards her staff. Her fingers fell short—only inches away. She gritted her teeth, trying to stretch and close the distance. The blasts continued to storm around her. Her baby cried and wriggled beneath her. She stretched and stretched and stretched. Her arm was shaking uncontrollably. She let out a yell and reached a little bit farther, wrapping her fingers around her staff.

Partha rose to her knees, pointing the staff to the top of the trees. She closed her eyes, breathing in deeply. The air flowed down her throat to her stomach like a river before curving back up to her chest and then back out her mouth.

She felt the energy circulating within her. She felt it running from her heart, up through her arms, and into the sphere. She let her mind focus, letting the energy continue to flow through her. Every muscle in her body pulsed. A blue light shot out from the sphere enclosing her and her baby like a shield.

The three men crashed through the dense trees to where she was standing, but stopped abruptly.

"Where'd they go?" one of them asked.

"I don't know. I could've sworn they went this way!" another said.

"Do ya hear anything?" The third asked.

"No, I hear nothing." The first man pointed his Captor at where Partha was standing. "They were right here."

Partha held her breath, every muscle in her body aching.

The third man took a step forward. "Let's keep moving. The queen will not be happy if we let them get away."

The three men ran forward, creeping deeper into the forest.

Partha felt the energy fading. She held it for a little longer. She could not chance wasting it all, but she had to make sure the men were out of sight.

Partha watched the glow of their yellow suits disappear into the darkness. When their footsteps faded, she let go of the energy and let out a loud gasp. Every muscle in her body screamed. She brought the sphere down in front of her face. *I used too much*, she thought as she turned her gaze towards the mountains, and then down at her baby. She scooped him up.

"We're going to make it, little one. We are going to make it." She nuzzled her baby with her nose.

Partha continued running towards the mountains.

But now the sphere on her staff glowed an even fainter blue.

Part One

The Hoarding

Year 913 A.Z.

Chapter 1
Jahrys

JAHRYS GRENT DODGED a blow from his enemy. He was knocked off balance, but he found his ground and leapt forward, swinging his sword. A loud crack echoed throughout the forest as the two swords collided. Jahrys let out a grunt. He used all his strength to push his sword towards his enemy. The sweat poured into his eyes, causing them to burn, but Jahrys held his gaze. His heart was racing, and every beat sounded like an elephant's foot pounding the earth. His muscles were aching, but he continued to hold his sword.

His enemy broke the bond, and swung at Jahrys; it sounded like a whip slicing the air as the sword came down on him.

Jahrys rolled to the side, missing the blow by inches, as his enemy's sword smacked the ground. Fixing his feet, he steadied himself.

His enemy was on him again. This time he was swinging his sword left and right, left and right.

Jahrys parried the attacks as he stepped backwards. Each step had to be placed perfectly or else he would—

A root appeared out of nowhere. Jahrys stumbled, falling on his back. He let out a yell of pain. He tried to regain himself, but when he raised his head, a wooden sword was pointed directly at his heart.

"Looks like I win again," his best friend, Kevrin Danell, boasted. Playfully, he poked Jahrys with the point of it.

Jahrys flicked it away in frustration. "You got lucky this time."

"Isn't luck part of the game?" Kevrin asked, giving him a sly smile. He lowered his wooden sword and shot a hand out towards Jahrys.

Jahrys took it, and groaned on the way up. Pain shot through his lower back. "I think a stick dug into me."

"Maybe it will turn into a scar just like Sir Piller Lorne's to brag about," Kevrin laughed.

"No scar will ever look half as menacing as Sir Piller's. Have you seen it in person?" Jahrys asked, as he brushed the dirt off his back.

"I've only heard the stories," Kevrin said, as he walked over to his log to sit down and drink from his waterskin. "I heard on his first night in the Poolesguard he took out three men single-handedly to save a little girl, and when he was just eleven years old, he saved his father's shop from a crazy old fool who had tried to rob them!"

Jahrys walked over to his own log. He leaned his wooden sword up against it and grabbed his own waterskin. He sat down on the ground, his back leaning up against the log. He felt his heart still racing in his chest, and his breathing was hurried. He took a sip of water to cool off before he answered. "The stories soften it up. I saw his scar."

"You saw his scar? In person?" Kevrin leaned forward on his log. His ears pricked up like a dog's.

Jahrys took another sip of water and began to unstrap the pads around his legs. "I sure did. He was searching the streets with the Poolesguard, looking for a wanted man who had escaped the castle. Sir Piller walked right past me on my way to my father's shop. His scar ran all the way across his face like this…" Jahrys drew a jagged line with his finger from his forehead to his chin.

Kevrin's jaw dropped. "I hope I get to see it one day."

Jahrys watched Kevrin trace a line on his own face, as if imagining what it would be like to have his own facial scar.

"I still think Galagar Poole is the bravest knight of Astenpoole," Kevrin stated, as he began to unstrap the pads around his shoulders and arms.

"You can't compare a man who lived three hundred years ago to him," Jahrys shook his head, tossing another pad into the pile he had started on the ground. He wiped his sweaty brown hair from his eyes before working on another pad around his right knee. "Times were different back then."

"Well I still think it's astounding a guy could go from begging on the streets to becoming King of Astenpoole."

"Okay, well, if we're talking about three hundred years ago, then I'll throw Palor A'kal into the mix. He may not have been a king but he was a true hero!"

"Palor wasn't even officially a knight," Kevrin pointed out, struggling with a pad on his wrist.

"No. But I still think he deserves a place in the Hall of Heroes. The guy tried to stab King Alas Danor after walking in on him beating his own daughter. And he got banished over the Western Mountains for it! He threw everything away for Princess Melaine."

"Well, then, what about his brother, Sible, who actually succeeded in murderering King Alas?"

"I guess he deserves a spot on the wall, too."

They both came to an agreement about that.

"And what about Old Lan?" Kevrin asked, his face serious.

Jahrys's hands stopped working on the pad around his knee. He looked at Kevrin and burst out laughing. Kevrin joined him.

The two boys finished taking off their pads and leaned back to enjoy the fresh air. The trees swayed side to side above their heads. Birds scrambled back and forth to different branches. Insects were little black specks circling over their heads, buzzing and spinning. The day was perfect.

Snap.

Jahrys and Kevrin spun around.

"Well if it isn't Jahrhead and Grammy's Boy," a tall, muscular boy named Rallick Henner said, appearing from behind a tree. Two other boys accompanied him: Stade Crar and Taygar Flebb. Stade was tall and skinny, and Taygar was fat and had no tongue.

Jahrys let out a groan. *Just what I needed.* "What do you want, Rallick?" he asked rudely.

Rallick stepped forward, puffing out his chest, leaving Stade and Taygar to glare menacingly from behind, but Rallick's glare was the worst. "I came for my fifty pooles you owe me from our game the other day." He held out a hand, as if expecting it immediately.

Stade and Taygar sniggered and crossed their arms behind him.

Jahrys stayed put. He didn't have any pooles on him, and he didn't want to give in to Rallick's harassment. Jahrys knew he got a rise out of it. "I *told* you I would get it to you when I can. Why don't you go bother someone else?" Jahrys snapped, waving them away.

"I want my coin…*today*," Rallick demanded, taking another step forward, more threateningly this time. "Are you deaf, Jahrhead? I said I—"

"He said he would give it to you when he can," Kevrin stood up. His fists were clenched tight, his nostrils flaring.

"Shouldn't you be back home taking care of that sick grandmother of yours? Or have you finally seen the light and realized The Sickness has taken her?"

Kevrin grabbed his wooden sword and pointed it at Rallick. "That isn't funny."

All three laughed at the sight of Kevrin's sword.

When Kevrin realized how ridiculous he looked, he lowered his weapon, his face reddening.

Jahrys lifted himself up. He placed a hand on Kevrin's tense shoulder. "He isn't worth it, Kevrin. Let's just go."

"Go?" Rallick mimicked. "Are you afraid, Jahrhead?"

"I am *not* afraid," Jahrys turned and puffed out his chest. *A knight is never afraid.*

"Tell you what," said Rallick. "If you can land one blow on me with that stick you call a sword…I'll walk away and forget you owe me anything." He turned back to Stade and Taygar. "Doesn't that seem fair?"

"Sounds fair to me, Rallick," replied Stade, nodding his head mindlessly in agreement.

"Hargh!" agreed Taygar, his lips moving in odd directions as the fat under his chin jiggled.

"And better yet,"—Rallick's lips twisted into a smile—"I won't even use a sword against you." He lowered his hands to his side as if he was offering peace.

Jahrys wanted to knock that smirk off his face. Why couldn't Rallick just leave them alone? Jahrys felt his temples pulsing, and his fingernails were digging into his palms.

Kevrin placed a hand on Jahrys's shoulder. "Come on. Like you said…he isn't worth it."

Jahrys didn't listen. He picked up his wooden sword, and gripped it tight in his hand. "If Galagar Poole had turned away, he would never have been the King of Astenpoole. If Palor A'kal had turned away, he wouldn't have saved Princess Melaine. If Sir Piller had turned away, that little girl would be dead. I will *not* turn away," he muttered.

"Jahrys—" Kevrin tried to stop him.

But Jahrys charged forward, closing the distance between him and his enemy in a few short strides. Everything around Jahrys seemed to fade away, including the leaves that rustled up around his legs as he ran. His mind was focused on Rallick…and that awful smile.

He raised his sword high above his head and swung it down, and—

"Jahrys…Jahrys? Are you okay?"

Jahrys tried to open his eyes, but his left eye was throbbing. A hand shot up to feel it—his eye was as big as an apple.

There were two Kevrins leaning over him. "Jahrys?"

Jahrys groaned as he attempted to lift his body. His head fell back and he clutched his swollen eye. "What happened?"

"Rallick landed a nasty punch to your eye," Kevrin said, biting back an 'I told you so'.

"Better luck next time, Jahrhead." Rallick and his cronies laughed, walking away. "I'll be back for my pooles." Their sniggering echoed through the forest as they faded away into the trees.

"Don't let it get to you," Kevrin said. He held out a hand. Jahrys took it.

"Let's get you to The Arcalane. Willem will have some ice you can throw on your eye." Kevrin helped Jahrys to his feet.

"I'm fine." Jahrys wasn't in the mood to see Innkeeper Willem.

"It's going to swell."

"I don't care."

"Are you okay?"

"How am I ever going to be a Knight of the Poolesguard if I can't even win a fight against Rallick? He didn't even have a weapon in his hand!" Jahrys threw his hands in the air in disgust. "Every knight who ever existed would be ashamed of me."

"I'm not ashamed of you. I'm proud!"

Jahrys ran a hand through his tangled hair, too ashamed to respond.

Kevrin continued, "You always talk about wanting to be a knight. Well, you stuck up for me, Jahrys! And I think that's what being a knight is all about, being there for others who are in need. When Isabella Danor was in need, her knight Galagar Poole was there for her. When Melaine Danor was in need, her knight, Palor A'kal, was there to protect her. When that little girl was surrounded by those three dangerous men, Sir Piller was there to save her!"

"So you're the princess in this scenario?"

"You know what I mean," Kevrin scoffed.

Jahrys chuckled. "Thanks." He patted his friend on the back. "When I get older, I'll be just like Sir Piller Lorne: fearless, strong, and wise. He wouldn't be afraid of Rallick and his dumb friends. He isn't afraid of anything!"

Junkland

"Everyone must be afraid of something," Kevrin argued.

"Not him. One day I'll be a Knight of the Poolesguard, saving princesses and those in need from people like Rallick!" Jahrys was sure of it. "I will be fearless and strong and wise."

Kevrin gave up arguing. "I think that punch has gone to your head. Let's get you back before you start telling me you're going to give up chasing girls."

Jahrys glared at him.

Jahrys and Kevrin stuffed their pads into their bags and grabbed their wooden swords. They followed a dirt road that took them to the edge of Kaluk. The trees of the forest hung over their heads, a leafy arch, blocking the sunlight from the clear, blue sky. A breeze lightly swayed the branches, making a soft scratching sound.

Jahrys took it in, it was all so beautiful.

It was finally the end of the stormy season and the beginning of the long summer. It had been too long: the winds howled throughout the kingdom, making it difficult and dangerous to walk outside; the waves of the Farrest Sea were too rough to sail; the clouds lingered creating a never-ending gray sky. It had been too long. Too long of daydreaming of being a knight and not being able to train. The only thing Jahrys could do in those long, drastic years was work in his father's shop, wasting the days away.

A stone bridge appeared from behind a line of trees, arching over the Seaport River. Jahrys and Kevrin walked over it, nodding to a couple riding a cart pulled by two horses. The wheels clicked and clacked over the stone.

There was a sign that stood on top of a long wooden pole in the center of the bridge that showed Palor to the west, Danor to the north, Astenpoole to the northeast, Sible to the east, and Kaluk to the south. Jahrys and Kevrin headed west, toward Palor.

The castle of Astenpoole was seated high on top of a hill in the distance. The white stone glistened in the sunlight. It looked beautiful against the light blue background of the sky. The towers of the Castle Keep shot straight up, even higher than the castle walls.

Jahrys had never been inside the castle before, but every day he dreamed of what it would be like. He could only imagine how many knights were behind those walls, and he fantasized about the beautiful Princess Alana. Jahrys didn't actually know if she was beautiful or not—he had never seen her. He only heard the stories about her beauty from the people in Palor.

The streets of Palor were filled with people arriving from different parts of the Four Cities. Everyone was busy setting up for the royal wedding that was to take place seven days from now. Tents were flying up, stages were being built, and the inns were bustling with visitors.

Jahrys had never seen Palor this crowded before. It wasn't even this crowded for celebrations during the Coming of Zalus; the most sacred day of the year. It was once a year when the full moon rised high in the sky, and the Four Cities gathered in Palor to worship and celebrate Zalus and the day he came down from the Western Mountains.

Apparently, the roads weren't even this crowded when King Leoné had married Asha almost fourteen years ago. Jahrys had heard stories from people who visited his father's shop telling him how crowded it was then, and it didn't compare to this.

Jahrys and Kevrin finally got to Zalus Road, the main road of Palor.

"I'm going to stop by The Arcalane to talk to Willem about a few things we need to do before the wedding. You sure you don't want to come in and ice that eye?" Kevrin asked, giving him a worried look.

Jahrys could only imagine how many drunk people were at the inn. "The last thing I want to do is be surrounded by drunken fools. I'm going home."

"I'll see you tomorrow for some more training then?"

"As soon as my father let's me off at the shop."

Kevrin nodded and set off towards The Arcalane, up by the castle gate.

Jahrys continued in the other direction on Zalus Road, towards the mountains; his home was all the way at the end of the road, but the view made up for the trip. The Western Mountains loomed in the sky. The sun was beginning to set behind their tall peaks. There was nothing in all of Astenpoole that compared to the sight of the Western Mountains. Not the endless blue of the Farrest Sea, nor the rainbows that formed under Zalus's Tears, not even the great walls and towers of the castle. Jahrys's breath was always taken away when he looked at the peaks fading into the clouds.

No one had ever been over those mountains and returned to tell the tale. Trekking the mountains was usually used as punishment; like when Palor A'kal was banished, King Alas sent him over the Western Mountains, never to return. And as the stories said, he never did return.

"O'Jahrys!"

Jahrys cringed at his full name. He turned his head and saw a large Danorian man waving to him from across the road. Jahrys crossed, dodging the busy traffic composed of carts, horses, visitors, workers, and drunken fools.

"Come here, my boy!" the Danorian man took his hands from the cart he was pulling and wrapped his large arms around Jahrys, squeezing him into his round belly.

"Nice to see you too, Frayel," Jahrys said, struggling to breathe.

"It's been too long," Frayel let go of Jahrys and smiled, showing his crooked teeth.

Jahrys let out a gasp of air.

"Let me have a look at ya," Frayel said in his thick Danorian accent. He scanned Jahrys up and down. "By Zalus, you have grown. The ladies must be all over ya! You got a lady, O'Jahrys?"

Jahrys shook his head.

"Well, keep your eyes open. They'll be sprouting all over ya soon enough," Frayel chuckled. "This weather is something, ain't it? I bet you were a little boy last time there was a long summer."

"I was. My parents already took Kevrin and me to the Sandy Shore a month ago, as soon as the storms began to die down. It was my first time feeling the sand in nearly nine years. My parents used to take me every year when I was little. We used to watch the ships coming in and out of Seaport."

"How are the folks doing?" Frayel asked.

"Father still drives Mother crazy. Nothing new."

"Your father always knows how to get your mother going." Frayel laughed. "His Grent Wine has been the talk of the Four Cities this past year. Now that the stormy season is over, I'm sure business has been good for your father down at Grent Wine and Woodwork?"

"It sure has. That's all my father has been doing lately. He even had to cut back a few orders of his woodwork for customers in order to spend more time making wine."

"Your father always does too much for himself. I hope he's not working you too hard, O'Jahrys."

"Too much is an understatement!"

"Well, business should be good for y'all this week. It's only a week away from the wedding, and the streets are already filled with people from all parts of the Four Cities. I brought some of my own stuff from my farm in Danor to sell." Frayel pointed his thumb over his shoulder, towards his cart. It was filled with a cage of chickens, fresh fruits, and vegetables. "I'm hoping to make a good amount of pooles to spend on my loving Astonia," Frayel smiled at the sound of his wife's name.

"I'm sure you can buy her something nice here. Palor has a lot of nice markets."

"I'll be keeping my eye out then," Frayel chuckled. He glanced at the fading light from the sun; the last bit of sunlight was beginning to disappear behind the mountains. "Well, I best be heading off now. My Astonia is waiting for me back at our tent. I shall be stopping by your shop to grab me some of that Grent Wine! Tell your father for me, will ya?"

"I will. It was nice seeing you."

"So long, O'Jahrys!" Frayel waved goodbye. He tugged his cart up the road.

Jahrys cringed again at the sound of his full name, but waved goodbye. He continued his journey home. The crowd began to diminish the farther he walked away from the castle.

Up ahead, the golden palms of Zalus were glistening from the last bit of sunlight on top of the large church. The church was decorated and cleaned up nicely for the festivities; it had a reputation to live up to, because Palor was the holiest place in all of the kingdom.

At the end of Zalus Road was where Zalus came down from the Western Mountains, 913 years ago, and raised his palms high into the sky, creating life. During every Coming of Zalus, everyone would travel to Palor to celebrate and attend Pastor Allen's ceremony.

Pastor Allen was a kind man, but ever since his daughter had died from The Sickness, he had been slightly off.

The pastor was known for his preachings after hours on the steps of his church. Jahrys was approaching the grand steps now. He tried to keep his head down, not wanting to draw attention to himself if Pastor Allen was out that evening preaching from the steps. He just wanted to get home.

His luck had failed him. Pastor Allen was out.

Jahrys dropped his head lower and looked away. *By the palms of Zalus, don't let him see me.* But something made Jahrys raise his head in curiousity.

Pastor Allen's voice was filled with fear. He was yelling out to the road, but there was no one there except for Jahrys. The pastor's eyes were deep, black pits. He was flailing his arms around like a tree during the stormy season, and his face was whiter than the clouds.

It was the words that scared Jahrys the most.

"With dusk comes the dreadful night, when giant walls block out the light. Yellow rain will fall. A storm of eternity! Taking it all as the innocents lose energy. Oh Zalus! Come down from the Western Mountains with your palms of light. And save us from the darkness that will bring us all an endless night."

Jahrys was frozen; he didn't know what to do, he was shocked at Pastor Allen's dark words.

"You there!" Pastor Allen pointed a trembling finger towards Jahrys.

Junkland

"Pastor Allen?" Jahrys called out. "Pastor Allen, are you—"

"A darkness is rising and will come over these mountains. The blue from the Farrest Sea and skies that surround us, the red from the fire and energy that keeps us warm, and the yellow from the sun above our heads and soil beneath our feet, will all be sucked into darkness. Pray for Zalus's return, for he is the one who can save us!"

With the last word, Pastor Allen collapsed. He toppled down the grand steps, and landed hard onto the cobblestone road.

"Pastor Allen!" Jahrys yelled, dropping his bag and sword, running over to the pastor. He bent down and scooped the pastor's head up with his arm. "Pastor Allen?"

Pastor Allen's eyes shot open. "Zalus?" he whispered. "Zalus...have you come?"

"Pastor Allen, it's me...Jahrys."

The pastor's hand shot up, grabbing a fistful of Jahrys's shirt. He yanked him down, hard. Jahrys could hear how fast the pastor was breathing.

"Have you prayed, O'Jahrys? Have you prayed for Zalus's coming?" Pastor Allen's fist was shaking as he gripped Jahrys's shirt into a knot.

"I—" Jahrys didn't even have time to cringe at his name.

"Pray my boy. Pray for Zalus. He is the one...the only one who can save us." Pastor Allen began to cough.

"It starts with..." Pastor Allen's eyes began to roll behind his head.

"It starts with what Pastor Allen? It starts with what?"

"It starts with..." Pastor Allen's head toppled over into Jahrys's arm as he lost consciousness.

Chapter 2
Alana

IT WAS THE end of the stormy season and the beginning of the long summer; the air felt crisp and clear, the birds were singing sweet melodies, and the city of Astenpoole was alive.

Alana Poole breathed in the Astenpoole air for what seemed the first time in her life. She had forgotten how good it felt. She had been cooped up inside her bedchamber within the Castle Keep for far too long.

The streets of Astenpoole were busy with people setting up for the wedding festivities. She saw a group of men hammering wood and stakes as they built a stage. Another group of people were helping to lift a tent from the ground. A man was herding sheep and goats up Pooles Road. Women laughed and children ran around in circles, chasing dogs and cats.

Alana took a turn onto a side road, heading towards the small town of Riverside.

She was dreading the wedding. She didn't want to deal with any more of Mother Claraine's nagging about dresses she must try on or her handmaids examining and judging her body. But most importantly, she didn't want her father to marry Nadia. He was marrying her for all the wrong reasons—it was more for politics than true love.

The end of the stormy season brought calm seas, opening communication again between Farrest and Astenpoole. Her father wanted to strengthen the ties between the two kingdoms, and the best way to do it was with a marriage. Her father had agreed to marry a widowed lady, Nadia, from Farrest.

Everything about Nadia made Alana gag, even her name. Nadia would never replace her real mother. Alana would make certain that never happened.

Alana walked over the stone bridge that brought her into Riverside; it was her favorite part of Astenpoole. Western Village was too busy. Northside was filled with strange folk. And Eastern Village was too quiet and deserted. Ever since her mother died from The Sickness, her father had ordered the Eastern Gate to be permanently closed. Her father didn't want Carriers coming inside the castle. The Western Gate remained open, but it was heavily guarded; it took numerous security checks to enter and leave.

Alana found a pleasant place by Seaport River. It was quiet, the shade blocked the hot sun, and she was alone. She folded her skirts as she sat down on the hard ground. The gentle lapping of the river put her in a soothing trance. Birds chirped a song over her head, bees buzzed in harmony from flower to flower, and squirrels and chipmunks skittered from one tree to the next. Her eyes glided over a long stick a few feet in front of her. It reminded her of a sword. Alana stood and walked over to it, picking it up. She began to swing it around, trying to recall her lessons from Sir Mazo Dapher.

"Breathe. Swing. Don't miss," Alana recited.

Sir Mazo had been a knight in her father's Poolesguard. Alana had loved her lessons with him; he was filled with knowledge and experience. But after her mother had died, her father had put an end to her lessons with the knight and forbade Alana to leave the Castle Keep. Alana had hoped her father would break out of this cautious phase and she would be able to start her lessons back up with Sir Mazo. But all hope of training again slipped away after Sir Mazo was taken by The Sickness.

"Breathe. Swing. Don't miss." Alana repeated his words again and again as she continued to breathe and swing.

With the birds singing, the river humming, and the insects buzzing, she found a rhythm. She took a step and swung her sword. She felt free.

"Step, step, swing. Step, step, thrust." Alana repeated outloud as she moved around the riverbank. Her feet twirled and spun beneath her just like a dancer. "Step, step, turn, and swing."

"I'm impressed," a man said behind her.

Alana lost her balance mid-step and tumbled forward. She let out a groan as she flipped her hair back away from her eyes to see who distracted her. Her stomach dropped.

"Sir Benjamin, I—how did you find me?" she jumped nervously to her feet, fixing her skirts. Sir Benjamin Burrow was one of the seven current Knights of the Poolesguard. He was tall, a man of twenty-eight, and muscular. His blond hair fell perfectly around his face. He was a man that always held the attention of the young ladies. They would always blush and giggle as he passed them on the streets.

"A beautiful day after nine years of gray...I had a feeling you wouldn't be staying inside the Castle Keep. Your father may be oblivious, but I'm not."

"I-I'm sorry...I didn't mean to get you into trouble," Alana wiped the dirt from her hands onto her skirts. She picked up her stick she had dropped.

"What your father doesn't know won't hurt us. Your secret is safe with me, my princess." Sir Benjamin smiled at her. His white teeth glistened.

Alana let out a sigh of relief.

"Now, put that stick down," Benjamin ordered.

Alana listened. She tossed the stick into the river. She knew freedom was too good to last. Benjamin would take her back to her bedchamber where she would spend the rest of the day listening to Mother Claraine's annoying rants about Zalus knows what—her dresses, probably.

"Let's see what you can do with this." Benjamin tossed her a scabbard.

Alana lifted her hands just in time to catch it. She was surprised as she unsheathed a wooden training sword. She looked at it in awe.

"Are you going to teach me?" she asked, getting excited.

"If you will let me," Benjamin smiled at her.

"But…Father—"

"Like I said before, your secret is safe with me," Benjamin winked. "Now, sword at the ready, out in front of you."

Alana raised her training sword by her hip.

"A little higher. A little more. Almost there…and…stop. Perfect."

Alana had her sword up to her chest. Her arms were already wobbling from the weight.

"Good. Now bend your knees."

She bent her knees. "Like this?"

"A little too much."

Alana relaxed her knees.

"Yes! Good. Now…watch out!" Benjamin dove forward, swinging his own training sword down hard.

Alana lifted her sword and blocked his blow. A loud clang echoed off the trees around her. Alana's hands stung from the vibration, but she winced away the pain.

She stepped back and swung at Benjamin. She felt more alive than ever.

They practiced and practiced until the sun began to sink below the Western Mountains.

Alana was dripping sweat, and she could feel the dirt that covered her face. Her muscles ached, her chest rose and fell rapidly, and she was breathless. She was covered in bruises from her failed attempts at blocking Sir Benjamin, and the numerous times she had fallen.

"Sir Mazo taught you well," Benjamin said, wiping the sweat off his brow.

"He was a great teacher." Alana's legs were wobbling.

"Yes...yes he was," Benjamin agreed. "Well, we best be getting back before your father finds out you're missing."

"Thank you for the lesson today, Sir Benjamin. I hope we can do it again soon?" she asked politely, hoping he wouldn't say no.

"Perhaps," Benjamin gave her another wink.

Alana laughed and gave her training sword back to the knight. They walked back, crossing the bridge that took them into Western Village. Alana told Benjamin she would walk to her bedchamber alone; she didn't want Benjamin getting into trouble on her account if they were found together. Benjamin agreed to meet her back at her bedchamber. They parted ways.

Alana headed to the abandoned house off Pooles Road. Inside, behind a large painting of the Western Mountains, was a secret passageway that led into the Castle Keep. She had to climb down a ladder that took her to a tunnel. She had to crawl through darkness and dust, but she was used to it by now. It was her only way of escape from her father's strict rules.

While there were many twists and turns in the tunnel, she had memorized them all. Eventually she came to a stop inside the tunnel. She flicked a switch on the wall and pushed. Light poured in as she stepped down into her bedchamber and swung the bookcase shut. She waited for it to click back into place. She barely had a second to unwind before there was a knock at her door.

Knock. Knock. Knock.

Her heart dropped. She was still covered in dirt and sweat.

"Who is it?" she tried to make her voice sound calm.

"It is Mother Claraine, my princess, it's time for your fitting," her hoarsed voice yelled through the door.

How long was I gone? "Just a minute!" She yelled back, glancing out the window to see it was well into the evening now.

Alana quickly stripped down, throwing her dirty clothes underneath her bed. She dove into her closet, picked the first sundress she could find, and threw it on. She took one quick glance in the mirror; her hair was a mess, and she was still dirty, but there was nothing she could do about that. She hoped her father wouldn't see her, and Mother Claraine wouldn't make any comments.

Alana opened the door and smiled down at Mother Claraine. She was an older lady, in charge of running Alana's daily life: from her sewing lessons, to her cooking lessons, as well as her fittings.

"Ah, my princess looks…" She was going to say stunning, but Mother Claraine had a frog stuck in her throat when she looked Alana up and down. "My princess, you look—"

"Sweaty. I know. Let's get this over with."

Mother Claraine mumbled to herself as she walked in, probably about her dirty face and hands. Three handmaids followed Mother Claraine in.

Alana peaked through her bedroom door as it was shutting, and saw Benjamin standing guard outside, he gave her a little wave.

The three handmaids began to undress Alana. When she was completely naked, Alana could tell they were trying to keep their comments to themselves on how dirty and bruised her body looked.

But Mother Claraine couldn't take it anymore. "Alana! You are bruised from head to toe and you have dirt everywhere! Even in your hair! By the palms of Zalus, what were you doing?"

When Alana refused to answer her, Mother Claraine threw her hands up in frustration, and told her handmaids to bring her up a bath. They spent the next half hour scrubbing Alana down. She didn't know why she needed a bath—all she was doing was trying on a dress for the wedding, which she didn't even want to attend.

After Mother Claraine's handmaids were done scrubbing her body, they dried her off, and stood her in front of the mirror. She was still covered in bruises and a few scratches, but she was clean.

Mother Claraine whipped out a thin piece of rope from an inner pocket and measured every inch of Alana's body. She then signaled to her handmaids, who flung the dress over her as if she was a little girl. Mother Claraine again made her measurements, and examined every nook and cranny of Alana's dress, muttering to herself. Alana couldn't wait until this fitting was over.

Knock. Knock. Knock.

Alana groaned. *Why can't I just be left alone?*

"Who is it?" Mother Claraine spoke for her.

"It is Leoné. I would like to see how pretty my daughter looks…if you don't mind."

Junkland

"Of course, of course!" Mother Claraine said excitedly. She motioned her handmaids to back away from Alana as she opened the door.

Her father ducked under the doorframe and stepped into the room. He stood behind Alana in the mirror, placing a large hand on her shoulder.

Mother Claraine was biting her nails in the corner, waiting for Leoné's response.

"Alana, you look beautiful! The more you grow, the more I see your mother in you. You have the same eyes as her, as blue as the Farrest Sea. I—" he paused when he glanced down at her bare arm. "What's this?" Her father held her right arm and examined it.

Alana's heart dropped. *No…*

"OUT! I WANT EVERYBODY OUT!" the room quaked with his voice.

Mother Claraine hurried herself and the three handmaids out the door.

Her father's grip tightened around her wrist.

"Father…please—"

"How many times?" he let go of her wrist and examined the other bruises on her body. "How many times must I tell you? You are *not* allowed to leave this Castle Keep without my permission!"

"But you never give me your permission! You keep me trapped inside here as if I'm a little girl. I'm fourteen! This is not fair…"

"Fair? Do you think it's *fair* that The Sickness is still running rampant throughout the kingdom? Or that the Carriers have infected us inside the castle? Do you think it's *fair* that one of those Carriers infected your mother? Killing her!" He choked down a sob.

"You don't know that, Father! For all we know, it could have been someone from Astenpoole, someone from inside the walls!" Alana felt the tears start. *Why does he always have to bring up Mother?* She thought. She felt as if he was blaming her.

"Don't give me that nonsense. You should be smarter than that. We all know the first signs of The Sickness came from Palor. And—" Her father shook his head. "I don't need to be explaining myself to you. I'm your father and the king, and you *will* listen to me. And where was Benjamin?"

"He was with me!" Alana cried out.

"But he did not get my authority to take you outside the Castle Keep. I will have a word with him."

"Please, Father! It wasn't his fault. Please don't blame him." Alana felt tears rolling down her face.

Her father let out a deep sigh and placed his hands gently on the sides of her burning cheeks as he looked into her eyes. "I am doing this for you, Alana, to protect you. I can't live with myself if I have to watch your body burn, too—just like your mother's. I can't lose you both." He sighed, his eyes moistening. "I have lost my brother, my parents, and my wife. You're all I have left. Do you understand that?"

"I understand." Alana let her head sink in disappointment. She would never win this fight.

"Good. Now let Mother Claraine finish. I will see you for dinner." Her father left for the door, but turned around before he opened it and said, "No more funny business. Please…stay inside the Castle Keep." He left.

Mother Claraine and her three handmaids crept back in. They continued their measurements, but were much quieter than before.

Alana ignored them. She stared into the mirror in front of her, letting the tears roll down her face as she thought about her mother.

Chapter 3
Jahrys

JAHRYS GOT LITTLE sleep the next few nights; Pastor Allen's words haunted him. Jahrys laid awake for hours each night trying to puzzle together what the pastor had meant.

After Pastor Allen had passed out, Jahrys brought him into the church and laid him down on a pew. Jahrys had wet a cloth from Pastor Allen's office and placed it on the top of the unconscious pastor's forehead. Jahrys waited, expecting answers, but when Pastor Allen regained consciousness, he did not remember a single thing.

'Yellow rain will fall…' What did he mean by that? Jahrys thought as the morning light seeped through his window. A bird began to chirp loudly outside.

Jahrys let out a groan. His clothes were stuck to his body as he flung the sheets off. He let out another groan. *Not again.*

He peeled the clothes off his body, tossing them into a dirty pile in the corner of his room, on top of more soggy clothes. He still wasn't used to the warm weather that came with the end of the stormy season. It seemed he sweat more than he slept each night. The stormy season always brought a cool breeze off the shore of the Farrest Sea. But now, without the strong winds, Astenpoole and the Four Cities were a melting pot.

Jahrys let out a moan when he felt every muscle in his body ache. Jahrys and Kevrin had gone three straight days of practicing their sword fighting, and it was beginning to catch up to him.

At least the pain in my eye is beginning to fade, he thought. He gently touched his eye, testing it out. To Jahrys's relief, Rallick, Stade, and Taygar had not bothered him and Kevrin since that day.

Jahrys put on a pair of brown, woolen pants. They weren't pants anymore, though, as he had ripped them up to his knees. He then put on his faded blue tunic and wrapped a belt around his waist. He muffled up his long, wavy brown hair and walked over to his window to look at Astenpoole and the Castle Keep. He watched the sun slowly rise above the six towers of the castle.

The castle walls were recently cleaned, and banners were now draped over them. Every banner had a different sigil. There was a patch of farmland for Danor, mountains for Palor, a tree for Kaluk, and a wave for Sible. The palms of Zalus was Astenpoole's sigil, with the four sigils of the four cities in the opened palms.

The wedding was to take place early that afternoon. Jahrys was staring out at the castle, wondering how many people must be gathering inside the walls. He could picture all the knights in their shining armor, holding swords at their sides while keeping a diligent eye on the crowds as they looked for suspicious activity. *One day I'll attend a royal wedding as a knight*, thought Jahrys, as he rubbed the knots in his shoulder.

Only a select few, mainly lords—including Lord Wayve Hupperton of Palor, Lord Ide Velton of Sible, Lord Henrick Cornvall of Danor, and Zal Jav P'avka of Kaluk—and people of importance in the Four Cities, would be able to attend the royal festivities within the castle. And even they had to go through numerous stages of security just to enter the Western Gate.

Ever since Queen Asha died from The Sickness four years ago, King Leoné limited the access in and out of the castle walls; it was nearly impossible to enter and to leave these days. He wanted to ensure that whoever entered the castle wasn't a Carrier.

But Jahrys was confident that The Sickness was fading, especially with the end of the stormy season. His family was blessed to have not fallen victim to it, but they knew many who had; Kevrin's grandmother was one of them. According to Kevrin, she was still alive, but barely.

Jahrys laced up his brown boots and walked down the creaking stairs. His parents were already in the kitchen. Just like the rest of Jahrys's house, the kitchen was small, but it was large enough for them. Jahrys's mother was cutting up sausages and cooking eggs over the stove, and his father was examining a wooden chair he was holding upside down by the two front legs.

"BUCUUUUUCK!"

A chicken ran out from under the table towards Jahrys as he entered the kitchen. The bird wobbled up to his boot and began to peck at it. Jahrys heard the jingling of keys.

"Good morning to you, too, Miller." Jahrys bent down to pick up the funny looking bird. He took the ring of keys from Miller's mouth. "Trying to escape again?" he asked the large-eyed chicken.

Miller stared at him for a few seconds before deciding to peck at his fingers. Jahrys placed Miller back on the ground and watched him wobble out of the kitchen, into the living room.

"Ah, O'Jahrys, you're up," his father said, taking his eyes off the chair for a second to look at his son. "Today is going to be busy, busy, busy."

"For the thousandth time, will you call me Jahrys?" He was tired of repeating the same thing to his father. Jahrys never liked the full name he was given, but he could live with Jahrys.

"But that was your granddaddy's name! O'Jahrys the Bear, as they used to call him. His arms were as thick as a tree, and he was as big as a bear. As hairy as one too, as a matter of fact." His father gave a little chuckle, his mustache bouncing. "He had Palorian blood all through his veins."

"I never even met him," Jahrys said, as he walked over to his mother to say good morning.

"Well, he taught me everything there is to know about carpentry. He sure did. The man could have built a whole city if he wanted."

"I'd be lucky if I didn't splinter myself building a birdhouse."

"Good morning, honey," his mother said, turning to greet him as she finished cutting up the last sausage. His mother had blonde, graying hair and the trademark pale Danorian skin. "What happened to your arm?" she put down the knife and rubbed her finger gently over a bruise.

"It's nothing," Jahrys lied, pulling his arm away.

"Were you and Kevrin playing with those sticks again?" his mother asked, scolding him with a pointed finger. "You know I don't like it when you guys fight. You are going to get another black eye!"

"They aren't sticks," Jahrys defended.

Junkland

"I don't care what you call them," she placed a firm hand on her hip and turned to his father. "Don't you agree, Alv?"

His father lifted his eyes from his chair, confused as to what the topic of conversation was about. "Listen to your mother, O'Jahrys."

"But how else am I supposed to train to be a knight?"

His mother opened the cabinet above her head and handed Jahrys three plates. "You can start by setting the table. I need a knight in my kitchen…Sir Jahrys," his mother ordered.

"Yes, Mother," Jahrys did not hesitate, but walked gloomily over to the table, placing the plates down.

"Look at this, O'Jahrys," his father was tracing the carving on the leg of the chair he was examining: vines ran bottom to top on each leg, with an occasional rose carved between the vines. "Look how perfectly symmetrical they are. You can't find art like this anywhere else in the Four Cities or Astenpoole. No, you can't! This is the work of patient, Grent hands. It runs in our family."

"Put that chair away, Alvys," his mother ordered. "We're about to eat."

"It's going to be busy these next few days, Eve," his father said, without taking his eyes off the chair. "We need to make sure we have everything prepared for the festivities after the wedding this afternoon."

"You've been working all morning! Put it away and work on it after we eat," his mother repeated, looking stern, yet still beautiful.

"Dammit woman, you make it so hard not to listen to you." He gave her a little smile, his graying mustache rising and falling. He carried the chair to the living room and sat down at the table as Jahrys's mother served the food.

Jahrys wanted to bring up what happened with Pastor Allen the other day, but he was having a hard time figuring out how to word it without freaking out his mother and father. He decided to go for it. "I was walking past the church the other day and Pastor Allen said—"

"Oh, now you listen close, boy," his father interrupted, pointing his fork at Jahrys. "That man has screws in his head. Don't listen to anything he says, you hear?"

"But—"

"Well," his mother cut him off as she joined them at the table, "what your father is trying to say is, don't listen to anything he has to say outside of the church, honey. Pastor Allen has been having a hard time ever since his daughter passed away from The Sickness."

"He's a loon," his father said, throwing his hands into the air. "I don't know why we go listen to him every week and hear him talk about some Western God. He needs—"

"Be quiet, Alv," Jahrys's mother interrupted.

"I'm just say—"

"We go because that's what families are supposed to do. Now eat your damn breakfast!" His mother snapped and shook her head. "Zalus forgive us."

With that, Jahrys did not bring it up again.

After a long silence of chewing sausages, Jahrys's father said, "We're going to need at least a hundred cases from the cellar out back for this afternoon. After the wedding is done, people are going to want to celebrate and get really, really—"

"Alv! Don't talk like that in front of Jahrys," his mother shouted, jabbing a fork at his father.

"Come on, Eve. I had my first drink with my pop when I was thirteen years old. The boy is almost a man grown now." He turned to Jahrys, lowering his voice so his mother couldn't hear. "Uh, how old are you now son?"

Jahrys rolled his eyes. "Fifteen."

His father shot up and placed a hand in front of Jahrys as if he was a showcase. "You see! Almost a man grown."

"Yea….*Almost*." His mother stressed. "But until then, no talking like that in front of our son."

"As you say, my lady," his father said, waving his hand like a servent.

Jahrys rolled a piece of sausage around his plate, waiting for the next awkward topic of their morning conversation.

His father turned to him, pointing his fork. "Later today I will show you how to make a perfect chair, O'Jahrys. That will be our back up if we run out of cases of wine tonight. You can never have too much wood. Isn't that right, honey?" He asked, winking at his wife.

His mother's fork fell to her plate and her face shot up at his father, giving him a devilish stare, but she was blushing.

"Uh…right…" his father looked away from her, "never mind." He paused, and then announced, "Well…this will be our chance to make a fair amount of pooles. We mustn't mess up this opportunity."

Jahrys stared at his plate uncomfortably. He felt Miller pecking at a few crumbs by his feet.

"I promised Kevrin I would go…" Jahrys stopped himself before he gave his full plan away. "I promised I would go fishing with him down at Zalus's Tears before we open shop," Jahrys told his father, as his mother gave him a suspicious look.

"As long as you're back in time to help me, O'Jahrys, I don't care what you do," his father replied.

"As long as you aren't playing with those sticks," his mother added.

"I promise, we are going fishing," Jahrys lied.

"How's Kevrin doing by the way?" his mother asked. "We haven't seen him since our trip to the Sandy Shore."

"He's been busy helping out his grandmother. I don't think she's doing well."

"That's a shame. And to think, The Sickness is just beginning to die down. She must have caught the tail end of it. We should go over there and help out. That's a lot of responsibility for a fifteen-year-old boy to do without any support. Don't you think we should do that, Alv?" his mother turned to Jahrys's father.

"Huh?" his father's eyes were back in the living room, on the chair he had been examining earlier.

"About Kevrin's grandmother," his mother repeated, getting irritated.

"Oh, the woman we still have yet to meet?"

"Kevrin said she's too old to leave the house. And now that she's sick…it's impossible. He has been helping Willem around The Arcalane for a few extra pooles to provide for her." Jahrys was getting annoyed at the subject. Truth be told, Jahrys had never met Kevrin's grandmother either. Kevrin always acted strange when Jahrys would bring her up.

"Oh, that poor boy. Bless his soul," his mother said, placing a hand over her heart. "After the celebrations settle down, we'll go over there and help."

"I don't think he wants us to get involved—" Jahrys started.

"Nonsense. I'm sure Kevrin would appreciate the help. Don't

you think so, Alv?"

"Huh?" his father was preoccupied with his meal.

"Oh, never mind," his mother said, giving up on repeating herself.

When Jahrys had finished everything on his plate, he turned to his mother and asked, "Can I go meet up with Kevrin now by…the lake?"

"Yes, just make sure you're back in time to help your father," his mother said, leaning over and kissing Jahrys on the forehead.

"We need to make sure everything's ready in time for the celebrations, O'Jahrys," his father said.

Jahrys cringed at his full name.

"Don't forget," his father continued. "Everyone will be celebrating. King Leoné and his new wife, Nadia. I bet she is a poole and a—"

"Alvys!" his mother interrupted.

"What?" his father gave her an innocent look.

His mother rolled her eyes, ignoring him. "I still can't believe it has been four years since Queen Asha's death. Such a shame. Her daughter must be so devastated. I hope Nadia brings both her and her father happiness," his mother said.

"Aye and maybe Princess Alana will marry O'Jahrys, and we will become part of the royal family with King Leoné, ha!" his father gave a big chuckle and nudged Jahrys with his elbow. "That would solve all our money problems. No pressure, son."

Out of all the things he chooses to listen to, thought Jahrys.

"Just because the boy isn't courting yet, doesn't mean you have to tease him, Alv," his mother scolded.

On that note, Jahrys quietly slid out the back door of the kitchen, with Miller following.

Jahrys grabbed his bag and wooden sword that had been leaning against his house. He stayed clear of the vineyard and crossed the yard to the back gate. He opened it and curved around to Zalus Road, Miller crisscrossing between his legs as he walked.

He walked up the road, towards the castle. The streets were filled with people, wagons, tents, and animals. Jahrys avoided the crowd building in front of Pastor Allen's church and headed right, down a back alleyway. He weaved through a maze of buildings until he reached the bridge that crossed over Seaport River into Kaluk.

At the first sight of the forest, Miller took off and began circling the trees. Jahrys laughed as he watched the chicken play as he walked.

When they arrived at the meeting spot, Jahrys sat down on his log. He dropped his gear onto the ground, causing a bunch of leaves to crinkle.

Miller ran off to a nearby tree and began to peck at it.

I wonder what goes through that chicken's head, thought Jahrys, as he began to put on his training armor.

The forest came alive around Jahrys as the animals got used to his presence. A collection of sounds bounced off the trees: insects humming, birds chirping, squirrels and chipmunks scurrying through the fallen leaves.

Miller became bored with the tree and began chasing a mouse around Jahrys's log.

Where is Kevrin? He should have been here a while ago. Jahrys was beginning to worry.

After another ten minutes of waiting, Jahrys heard the stomping of leaves coming from the bridge up ahead. It sounded like someone was running.

"You best be running!" Jahrys shouted through the trees as he stood up from his log. "Do you know how long I've been wait—"

Kevrin came sprinting towards him. Jahrys could see his bloodshot eyes from where he was standing. Kevrin's hair was a sweaty mess, his skin was whiter than the clouds, and his body was shaking.

"Jahrys…Jahrys! I have to tell—" Kevrin tripped over a branch, falling face first to the ground.

"Kevrin?" Jahrys yelled. He ran over to his friend, rolling him over. "Kevrin…are you all right?"

Kevrin's eyes had rolled back, only the whites were showing. He was shaking uncontrollably, and foaming at the mouth as he kept repeating, "Tell…tell…tell."

"Kevrin?" Jahrys yelled. He didn't know what to do.

Jahrys struggled to pick Kevrin up, but he got him over his shoulder. "Come on, Mill. I have to take Kevrin to Willem. He'll know what to do." He ran as fast as he could back towards the Seaport River, over the bridge, and back to Zalus Road. Miller followed closely behind, occasionally flying to catch up.

Jahrys sprinted all the way up the road towards The Arcalane. His shoulders and back were aching, but he didn't slow down. He ran, weaving in and out of the crowd of people.

When he arrived at The Arcalane, Jahrys kicked open the door. He ran straight to the bar where Innkeeper Willem was standing.

"My boy! How are—" His words were cut short when he saw the look on Jahrys's face. "What's going on here?"

"It's Kevrin! I don't know what happened. He just…collapsed." Jahrys didn't know what else to say.

Willem turned to a thin man with a crooked nose next to him

behind the bar. "Havrick, you're in command."

"I'm on it, boss," said the bartender with the crooked nose.

Willem turned back to Jahrys. "Bring him to the back. Quickly now!"

Jahrys rounded the corner and brought Kevrin to the back room, laying him down on a table in the center. Miller scurried under the table.

Willem barged in, carrying a bucket of water and a wet cloth.

"Move aside," he ordered. He placed the wet cloth on top of Kevrin's sweaty head. "Tell me what happened."

"I was waiting for Kevrin in Kaluk. He showed up, sprinting towards me, and yelling he had to tell me something…but then he collapsed."

"Tell you something?" Willem repeated as he patted Kevrin's head with the damp cloth. "Well…what did he tell you?"

"Nothing. He didn't get a chance to tell me."

"Ah. Well, we'll have him up and running in no time, don't worry my boy. It looks like he had a slight seizure."

"BUCUUUUUCK!" Miller yelled, from below the table.

Jahrys turned to the chicken, realizing he was going to be late helping his father. He turned back to Willem. "Willem, what time is it?"

"It's close to midafternoon now," Willem answered.

"By Zalus! Will you look over Kevrin for me? If I don't open up my father's shop…he'll kill me!" Jahrys exaggerated.

"I've never heard of good old Alvys killing anyone," Willem teased. "Get going, my boy. Kevrin will be safe with me."

"Thanks, Willem." Jahrys shouted as he ran out the door, Miller following. They ran out of The Arcalane and sprinted back down the road, towards the Western Mountains that rose high up in the sky, past the clouds.

Chapter 4
Alana

IT HAD BEEN four years since her mother's death, but the pain was as real as if it had happened yesterday. Alana remembered her perfectly, as if she was still standing right in front of her. Her mother had been so beautiful. She had had long curly blonde hair, eyes as blue as the Farrest Sea, brighter than the sky, and soft pink skin. She also had been loving and caring in every way imaginable.

Alana could see her mother's features in herself as she looked in the full-length mirror in her bedroom. She didn't have the blonde hair, nor the rosy pink skin as her mother, but she had her blue eyes and the shapes of their faces were the same. Every time she looked in a mirror, it felt like her mother was a part of her.

She had been ten at the time, young and confused as to what was happening to her mother. A day never went by when Alana didn't think of her.

She missed when her mother used to take her to the shops in Western Village, when her mother used to tell her old fairy tales of princesses and princes by the Seaport River, when her mother would

Junkland

always stick up for her when she wanted to do something adventurous. Her mother always wanted to do something thrilling, unlike her father. Her mother was so brave.

Now, without her mother, she was trapped. Everyone held an expectation over her head, and Alana didn't have her mother to defend her. Everyone expected Alana to be as perfect as Simona Poole, Lydia Poole, Valerina Poole, Ivah Poole, Isabella Danor, Melaine Danor—all the princesses and ladies that had graced the castle before her.

Mother Claraine told her the stories about how beautiful, smart, and well-mannered they had been. They would never have disobeyed their fathers—running away to play with swords! Oh please! They were beautiful and kind, but stationary. No one ever talked about how those women were defenseless against outlaws who had come from the Farrest Sea to take them away; or when a treacherous king would beat them without regret. No one talked about that. All Mother Claraine would talk about was how they grew up to become beautiful queens, just like Alana would one day.

Alana spat on that thought.

She didn't want to become Queen of Astenpoole; that was the last thing in the world she wanted. She would rather be a normal girl, where no one recognized her. She wouldn't even mind running away. The thought had crossed her mind numerous times.

Knock. Knock. Knock.

"Alana? We're going to be late. Are you ready yet?" it was a man's voice.

Knock. Knock. Knock.

"Almost!" she said, as she was brought out of her thoughts.

"Hold still," snapped Mother Claraine as she continued to pin her dress. "I need to fix this before you leave."

Alana tried to stay still. She looked into the mirror again.

She was wearing a beautiful light pink gown with a floral design on the corset, and smooth silk everywhere else. While it was sewn specifically for her size, the dress had torn when it had been pulled over her chest.

Mother Claraine let out an impatient groan. "By the palms of Zalus, Alana! Did your bust double in size over night?"

"I...I don't think so," Alana said awkwardly. She had been feeling uncomfortable with this fitting, and now, even more so.

Knock. Knock. Knock.

"Alana! If you don't come out right now, I will be forced to—"

"WILL YOU SHUT YOUR PIPE!" Mother Claraine screamed through the closed door.

There was absolute silence as Mother Claraine took one last shot at pinning her dress. "By Zalus, I got it! Take a look."

Alana did a tiny spin while she looked at the mirror. "It's wonderful! Thank you, Mother Claraine."

"Just keep those breasts of yours in check until this wedding is over."

Alana gave her an awkward smile as she walked over to her bedroom door and opened it.

"Well now, don't you look like a beautiful young lady," said the knight standing before her.

"You look very handsome yourself today, Sir Benjamin." Alana gave him a little curtsy.

"My princess is too kind. I look this way every day." The handsome knight gave a little chuckle. "Shall we be off before your father kills me for how late we are?" he asked, offering his arm to her. She smiled and took it.

Benjamin always knew how to cheer her up. He had been her personal guard for almost four years now. After her mother's death, her father had assigned Benjamin to watch over her. As much as she protested this, she had grown to enjoy his company. Especially on a day like today when she felt more alone than ever missing her mother. Her knight had become a close confidant and companion, almost like a brother.

Benjamin escorted her out of her tower and into the Village. They took the path towards the courtyard in the distance, one of her favorite places in the Castle Keep. Houses and shops lined both sides of them.

The path opened up to the courtyard where trees and beautiful gardens lined the roads throughout the great, green yards. People would gather here to relax, pray, and now that the long summer was here, escape the Astenpoole heat. The courtyard was completely deserted today, however. Everyone was either at the wedding or setting up for the celebrations that would occur later that night.

Giant tents had been set up in the middle of the courtyard. The majority of the tents contained tables, chairs, and bars. A large stage was set up near the fountain.

The fountain sat in the center of the courtyard. To say it was a large fountain would be an understatement. This fountain could be mistaken for a pond; it was huge! A marble statue of Zalus stood on a platform in the center of the water. He was raising his palms to the sky as water sprayed out of them like a waterfall. Galagar Poole built it nearly three hundred years ago, when he returned the worship of Zalus to Astenpoole after King Alas Danor banished it years before.

"May I ask you something, Sir Benjamin?" Alana asked as they walked past the statue.

"My princess may ask me whatever she likes." He did a little bow and waved with his hand to urge her to continue.

"Do you believe?"

"Do I believe in what, my princess?" He wasn't following.

"Do you believe in Zalus? The Western God?"

"Well of course I believe. He's why we're here now, walking to your father's wedding. He's the reason why we're talking to each other right now, and the reason why we're practicing sword fighting. Without him, I wouldn't be a Knight of the Poolesguard. He came down from the Western Mountains, raised his palms high toward the sky, and life poured out of them. Zalus is the creator of this world. His blood is our blood." He sounded very confident.

"But where is he now?"

"Beyond the Western Mountains, watching over us, my princess."

"Well if he is watching over us, then why did he let The Sickness take my mother?" she felt her voice rising. She felt nauseated. Alana placed a hand on her stomach.

The handsome knight was caught off guard by her sudden change in tone. He stopped and faced her. "Is my princess okay?"

"Yes...I'm fine," she took her hand away from her stomach and looked at Benjamin.

"You see, Alana, some things in life are beyond the control of people, and even beyond the control of Zalus. I'm sure if Zalus could've saved your mother, he would. But I assure you, your mother is at peace now, and watching over you beyond the Western Mountains. Zalus is taking good care of her, I promise. And one day, you two will meet again." He held up his palm. "I swear by my

Junkland

honor as a Knight of the Poolesguard. Believing is what gets me up in the morning. It gives me a purpose."

But what do I believe in? Alana wondered.

Ding. Ding. Ding.

Benjamin turned to the sound of the bells. "Let's keep moving. Your father is going to have my head at our lateness."

They walked underneath the Village Gate and followed the road to the Great Hall. Alana and her knight took one step at a time as they climbed the steep, grand steps that brought them up to the giant oak doors.

The two brothers, Sir Krist Perriwill and Sir Martellus Perriwill, were there to greet them at the doors.

Benjamin gave them both a slight nod, "Krist, Martellus, I have brought the princess."

"What took you so long?" Krist asked, frustration in his voice. "The king is furious! He won't start the wedding without her. Let's get you inside, Alana." Krist motioned to his brother. "Are you going to just stand there like a fool, or open the door for Princess Alana?"

"I thought that was your job," Martellus said sarcastically. He turned to Alana, ignoring his brother. "May I say you look stunning today, my fair lady." Martellus said, giving a little bow.

Benjamin huffed. "Do I have to do everything myself?" He walked to the doors and flung them open. "After you, my lady." He waved his hands urging her towards the doors.

Alana gave Krist and Martellus a sweet smile and said, "Thank you Sir Krist, Sir Martellus," and walked through the double doors.

Before the doors closed behind her, she heard Krist slap Martellus on top of the head and say, "You are the dumbest knight in all of Astenpoole! I don't know why Piller pairs us together for every single task. I'm going to have a…"

The doors closed behind them. They were now in the entranceway of the Hall of Heroes. Past kings of Astenpoole and knights stared at her in their portraits on the walls. There was the first King of Astenpoole, Alas Danor the Voyager, also known as the Destroyer, followed by Galagar Poole the Uniter, Gabriel Poole the Divider, Caverin Poole the Simple, Aygor Poole the Strong, and dozens more. And in the center of the room was her father, Leoné Poole. Alana had heard rumors that people had begun to call him Leoné Poole the Abandoner, and she wasn't sure how she felt about that.

Footsteps echoed down the hall.

"Where have you been?" it was her father approaching them.

"I…uh…you know Father…lady things." She used that excuse for everything. Her father struggled to relate to his only daughter. He only had an older brother growing up, but Timmon Poole was an uncle Alana had never met.

Her father put a hand up to stop her. "Say no more. I don't want to hear about it." He walked over to his daughter and wrapped his arms around her. He gave her a kiss on her forehead. "I know this must be hard for you, Alana. But I'm so proud of you. I hope you know that."

Alana tried to smile. She didn't know what to say. She wasn't happy for him about this wedding.

Feeling the tension, her father turned to Benjamin. "Thank you, Sir Benjamin, for escorting my daughter here. Now, let's go start this wedding."

Together, they walked down the long hallway in the Hall of Heroes and entered the throne room. A wave of sound hit Alana. Hundreds of people filled the pews that lined either side of the room, a red carpet dividing them. People were hanging over the balcony that wrapped around the perimeter of the throne room, trying to get a better look. The carpet extended across the room, and ended at the steps to the altar. Usually the steps led up to the High Seat, or the Wave, as some nicknamed it, since the throne was in the shape of a giant wave, but an altar had taken its place for today.

There were freshly shined pillars supporting the balcony. Archways covered the first floor beneath the pillars. Carvings of stories were designed into the white marble of both the pillars and the archways. On the high ceiling, there was a painting of Zalus on his knees before the Western Mountains. His palms were raised to the sky and a baby laid upon them.

Alana and her father walked up the red carpet followed by Sir Benjamin. Her father took his spot at the altar as Benjamin guided Alana to the right front pew, following behind her. She slid in next to Sir Devan Lark. Sir Arnold Beck and Sir Hollow Tryant were to the right of Sir Devan. They were all brothers of the Poolesguard. The Captain of the Poolesguard, Sir Piller Lorne, stood guard at the bottom of the steps, his long sword in hand.

"Princess." Devan gave a slight nod as he greeted her.

The two younger knights on the other side of Devan waved.

She gave both of them a small wave back.

Suddenly, the sound of an organ began to echo throughout the hall. All eyes turned to the back of the room.

There she was—Nadia, the future queen. She was standing at the entrance. She was wearing a beautiful white wedding gown, but it did nothing to accentuate her features. The white clashed with her pale skin and her cropped black hair. Her eyes even seemed to glow a faint yellow. Alana always thought she looked like a man with her short hair and the prominent bones in her face. Nadia definitely didn't have the beauty that her mother had. She didn't know what her father saw in her. But she kept her mouth shut. She just assumed that all the women across the Farrest Sea looked like that.

Nadia began the long, slow walk to the altar as the organ played the classic wedding song. Nadia's heels echoed throughout the throne room as she ascended the steps to the altar. Her own knights parted to the side and waited below the steps.

The music stopped.

Alana's father smiled at his soon to be wife, but she only gave him half a smile back. Neither of their smiles reached their eyes.

The priest began the long ceremony.

The minutes felt like hours to Alana, but eventually the priest finally said the words she was dreading. "Do you, Leoné Poole, King of Astenpoole, take the hand of this lovely lady to be your lawfully wedded wife and queen?"

"I do," her father said. His voice echoed loudly throughout the hall.

Alana's chest tightened. She suddenly felt short of breath. She began to sweat.

The priest turned to Nadia. "And do you, Nadia of Farrest, take this man to be your lawfully wedded husband and king, and to carry out all the duties that are required from the Queen of Astenpoole?"

"I do." Nadia smiled with her perfect white teeth.

Alana felt her chest tighten even more as if it was coiling into a tiny ball.

Junkland

"By the power vested in me and through the life that flows through the palms of Zalus, I now pronounce you husband and wife, king and queen of Astenpoole. May you grow old and one day find peace together beyond the Western Mountains." The priest clapped his hands together as if to pray and gave a bow towards the altar and the newly wedded couple.

Her father and Nadia kissed in front of hundreds of eyes. The hall erupted in polite applause—except Alana.

She wanted to run, to get out of there, to never look at her father again. She wanted to escape the walls that constricted her, to escape the castle.

Alana tried to push past Benjamin, but her legs gave out before she could go one step as she collapsed to the floor.

The back of her head slammed down hard on the wood of the pew. She found herself lying on her back looking up at an open window, high above the balcony—freedom! But it was so far away.

Alana's vision was slowly fading, but she saw something black sitting on the window's edge looking down at her. It looked like a crow—but suddenly her world blurred as it spun around her, gradually growing black and silent.

Chapter 5
Jahrys

JAHRYS'S FATHER HAD been furious when he showed up late. His father had to carry all the wine cases from the house to the shop by himself. And, as soon as he got there, he was met by a huge rush of people who wanted to complete their purchases before the festivities began.

Jahrys tried to explain to his father what had happened to Kevrin, but his father only told him he was selfish and irresponsible.

For his punishment, Jahrys had to clean all the windows in the shop—and there were too many to count! He had to climb on top of a high ladder to reach the top ones. It seemed each time he climbed up, the store bell would ring, and he would have to climb all the way back down to help a customer. Jahrys cringed every time that bell rang above the door, it seemed to be neverending. All he wanted to do was finish so he could get out and enjoy the festivities…if his father would even let him leave.

Miller had been watching him, but he eventually became bored and scurried off to watch his father handle the cases of wine and woodwork.

Ding. Ding. Ding.

Jahrys groaned at the sound of the bell ringing *again*. He was only through half of the windows. He threw his rag into the bucket of water, splashing water onto his face. He groaned and wiped it off with the back of his hand before climbing down with the bucket swinging in his hand.

A rather large, pale man was standing at the counter—Frayel.

"O'Jahrys! How're you doing?" Frayel asked, giving Jahrys a hard pat on the back as Jahrys walked past him to get behind the counter. "I came by for my order."

Jahrys tried to keep a smile as he put down the bucket, splashing himself yet again with the dirty water. He wiped his hands over his already damp clothes. "Hello, Frayel. I've just been helping Father around the shop. What was your order again?" Jahrys asked, fiddling through the list of orders.

Frayel placed a note on the counter. "I got it right here. Two bottles of Grent White and a birdie house for my lovely Astonia. My Astonia does love her birdies back home on our farm—that she does."

Jahrys picked up the note and read it over. He went to the back to find Frayel's order.

"You Palorians sure know how to throw festivities," Frayel continued to talk, his voice booming all the way to the back of the shop. "We Danorian can't keep up with ya'll. I tell ya, after these festivities, Astonia and I are going straight back to our farm. The city life is no life for me—no it ain't. What about you O'Jahrys? Are ya not celebrating tonight?" asked Frayel in his thick Danorian accent.

"I have to help my father close the shop tonight," Jahrys said, disappointed. He was still searching the shelves for Frayel's name.

"Is that so? Where's your father? I wouldn't mind having a word with Alvys. A young boy like you should be out celebrating. I'm sure there will be plenty of fine ladies. You don't want to be missing that, now do ya?" Frayel let out a chuckle. "You got a lady, O'Jahrys?"

Jahrys sighed as he lifted a box filled with Frayel's order from a top shelf and carried it back to the front. "I already told you, Frayel. I do not."

"Ah, well you're too young to be tied down anyways. How old are ya again, O'Jahrys?"

"Fifteen," Jahrys answered, as he placed Frayel's order on the counter.

"By Zalus! Fifteen? I'm getting old," Frayel slapped his head playfully.

"Two bottles of Grent White and a birdhouse for your wife. Is that all?" Jahrys was getting impatient.

"Hmm, I've always wanted to try a bottle of Grent Red; I've heard good things. Might as well give me one of them, too. I'm sure the missus will love that," Frayel chuckled.

Jahrys went back to grab a third bottle and added it to the order when he returned. "Okay, Frayel. Two bottles of Grent White, a bottle of red, and a birdhouse. Is this all?"

"Hmm."

By Zalus. Jahrys tried to hold in a groan.

"Yep. That's all. Don't want to be giving my loving Astonia a heart attack with all these gifts. I'm going to be one lucky guy tonight, O'Jahrys. Remember, the ladies love gifts."

"Ladies love gifts," Jahrys repeated to please Frayel. "Thank you for the advice." Jahrys made sure the bottles of wine and the birdhouse were secure in their traveling box. "It's fifteen pooles each for the two whites, twenty pooles for the red, and fifty pooles for the birdhouse."

"By Zalus! Good thing business has been good the past few days," Frayel chuckled to himself as he fumbled through a small pouch of coins. "Here ya go," he handed the coins to Jahrys.

"Thank you. I hope you enjoy the rest of your stay in Palor."

"Thank you, O'Jahrys. I hope your father comes to his senses. Goodbye, my boy." Frayel left the shop, carrying his box.

Jahrys let out a long sigh. He picked up his bucket and climbed the ladder to finish his punishment.

He watched everyone running past the shop through the windows. They were either heading up the road to The Arcalane or to a festival along Zalus Road to celebrate the wedding. Jahrys quickened his pace, hoping to get done in time to join his friends.

Jahrys's forearms were throbbing after he finished the last window. He threw the rag into the bucket and more water splattered onto his face. He wiped it with the back of his hand and climbed down the ladder. He placed the bucket down and walked behind the counter. He plopped down on a hard wooden chair, letting out a long, deep sigh as he let his body sink into the chair.

Boys his age constantly ran past the shop, laughing as they ran up the road. Annoyed, Jahrys started to hum to block out the noise, but it was as if the laughter was competing with Jahrys; no matter how loud he hummed, the laughter was always louder. *I am going to be the only one missing out on all the festivities tonight*, thought Jahrys, as he gave up on his humming.

When there seemed to be no more customers, Jahrys opened up

a drawer and pulled out *The Knightly Tales of Astenpoole*. He had read it nearly a hundred times, but the stories never got old.

He re-read the famous story of Palor A'kal. He almost had it memorized at this point.

The story started many years ago, when Astenpoole and the Four Cities didn't even exist, and the land was covered in thick forests from the north to the south. Back then, the land between the mountains and the sea was known only as Kaluk.

Alas Danor and his new bride, Lady Kathrin, had sailed from across the Farrest Sea, landing on the forest-infested shores. He had proclaimed himself king of this new land and chopped down trees and mined the large stones near the mountains to begin building his new home—a castle—for him and Kathrin. Lady Kathrin soon became pregnant, but died during childbirth. Thankfully, their baby, a beautiful girl named Melaine, survived.

The Kalukians had been outraged at this intruder. They had lived in the forest of Kaluk since the dawn of time—before years were even recorded. They were there to see Zalus come down from the Western Mountains with his palms of light, worshiping him and using his name as a title for their leaders. And now they were being pushed out of their homes as the trees disappeared.

Paluk A'kal, the Zal of the Kalukians, had revolted against Alas Danor and his army. The Kalukians would no longer accept the foreign king and his child.

The War of Two Worlds had begun. Many died fighting the strenuous two year war.

In the end, Alas Danor had won, slaying Zal Paluk A'kal. Alas had taken Paluk's pregnant wife, Zala, to be his new queen in order to maintain peace among the Kalukians. He had fostered Paluk's son, Sible, and allowed Zala to nurse her newborn son, Palor. His own daughter, Melaine, close in age to baby Palor, was treated kindly by Queen Zala.

King Alas Danor ruled the land of Kaluk. He banished the worship of Zalus and slaughtered anyone who spoke freely of the Western God. He had continued to deforest the land, and his castle continued to grow in size. Many Kalukians disappeared, traveling farther south of Kaluk to live in the remaining forest.

King Alas and Queen Zala had a child of their own, the beautiful Princess Isabella Danor. The two princesses viewed each other as sisters, and all the children were raised as siblings. It was said that Melaine and Palor had a special bond, being the closest in age.

Years later, when they were almost grown, Palor walked in on King Alas beating his own daughter, the Princess Melaine. Filled with rage and love for his stepsister, Palor had attacked the king, stabbing him numerous times. But to Palor's ill luck, the king had been saved and healed of his wounds.

Palor was thrown into the dungeon while he waited for his death sentence. King Alas Danor knew he couldn't kill Palor, however. That would only cause another war with the Kalukians. So he decided to banish Palor over the Western Mountains.

To this day, no one knows what happened to Palor—if he ever made it over the mountains, or if he died trying. Though no one ever forgot his love and sacrifice for his stepsister.

Tragically, that same year, Princess Melaine died from a head injury when she fell down the stairs. Rumor spread that the king had pushed her down the steps.

Sible, enraged by this rumor and by the banishment of his brother, stabbed King Alas to death. Sible suffered knife wounds from the king's guards, and died as well.

Such a tragedy, thought Jahrys, as he finished the story. *They were all so brave.* Jahrys took a second to reflect before moving onto the next story—another one of his favorites, this one about Galagar Poole.

Galagar Poole was a poor boy who lived in the streets of Kaluk during the reign of King Alas Danor. His parents, both Kalukian, died when he was young. The only thing Galagar had owned were the clothes on his back and a lute that once belonged to his father. He would practice the lute day and night, listening to songs he had heard on the street and trying his best to mimic them. Once he was good enough, he began to perform in public, making a few pooles here and there, just enough to live off.

One day, King Alas Danor had been traveling and noticed Galagar playing his lute in front of a small crowd. The king had been impressed with the boy's skill. He had approached the boy and asked him if he would like to play for him at the Castle Keep. In exchange, he would provide the boy a place to sleep and food to eat.

Galagar, of course, did not hesitate to accept. He had never thought he would ever play for a king. He would play while King Alas ate, while he thought, and even while he slept. And he even got to play at some royal gatherings and parties. Most importantly, he was able to play freely in the courtyards for the common folk.

What Galagar really ended up enjoying, however, was playing for the Princess Isabella. She was two years younger than Galagar and very beautiful. Galagar described her as prettier than any sunset falling behind the Western Mountains, prettier than the pink and orange clouds that would swirl like candy during sunrise, and prettier than the millions of diamonds that would sparkle off the Farrest Sea.

Junkland

He was in love with her.

One dark and humid night, while the castle was sound asleep, outlaws had found a way inside the castle. They had snuck their way into Princess Isabella's bedchamber. No one heard them enter and no one heard them leave: except for Galagar.

Galagar had heard struggling outside of his window that night. He looked out and saw the outlaws carrying an unconscious girl across the courtyard—the princess! Galagar lifted his mattress and picked up the sword he kept hidden underneath. The one that he had stolen from the armory so he could practice in his spare time, and use if he ever needed it. He sprinted down the steps and burst open the doors that led to the courtyard. He ran after the three outlaws.

Some tales say he killed all three with a single stroke of his sword. Others say it was one, clean stroke per outlaw...but it didn't matter. Galagar Poole killed the outlaws and saved the princess. The entire castle had woken up at that point to discover the new hero. The king had rewarded Galagar with his knighthood the very next morning.

Some years later, Galagar proposed to Isabella and was warmly invited into the royal family. After King Alas was murdered by Sible, Isabella and Galagar were named the new queen and king of the land. Zala, the queen mother, became heartbroken over the demise of her family and soon passed away. Isabella, now with no family left, took Galagar's family name and became known as Queen Isabella Poole. The now king, Galagar, renamed the land and castle, Astenpoole, after his own father, and brought back the worship of Zalus.

Kalukians began to reappear from the forests of Kaluk when King Galagar promised their lands would be untouched and no more trees would be removed. That was how Galagar Poole got his nickname—the Uniter.

Jahrys leaned back and stared at the ceiling after reading the story. He daydreamed about saving a princess and killing outlaws with his own sword. He wanted to be just like Palor A'kal and Galagar P—

"What are you reading?"

Jahrys shot forward, frightened at the sudden voice. Jahrys's father popped out from the back of the shop. Miller was circling his legs. His father leaned over to look at the cover of the book. "*The Knightly Tales of Astenpoole?*" his father laughed. "Why are you wasting the space in your head with these silly fantasies, O'Jahrys?"

"For the thousandth time, call me Jahrys!" he yelled at his father. "And they aren't fantasies. These are real stories about real heroes," he said, irritated at his father for not understanding.

"Ha! If you want a real hero, you should read this…" His father walked behind the counter and pulled out a drawer. He handed his son a book.

Jahrys read the title. "*Govad's Guide for Building the Perfect Chair?*" Jahrys rolled his eyes. "Really?"

"The man knows his stuff, I tell you! The man knows his stuff." His father pointed a finger at Jahrys as if he was teaching him a lesson.

When he noticed Jahrys's disinterest in his choice of book, he changed the subject. "You know, I met King Leoné a few years back when you were just a little boy."

Jahrys's ears shot up. "You met the king?"

"I sure did. When I started selling wine, word spread quickly into

Astenpoole. King Leoné sent a messenger directly requesting I personally bring him an order of my wine so he could try it. So I made my best batch of wine and carried it to the southeast tower in the center of the Castle Keep to deliver it to the king." His father stood up proud.

"What was he like?" Jahrys asked curiously. He had never seen the king before.

"King Leoné was taller than any man I've ever laid my eyes upon. His sword was twice the size of my arm, and he was as large as an ox. But! He was nicer than any man I've met.

"He took a sip of my wine and was astonished. He shook my hand and told me to bring him a hundred more cases so he could share it with his family and friends inside the castle."

"That's…I never knew," Jahrys said, ashamed he didn't know this about his own father.

"I guess my point is…heroes don't always have to wear armor and carry swords, O'Jahrys. A hero can be anyone who simply makes a king's day by a taste of his wine." His father smiled at Jahrys and turned to look at the windows. "Well, I have to say, you did a good job on the windows." He turned back to Jahrys. "Thank you, son. I know I was a bit hard on you earlier."

Jahrys watched his father's eyes examine his face. "Your eye is looking better." His father pointed out. "You know, son, your mother doesn't like your sword fighting with Kevrin. And by Zalus! All this talk about becoming a knight…you're going to give your mother a heart attack."

Jahrys turned his head, not wanting to hear what his father had to say.

"But I remember when I was your age," his father chuckled and continued, "yep, I remember I used to dream about being a sailor. That I would build my own boat with my bare hands and sail across the Farrest Sea to distant lands and adventures that were beyond the horizon, just like King Alas Danor had done."

Jahrys turned back to look at his father. He didn't know his father had any dreams. "Why didn't you?" Jahrys asked curiously.

His father placed a hand on Jahrys's shoulder. "I grew up. And those dreams faded. Now, I have your beautiful mother and you as my wonderful son. That's the best dream Zalus could have given me."

Jahrys's head dropped again, disappointed.

His father wasn't done, though. "Don't grow up, Jahrys."

Jahrys looked up, surprised at this sudden change and how his father said his name.

"Keep dreaming. The world needs people like you now more than ever. People who believe in themselves." He pointed a finger at Jahrys's chest. "Because when the world goes dark, the dreamers will be the ones who find the light."

There was an awkward silence. Jahrys had never heard his father speak this way before.

Laughter came from outside as more kids ran up the road as the last bit of sunlight was hanging onto the day. Jahrys stared out the window, wishing he could join them.

His father must have noticed the disappointment in his eyes. "Look at the time," he said. "Why don't you head on out and join your friends. I'll close up shop tonight."

Jahrys's head spun back to his father. "What?" he couldn't believe what he just heard.

"Go! A kid your age shouldn't be cooped up inside the night of a royal wedding."

Jahrys jumped up from his chair. "You really mean it?" He still couldn't believe it.

"Yes. Go! Before I change my mind…" His father waved a hand towards the door.

"Father—"

"No need. Miller will help me close up."

"BUCUUUUUUCK!" Miller yelled when he heard his name. He had the keys to his father's shop already hanging from his beak.

"You see?" his father waved a hand at Miller.

Jahrys laughed.

"Thank you, Father!" Jahrys threw his book back inside the drawer and sprinted around the counter. He gave his father a hug, patted Miller on the head, and threw open the front door. But before he walked out, he turned back to his father. "You should build your boat."

His father looked at him and smiled. "Perhaps I will…perhaps I will."

Jahrys turned to walk out the door.

"Hey, Jahrys…" his father called out before he left.

Jahrys turned back again. He was afraid his father had changed his mind.

"Don't tell your mother," his father said chuckling, but then he gave him a serious look.

Jahrys motioned his fingers across his closed lips, letting his father know his secret was safe with him. He turned and walked out of his father's shop.

The sun was almost gone behind the Western Mountains, but the night was young. He traveled up the road, towards The Arcalane.

Music filled the air along with drunken laughter, shouting, and yelling. The city was alive.

He couldn't wait to see Elyara, Gabe, Kat, Tarl, and all his other friends at The Arcalane. He was also hoping Kevrin had made a recovery and would join them tonight. It was going to be a night to remember.

"AHHH!"

Someone was screaming. Jahrys turned his head. It sounded like it was coming from a market square off to the side. He heard the sound of struggling.

"HELP!" It sounded like a girl.

Jahrys didn't hesitate. He ran towards the yells.

Chapter 6

Piller

DEVAN RAISED HIS mug from across the table with his stocky arms. "Cheers to good friends and peace in Astenpoole," he cheered. He was already drunk.

The other five knights joined Devan at the center of the table. The mugs collided with a loud clunk. Beer spilled over Piller's mug and onto his left hand. He flicked his hand to the side, getting as much beer off as he could. He lifted his drink to his mouth and took a sip. He placed it back down on the table as the others did the same.

"Ah. Now that's refreshing after a long day." Devan leaned back in his chair with his arms behind his head—his long brown beard, flicked with gray, was lying on his chest. Piller glanced at Devan.

At forty-two, Devan was the oldest knight in the Poolesguard. He had been next in line for captain after Landerin Raneir was forced to resign. However, Devan had turned down the opportunity. He claimed he had seen what the role does to great men and wanted no part of it.

So that was how Piller had become the ninth captain of the Poolesguard at the age of thirty-four. *Maybe I should have turned it down, too,* Piller thought, as he rubbed the pin on his leather tunic with his fingers. The metal pin was shaped into the palms of Zalus, signifying him as the captain.

"This would be a great night for a game of Pooles and Palms, don't you think?" Devan asked the question around the table.

"Ha," Krist laughed, waving his muscular arms into the air. "So you can just cry again when you lose all your pooles? I don't think tonight is the night for that. We're here to celebrate the new marriage."

"I agree," Arnold, the youngest knight of the Poolesguard, chimed in. "I don't want a repeat of the other night to be quite honest. I don't think my ears could handle that much yelling and antagonizing again."

"Maybe if you all weren't a bunch of rotten cheaters trying to rob me." Devan spat. He took another sip from his mug, white foam covered his beard when he brought the mug down. He wiped it clean with one of his large hands.

Piller turned his head towards Devan. "We weren't cheating you. And besides we're down a player anyway." Piller scratched the scar on his left side that ran from his forehead down to the right side of his jaw.

"Where's the princess lover anyway?" Martellus said sarcastically, as he moved a strand of black hair from his eye.

"*Benjamin* is guarding the princess's bedchamber," answered Piller, as he stressed Benjamin's name.

"That poor girl," Hollow shook his head. "Must be a lot of pressure on her with her mother gone and all." He took a large gulp from his mug. Hollow was the second youngest knight in the Poolesguard and like Arnold, this was his first year.

"I knew she wasn't taking her mother's death lightly. Heck, I didn't take my own mother's death lightly. But to collapse at your own father's wedding—" Devan pushed a hand through his thinning hair. "By Zalus, who would have thought it was that bad."

Piller looked down. He thought about his own mother and how he had felt when she had died. He felt pity for the young Princess Alana.

"She has been the talk of the party tonight. I don't think any of us were prepared for that. Who is taking care of her?" Arnold asked. He had to raise his voice over the noise inside their tent.

"Galla went to her tower shortly after the incident. She has been giving the princess some fresh herbs to calm her down," Piller said, as he looked around at his brothers. All their eyes were sitting on their drinks, cupped between their hands. "The princess is resting now."

A serving girl approached the knights at the round table. "Would you good sirs like another round?"

"My good dear! Do I look drunk yet?" said Devan hotly, waving his empty mug into the air. "Fill us up again with your finest ale!"

"I would like a water actually, miss," Krist said politely.

Devan turned to Krist and spat. "When are you going to be a real man and drink with us?" He turned back to the serving girl. "Get this muscle man an ale, will ya?"

The serving girl gave a nervous chuckle, took their mugs, and walked away before Krist could protest. She walked towards the bar underneath the tent.

"Will you look at that," Devan was staring at the serving girl as she walked away. "She has curves as wavy as the Farrest Sea."

"Leave her be!" Krist yelled at Devan.

Devan gave Krist a bold look. "Are you telling me you don't find *that*"—he pointed to the serving girl who was grabbing the drinks from the bartender—"remotely attractive?"

"I...yes...I mean—"

"Ha! Then shut your trap. She's coming back now."

When she returned, she handed them all new mugs. Krist was pleased he had received the water he had requested, and a little wink to go along with it. He blushed.

Devan didn't notice. He gave her an innocent look. "What does a knight like myself have to do for a dance with a pretty girl like you?" Devan asked, drunkenly.

She smiled at Devan. "I'm flattered, sir. But I'm working until the end of the party. But"—she placed a hand on her hip—"you can start by referring to me as a lady and *not* as a girl." She turned and walked away, giving him a sassy smile over her shoulder.

"By the palms of Zalus," Devan didn't take his eyes off her. "I think I'm in love."

Piller rolled his eyes. *He's a drunken fool*, he thought to himself.

While the brothers continued to discuss the princess, Piller let his eyes wander around the courtyard. They were seated in one of the five large tents that surrounded the dance floor.

The water that flowed from Zalus's palms glowed in the slowly setting sun. A beautiful mixture of pink and cream orange swirled in the sky. As the day transformed into night, the courtyard began to glow in the warm candlelight.

A blend of talking and yelling flowed throughout the yard. Women flirted with men, children ran and giggled under tables, dogs barked and chased other dogs, and old men told stories of their younger years to all that would listen.

"Aye! Zatum!" Piller's attention was brought back to the table as Devan shouted to a boy who was hurrying out of the tent. "Who invited you to this wedding?"

The boy was shaking from head to toe. He looked nervous and out of place. "I...I...the king...invited me, Sir...I am...his messenger...S-S-Sir."

"Har! Just be messing with ya, kid," he slapped Zatum on the back. "Now get runnin' off. Don't be keepin' the ladies awaitin'." He waved Zatum away. The boy hurried out of the tent, giving a nervous glance behind his shoulder.

The dance floor was picking up as the band began to play their third set of the night. The newly weds entered the dance floor. King Leoné twirled his new wife around as people gathered around to watch. The band felt the vibe of the crowd and increased the tempo of their song. The dance floor soon became wild. All the women from Piller's tent piled out onto the dance floor.

"Well," Devan sat up from the table. "I don't know about you lot, but it isn't every day I get to be a free man." He took one last, large gulp to finish his mug. He wiped the foam off his beard and then patted down his cherry colored robes. "Now if you excuse me, I'll be out there looking for a woman to warm my bed tonight. Har!" Devan stumbled off to the dance floor, mumbling drunken nonsense to himself.

Two lovely ladies, who looked to be identical twins, approached their table. They were both wearing the same yellow sundress. They both skipped over to either side of Martellus and leaned into his ears—whispering something too quiet for Piller to hear.

Martellus laughed. "Woo! Sheila! Nayna! Let's start with a dance first."

The twins giggled and each took one of Martellus's hands.

Martellus rose. "Well boys. Looks like I'm being summoned." He gave a farewell smile. "Watch my beer," he winked at Krist, as the twins dragged him to the dance floor.

Krist chugged his water and slammed it onto the table. "Damn him. I don't know how he does it." He shook his head in disbelief.

Piller, Hollow, and Arnold exchanged glances across the table, laughing silently.

The four remaining knights turned their gaze to the dance floor, watching their brothers make fools of themselves. Devan was talking to a thin, tall blonde at the corner of the squared floor. She looked young, but she was at least a full head taller than he was. He would have to get on his toes to even attempt to kiss her.

Piller could only imagine what outdated stories he was telling her.

Martellus was twirling Sheila around with one hand and Nayna with the other. His footing was excessively better than his partners. *He's so different from his brother,* thought Piller, laughing to himself.

Suddenly, the crowd began to back away from the center as a man stumbled from a tent onto the dance floor. It was Landerin Raneir, the old Captain of the Poolesguard; he was better known as Old Lan these days.

Old Lan spun drunkenly around, his arms swinging above his head like a mad man. His mug was still half-full in his right hand, and he showered the crowd around him with ale. The women shrieked and yelled as beer rained down on their clothing. Old Lan was trying to sing along with the band, but he was failing profusely. His moment of fame ended quickly when he tripped over a woman's foot. He went down face first and made no sort of effort of rising back up. Two of his friends dragged him off the dance floor.

Piller felt pity for the old knight. He had lost his entire family in The Sickness. Piller felt especially bad because it was mainly his fault for Landerin's forced resignation as captain a year ago. Landerin was now a common guard at the Western Gate. Piller had thought he was doing Landerin a favor when he had turned him in for being drunk on duty. But now he wasn't so sure.

When the band ended their song, the singer spoke to the crowd. "All right, all right. It seems things are getting a little rowdy out there. We're going to bring it down a notch. Here's an old classic."

The band started their next song. It was slower—more romantic. Men grabbed their women and pulled them to the dance floor, dancing slowly to the peaceful melody.

> *Under this mountain and starry sky,*
> *Is where I leave you and say goodbye.*
> *Do not cry, for I shall be back soon,*
> *Love will bring me back to Astenpoole...*

Piller's heart dropped. He knew this song. It was the song his mother sang to him when he was a young boy. She would sing it to him after she told the story of Palor A'kal and Princess Melaine; it was the song Palor sung to Princess Melaine when he said goodbye to her beneath the mountains.

It was also the song Piller's mother sang right before she died.

Piller rose from the table. "Please excuse me," he said to the three remaining brothers.

"Are you okay, Cap'?" asked Krist, looking worried.

"Yes…I'm fine. Just going to go for a walk. I'll catch up with you all later." He turned and walked away from the festivities.

He left the Village and walked down King's Road. He passed the magnificent architecture of the Great Hall on his left, and the armory on his right, before leaving the Castle Keep underneath the King's Gate. He followed a path that wrapped around the north part of the wall, passing through Northside and bringing him to the Eastern Village. The streets were deserted. Everyone was either celebrating inside the Castle Keep or out in the Western Village at the bars on Pooles Road.

It was silent on the eastern side of the castle. It was as if all the noise had been sucked away. It was also dark, save for the faint candlelight glowing in the graveyard on a hill not too far away. Piller followed the path towards the rusty gate of the graveyard.

Not many people came to this side of the castle anymore, not since King Leoné had permanently shut the Eastern Gate four years ago to prevent Carriers from entering the castle. It was a shame, really. Piller had always enjoyed the eastern side of Astenpoole, with its peaceful courtyards, its view of the Seaport River, and the talk of sailors from the Farrest Sea.

Piller walked up to the gate of the graveyard, opening it with a loud creak. It slammed shut behind him. He followed the path straight up, taking a right that wrapped around the hill. The tombstones resembled a tiny city. He had to step off the grass to get to his destination. Three gravestones were before him. He knelt down in front of the stones.

The first stone read:

Junkland

> *Cladus Lorne*
> *848 A.Z.–890 A.Z.*
> *May you find peace with Zalus*
> *Beyond the Western Mountains.*

The stone to the right read:

> *Malah Lorne*
> *849 A.Z.–901 A.Z.*
> *May you heal and find rest*
> *With your love, Cladus,*
> *Beyond the Western Mountains.*

Piller wiped a tear from his eye, laying a finger over the smooth bump from his scar. He was grateful he didn't have to burn his parent's bodies and that he could still be with them here. His mother had died before King Leoné passed the law that all victims of The Sickness were to be burned after death; he was thankful for that at least. His father was murdered when Piller was only eleven years old. He had failed to save them both.

"I'm sorry, Father." His head sank down to his chest. "I'm sorry for not being strong enough to save you. I'm sorry, Mother. For not being able to protect you. I have failed you both." Piller lifted his head. "I wish you were here with me tonight. To see me as Captain of the Poolesguard." He took in a deep breath. "I'll make you proud...I promise." He lifted his gaze towards their graves. "Dammit, I *will* make you proud," he whispered.

After Piller was finished, he stood up and looked at the third tombstone next to his mother's. His heart hurt as he thought back to his first night on duty and to that little girl. "I hope you are resting peacefully beyond the Western Mountains, little one." He bent down and kissed the tombstone and whispered, "I'm sorry."

The little girl everyone thought he had saved...*she'd be a young woman now*, he thought.

AHWOOO. AHWOOO. AHWOOO.

Piller turned his head back to the Castle Keep. *The King's Horn,* Piller thought. *Something is wrong!* The King's Horn was only blown in time of great need within the Castle Keep. Piller sprinted as fast as he could to get back to the festivities.

When he arrived back at the festivities, he had to weeve through worried people until he found King Leoné.

"Piller, where have you been?" King Leoné demanded, looking worried.

"Forgive me, Your Grace. The King's Horn—What has happened?" Piller asked.

"It's Alana," Leoné said in a worried voice. "She is missing!"

Chapter 7
Alana

SHE WAS FREE! Alana breathed in the fresh air as she walked away from the castle. Each step she took made her feel a hundred times happier, and the pain in her head from when she fell was completely forgotten. The Western Mountains looked larger than ever as she gazed up at the white peaks that faded into the clouds. The sun was high above her head, warming her body.

Alana had been taken back to her bedchamber after she had fainted during her father's wedding. Galla the Healer came to her with bottles of herbs that she forced Alana to take and an ice cloth to place on her head.

After Galla and Sir Benjamin left her to rest, and everyone was out enjoying the festivities, Alana escaped through the hidden door behind her bookcase in her bedchamber. She had finally used the secret passageway she had found to escape Astenpoole. She needed to be free and as far away as possible from her father—and from Nadia.

Alana took in another deep, flowing breath. She breathed out, forgetting everything about the wedding, her father, Nadia, Mother Claraine and her handmaids, and Galla's disgusting herbs.

She had on black woolen trousers underneath an old green long-sleeved dress, with a dark cloak over both. She had tried to wash herself off a bit in the Seaport River before she crossed the bridge that had taken her into Palor, but she knew she wouldn't be able to get all the dirt and dust off of her face and clothes from the tunnel. She hid her face under the hood of her dark cloak.

The streets were filled with people drinking ale and wine, talking about good times, singing and dancing by the stages, and playing card games. People scurried around like ants, weaving in and out of all the shops that populated the road.

"Good evening, my lady," a large man tipped his hat to her. He was pulling a donkey.

"Good evening," she replied, giving him a nice smile.

"Hello, my dear," a plump old lady said to her while passing. She was holding a basket of vegetables pressed against her bosom.

Alana smiled at her. *They don't recognize me,* she thought as she cautiously pulled her hood off her head.

She twirled around the streets of Palor, her bag flying over her shoulder. Alana continued down the road as the lemon colored sun gradually turned orange, sinking deeper behind the Western Mountains.

The middle of the cobblestone road eventually became too crowded. Alana pushed herself out to the side so she was able to breathe. She popped out through the wall of people into the entrance of a market square. Tents and shops lined the square with women, men, and children appearing and disappearing from all the entrances and exits. There was a statue of Palor A'kal in the center;

Junkland

it wasn't as large as the statue inside the Castle Keep, but Alana liked this one more because of its simplicity. Kids were skipping on the lawn next to the statue as their mothers kept a weary eye on them.

Alana crossed into the market square.

"Get your fresh stew here! Fresh stew," a man with a large beard yelled off to the side.

"Diamonds and pearls! I have diamonds and pearls," a woman shouted.

"Fresh roots, my lady?" an older woman asked, resembling Galla the Healer. She held out a root that looked like it was just plucked from the ground. Dirt was crumbling off it and small roots, like tiny hairs, were poking from the sides.

"No, thanks," Alana smiled and continued walking.

"Squirrels and rabbits. I got squirrels and rabbits right here," a man banged on a cage filled with shaking rodents as he yelled.

Alana walked down the market, peaking inside all the tents and trying her best to avoid all the hagglers.

"My lady, you would look lovely in this dress," an extremely large woman said, approaching her, holding a beautiful plum colored sundress in front of Alana's body. "You *must* try it on."

Alana almost said no, but caught herself. *Why else did I come out here if not to enjoy myself?* "Sure! I'll try it on."

"Come, come, come." The lady placed a gentle hand on Alana's back as she guided her inside. Clothes hung on racks that filled the tent. Women of all ages were browsing the racks.

The lady showed Alana to a dressing room. "This one right here, my sweet."

"Thank you," Alana said politely as she took the dress from the lady's hands and stepped into the dressing room.

Alana tossed her bag to the floor and stripped down to her undergarments, tossing the cloak and her clothes onto her bag in the corner. She slid into the sundress, untucking her hair which had got caught behind the dress. She turned to look at herself in the full-length mirror. The dress had a beautiful pattern of marigold yellow flowers over a background of plum purple. There were pockets on the side seams. The length was just above her knees, something that would be considered inappropriate inside the castle, but with her calves bare, she felt free. She gave herself a little twirl before exiting the dressing room.

"Ah, my sweet," the large lady said, putting a fat hand over her mouth. "You look absolutely marvelous!"

I need to replace Mother Claraine with this lady. "Thank you. How much is this dress?"

"Well, originally, it was a hundred pooles, but since you look just absolutely stunning in it…I only ask for fifty."

Alana fumbled inside her bag, searching for her money purse. She took out a few coins. "Here is fifty pooles for the dress…another fifty pooles for your service…and another twenty to wish you the best."

"My sweet—I—thank you! By the palms of Zalus, I thank you!" The lady squeezed Alana so tight that she thought her insides were going to burst. Her face was crushed into the lady's large bosom as she struggled to breathe. "May the palms of Zalus shine light on you and your family."

Except for Nadia, thought Alana, as she broke free from the embrace. Alana went back to the dressing room to put her old clothes into her bag. She exited the room, waved goodbye, and walked back out into the market in her new dress.

A band began to play in the center. There was a man with a lute, a few horns, and a drummer. The melody they played was gorgeous. Children were dancing in front of the band while mothers applauded and laughed. It reminded Alana of the times her mother took her to the Western Village to listen to the music on the street.

The music followed her around the market as she continued to curiously look into all the shops.

When the sun had finally begun to fade behind the mountains and the shops began to close, Alana started her way back. She didn't want someone realizing she was gone. She walked back towards the main road. She knew she would have to face her fears inside the castle eventually. She couldn't stay away forever.

The main road was almost upon her as she passed the last tent in the market square. Curiousity tempted her to look inside.

Alana stopped in her tracks. Something shiny had caught her eye. She made a detour into the tent and walked over to a small table that displayed the most peculiar necklace Alana had ever seen. The necklace had a blue pendant, but she could not make out the type of stone. It wasn't sapphire, nor was it a blue diamond. She picked it up to get a closer look at the gemstone—it was round, a perfect circle, like a full moon on the nights of the Coming of Zalus. It was an even darker blue than she first thought, like the water of the Farrest Sea, or better yet, like the eyes of her mother's. *Is that what it reminds me of? Her eyes?* She thought as she stared into it.

Alana had never seen a necklace as beautiful as this before, even in the most expensive jewelry markets in the Village. *I wonder how much this costs.* Alana placed her bag on the ground and searched for a price tag.

A hand suddenly shot out, catching her wrist.

Her heart leaped in surprise.

"Trying to steal from Hugo are we, little girl?" The man was huge and his eyes were wide with fury. His dark mustache was curled in anger. "I shall cut off this little hand of yours to teach you never to steal from Hugo's shop again!"

"But I was just looking for—" Alana began. She struggled to free her hand but his grip was too tight.

"Silence, little girl!" He had taken out a long curved blade from his belt with his free hand and slammed her arm hard onto the table.

"AHHH!" Alana winced from the pain. "Please! I was looking—HELP! Please…"

Everyone in the market busily carried on, minding their own business, not paying her any attention.

Alana saw the long blade rise high into the air. All the jewelry in the room reflected off the steel, blinding her. Everything seemed to move in slow motion. Alana's heart was about to jump out of her chest, her mind was spinning, and her body was shaking. She was too scared to scream anymore. She watched as the blade hung in the air for what seemed an eternity before it came swinging down. She turned, looking the other way; she was too scared to look.

Thump.

Hugo groaned. "What the…"

Alana spun around to see that her arm was still attached to her body. There was a rock lying on the table.

Hugo was rubbing the back of his head, distracted as he looked around for the culprit.

The grip loosened on her wrist.

She wriggled free, but she felt a new hand grab her. She tried to break loose and was about to let out a cry when she heard a whisper in her ear.

"Stay quiet…grab my hand."

Alana looked up. From the corner of her eye she saw a boy, and without thinking, she gave him her hand. He pulled her out of the tent and back out onto the road, leaving her bag behind.

"Somebody stop them! Thieves!" she heard Hugo yelling.

She saw a group of men, almost the same size as Hugo, chasing after them, each with long, curved blades. *If they catch me…they will find out who I am!*

The boy's rough hand tightened around hers. She felt her heart racing inside her chest as the boy brought her down a maze of alleyways off the main road. The shouts from Hugo's men were close behind.

The boy tugged her to the right as they popped out into another market square, this one even more densely filled with people. The boy flung her up against a nearby wall and signaled her to be silent.

Sweat dripped down Alana's neck and her body was shaking. She felt the boy's warm breath against her cheek; his chest was against hers. She could feel his heart beating. She realized he was just as nervous as she was.

Hugo's men broke out into the market. Alana and the boy looked away from the street, staring at each other. After a few long seconds, they both turned back and saw that Hugo and his men had run right past them.

Alana let out the breath she felt like she had been holding in for hours. She turned to face the boy. He looked to be about her age, maybe a little older. He was handsome, his skin was tan, a perfect match against his brown, wavy hair. What really caught Alana's attention was how blue his eyes were.

"Uh, do you mind? I can't feel my arm…" The boy broke the silence.

Alana looked down and realized she was digging her fingernails into the boy's skin. She quickly released him. "I'm sorry!" she turned away embarrassed. "I didn't realize…"

"No need for apologies, Miss…"

"Bellsworth," it was the first name that popped into her head. "Lily Bellsworth."

"Ah…Miss Bellsworth. I am guessing no one taught you to never steal from Hugo's shop?" he said, teasingly.

"I didn't steal from him." Alana's voice rose as she defended herself.

"Then what's *that*…" The boy pointed at the necklace dangling out of her closed hand.

Alana blushed as she looked down, opening her hand to reveal the necklace. "I didn't realize I still had it…"

"You have great taste in shopping, I see," the boy leaned over to look at the blue pendant.

"It just reminded me of…" she was silent for a second, her eyes lost in the blue as images of her mother flooded her mind. She jerked her head back up to face the boy. "I didn't mean to steal. I'm going to return this right now." She snapped her hand shut, placing the necklace into the pocket of her dress. She turned to walk back towards the main road—wherever that was.

The boy grabbed her wrist and pulled her back. "I wouldn't do that if I were you."

"And why shouldn't I? Who are you to tell me what I should and shouldn't do?" she barked at him, shaking her wrist free.

"Hugo has a hard time listening to people. And if I'm not mistaken, I think you'd be down an arm right now if it weren't for me." The boy gave her a sly smile.

"Fair enough. Thank you for saving me, but I really must be getting back now. My father needs me." She turned away, still not sure where she was supposed to go.

"Wait—"

Alana impatiently turned back around. "What?"

"One drink," it was all the boy said.

"Why should I get a drink with a boy I don't even know?"

"Because I saved you and you want to reward my brave heart." The boy gently took her hand as if she would run away at any second. "One drink, and I can show you a side of Palor you've never seen before."

Alana stared into the boy's trusting eyes. She liked him, but she knew she must be getting back; it was late, and they would soon discover she was missing. *But isn't this what I left Astenpoole for? For adventure?*

Alana let out a long exhale. "Okay...one drink," she held up a serious finger, "and then I must be getting back."

Chapter 8
Alana

AFTER TRAVELING BACK to the main road, Alana and the boy walked towards the castle. The sun was completely gone now and people were stumbling all over the streets. Music still echoed in the night air as people laughed and told stories.

"You're going to love this place," the boy said to her.

They stopped in front of an old inn that looked like it was about to collapse at any second. People were stumbling in and out of the door. The sign at the front was swinging lightly with the gentle breeze. The sign read: *The Arcalane*.

They walked inside. The volume increased dramatically. People were yelling, screaming, shouting, arguing, and singing all at once. Mugs were swinging in the air, spilling drinks on people's heads. The room smelled like ale, with a faint haze of smoke. People constantly walked up and down the stairs on the right side of the bar, coming and going from their rooms. The bar ran almost the entire length of the room. The opening to the left led to a back room around the corner. Two pillars sat in the center that ran up to the ceiling. The

Junkland

high tables and chairs that surrounded them were filled with people laughing over their drinks. A dozen booths lined the windows, and a huge stage sat against the left wall. The band was in the middle of a song that Alana did not recognize. People were dancing, twirling, spinning, and jumping all around the stage.

How does all this fit inside this tiny inn? She thought to herself.

"Come on. Let me grab you that drink," the boy smiled at her, taking her hand as he dragged her through the crowd to the bar.

"Two of your finest ales, Havrick," the boy said to the man with the crooked nose behind the bar.

"Of course, my friend! How's your father doing?"

"He's closing up shop now. We had a lot of business today."

"Ah, that's good to hear," the man named Havrick said, as he slid the boy the two mugs.

"That'd be ten pooles."

The boy handed the bartender ten coins and turned, handing Alana her drink. She stared at the mysterious drink in her hands; she had never tried alcohol before. They told her it wasn't lady-like at the castle—that it was for dried up women who had nothing better to do but drink their sorrows away.

"Cheers!" the boy clacked his mug against hers, a bit spilling over onto her fingers. The boy took a sip. Alana followed.

She couldn't help but gag. It was terrible. The most bitter tasting drink she had ever had. *Why do people like this?* she wondered.

The boy laughed.

"Never had ale before?" the boy asked, trying to sound polite, but Alana knew he was mocking her.

Alana shook her head while cringing her nose.

"The first sip is always the worst. The second sip will be better...I promise." The boy took a second sip from his mug, spilling it yet again, almost all over her new dress, but it only splattered the floor.

"I still don't know your name?" Alana asked curiously, shaking the ale off her fingers.

"My name is—"

"O'Jahrys!" a giant man with a huge mustache and thinning hair slapped a hand on the boy's back.

Alana noticed the boy grimace and turn the color of a tomato at the sound of his name. *I don't blame him. It's such a funny name.*

"I see your father didn't punish you too hard tonight?" The large man placed two hands on his belly and chuckled.

"Trust me, Willem," said Jahrys. "I'm just as shocked as you are."

The man named Willem turned to Alana, eyeing her with his large eyes as he ran a thumb and index finger through his mustache. "And who is this fine lady you got here, O'Jahrys?"

"Willem, this is Lily. Willem is the innkeeper and owner of The Arcalane," the boy said.

"It's a pleasure to meet you," Alana extended her hand in greeting.

"No my lady, the pleasure is mine," he bent down to kiss her hand.

Alana blushed.

"She's a beauty, O'Jahrys. Don't screw it up," he gave the boy a playful nudge. The boy turned red again.

"How's Kevrin? Is he around?" the boy asked.

"Ah. He ran off when he woke up. Didn't say much either." Willem turned to the crowd and pointed to a Kalukian girl talking to a group of people around a high table. "His lady friend is over there, though. Maybe she'll tell you more." The large man turned to Alana. "It was a pleasure meeting you, my lady. This here boy is a good lad. He'll treat ya well!" Willem left them alone, chuckling to himself as he walked away.

"O'Jahrys?" Alana giggled.

She watched as his face reddened.

"Yea, yea. Get it out of your system."

"Do you have a nickname…O'Jahrys," she put a hand up to her mouth to try and stop her giggles.

"Jahrys." He smiled at her.

"Okay…Jahrys. Besides spilling more ale all over me, what are we to do?" she asked, looking around the crowded room.

"Come on. I'll introduce you to some more people." Jahrys grabbed her hand again and dragged her towards the tables in the center.

"Jahrys!" the Kalukain girl smiled at him as they approached her table. Her hair was darker than the night sky, and her skin and eyes were only a shade lighter. She was beautiful.

"Lily…this is Elyara M'ava," Jahrys introduced them.

"Nice to meet you, Lily," Elyara said in her thick Kalukian accent, leaning over to kiss Alana on both her cheeks. Alana blushed; she wasn't used to the Kalukian culture.

"I like your dress. That must have cost a fortune. Are you from the Manor?" asked Elyara.

"Yes…my parents own a house on Ocean Lake," she lied.

"Ah! I had a feeling you were from High Point. You Sibleman wear fancier clothes than people inside the castle," Elyara said, feeling a piece of fabric from Alana's dress.

Alana didn't know if she should feel insulted or complimented.

"Are the stories true about the sea monster?" Jahrys asked Alana curiously.

"Sea monster?"

Jahrys's eyes lit up. "You're telling me you live by Ocean Lake and you haven't heard the stories about the Octa Monster?"

Alana shook her head, she regretted asking.

Jahrys couldn't believe it. "Would you like to tell it, Elyara?"

Elyara took a sip from her mug and began, "The Octa Monster is believed to be left over from the First Age, back before this land was known as Astenpoole, even further back, before it was known as Kaluk. The land below the Western Mountains, from Danor to the southern tip of Kaluk, from Palor, to the edge of High Point, was all covered by the ocean. It was an age where sea monsters were the kings of the world.

"As time sped forward, the water level began to lower, and land sprouted below the Western Mountains. The Kalukians eventually populated the newly forested land and the water was pushed back to what we now call the Farrest Sea. However, a small part of the ancient sea never left this land. Ocean Lake is the last remaining body of water from the ancient times, filled with salt water—a small ocean.

"Sailors and fishermen have told stories of sighting a sea monster that has survived all these years and lives in the deep waters of the lake. A sea monster with tentacles that rise above the waters, wrapping around whatever it can grasp onto, and taking it down to the deep depths of the watery abyss. There have been so many sightings of this monster with eight tentacles that they gave it the name, the Octa Monster."

Junkland

Elyara leaned her head back, taking a large sip from her mug, and slammed it down hard on the table.

"That's quite a story." Alana was shocked she had never heard it before. "I've never seen the Octa Monster, though."

"Keep your eyes peeled. The world's full of little secrets. What brought you to Palor anyway? The festivities?"

"My father…is…ill," she was struggling to come up with a quick lie.

"Ill?" Jahrys repeated, concerned.

Alana quickly came up with a story. "Yes. He's ill and I've heard Palor has an herb called Iliken."

"Ah. Yes. The herb that helped cure The Sickness. That's sure to clear him up," Elyara assured her.

"You're Kalukian?" It was the first thing Alana could think to say. She needed to change the subject from herself.

"From head to toe," Elyara giggled. "I like her Jahrys. Don't mess it up."

Jahrys's face reddened yet again.

"Have you heard from Kevrin at all?" Jahrys asked Elyara.

"Not a word. I heard what happened earlier, though. That doesn't sound like my Kevrin." The serving girl brought over new mugs for the table. Elyara grabbed her new mug and took a large gulp.

Alana was barely on her second sip of her first mug. She followed Elyara and brought the mug up to her mouth. Jahrys was right. The second sip tingled her lips and made her feel warm inside, much better than the first.

"I guess we'll find out tomorrow," Jahrys sighed, looking worried about this friend, Kevrin.

Elyara leaned over the table towards Alana. "You need to see these two together, Lily. Kevrin and Jahrys look so alike!" Elyara giggled, keeping her voice low.

"That is not true." Jahrys overheard her and stepped in. "Kevrin has black hair and I have brown. I would also say that I'm more handsome."

"Keep telling yourself that," Elyara teased him.

"Jahrys!" a pale boy at the table spun around to face them. The rest of the people at the table turned around, too. They had been preoccupied with the band. "Who's your lady friend?"

All eyes were on Alana. She tried her best not to look nervous.

"Everybody, this is Lily Bellsworth. Lily, this is Tarl Frast, Gabe Glumberman, and Kat Laver." Jahrys pointed, matching the name with the person.

They all greeted Alana kindly. "It's a pleasure to meet you all. Everyone is so nice here."

"That's Palor for you!" they all said in unison and laughed.

Alana giggled and took another sip from her mug.

"Have you managed to steal a case of wine from your father yet?" the boy named Gabe asked Jahrys from across the table. He was slightly overweight. His skin was as white as the inside of a coconut. Judging by his slight accent, Lily guessed he was Danorian.

"I don't think it's going to happen any time soon," Jahrys said.

"By the palms of Zalus." Gabe banged his hand against the table playfully. "You're disappointing me, O'Jahrys. The things I'd do for Grent Wine."

Jahrys gave Gabe an evil stare.

Grent Wine…where have I heard that name before? Alana thought. Suddenly, it came to her. *From Father!* "Are you the son of Alvys Grent?

Junkland

The famous winemaker?" she asked curiously.

"Ha! You hear that Jahrys? Your father is famous!" Tarl laughed. He had a slight Kalukian accent, but his skin was a much lighter shade than Elyara's.

Jahrys ignored him. "Yes, he's my father." He tried not to sound too proud.

"My father, K—" she stopped before she gave herself away "—Kane, loves your father's wine! It's all he talks about." Alana laughed, feeling her head start to spin as she took another sip. "Out of all the boys to save me…"

"Save you?" Kat chimed in. She placed a hand on Jahrys's chest as if he was on display. "Jahrys can barely save himself from getting into trouble with his father."

The table chuckled.

"Who told you about today?" Jahrys asked, annoyed.

"Word spreads quickly around The Arcalane," Kat said. "You should know that already." She gave Jahrys a flirty smile.

Alana felt a small bite of jealousy.

Alana stood up straight and let the ale do the talking—she had almost finished her mug, and she could feel the change in her. "Jahrys saved me all right. I was accused of stealing a fancy necklace from a man called Hugo—"

She was interrupted by a sound of disgust from around the table. Apparently Hugo was unliked all around.

Alana pulled out the necklace from her pocket to show everyone. The blue pendant glimmered in the light. Every eye around the table stared at it in wonder.

"I've never seen a gemstone like that before," Elyara admitted. "It's beautiful! The color is so unique, as well as the shape of the stone. It's so...moon-like."

"How did he save you?" Gabe interrupted, anxiously leaning on the table with his elbows.

Lily pulled the necklace away from the curious eyes and slid it back into her pocket before she continued. "I was only looking at the necklace when Hugo slammed my arm onto the table and took out a blade. He was about to cut my arm off when Jahrys saved me! He distracted Hugo, and swept me away. Hugo and his men chased us down a maze of paths, but eventually we lost Hugo and his men. Jahrys is a real hero. I think he would make a fine Knight of the Poolesguard!"

Alana watched as Jahrys's face lit up at the sound of that. He smiled at her, and she felt the blood begin to rush through her body as she smiled back.

"Wow! Is that all true, Jahrys?" Gabe asked, in awe.

Jahrys puffed up his chest. "It sure is."

"To Jahrys!" Elyara lifted her mug in the air. "A real knight of Palor."

Alana followed everyone and lifted her mug. "To Jahrys!" they all yelled, clanking their mugs together.

"A real knight of Palor?" a deep voice broke their laughter. "You aren't talking about Jahrhead over here, are you? He can't even use a sword correctly." A tall boy placed his hand firmly on Jahrys's shoulder. Two boys, one skinny, the other fat, were laughing up a storm behind him.

"Piss off, Rallick." Jahrys threw Rallick's hand off his shoulder.

"Oh come on, it wasn't that hard of a punch, now was it?" Rallick teased.

"It left my eye black for a whole week," Jahrys said, irritated.

Junkland

Alana looked closely and did notice the fading yellow bruise around Jahrys's left eye.

"Leave him alone, Rallick. Go play with Stade and Taygar," Elyara said.

"Go back to the forest, you damn forester!" Stade cursed at her.

Elyara grabbed his hand and twisted it behind his back as she jumped to her feet. "What did you call me?"

"Hargh!" Taygar yelled behind them in fear.

"You heard me." Stade panted the words as his face turned red, his wrist twisting even more.

"Let him go!" Rallick stepped forward, but Jahrys blocked the way. "You really want to do this again, Jahrhead? Remember what happened last time?"

"What's going on here?" Innkeeper Willem marched up to the table. "I'll have no fighting in my inn. We are celebrating the welcoming of our new queen. Elyara, release Stade."

Elyara groaned and threw Stade's hand away.

"And you, Rallick. Back away from my boy. If you lay one finger on him…you will answer to me," Willem threatened.

"Watch yourself, Jahrhead," Rallick said as he walked away with Stade and Taygar.

The tension broke and they all joined back at the table, enjoying their drinks. Alana smiled as she finished her mug. *It doesn't taste so bad after all…*

She turned to Jahrys and smiled.

He smiled back, leaning over to talk to her. "Are you enjoying yourself?"

Alana gave him a flirty nod. She could smell the alcohol on his breath. "You have interesting friends," she laughed.

"I can't disagree with you there," he chuckled. His mood suddenly changed. "I wish you could've met Kevrin. You would have liked him."

"I bet I would have," she assured him.

"How's everyone doing out there?" The singer of the band shouted out to the crowd. He was answered with a drunken roar of applause. "So, to get the night going and to honor our new queen, Nadia Poole, we are going to play an old classic."

" 'Drunken Day at The Arcalane'!" A drunk man yelled out somewhere from the front. "Com' on, Felix!"

The singer, a Sibleman named Felix, laughed. "Someone get that guy another drink. 'Drunken Day at The Arcalane' it is!" Felix turned to his band. "Ready, boys? Start it up!" he threw his hands into the air.

The horns blasted, the strings echoed off the walls, and the drums shook the tables as the band began to play the song.

Felix began to sing and everyone in The Arcalane joined him.

> *Cheers, cheers to all the girls in here,*
> *We toast to you with all our beer,*
> *We chug and chug until we're done,*
> *Now fill us up again my dear.*
>
> *Cheers, cheers to all the girls in here,*
> *We hope you stay so close and near,*
> *We chug and chug with you for fun,*
> *Now fill us up again my dear.*
>
> *Just a drunken day at The Arcalane,*
> *A drunken daaaaaay at The Arcalaaaaaane.*

"Care to dance?" Jahrys offered his hand to Alana as the song continued.

Dance? That word stung her. *The last person I danced with was my mother.*

"I would love to dance," Alana smiled, taking Jahrys's hand.

Hand in hand, Jahrys guided her to the dance floor. Elyara, Kat, Tarl, and Gabe followed them.

"Ready?" Jahrys asked.

"Wait—"

But her words were taken from her when Jahrys pulled her close to him, and then spun her around and around. She twirled and spun and flew. Jahrys guided her through it all. It was the best dancing she had ever experienced. They danced close together and far apart, but always together. Alana caught onto the words and began to sing along with all the people in the inn.

The band continued to sing the crowd pleaser, even though the song was really only the repetition of the same few lines. The crowd was getting drunker by the minute.

> *Cheers cheers…girls here,*
> *We toast you…with our beer,*
> *We chug…chug…til…we're done,*
> *Another…dear!*

Alana took a large swig from her new mug, and then slammed it down on a nearby table. She felt her whole body tingling with excitement. She ran back over to Jahrys and jumped into his arms. He held her up and spun her around and around. She let her heart take her away.

They stumbled out of The Arcalane, laughing and giggling in each other's arms. Jahrys was mostly supporting all of Alana's weight.

"Did you see Gabe's face after Kat said no? I can't believe it!" Jahrys laughed.

"Ha! I know! Kat was…was furious!" Alana giggled and hiccuped.

"You're drunk, my lady," Jahrys laughed.

"Maybe…just a little." Alana looked up at the night sky. "What…what a beautiful night." A million stars sparkled over her head. "So pretty."

"You think this is pretty?" Jahrys held out a hand. "Follow me."

Alana studied Jahrys's hand before taking it, and then looked up at him, smiling.

Jahrys pulled her back down the road.

Alana didn't resist.

Chapter 9
Jahrys

JAHRYS TIGHTENED HIS grip around Lily's hand as he guided her onto the boat that was rocking gently on the Seaport River.

"Watch your step," Jahrys said, as his arm guided her. "I don't want you falling in."

"I didn't have *that* much to drink," Lily proclaimed.

But Jahrys wasn't about to take her word on that.

When Lily was safely on the boat, Jahrys walked over to the pillar and untied the rope. He placed one foot in and the other foot pushed against the wall at the end of the dock. The boat rocked gently as it floated into the center.

Lily looked around nervously.

"It's okay, we won't tip," Jahrys promised.

"I wasn't worried," Lily said, giving him a small smile.

Jahrys coiled the rope and placed it at the bottom of the boat. He readied the sails and thanked Zalus for the wind. He was glad he wouldn't have to paddle.

He walked behind the helm and guided the ship away from the

docks, into the center of the river. The Seaport River was not very wide in this part of Palor, but it opened up closer to Zalus's Tears and over to the east by Seaport. That was where him and Kevrin would usually go fishing.

Lily had sat down, leaning back in the base of the boat. She was looking up at the balconies that flew above their heads.

Jahrys watched as the wind blew Lily's beautiful brown hair into a tangled mess, carrying the scent of flowers. Jahrys grew dizzy from the soft fragrance of her hair, like lilacs carried in a long summer breeze. The moonlight outlined her perfect cheekbones and olive skin. Her lips were slightly parted. She was gazing at everything in wonder.

It's almost as if she has never been outdoors her entire life, Jahrys thought as he was stuck in his trance. *She is beaut—*

The boat veered sharply to the right. Jahrys tightened his grip on the helm, and guided the ship forward, avoiding crashing into the walls that paralleled the river.

Jahrys looked up to see Lily staring at him with large eyes. "Sorry. I was...distracted."

"Eyes on the water, O'Jahrys," she said, teasingly.

Jahrys felt his face redden.

"Would you like to steer?" he asked, offering the helm.

"Steer? Are you serious?"

"It's quite easy."

Lily laughed. "Yea...after you almost crashed us into the wall from your *distraction*," she said, making quotes with her fingers.

Jahrys felt himself blush yet again.

"Sing me a song," Lily said, after an awkward pause.

"A what?"

"You know. Words set to music…"

"I know what a song is!" Jahrys shouted.

"Well, from the stories I've read, sailors usually sing to entertain their guests on their ships."

"Well, I don't know what kind of stories you're reading, but I am *not* singing." Jahrys crossed his arms. The boat veered right again and Jahrys shot his hands out to catch the helm.

Lily laughed. "Tell you what…" she stood up and walked over to Jahrys while keeping her arms out for balance. She stood next to him. The rocking of the boat made her lean forward, brushing her arm against his. Her skin was smooth, as if it was made of pieces of silk. "…If you sing me a song, I'll take the wheel."

The thought of her standing so close to him was too good to pass up. "You got a deal, Miss Bellsworth."

Gently, Jahrys took her left hand and placed it on the helm as he stood behind her. He reached for her right hand, praying to Zalus that she didn't notice how sweaty his palm was, and placed it on the opposite side of the helm. He felt awkward holding her hands there, so he quickly let go.

The boat veered right.

Lily let out a frightened scream.

Jahrys shot his hands back. He placed them over hers as they gripped the helm together.

They both steered the boat forward as his nose was filled with the scent of her hair.

"Sorry, but I think it would be best if I helped you," Jahrys reasoned.

"Don't be sorry," Lily leaned back and smiled up at him. "I like your hands there."

Jahrys stared into her face, her blue eyes were glistening. Her lips were lightly parted again. Jahrys wanted nothing more than to kiss them. He leaned forward.

Lily backed away, her eyes wide open. "I believe you owe me a song, Sir Jahrys."

Jahrys felt like an idiot. "I...okay..."

Lily faced forward, staring out into the water, waiting for him.

Jahrys held onto her hands, helping her guide the boat as he fumbled through a mental list of songs he knew. *What do I sing? Does she want a love song? Maybe a song about the sea? By Zalus, help me! I've never sung for anyone in my life!*

Lily let out a sarcastic cough to signal she was waiting.

Jahrys took a deep breath in. *Here goes nothing.* He began to sing.

> *Trust me as I take your hands,*
> *And I will bring you to distant lands.*
> *Far beyond the lined horizon,*
> *Past the wall your mind's in.*
>
> *I'll open your eyes to the world,*
> *Away from Palor, past the farms of Danor.*
> *We'll find adventure no man's encountered—*
> *Discovering new lands where we'll be the founders.*
>
> *We'll roam the world, find perfect views—*
> *Sail the Farrest Sea to somewhere new.*
> *But any place won't feel as good,*
> *Unless it is a place with you.*

Lily was looking at him with sparkling eyes when he finished the song. "I've never heard that song before."

"Galagar Poole sung it to the Princess Isabella," Jahrys lied.

"It was beautiful. What's the name of it?" she asked, curiously.

Her face seemed like it was inching towards his. " 'A Place With You'."

Was he imagining it or was she even closer now? Her eyes were staring at him, hypnotic. It was as if they were signaling him, calling him.

All Jahrys was thinking about was how sweet she smelled; she smelled like roses and berries and lilacs—like a beautiful summer day. He was thinking about the warm heat of her breath against his neck and about how much he wanted to kiss her.

Jahrys leaned in again.

The boat tilted violently to the right.

Jahrys toppled on top of Lily.

"The wheel, Jahrys! Grab the wheel!"

Jahrys came to his senses and whipped around to see the wheel turning dangerously. He jumped on it, rotating the wheel in order to steer the boat forward.

They both laughed.

As much as he regretted it, Jahrys thought it best if Lily took a seat at the front of the boat while he focused on sailing; he didn't want to kill them.

The river began to widen as Jahrys approached their destination. A light roar began to echo in the distance.

"What's that?" Lily asked curiously, as she leaned over the bow, peering into the night.

"You'll see," Jahrys said.

The river opened up into a giant lake. A waterfall crashed down across from them, falling from a cliff that protruded out of the Western Mountains. A cloud of mist covered the water of the lake.

"Welcome to Zalus's Tears. The most beautiful spot in Palor," Jahrys said, as he gazed at her instead of the waterfall.

Jahrys steered the boat into the center of the lake, keeping clear of the misty cloud.

When the boat was still, he walked over to the front, placing his hands against the rail. Lily walked over and joined him.

They both stared up at the endless night sky. With no clouds in sight, it was perfect for stargazing. Millions of stars stared back at them, sparkling. The stars looked like diamond clouds that swirled in spirals around their heads. Every so often, a shooting star would streak across the black abyss.

The boat rocked lightly in the water as Jahrys and Lily enjoyed the view. The chirping of crickets, the croaking of frogs, the splashing of the occasional fish, and the thundering of the waterfall surrounded them.

"I've never seen so many stars in my entire life," Lily said in amazement.

"It makes you feel small, doesn't it?"

"What does?"

"The stars," he pointed up. "It makes you feel like an ant when you look up and realize there's so much more out there." He opened his arms wide into the night, as if he was about to hug the sky.

Lily playfully slapped his hand away from her view. "Which one would you travel to?" she asked, turning her head towards him.

Jahrys looked up and thought for a minute. *They all look exactly the same.* "Hmm. I think I'd pick that one." He pointed up, at random.

Lily tried to follow his finger towards the sky. "The bright one?

Why did you choose that one?" she asked, curiously.

"Um...because...even though it's surrounded by so much darkness, it's able to find the most light. There must be something special about it."

"Those are wise words, O'Jahrys," she giggled.

He cringed at the sound of his name, but ended up laughing with her. "Yea...they are wise words," he said more to himself, thinking about what his father had said to him earlier.

"Okay, your turn. Which star would you travel to?" he asked.

"Hmm. I'd pick...that one!" she pointed up towards the sky.

"Which one?"

"That one! Way up there," she dragged his finger as best as she could to the star she had picked.

"That one? You can barely see it! Why'd you pick that one?"

"Because sometimes it's nice to be unnoticed. It looks like a place I could run away to...and no one would ever find me."

"I would find you," Jahrys accidentally said outloud.

Lily turned to face him, staring deep into his eyes.

Jahrys felt his heart skip. He felt like he couldn't breathe. It felt like his stomach dropped all the way down to the bottom of the lake. He wanted to kiss her, to pull her close, to—

Lily kissed him lightly on the lips.

Jahrys's body tingled from head to toe as he felt the blood rush through him.

She backed away, giggling.

Jahrys was sure his face must look foolish. He had never kissed a girl before.

They stared at each other, smiling. Her eyes sparkled more than the stars. He felt her stomach lightly pressing against his as she breathed. Her chest was lightly grazing his own.

Jahrys wrapped his arm around Lily. The boat rocked and Jahrys lost his balance, bringing Lily down to the deck with him. They laughed and he rolled her onto her back. He was looking down at her. Jahrys didn't know what part of her he liked best: her smile, her eyes, her cheeks, her chin, her nose, her freckles, her hair, every feature of her was perfect—especially her lips.

He leaned in and kissed her, slowly. He wanted to savor every moment. Her lips were warm and smooth. They soon found a rhythm.

Jahrys felt Lily's fingertips creeping towards his neck. She ran them through his hair. Her mouth rose to the side of his head. She breathed into his ear and gently nibbled it. At first, he was surprised, but the shivers she sent down his spine made him want more.

He found her lips again, kissing her harder. He felt her breathing begin to deepen and her body curved beneath his. He wrapped a hand around her lower back. Jahrys kissed her cheeks, her neck, her nose, her chin, her forehead, and her lips again and again and again.

Lily tangeled her legs around Jahrys's to the point where Jahrys was worried they would never untangle—and he was fine with that.

They eventually sat up, brought out of the moment by the sound of fireworks. They looked around, enjoying the view. The castle was lit up in the distance, and fireworks exploded in the sky, painting the night above Astenpoole.

"I've never seen the castle this way before," Lily admitted. "It's beautiful."

"Not as beautiful as you, though," Jahrys smiled at her.

Lily shot him a playful look, but she returned the smile and leaned over for another kiss.

Jahrys sailed them back to their starting point. He docked the boat, and Lily helped him tie it up, as she was feeling more confident on the water.

After they were finished, they stood hand in hand next to the river.

"Thank you…for saving me today. Palor is absolutely stunning," she played with Jahrys's fingers. "Jahrys…there's something I need to tell you…" Lily suddenly looked nervous.

"What is it?"

"I—"

AHWOOO, AHWOOO, AHWOOO.

Lily and Jahrys both shot their heads toward the castle.

AHWOOO, AHWOOO, AHWOOO.

Lily broke away from Jahrys. "I really must be going. I…I'm sorry!" She turned and ran down the road.

"Wait!" Jahrys yelled out to her. "Will I see you again?"

Lily shot him a quick glance over her shoulder. "Meet me at sunset in three days!"

"Sunset in three days…" Jahrys recited her words, afraid he would forget them. "Where?"

"Outside The Arcalane!" she shouted back.

Jahrys watched as she took off, disappearing into the darkness.

Something sparkled on the road, not too far from where Lily had disappeared. Jahrys walked towards it and picked up the necklace Lily had taken from Hugo's shop. He looked up, ready to call out to her, but she had disappeared down a side road.

What just happened? He thought, as he looked down at the blue, full moon shaped gem, tracing its outline with his thumb.

Chapter 10
Jahrys

JAHRYS WAS HURRYING up the road filled with excitement. He couldn't wait to smell her hair, feel her skin, watch her smile, and listen to the music of her voice.

Three days had felt like three years. He had spent the days working in his father's shop and helping his mother around the house. He still hadn't heard anything from Kevrin, so his sword fighting had been put on hold. It was probably better anyway, gave his mother a break from yelling.

The roads of Palor were beginning to empty of the travelers and merchants from the wedding festivities. However, there were still some who couldn't get enough of Palor and lingered behind. Jahrys still had to weave in and out of the busy streets.

"Chickens here. Get your chick—Jahrys!"

Jahrys turned to see Frayel holding a live chicken in his right hand, and a butcher's knife in his left. The dangling chicken cocked an eye up as Jahrys approached.

"Hello Frayel, I thought you were heading back to Danor after the wedding?"

"Ha! Did I say that?" Frayel said in his thick Danorian accent. "Me and my Astonia had so much fun, and business was doing us wonders, so we decided to stay a few more days."

"I'm glad. Palor is a great city," Jahrys said.

"Did your father end up letting you out for the festivities?" Frayel asked, pointing the bloody blade at Jahrys.

"He did," Jahrys moved to the side to avoid the blade.

"By Zalus, I knew Alvys would come to his senses. Good for you, boy." Frayel turned to nudge Jahrys with his giant elbow. "Meet any fine ladies?" he chuckled.

"I did, actually."

"That's my boy! I bet she's a poole and a half."

"She is pretty," Jahrys wished he hadn't said anything. "Are you selling chickens today?" He asked, trying to change the subject.

"Ah, yes. This here guy is the next one for sale. Will you be needing anything today, my good boy?" The chicken cocked an upside-down-eye at Jahrys and squawked at him. "Usually I be selling them for fifty pooles but for you, my dear lad, I'll give you this fine chicken for only five."

"Erh, no thanks. Not today. We already have one at home to deal with." He pushed the chicken away from his face. It squawked again, her head moving in all directions. "I'm actually meeting up with someone down the road."

"Aye, it wouldn't be that girl now would it?" Frayel gave Jahrys a playful nudge. Frayel gave a chuckle after seeing how red Jahrys had gotten. "So be it, my boy. Keep your secrets. Tell your father to keep that wine coming. Me and Astonia, we finished all three bottles the night of the wedding. That wine is sweeter than a woman's kiss."

Frayel chuckled.

"I will tell him." Jahrys actually had never tasted the wine before. He wanted to save his first taste with his father, but his father and mother assumed he didn't drink yet.

"Your father was blessed with that small piece of land of his. You can't make wine like that anywhere else in *all* of Astenpoole and the Four Cities. Not even up in Danor where the farmland is fair and moist. What's his secret, aye? I'm guessing it's from living so damn close to that mountain."

"No secret. It's just his passion. He spends hours out in the yard when he isn't in the shop," Jahrys explained.

"Hmm. Well, you're a good lad, O'Jahrys. Don't ya forget that." Frayel pointed at Jahrys's chest with his hand holding the chicken.

Jahrys cringed at the sound of his name, and at the poor chicken.

"You best be off. Don't want to be keeping the lady waiting." Frayel gave a wink and chuckled to himself. "Tell your folks good ol' Frayel said hello."

"I will. It was nice seeing you." Jahrys waved goodbye. He turned to continue his trip up the road to meet Lily.

A crowd was forming outside The Arcalane when he arrived. Everyone was talking loudly and enjoying themselves.

Jahrys plopped into a chair outside, taking in the beautiful day. He peered inside a window to see the inn filled with people, but saw no sign of Kevrin.

Jahrys fumbled with Lily's necklace inside his pocket; the gem was smooth against his thumb. His heart jumped with every brunette girl that passed him. It was close to late afternoon, and the sun was beginning to set behind the Western Mountains. Jahrys was beginning to worry.

Junkland

She should be here by now. Jahrys turned his head, looking up and down the road. *What if she doesn't come?*

Jahrys shook his head to throw away those thoughts. He sat back in his chair and waited. *She will come.*

He watched people push carts back and forth on the road, mothers tugging on their crying children, men and women shouting, trying to get their final sales in before sundown, and horses clacking with their carts around the streets.

Jahrys let out a long sigh. He was now officially worried. The sun had completely set behind the mountains. Maybe Lily wasn't interested in seeing him again? Maybe he had come on too strong? *Why am I such an idiot? I should have called it a night after the drinks. I probably scared her off.* Jahrys knew the boat ride was a bit excessive, but he couldn't help being a hopeless romantic.

Suddenly, a loud hum echoed from the mountains, shaking the table in front of Jahrys. Jahrys felt the vibration beneath his feet. The metal of the chair quivered against his back.

Jahrys looked up, towards the mountains. A yellow light glowed above the rooftops of the houses at the end of the road. He looked around to see if anyone else had noticed, but everyone was busy with their drinks and their conversations. *It's probably just fireworks*, Jahrys tried to tell himself, but he wasn't so sure.

There was another hum, but this time, it was much louder and more distinct. *Definitely not fireworks.*

The sky down the road flashed a blazing yellow. The earth shook again around Jahrys.

The crowd suddenly went silent, everyone's attention turned towards the mountains. Some people were even smiling, thinking it was some kind of show.

Something didn't feel right, however. It was now three days after the wedding. All the fireworks had already been used up. There was nothing left to celebrate.

"RUN!" a voice screamed from the dark road ahead.

Everyone stared down the road with curious faces.

Jahrys pushed his chair back and rose to his feet to join the crowd.

A man appeared from the darkness of the road. He was limping, but trying to run. He was holding his arm, and blood was dripping from his face and neck. His ear was missing. It was hard to make out who it was.

"RUN!" the man yelled again as he came into view.

Jahrys's stomach dropped. *Frayel*.

"RUN TO THE CAS—"

A yellow blast appeared at the center of Frayel's stomach. He let out a frightening scream as his insides exploded onto the road. Frayel's blood sprayed Jahrys and those near him.

Frayel's face went white as he fell to his knees and toppled over to his side.

Jahrys heard another deep, low hum that shook the earth.

VHRUUUUMMMM.

A beam of yellow light shot out from the darkness behind Frayel, encompassing his body like a bubble.

Jahrys's world was blinded.

When his sight came back, Frayel's body was gone.

That was when the screaming began. Everyone pushed and shoved in all directions. More light was shooting from the darkness.

Jahrys turned and ran. If Lily was still meeting up with him, she might be up the road. He had to find her.

People were dropping left and right when the yellow blasts hit them. Jahrys pushed his way through the chaotic crowd. Blasts flew over his head. The heat tickled the side of his face. Buildings began to flame and the fallen bodies disappeared around him.

He didn't slow down. He ran as fast as he could towards the castle gate up the road, keeping an eye out for Lily.

"Lily!" Jahrys screamed over the cries for help. "LILY!"

No answer.

A blast hit inches from his foot and Jahrys went flying into the air. The breath was taken from him as he landed hard on his stomach. He pushed himself back up, heart pounding in his chest.

"LILY!" he yelled louder this time.

"Over here, Jahrys! I'm over here!"

Jahrys spun his head in all directions, searching for the sound of her voice. He had to shield his eyes to cover himself from the blinding light and fires from all the buildings. He coughed from the smoke.

And then he saw her. She was on the other side of the chaotic crowd, standing below a tall shop.

Jahrys dove into the crowd. He was bounced around left and right, left and right. Someone's elbow smashed against his face, but he pushed through and broke free of the crowd.

"Jahrys!" Lily yelled over the screams. She was only twenty feet away.

A blast exploded into the building above Lily's head. Heavy debris tumbled down, heading straight for her.

"Look out!" Jahrys sprinted forward, the debris about to crush Lily's body. Jahrys dove into her, wrapping his arms around her as they went flying. Jahrys pushed her to the ground, covering her with his body. The debris from the house crashed onto the road behind them.

Jahrys lifted himself off her. "Are you hurt?"

"I'm fine. Jahrys…your face, it's covered in blood!" Lily brushed his face with her fingers. "Are you okay? What's happening?"

"Yes. Yes! We have to go!" Jahrys grabbed her hand and pulled her up the road towards the castle.

They ran together hand-in-hand as fast as they could. They were heading towards the castle gate. It was the only place he could think to go.

They made it to the Western Gate, but they were still a hundred feet away. A frightened mob of people blocked their path to the entrance. Yelling and shouting filled the air.

"Let us in! We'll die out here! You have to let us in!" the crowd yelled.

"What's happening?" Jahrys turned to a frightened old lady next to him. "Why can't we go through?"

"Tis' the guards. They won't let us pass. By Zalus, we're all doomed!" she wailed, her hands waving madly in the air.

"Come on." Jahrys grabbed Lily's hand, pushing his way to the front. He had to get them through the gates to safety.

"By the order of King Leoné Poole, you *must* step back! No one else is allowed inside the castle!" it was a knight who spoke. Jahrys recognized him from The Arcalane. Innkeeper Willem refered to him as Old Lan. He was the previous Captain of the Poolesguard.

"Step back!" the old knight yelled again.

Jahrys saw a wall of knights on both sides of Old Lan. They were holding spears and shields, blocking the entrance to the castle.

The crowd was getting violent. People were throwing rocks at the knights and screaming, "Let us in! Let us in!"

The screams and yells behind them were getting louder as the earth continued to shake—the humming blasts were getting closer.

"Follow me. I have a plan," Lily said, pulling Jahrys through the crowd, closer to the castle gate.

Jahrys didn't know what she planned on doing, but he followed. He held tightly onto her hand, staying close behind her.

A man bumped hard into Jahrys.

"Get out of my way, will ya?" the man yelled, shoving Jahrys.

Jahrys stumbled backwards and felt Lily's hand slip away.

"NO!" Lily screamed. "NO! JAHRYS!"

Jahrys didn't know what was happening. He regained his balance and looked around for Lily—but she was gone.

He panicked, trying to push through the crowd, trying to catch a glimpse of her.

"Lily!" he yelled out. "LILY!"

"JAHRYS! HELP!"

Jahrys saw her brown hair through the crowd.

"Move out of the way!" Jahrys yelled to a man and a woman standing in front of him. He had to get to her.

"Aye, watch yourself, boy," the man glared at him in anger.

"JAHRYS!" Lily's scream drowned out the chaos around him.

Two knights were dragging her towards the castle gate. She was kicking and screaming, trying to get away.

Craaack.

The gates slowly began to rotate together.

No! Jahrys pushed as hard as he could through the crowd, but it was no use. The more he pushed, the farther back he went. He was helpless, watching Lily disappear as the gates inched closer together.

Everyone was still screaming and begging for help. Even the knights began to give worried faces when they realized the gates were pushing them outside the castle. Everyone began to fight for the remaining space behind the closing doors.

Boom!

The gates slammed shut and everyone was silent.

Chapter 11
Piller

THE DICE WERE bouncing back and forth while Piller shook them vigorously from hand to hand. *By the palms of Zalus*, he thought, *give me something good*. He gave his cupped hands one last shake and sent the dice bouncing across the tabletop. The first die landed on a two. The second was spinning on its corner. Four pairs of eyes were watching it carefully as it spun and spun and spun.

It landed on a one.

"That makes three!" Piller shouted.

"I could have sworn that was going to land on a two. Damn you, Piller," said Devan as he sat back in disgust.

"You want me to lose points on myself?" asked Piller in disbelief.

He reached his right hand over to his personal deck on the table. He counted aloud as he went through the cards. "One, two, three." He pulled the third card from his shuffled deck.

"A five." He placed it in front of his king. He now had an army of five to protect his king and castle if one of his brothers attacked.

"At this point, I just want to win my pooles back," groaned Devan. "You guys have been running me dry all night."

"You have been running yourself dry all night," said Hollow. He turned to Piller. "Pass the dice if you're done, Captain." He held his right hand out. Piller passed him the dice.

"I'm going to start my turn by attacking my army of ten on Devan's defenseless castle," Hollow said, as he talked through his turn.

"Damn you all," mumbled Devan as he took away one of his large clear red rocks from his castle. He now only had one remaining. "Would you like to take the other one while you're at it?"

Hollow took the dice and rolled a three and a five. He took the eighth card from the top of his deck. It turned out to be an army of three. He placed it on the table next to his current army of ten.

"Give me those damn dice will ya?" Devan grabbed the dice from the young knight. He began to shake them back and forth. "I'll show all of you. This will be my come back and you'll all be sorry when I take all of your pooles."

"By Zalus! Just roll the dice," yelled an impatient Arnold, who was the fourth player at the table.

Devan tossed the dice. All eyes were glued to them as they went spinning across the table. When they stopped, Devan's jaw dropped at the outcome. "Ah! By the palms of Zalus, you've got to be kidding me."

"Looks like you lose," Arnold smirked.

Everyone tried to hold in their laughter.

"It's like the dice are working against me. Two fives? Are you kidding me? Two fives? I want a reroll." Devan was furious.

"There will be no reroll, Devan," said Piller.

Devan grunted, taking the dice anyway and rolling them.

"This...this must be some sick joke." The dice landed on two fives again. "You guys have rigged the dice. Let's pull a number on poor old Devan. And here I thought we were brothers."

Hollow let out a laugh that he was trying desperately to hold.

"Oh, you think this is funny?" Devan pushed his chair back and stood up over the boy, "robbing from a good old friend? Well it ain't!"

"There won't be much left of a Poolesguard if you guys keep playing this stupid game," remarked Krist from the corner of the room. He was sitting on a chair, sharpening his sword with a whetstone.

"Yea, it'll just be me, good old Krist, and the princess lover, Sir Benjamin the Beautiful," Martellus chimed in from the other corner of the room, looking up from his book called *The Tales and Myths of the Western Mountains*.

"I'll run away if that's ever the outcome," Krist said to his brother.

"One less soul to be humiliated by the new queen," chuckled Martellus, as he raised his feet back up onto the chair beside him.

"By Zalus," Devan grunted, his long beard giving a bounce, "don't you get me started on that foreign broad, boy. She has no reason to be here. I don't like to be told what to do, especially by a woman. Especially a woman like her! She has Leoné tied up like a puppy."

"I kind of like her," said Hollow, placing his cards face down onto the table.

Arnold chimed in. "We know you like her. We've all caught you staring at her ass during—"

"That's enough!" Piller yelled as he stood up, "I will not have you insult our new queen." He gazed around at his brothers of the Poolesguard. *What kind of fools have I gotten myself involved with?*

"Devan, either put down some more pooles or leave the game. We don't—"

The door of the common room burst open. A young boy flew in. He was panting and sweating. "S-S-Sir Piller," the boy said, gasping for air.

"Settle down, lad. Catch your breath." He walked over to the boy and placed a hand on his skinny shoulder. "Krist, get Zatum some water, will you?" He looked into the frighten boy's face. "What is it? What's wrong?"

Krist brought over a cup of water and handed it to Zatum. The boy took it and brought it up to his mouth with shaking hands. It spilled on his chin and down his neck. He managed to get in two gulps before he was ready to talk. Zatum wiped his mouth clean.

"The king…the king needs…he needs to see you. Now! We are under attack!"

"Attack?" Piller repeated as if it was a word he had never heard before.

"Don't ya hear the horn, Sir?" the boy asked, surprised.

They all stopped to listen.

AHWOOO, AHWOOO, AHWOOO, AHWOOO.

Four times means outside the walls. But we haven't been attacked from outside the walls since the War of the Great Pact, when the group of Kalukians thought King Galagar Poole was a traitor. But that was almost three hundred years ago! "Outlaws? Is it outlaws, boy? From the Farrest Sea?" Piller asked the frightened boy.

"N-n-no Sir. Not outlaws, Sir. They came from the mountains." The boy looked around nervously. All eyes were on him.

"By Zalus…" Devan's eyes went wide.

Piller could feel the fear in the room.

"The mountains?" Martellus repeated. He put his book down. "No one's ever come from those mountains. The tales say there are demons over there. Demons that can blow your head off with a snap of a finger. Demons that can—"

"That's enough," Piller yelled at Martellus, silencing him. He turned to his brothers. "Krist, Martellus, make sure Zatum stays safe in the common room." There was a moan coming from Krist, but a gasp of happiness from Martellus. "Hollow, Arnold, and Devan grab your swords and come with me."

"Aye, Captain," they all said in unison.

Piller fixed the pin on his brown leather tunic and grabbed his sword that was leaning against the wall by the door.

They marched down the long circular steps of the northwest tower. When they were outside, the ringing of the bells and the sound of the horn echoed loudly off the walls. They heard screaming far off in the distance, and the night sky was tinged with yellow.

The king was waiting for them across the yard. He was sitting on his horse on King's Way. They crossed to meet him.

"Your Grace," all four brothers took a knee.

King Leoné jumped off his horse. He towered over them.

"Get up, get up. We have no time for this." Leoné sounded frightened.

"What is it, Your Grace?" Piller asked. "Who's attacking us?"

"I don't know, Piller. They've come from the mountains. In all the history of Astenpoole, nothing has ever come down from those damn mountains." He turned his gaze west to the yellow night sky.

"Should we summon our Army? Should we fight, Your Grace?"

Piller asked.

"No. They are using weapons that are beyond us. We cannot fight."

"What kind of weapons?" asked Hollow.

"We don't know. Some yellow light," Leoné's eyes were wide with fear.

"Yellow light?" Devan chuckled as if it was a joke. "Have you gone mad, Your Grace? Let's fight and show them what Astenpoole has to offer."

"No! We will *not* fight!" yelled Leoné.

"But, Your Grace, we need to do something," said Arnold in desperation.

"Close the gates," Leoné demanded.

"What?" all four of the brothers gasped.

"You heard me." Leoné turned to Piller. "I need you to ride down to the Western Gate and tell them to close it immediately. We cannot have them breach the castle."

"We're just going to hide inside the walls? What about the people outside?" Piller raised his voice. "They'll die!"

"I'd rather have a few people die than all of Astenpoole." King Leoné looked at each brother in the eye before continuing, "It's a hard decision, I know, but it has to be done. We need to save as many people as we can. If we let them enter through our gates…well…there won't be an Astenpoole any longer."

The brothers exchanged nervous glances.

There was a shout from across the yard behind them. "Your Grace! Your Grace!" Benjamin was sprinting towards them.

"What is it, Benjamin?" Leoné asked the knight.

"Your Grace. The princess, your daughter…she's gone!" he was leaning over with his hands on his knees.

"By Zalus," Leoné cursed. "How many times do I have to teach that girl to stay put? Arnold, come with me. You will help me and Benjamin look for my daughter." The king turned to Piller. "Piller. You have the command. Get those gates shut!"

"As you command, Your Grace," Piller knelt down again. *Close the gates? How can they close the gates and desert all those people?*

He rose to his feet and turned to Hollow and Devan. "Let's move."

The brothers received their horses from the stables and hurried through the King's Gate and down Pooles Road. People were screaming left and right, running as fast as they could from the Western Gate. Piller could tell who came from the outskirts due to the ragged clothing.

These poor folk, he thought, as he kicked his horse to go faster. He galloped down the road with his two brothers following close behind, the wind rushing in his face.

When they arrived at the gate, Piller only saw chaos. A crowd of people were pushing their way through the gate, while knights tried to keep them from piling in. Old Lan was in the center of the knights, holding the crowd back.

"Step back!" he heard Old Lan yell at the frightened crowd.

The ground suddenly began to shake beneath their feet. Piller's horse spooked, sending him flying to the ground. He hit the hard cobblestone road, and a shooting pain spread across his back. Piller let out a groan.

Hollow and Devan jumped off their own horses to help Piller up.

"What was that?" Hollow asked.

There was a deep, low hum that echoed off the walls.

The sound was moving closer. The panicked crowd grew even more unruly. Everyone charged forward, knocking down the knights as if they were as light as feathers.

"Cap'? Captain?" yelled Devan, but Piller didn't seem to hear him. "Piller!" he yelled again over the screams.

The earth shook again beneath their feet.

Piller turned to his two brothers.

"What are the orders, Captain?" asked Devan, fear prominent in his eyes.

"We close the gates." It was as if someone else was speaking for him.

"What?" asked Hollow over the noise.

"WE CLOSE THE GATES!" Piller looked up the wall. "Follow me."

They pushed their way through the gatehouse tower and climbed the stairs to the top. Piller used all his force to open the door and stormed inside. "CLOSE THE GATES!" he yelled.

"What? Close them?" the gatekeeper stood motionless and confused.

"By the king's orders I need you to close this gate," Piller repeated himself.

"All right, all right. Old Riago don't be wanting any trouble. What the king wants is what the king gets."

Riago ran over to the wheel and began rotating it.

The brothers stepped outside onto the wall. They watched below as the gates began to slowly rotate together, pushing both the knights and the chaotic crowd outside of the castle.

Confused screams and shouts came from below as the gates continued to come together. Piller raised his eyes towards the city of Palor. The sky was illuminated with a yellow glow. In the distance, houses were on fire and people screamed.

VHRUUUUMMMM.

The earth shook. Beams of yellow light shot across the streets below.

Piller watched as the people, including the Astenpoole knights, fought for the small space remaining between the gates.

Old Lan was banging on the gates, yelling for them to re-open. Old Lan looked up the wall and found Piller's eyes. The old Captain of the Poolesguard gave Piller a look so cold, it sent a chill running through his bones.

By the palms of Zalus, was all Piller could think as he watched the gates shut. *What have I done?*

Chapter 12
Jahrys

JAHRYS HOPPED HIS back fence and ran through the vineyard. His lungs felt like they were about to cave in. Sweat soaked his clothing. He had no idea what was happening. He had just watched Frayel's body disappear from thin air, he had just let the girl of his dreams slip away, and he had just watched the king abandon his people.

By Zalus, what is going on? Jahrys wondered as he ran up his back steps. He would not let his parents suffer too.

He stopped abruptly at his back door, as he heard shouting from inside. He quietly opened the back door to the kitchen. Miller came flying out. Jahrys was about to yell out for him when a voice caught him by surprise.

"Where is he?" the deep voice asked. It was coming from the living room.

Jahrys heard his father reply. "I told you already. We don't know." There was fear in his voice. Jahrys had never heard his father sound this way before. "If you just let us go, we can go out and look

Junkland

for h—"

"Do you take me for a fool?" the deep voice threatened.

Jahrys silently crept to the other side of the kitchen. He peered into the living room. He saw two large men standing over his parents, who were restrained. His mother had a dazed look on her face, and blood ran down the side of her head. His father was crying.

The two men were wearing suits of armor Jahrys had never seen before. They were made of a metal he didn't recognize, and the lights on the suits gave them a yellow glow. Their helmets also glowed yellow. There was a breathing vent where their mouths were and dark holes where their eyes should be. They both wore boots and carried giant packs on their backs. A large circular yellow light encompassed most of the pack. A long tube ran from the pack to a device that Jahrys imagined was a weapon, but it was none he recognized.

The man closest to his father had two black stripes running down his helmet and was pointing the weapon at his father's head.

"I don't take you for a fool," his father said. "I just...I don't know where—"

"Hit her again."

"No! Please!" his father pleaded. "I'm telling you the truth! Take it out on me, just leave her out of it."

The other man marched over to his mother. He took his weapon and slammed it against the side of his mother's head. She fell hard to the ground. More blood began to ooze out of her head.

His father let out a wail.

"By the palms of Zalus, I beg you!" his father cried. "Please, leave her out of this!"

Jahrys couldn't take it any longer. He took a step forward.

"Fa—"

A hand flew over his mouth before he could finish what he was saying.

"Shh," a voice whispered in his ear.

Jahrys saw the man with the black striped helmet give a slight nod to the other. The man standing over Jahrys's mother lifted his weapon high into the air and brought it down hard on his mother's head one, two, three times. Each time the crunch of the weapon on her skull was louder.

"No! STOP!" Jahrys's father screamed.

His father struggled to his feet. He reached out for the man who was hitting his beloved wife, but before he could even touch him, the man with the black striped helmet pressed his finger down on the top trigger of his weapon.

A yellow blast shot out, hitting his father in the stomach. His father collapsed to the ground.

The man shot at his father a second time, and his father's legs flew into the air.

The person constraining Jahrys slowly guided him to the back door.

There were two deep, low hums as the two men pointed their weapons at Jahrys's parents, who were motionless on the living room floor.

The kitchen came to life, knives clattered onto the counter, chairs vibrated across the room and toppled over, plates slid out of cabinets and shattered on the floor.

VHRUUUUMMMM.

The light that filled the kitchen blinded Jahrys. He felt himself being pushed through the back door, his feet stumbling down the steps. He tripped and landed hard on the ground. He still couldn't see. He felt someone pull his arm, guiding him away from his house. He yanked away.

"Jahrys, we need to go…now!" a familiar voice called out.

"Kevrin?" Jahrys couldn't believe it, his vision clearing. He shook his head. "No! I have to save them." Jahrys struggled to his feet and ran for his home.

But Kevrin was faster. He grabbed Jahrys's arm and pulled him back. "Your parents are dead."

The words didn't seem real. Dead? How could his parents be dead? It just wasn't possible. Jahrys looked back at his home. *Mother…Father…*

"Come on," Kevrin gave Jahrys a nudge towards the yard.

Jahrys wiped the tears from his eyes and followed.

Before he left the yard, Jahrys took one more look at his home. It was completely dark inside now. The home that once brought Jahrys happy memories was now a melting pot for his burning heart.

Jahrys was about to turn back around to follow Kevrin, when something black caught his eye. A crow was sitting on top of the ledge over his back door, and it was watching him.

Chapter 13
Piller

HER WORDS ECHOED violently inside his head.

"Gone," she had whispered.

"Who is gone? What happened?" Piller had asked the frightened girl, who was shaking on a bed inside the Clinic. There were others there, too, all survivors from the attack. The injured were taken to the Clinic and the numbers continued to grow.

"All gone," the girl's eyes were bouncing right to left, right to left, as she stared up blankly at the ceiling. Sweat soaked the sheets from the bed she was resting on, and her dark hair was a tangled mess.

King Leoné had commanded Piller to find out all he could about the attack. Piller had thought the Clinic would be a good place to start. After a stressful talk with Galla the Healer, he eventually was able to persuade her to let him talk to her patients, but he was only allowed an hour.

Most of the patients were not in any state of mind to talk, and many of the others simply couldn't recall what had happened. But, he had found one who was helpful. The little girl was in the corner of the Clinic, and she was perfectly coherent, perhaps too coherent.

"Who is gone?" Piller had asked the girl again. He leaned in a bit closer. The girl began to mumble. Her eyes were as wide as the Farrest Sea. "Who is—"

The young girl's tiny arms shot out at Piller's tunic. He was shocked at how tight her grip was. Her fragile arms were shaking.

"They were right behind me. I saw them. They were there! I heard them, I tell you! I am not crazy!" The girl's eyes were large with fear as she dragged Piller closer to her face.

"I never said you were cr—"

The girl interrupted him. "I turned around and they were there before I started running. Oh! Yes they were. But we heard a blast and…and…"

"And what?" Piller tried to sound calm, but his rough voice made that difficult.

"We were on the road, heading back home. There was shaking and…and…a humming. Loud humming. I was ahead of my father, mother, and my brother…little Jax. Everyone began to scream and told me to run. So I ran. But then I heard a noise and when I looked behind me they were…they were…" The dark haired girl choked up.

"What's your name, little one?" asked Piller, feeling sympathy for the girl.

"My name is Dally," the girl said, choking on each word.

"What happened to your family, Dally?" Piller had wiped away the girl's tears that were running down her cheeks.

The way she had looked at him, the way she was talking, it was almost ghost-like. "They disappeared," the girl had simply said.

They disappeared? No one just disappears. The girl must be awestruck, he recalled thinking.

At that moment, Galla the Healer had noticed the girl's discomfort and shooed Piller away.

"Out. Be gone with you. And tell King Leoné to let these people rest." She waved a hand at him.

Piller stood up and smiled down at Dally. He brushed the hair from her face and gave her a little pat on the head. "Thank you, Dally," he had said.

He left before Galla the Healer could swat him with her hand.

The last words the girl had said were haunting Piller as he sat in the council room.

The council room was quiet. All the members of the Poolesguard sat around the round table in silence, waiting. It wasn't a large room. It was already snug with the seven of them in there.

There was a vent at the top of the ceiling letting in fresh, cool air. However, it was still hot and humid in the room.

He could see the fear in their eyes. The two youngest members of the Poolesguard, Hollow and Arnold, sat next to each other across from him. *I can't imagine what they're going through right now,* thought Piller as he waited in silence.

Piller turned his head to the left and stared at a large picture on the back wall. It was a beautiful painting of a sunset falling behind the Western Mountains; it was a sight Piller had only seen a few times from the castle walls. Most days it was hard to see the sunset behind the haze and the storms from all of the heat, especially during the stormy season.

His gaze dropped to Martellus who sat underneath the picture. He was tapping his fingers in an awkward rhythm on the table.

Junkland

Tap, Tap Tap.

Krist sat to his left. He was eyeing Martellus's fingers obsessively as if he was ready to chop them off.

Benjamin sat to the right of Martellus, not noticing the tapping or simply choosing not to care. He was staring down blankly at a wooden mug that he held cupped between his hands, probably thinking about the princess.

Leoné had been furious when they had found her outside of the castle walls during the attacks. The king had found the secret passageway Alana had been using to escape her room and had it sealed up. There was tension building between the princess and her father, and Piller wasn't sure what would happen between them.

There was heavy breathing coming from Piller's left. Devan sat in his chair, sleeping, with his beard rising and falling on his chest. Piller felt the droopiness in his own eyes. None of the knights had gotten much sleep the past few days.

After what seemed like ages, the thick wooden door bolted open, banging against the back wall.

Devan jolted up right. "What? Who?" Once he realized what was happening, he fixed his composure.

King Leoné rushed in, Zatum following him.

Piller stood up to help Leoné into his chair. Zatum took the seat next to the king at the head of the table, and took out a piece of parchment, a quill, and some ink from his bag. He dabbed the quill twice into the ink bottle and waited patiently.

Piller took his seat.

Leoné looked around the table at all the knights. He looked like he had aged ten years since the attack a few days ago.

He finally said, "This meeting has been called to discuss the matter of the attack that occurred three days prior." As Leoné talked, Zatum's hand glided back and forth across the parchment as his quill recorded the meeting. "Any news from the Clinic, Piller?" Leoné had turned to him.

Piller paused for a second, considering whether he should tell him about the girl who saw her family disappear. "There was one girl, Your Grace." Piller looked down at the table and then back at Leoné. "She saw her family disappear."

"Hmm. Disappear you say?" Leoné glanced over at Zatum's notes to check if he caught that.

"Yes, Your Grace. She said her family was walking behind her. There was shaking and humming. She heard screams and her family yelled at her to run. When the little girl turned to look behind her, her family wasn't there. She was convinced they had vanished."

"Vanished." The word hung in the air as Leoné looked down at the table. He ran his fingers through his beard, thinking. "Do you believe this girl, Piller?" Leoné asked him.

"I do, Your Grace."

"How can you believe such folly?" Devan broke in. "Do you hear yourselves? Vanished? People do not simply vanish."

"I think I have to agree with Devan on this one," said Krist, leaning his large arms across the table. "The girl must have been dazed from some of Galla's herbs."

"She seemed to believe it," Piller said, defending her.

"She's a little girl who just saw her entire family die from these men from the mountain," Devan argued. "You know how imaginative children are. She was probably in shock."

"Vanished or not, her family was attacked and murdered. We

have no knowledge about the weapons they were using, or where they came from and why they are here!" Leoné explained. There was frantic scratching on the paper as Zatum's quill zipped across the page.

"We're in danger," continued Leoné. "We need extra protection along the walls. No one goes in or out of this castle until we figure out how to defeat these invaders."

Leoné turned to Benjamin. "Benjamin. I would like you to keep an extra eye on my daughter. I do not want to find her outside of the Castle Keep by herself ever again. If I do, Zalus help you. Do you understand?"

"Yes, Your Grace. I won't let anything happen to her," Benjamin answered.

"Good, good. Krist and Martellus, I want you two to control the walls. You will replace Riago and Landerin, and arrange the men as you see fit. I want you to report any suspicious activity you find inside or outside the walls. And by Zalus, keep those gates *shut*." He stressed the last word.

"Your wish is my command, Your Grace." Martellus gave an awkward salute to Leoné.

"Yes, Your Grace," Krist responded.

"Hollow and Arnold, this must be a difficult time for the both of you, being new to the Poolesguard. I want Piller to take both of you under his company. You will do as he commands. Do I make myself clear?"

"Yes...yes, Your Grace," they both stuttered.

Finally, he turned to Devan. "Devan, you will stay by my side guarding myself and Nadia day and night." He broke his gaze with Devan and looked around the room at all the knights around the table. "Is that clear?"

They all nodded in agreement, except for Piller.

"But what about the survivors?" he asked, looking down at the old wooden table.

"Gala has been doing all she can for them," Leoné said.

"No. I mean the survivors in the Four Cities. The survivors we abandoned outside the wall. They are your people, too, Your Grace. They are a part of Astenpoole as much as we are." Piller took his eyes from the table and stared back at his king.

"Those folk responsible for killing Asha? Those Carriers?" Leoné spat, waving a hand in disgust.

"You have no proof that they caused The Sickness. For all you know, it could have started from within the castle walls." Piller could feel his heart pounding. *I need to convince him to help them. This isn't right.* "I know your frustration. My mother also died from—"

Leoné slammed both his hands onto the table, causing a loud bang. Everyone at the table jumped. "This isn't about your damn mother! You may be Captain of the Poolesguard, Sir Piller Lorne, but let me remind you who is the king."

"Put the past behind you, Your Grace. We all miss Asha. We all miss the ones we have lost in The Sickness. But we need to decide the fate of the kingdom. We need to save the people that we abandoned on the other side of *that* wall." He felt the words flow out of his mouth, having no control over his speech.

"What do you propose then?" The king glared at him.

Piller didn't have an answer prepared. He didn't expect himself to be in this situation. All eyes were on him. He needed to decide now, to figure out a plan. Sweat trickled down his forehead, barely missing his eye. He rubbed the scar on his face. His eyes roamed

Junkland

around the room, hoping for an answer. Zatum waited anxiously for Piller to begin talking, to say something, to write down his brilliant idea—but nothing came to him. The quill hung in the air, mocking him. Piller thought about the little girl he had failed to save. He thought about his dead father and his dead mother. He couldn't let them down. But what could he do?

"Piller? What do you propose we do?" The king repeated. "If you have no plan—"

"We need help." Krist's voice broke the silence across the table. Piller raised his head to look at Krist, who gave him a reassuring smile.

"Help?" Leoné acted as if he had never heard the word before.

"Yes, Your Grace." Krist stood up and continued, "If you refuse to open the gate, we can only survive for a year, maybe two, if we're lucky. We don't have enough food to live here forever. We need to feed an entire castle. We need help from the people outside of these walls."

"Yes." Martellus stood up next to Krist. "We need help from the outside, Your Grace. They can get us the resources we need to survive."

Devan was next to stand. "And the survivors outside the wall need our help, too," Devan grunted. "They won't be able to survive long out there with those...those *things*. We need to provide them with weapons and any kind of supplies they need."

"And how do you expect to help them?" Leoné asked.

"We need to set up some kind of communication between them and the castle." Piller broke in.

"Stations." It sounded like a little squeak from the corner of the room.

"What was that Hollow?" Leoné turned his glance to the young knight.

"We can build stations along the wall. To...to help," he stuttered nervously.

Zatum's right hand was flying across his paper. Piller had never seen someone write that fast before.

"Yes!" Arnold stood up now. "Let's build some sort of retrieval station along the wall that the survivors can reach from the outside. We can assign our people to work in the stations. They'll be in charge of communicating inside and outside the wall and be in charge of the jobs assigned to the survivors."

Benjamin was contemplating out loud. "Every time the survivors retrieve something we need inside the wall, we can give them something in return. Something they can use..."

"We can give them swords and shields," Piller said. "Any kind of weapon in exchange for resources. It's our only way of survival, Your Grace. We need resources if we're to stay here indefinitely."

Leoné thought this over for a long time. Silence hung in the air as he stared blankly towards the painting of the Western Mountains hanging on the back wall.

"Retrieval Stations you say?" He twirled his finger in his beard again. After a minute of thinking, he slammed his hands back down onto the table. "Yes! I like it. Piller, since this is your idea...you, Hollow, and Arnold will be in charge of setting up these stations."

Piller smiled. "Yes, Your Grace. I—" he glanced at the two young knights, "*we* will be honored."

Devan unsheathed his sword and pointed it to the center of the table. "To the Retrieval Stations! The last hope for Astenpoole!"

The other brothers unsheathed their swords and held them up

high to the center of the room.

    They all yelled together. "To the Retrieval Stations! The last hope for Astenpoole!"

Part Two
The Junkland
Year 916 A.Z.

Chapter 14
Jahrys

JAHRYS WATCHED THE teams stumble through the small door of The Arcalane. He was sitting on a stool with his back against the bar, sipping a warm ale. A light rain fell outside. It was getting dark. At least darker than it normally was during the daytime these days. As the years went by, it was getting harder and harder to tell the difference between night and day.

His other hand was fumbling around with the necklace he always kept in his pocket. His thumb traced the smooth outline of the gem.

The rain began to pick up outside, pounding against the sides of the inn.

Jahrys took another sip from his mug, listening to the rain outside while lost in his own thoughts. A day didn't go by where Jahrys didn't think of Lily. He wondered if he'd ever see her again—her blue eyes, the slight dimples on her cheeks, her beautiful smile…

Jahrys didn't get much sleep these days, not after the Hoarding. His exhausted body would always be overcome by the memory of Lily's soft hand slipping away from his three years ago, the screams of his dying parents, and the way Frayel's insides spilled onto the road.

A pain shot through Jahrys's foot, taking him out of his thoughts. He looked down to find Miller pecking his leather boots—each peck made a jingling sound.

"Don't you have something better to do?" Jahrys yelled down at the chicken.

Miller cocked a large, round eye up at him. A ring of keys were hanging from his beak.

"You know Willem isn't going to be happy when he can't find his keys." Jahrys pointed a scolding finger at the chicken. "Do you want him to have an excuse to feed you to the Retrievers?"

Miller cocked his head to the side, making no effort to drop the keys.

Jahrys shrugged. "Suit yourself."

Miller continued his pecking.

"Get out of here!" Jahrys yelled, kicking Miller lightly.

Miller scurried away and ran around the room, the keys jingling with every step.

Jahrys was still astounded that Miller was alive. Miller had miraculously appeared at The Arcalane a year after the Hoarding, pecking at the front door. Willem had opened it to find Miller standing there, as if the Hoarding had never even happened.

Miller was all he had left of his former life. That, and the dreadful screams and pleadings of his parents that were forever engraved in his mind. Jahrys could still picture his parents' faces before they died. How scared they had looked. He remembered his father pleading to the Hoarder with black stripes to leave his mother alone, to hurt him instead. Jahrys still remembered the blood that poured out of his mother's head as the Hoarder had crushed her with his Captor.

The Hoarding had taken so many lives: his parents, Frayel, and countless others from the Four Cities. Worst of all, the destruction continued as the years crept forward. The first year after the Hoarding, everything disappeared—doors, wagons, tables, cabinets, windows, boats, dead animals, and all the dead people. During the second year, everything reappeared in what the Retrievers have been calling, junk blocks. After the Hoarders were done doing whatever they were doing, they would empty their Captor Packs by shooting out junk blocks from their Captors. The junk blocks spread rapidly throughout the Four Cities, stacking up on top of one another, creating junk walls. By the third year, the junk walls became so high that they blocked the view of the Western Mountains.

Now his parents, Frayel, and all the others whose lives were taken during the Hoarding were part of the Junkland.

Jahrys glanced around The Arcalane. It was already busy and it kept filling up. A group of Retrievers were sitting at one of the booths by the corner in an intense game of Pooles and Palms. Other Retrievers were caught up in conversations scattered around the bar. Innkeeper Willem was busy serving drinks and maintaining the steady flow of Retriever teams that entered The Arcalane.

After The Arcalane was destroyed during the Hoarding, Willem didn't waste a second in rebuilding it. Instead of rebuilding it back to an inn, he built a massive shelter for protection against the Hoarders. He had added numerous bedrooms for survivors to live in. He barred down the windows and added metal siding along the perimeter. As the years went on and the storms got worse, he added a marble roof to absorb the rain, at least to the parts of the building that weren't already covered by junk walls. The inn quickly turned into the main headquarters for all the people in the Four Cities who had survived the Hoarding.

Word about The Arcalane spread quickly, and people traveled from Kaluk, Danor, and Sible to find shelter within. In exchange for a room, Willem only asked that people take up roles as Retrievers to provide for the inn or to help maintain it.

Jahrys heard the door slam open—a team had just arrived. Old Lan and his team rushed in, their suits dripping water onto the already dirty floor.

"Follow the procedure. Make your way to the showers in the back. Quickly now." Willem motioned, indicating for Old Lan's team to follow him.

Willem quickly directed them to the showers in the back where they would be stripped and thoroughly washed down. Their suits would be sterilized and stored for later use, until the storm passed.

This was standard procedure these days, as the Junkland was getting worse, and everything had to be kept clean.

"It seems these storms are getting worse and worse don't you think, O'Jahrys?" Willem asked after finishing with Old Lan's team and returning behind the bar. The rush of people was beginning to settle down. "It's like the stormy season all over again."

Jahrys took another sip from his mug. He turned to face the large innkeeper. "Do you think we'll ever see another long summer?"

Willem traced his mustache with his thumb and index finger. "Not if these Hoarders keep destroying our land. The junk walls are becoming so high, they are starting to block out any bit of sunlight that's able to push through those standstill clouds. Soon, we'll be trapped in an endless night without fresh food and water. The food and water we've collected over the years has already begun to go scarce. I fear at this rate we'll all be dead at the end of next year."

A shiver crept down Jahrys's spine at the thought. He took a heavy sip from his mug.

Willem continued, "If only that damn king would open the gate, we might have a chance of defeating these Hoarders."

"Why hasn't he?" Jahrys asked.

"Because he's a coward. He's a coward and afraid of anything happening to his precious daughter. Leoné is not like his father, Aygor the Strong. He wouldn't have abandoned us like this. No,"—Willem shook his head—"he would have fought for his people!"

"At least he's trying to help us with the Retrieval Stations," Jahrys pointed out. "Without the stations, we wouldn't have had any communication with the castle, and we wouldn't have collected all the weapons we used to kill the Hoarders."

Willem waved his hand in disgust. "Those Retrieval Stations are the king's way of telling us he only cares about himself. He doesn't care what happens to us out here. All he cares about is getting all the supplies he needs to survive inside that castle of his. Without us, they'd be dead inside those walls. We should be saving all this food for ourselves. Not giving it to those cowering behind the walls. Our teams have been traveling farther out to get resources for the king and for ourselves, risking lives. If we don't leave soon, we're going to die in this Junkland. We don't need more swords and shields. We have weapons that are beyond steel. We need to fight back or by Zalus, get our asses out of here."

"But if we leave, everyone inside the castle will die," Jahrys pointed out. *Lily will die. I can't leave her to rot inside those walls.* Jahrys placed his empty mug on the table. "And we barely know what's out there beyond Astenpoole."

Willem threw his hand in disgust. "To hell with them. It's time we search the great beyond. I—"

A boom of thunder cut Willem off. The walls of the inn shook violently. Silence fell throughout the inn as everyone looked around with worried faces.

"It's all right," Willem assured everyone in the inn. "Nothing to fear. I built this inn stronger than those castle walls. Nothing will tear it down."

The crowd settled down and continued with their drinks, chatter, and games.

Willem turned back to Jahrys. "I'm getting worried about Havrick. I sent the poor man out there with a team to bring back more Captors and Captor Packs. It's been over a week now. I need him back here to help me out with The Arcalane."

"I'm sure he's okay," Jahrys assured him. "If there's anyone I'd rather be stuck out in the Junkland with, it would be Havrick."

That seemed to put Willem at ease. "Thanks, O'Ja—"

The door slammed open once again. Another team entered. It was Rallick, Stade, and Taygar. Lightning flashed behind them, followed by a loud boom of thunder. It looked like the rain was coming down even harder now.

"Over here. Quickly now." Willem walked around the bar; waving a hand so they would follow him. "Follow the procedure. Any luck today?"

"We finished one job this morning, but couldn't finish our second because of this storm," answered Rallick, waving a hand toward the storm outside. His voice was deep and muffled as he talked with his helmet on. "There were no sign of Hoarders out by Danor. We're going to continue it tomorrow morning after this storm passes."

"Aye, before you set out, you'll need to help me patch up the marble roof," Willem said. "I fear one more storm like this will eat its way through the entire building." They disappeared around the corner into the back room.

Jahrys reached over the bar and poured himself another drink. He was starting to feel a slight buzz. *Yellow rain will fall,* he recalled Pastor Allen's words as he took a sip. Jahrys raised his hand in the air, the mug shaking. "To wherever you are, Pastor Allen. I hope you survived the Hoarding." *Or maybe you are better off dead.*

With that, Jahrys leaned his head back. He let the warm ale slide down his throat. He slammed the mug back onto the table and reached over for another round.

"Drunk already, Jahrys?" a familiar voice asked behind him.

Jahrys turned. Kevrin was pulling up a stool next to him, Elyara followed close behind. She wrapped her arms around Kevrin's neck and nibbled at his ear.

"Just enjoying myself. That's all." Jahrys continued to pour himself another drink.

"You know, O'Jahrys, we're never going to be good Retrievers if you're hungover every morning we go out," Elyara said in her Kalukian accent.

Jahrys cringed at the sound of his name. "For the last time Elyara, call me Jahrys."

"Just messing with you," she said, giggling.

"She's right, though," Kevrin said. "Other teams laugh at us. We've come out dry with three jobs in the last three months. We'll soon be out of food and Willem can't keep sneaking us stuff from the emergency supply." Kevrin reached over the bar and poured himself and Elyara a drink.

"Tomorrow's the day, guys," Jahrys assured them. "We're going to be the first ones at the Retrieval Stations and find a job we can complete." He took another sip from his mug.

"Well, I'll cheers to that," said Kevrin, lifting his mug in the air.

The three teammates clinked their mugs together and took a large gulp. When they were done, Elyara gave Kevrin a wet kiss on the cheek.

Jahrys turned away. He didn't want to see that. It only made him think of Lily.

"Well, if it isn't Jahrhead, his loyal sidekick Kevrin and his forester lover. Finish any jobs today?" Rallick stood behind them at the bar, finished with his washing. He leaned over and wrapped his arms around their shoulders.

"Piss off Rallick. We didn't go out today." Jahrys said, trying to shrug off Rallick's arm.

"Ha! I honestly don't know how you guys have survived this long." Rallick motioned at Willem for a drink behind the bar.

"Willem has been nice enough to help us out during our slump. But we're heading back out tomorrow," Kevrin answered.

"Anything to help out Alvys's son for all the wine he had provided my bar before the Hoarding, and Kevrin used to help me stock up. These boys were my heroes." Innkeeper Willem gave a little chuckle and went back to cleaning mugs. "I sure could use some of that Grent Wine, O'Jahrys. You don't think there's any lying around out there do you?"

"We've searched the remains of my father's shop, but it looks like we finished all the wine that was left in there. I'll keep my eye out for you, though." Jahrys turned to Rallick and said, "We're going to complete our first job tomorrow, you'll see."

"Well hopefully you have better luck at that than you do at Pooles and Palms. Just don't let the Hoarders get you or else Laura is going to have to save both your butts." He gave his best smile at Elyara.

"My name's Elyara, you idiot." She gave Rallick a dirty look. "At least they have a girl! Go back to your buddies. It looks like they miss you."

Jahrys looked behind Rallick and saw Stade and Taygar staring at Rallick from the corner of the room. Jahrys gave a little chuckle.

Rallick's face turned red. "Hey, just watching out for my fellow Retrievers, that's all." He patted Jahrys hard on the shoulder and said, "I'll be enjoying my nice reward of steak that was cooked fresh from the castle kitchens this afternoon." With that, Rallick took his drink and walked back to his teammates.

"We'll show him," Jahrys said, more to himself than to his friends.

Willem began to fill up a keg behind the bar. He saw the glum look on Jahrys's face. "This'll cheer you up. This came in today fresh from the castle, courtesy of Old Lan's team." Willem's mustache bounced up and down with excitement. It reminded Jahrys of his father.

A keg was the last thing Old Lan needed from the castle. Jahrys knew what happened when Old Lan got his hands on alcohol.

"Make sure you keep it away from him unless you want a repeat of last time," said Jahrys.

"Don't worry. I'll be keeping a sharp eye on Old Lan." Willem patted around the pockets of his clothing, looking for something. "Hey Jahrys, have you seen my keys?"

Junkland

"Nope. Haven't seen them," Jahrys lied.

"Strange. I must have left them upstairs. I—"

The door flew open again. It seemed to be another wave of teams, but there was screaming.

Jahrys, Kevrin, and Elyara twirled around to look.

"AHHH!"

Tarl and Kat rushed into the bar carrying their teammate, Gabe. His legs were flying in all directions beneath him. He was holding his hand out and blood was dripping onto the floor.

"AHHH! Cut if off! Just cut the damn thing off!" he screamed again.

"By Zalus," Willem mumbled to himself, "what happened?" Willem came around the bar to help carry Gabe.

"We ran into some Hoarders on the way back from High Point," explained a panicked Kat. "They chased us all the way back to The Arcalane. We were able to shake them loose, but one of them nicked Gabe in the hand."

Tarl continued for her. "The blast didn't fully take off his hand, but it's been getting worse. Look…"

Willem bent down to examine Gabe's injury. His hand was barely attached to his arm—his wrist was mangled. The glove that had covered it was burnt into his skin.

"Quick. Get him in the back. Now!" Willem ordered.

The rest of the bar was silent, watching the commotion. Willem escorted them to the back room. People looked around at each other awkwardly as Gabe's screams drowned out any noise from the room.

"Poor Gabe," said Elyara, shaking her head in sympathy. "That could've been us out there. We need to get some sleep so we're prepared for tomorrow. Who knows how long we'll be in the Junkland for."

Kevrin finished his drink, wiped his lips clean and said, "Elyara's right. I'm heading up to bed. Don't stay up too late, Jahrys. We have to get to the Retrieval Stations early tomorrow so we're guaranteed a decent job."

"I won't be too much longer," Jahrys lied, feeling too depressed to attempt to sleep.

"See you tomorrow." Kevrin and Elyara said, as they walked up the stairs to the right of the bar.

Jahrys sunk himself into his stool and zoned out from the screams and the light chatter around him. He continued to think of his parents. He thought about his mother, how loving and caring she had been. And when she would remember what he liked and didn't like to eat. He missed those little things. And he missed his father. He missed having someone teach him new things, like the art of carpentry, fishing, and how to make Mother smile. Even if it was things he didn't want to learn, Jahrys would always appreciate it later on down the road.

And then there was Lily. He would do anything to see her. How could he have let her slip away?

He fumbled around with the necklace in his pocket. His fingers lightly outlining the shape of the gem. *I'll make you all proud tomorrow*, he thought.

"BUCUUUUUUCK!"

Jahrys looked down and smiled. Miller was staring up at him. He had finally dropped the keys onto the floor.

"Finally got bored of biting metal?" Jahrys bent down and

scratched the chicken's round, bony head.

"BUCUUUUUCK!"

Jahrys laughed. "Me too, Mill. Me too."

Chapter 15
Jahrys

THE NEXT DAY started with a pounding headache for Jahrys. He rolled out of bed, still wearing the same clothes he had on the night before. Miller squawked as he was flung off the bed.

Jahrys's room was tiny, but big enough to fit a bed and a small dresser. A doorway led into an even smaller washroom.

I shouldn't have had all those drinks, Jahrys thought, as he stumbled his way into the washroom, ignoring the angry pecks at his toes from Miller. He dunked his hands into the bucket of water and splashed his face. He looked into the cracked mirror hanging on the wall above the bucket. His eyes were baggy and black, his tan skin looked pale, and his hair was a mess.

It had been another sleepless night for Jahrys. He had the same nightmares he had been having for the past three years. Once again, he watched his parents die, listening to their screams. Once again, he had felt Lily's hand slip away from his as he listened to her voice fade away.

Knock. Knock. Knock.

Junkland

Miller ran to the door and began pecking at it.

Jahrys turned and stumbled towards the door. He pushed Miller out of the way with his foot and opened it. Kevrin stood there and instantly tossed him a loaf of bread. Jahrys caught it as Miller scooted out under Jahrys's legs.

"Eat some of this and let's get going," Kevrin told him.

Jahrys took a bite and walked back over to his dresser. He gathered his bag he had packed the night before, and they both made their way down the creaking stairs to the bar.

There was no one in the bar except for Elyara, who had been waiting for them. *Good,* Jahrys thought, *everyone must still be sleeping.*

Jahrys, Kevrin, and Elyara walked around the bar into the back room. The back room used to be for storage before the Hoarding, but Willem had since enhanced it. Hooks now lined the right side of the wall, holding clean suits and helmets. Captor Packs were lined up against the left side of the wall. There was a separate room used for washing after teams returned from the Junkland.

The three teammates found their designated suits and slipped them on, double checking that their skin was not exposed to the air. They were tight, but the lightweight material made it easy to move around in. The suits had been collected from the dead Hoarders that had been killed over the years. The strangest thing had happened, though. The yellow lights on the suits, Captor Packs, and Captors that they had collected had changed blue. Every suit now had a blue tint. No one could explain it. Willem assumed it was some kind of sorcery.

The suits were crucial in protecting their skin in the Junkland. As the land became more and more dangerous, any open wound would instantly become infected, and they were running low on proper medicine to heal them. Survival was not guaranteed in the Junkland with an open wound. They also used the suits to protect themselves when fighting Hoarders.

They had also collected the Captors from the dead Hoarders. The technology was nothing they had ever seen before. It took them awhile to learn how to use them.

For the most part, using a Captor was straightforward: aim and click. There were two triggers on the handle. When the top trigger was pressed, it fired a fatal blast. However, the Captor had a limit. In order to recharge it, the Captor needed to be attached to the Captor Pack with the tube. Then, when the bottom trigger was pressed, it would fire a beam that would encompass any object it was pointed at. It was possible to use the Captor without the tube attached, but once the energy from the Captor was drained, it would not be able to fire anymore. There was a glass tube in the center of the Captor that glowed blue, showing the energy level.

When both buttons were pressed...Jahrys and the Retrievers still weren't sure exactly what happened. All they knew was when both triggers were pressed, the Captor would shoot out the objects from the Captor Pack in a compressed junk block. Energy was processed somehow, condensing the remains into a junk block.

Once their suits were firmly secured, Kevrin helped Jahrys and Elyara attach their Captor Packs to their backs. When the packs were clipped in, a circular blue light on the back lit up. Jahrys and Elyara then attached the long tube from the pack to their Captors. They checked the blue light on both their Captors to see if they were fully charged.

Kevrin never wore a Captor Pack because he claimed he wasn't the best at using a Captor. So instead, he was in charge of carrying all of their bags and supplies they wanted to bring.

The three teammates clipped on their helmets and walked back out into the bar, heading for the door. When Jahrys opened it, Miller tried to scoot out. Jahrys blocked his path with his boot.

"The Junkland is no place for you," Jahrys said through his helmet. His voice sounded distorted.

Miller stared at him with fearful eyes, his stick legs were wobbling beneath his round body. Jahrys must have looked like a monster to Miller.

Jahrys bent down to pet Miller with his gloved hand, but Miller squawked in fear and scurried away. Jahrys shrugged and walked out into the Junkland.

The air was hazy and thick. Shattered junk blocks that had fallen from the junk walls above covered the roads. It was quiet; animals were rarely seen or heard anymore. There were no horses either, since the roads were too unstable to walk.

The Junkland was lifeless.

They were only a few streets away from the castle wall, where the Hoarders hadn't polluted much of the roads, so it was easy to walk through. It wasn't as demolished as the lands farther out along the edges.

When they arrived at the closed Western Gate, Kevrin, Jahrys, and Elyara walked up the line of Retrieval Stations until they found the one they wanted. They approached a tiny wooden shed built into the stone of the wall. They walked up the creaking steps and opened the wooden door that was half off its hinges. It was dark inside and cramped, but Kevrin reached out and rang a bell.

Ring, Ring, Ring.

They stood patiently waiting.

A window shot up and light poured into the shed. A large man appeared. He looked the three of them over.

"Ah, if it isn't Kevrin Danell, O'Jahrys Grent, and the beautiful Elyara M'ava, come to see good old Riago. You guys are out early this morning." An old bald man stood behind the window, talking through the bars. He was so tall and large that he had to squat down to see them. "You haven't, by any chance, found any leftovers of your father's wine, have ya, O'Jahrys?"

"No, sorry Riago, not this time. I'll keep looking for you, though. How'd you know it was us?" They were all wearing their suits and had their helmets on.

"I had a hunch. Ah. The things I'd do for that wine. Your father was a true wizard." He coughed to clear his throat. "Well, what can old Riago do for ya this morning?"

"We need another job," said Kevrin.

"What happened to the one I gave you a week's past?" Riago asked while scratching his head.

"Erh, well, we couldn't find that man's family compass," Kevrin said with embarrassment.

"Hargh, Hargh," Riago let out a bark of a laugh. "Well, let's see what old Riago has for you today. Hopefully something a little easier then." He turned and started fumbling through some files to his right. "Hmm. No. Not this. Or this. Hmm." After a few minutes Riago said, "Ah ha! This should be a good one for ya." He slid a piece of paper beneath a slit at the bottom of the window. Kevrin took the piece of paper and examined it over. Jahrys and Elyara glanced at it over Kevrin's shoulder. It was a drawing of a white book with golden hinges.

"What is this?" Kevrin asked as he passed the drawing back to his teammates.

"It's a diary," Riago said. "A girl has been coming with the same job, month after month, with no success. Even Rallick and his gang couldn't find it."

Rallick failed to mention that at the bar, thought Jahrys.

"Bring that diary back here in one piece and the girl has left a hefty reward," said Riago, leaning over his desk.

"What kind of reward?" Elyara asked, curiously.

"All she told me was you would be highly rewarded."

Kevrin, Jahrys, and Elyara all looked at each other and nodded.

"We accept!" said Kevrin, taking the paper from Jahrys and folding it into his bag.

"You all have two weeks before Riago opens this job again to another team. So get moving," Riago said, shooing them away with a hand.

Kevrin, Jahrys, and Elyara turned to leave.

"One more thing," Riago yelled out behind them. There was a loud thump in a cabinet below the window. "Take these."

Jahrys reached down, opened the cabinet, and saw three knives.

"You guys are going to be needing all the help you can get. Hargh, Hargh." Riago let out a laugh as he shut the window and left Kevrin, Jahrys, and Elyara in the darkness of the shed.

Chapter 16
Jahrys

JAHRYS JOLTED UP, gasping for breath. His lungs felt like they were going to collapse and his heart was pounding in his chest. He was covered in sweat and his hands were shaking. *A dream, it was only a dream*, thought Jahrys as his lungs searched for air. He rolled over to his side and grabbed his leather waterskin. He drank it greedily. After he was done and his heart rate slowed, he tried to remember what the dream was about. *Screaming*, he thought. *All I remember is a woman screaming*.

His vision was blurred, but it was gradually coming back. His eye was stinging because a piece of his long, brown hair had whipped into it. He was still in his suit; he didn't want to take it off, just in case something were to happen during the night. His helmet was on the wooden floor next to him. His Captor Pack and Captor were next to his helmet. Lily's necklace was clenched tightly in his hand.

He lifted his head and looked around the musty room, still trying to calm down. The room was dark and the air was heavy and thick; it felt like it was engulfing his body. It was completely empty. There was no furniture, doors, or any household items; they were all taken during the Hoarding.

A small fire was to his left. Kevrin had made it last night when he had cooked some fish they had caught when they fished along The Pass that fed into Ocean Lake. It was a nice change from all the dry bread they had been eating the past week.

Kevrin had tried his best to make the fire small enough as to be unnoticed. He also wanted to avoid burning down the house they were currently residing.

The fire was now reduced to ashes and wisps of smoke. The red embers were dimly glowing. There was a pot next to the fire that was filled a quarter of the way up with water. Jahrys's bag lay behind him; he had been using it as a pillow. It wasn't the most comfortable sleep when compared to the other nights of their journey.

After leaving Riago's Retrieval Station, they had decided it would be a good idea to check High Point since Kat had mentioned her team had spotted Hoarders in that area. They had traveled to the east side of the castle where a boathouse had been built over the crossing of the Seaport River. The boathouse led into the castle, but this had also been boarded up—King Leoné had sealed it during The Sickness. However, the boathouse was still accessible from the outside. The Retrievers had rebuilt a few boats after the Hoarding and kept them hidden inside.

Jahrys, Kevrin, and Elyara had taken a boat down the river. The river had been flowing fast after the storm, so it only had taken them a little more than two days to travel down to The Pass that fed them into Ocean Lake.

The mist and fog from the lake had given them enough of a cover, so they had decided to camp along the shore, stocking up on fish, and searching the perimeter for any signs of Hoarders. The junk walls also protected them, forming a circle around the lake, towering high into the gray sky.

Jahrys had spent most of his time keeping an eye out on the water for any sign of the Octa Monster. He wasn't about to have a giant tentacle drag him to the bottom of the lake during the night. But the calm waves breaking on the shore had been soothing, and made it nearly impossible to stay awake. It had reminded Jahrys of the times his parents had taken him to the Sandy Shore.

When his teammates had decided to move on towards the Manor, Jahrys was sad to leave. However, he was excited to finally explore further into High Point where the mansions lined the edges of the cliffs. He had never been to the Manor before. He knew that Lord Ide Velton, the lord of Sible, lived in the Manor—or had lived there. Jahrys had heard Lord Ide's home towered above all the mansions at the edge of the cliff.

They had found a path through a junk wall and discovered most of the mansions crushed beneath the walls of debris. The junk walls had looked like large waves flowing from one mansion to the next. Junk blocks had been scattered on the ground at the base of the walls. Some of the blocks had shattered and debris filled the roads. But Jahrys had been disappointed when they had arrived on the eastern side of the lake; there had been no sign of Lord Ide's giant mansion.

The junk walls were even more massive here—perhaps because all the people had left, and the junk blocks hadn't been broken down for scraps. While the junk blocks were heavily compacted when the Hoarders released them, they could be taken apart with some work. It was a lucky day for a Retriever when useful items were found within a junk block.

After they had searched the area for most of the day for the diary, Jahrys, Kevrin, and Elyara decided to find a place to sleep. They had found a house that was still standing—sort of. The house had been tilted at an awkward angle; part of it had been raised in the air from the weight of the junk wall on top of it. They had climbed up the lopsided steps that had brought them onto a faded white porch. A burnt cherry colored door had been hanging off its hinges in front of them. Jahrys had been surprised to have even see a door at all.

Jahrys had grabbed his Captor that had been clipped onto his hip. He had turned the light on top of his helmet on, which was powered the same way as his Captor. He had used the tip of his Captor to nudge open the broken door. Kevrin and Elyara had followed close behind him. Elyara had also taken out her Captor and Kevrin had fumbled around his belt, looking for the knife Riago had given him.

The room had been dark. They had followed the light down the hall, stepping cautiously, trying to avoid the sound of creaks from the wooden flooring.

"You search the upstairs," Kevrin had nodded his helmet towards Jahrys, "Elyara and I will finish down here."

With the light still guiding him, Jahrys had ascended the stairs taking each step with caution, raising his Captor high. The clouds of dust had made it difficult to see past the point of his Captor. The air had been thick and made it hard to breathe, even with the air filter in his helmet.

Once he had reached the top of the stairs, he hung a quick right and continued down a narrow hallway, keeping his head low from the crushed ceiling.

There had been a door at the end, giving him a sinking feeling in his stomach. He had crept slowly towards the door, which felt like it was calling him. Was it calling him? The black door at the end of the hallway had a hypnotic aura around it. Sweat had begun to run down his forehead. However, he couldn't wipe it through his helmet, and so it dripped into his eyes.

He had finally reached the end of the hall and was standing in front of the door. It had seemed a lot taller than he had originally thought as it towered over him. He had placed one hand on the doorknob and pushed the door forward. The door had flung all the way to the left side with a loud creek before it crashed against the wall. Dust had flown up into a thick cloud, blocking his vision.

When the dust had cleared, Jahrys saw an image carved into the wall across the room. He had walked over to it and outlined the image with his fingers. He had traced it from the bottom all the way to the top. It looked like a temple. A grand staircase led up to the entrance where pillars surrounded the base. The roof of the temple rose high towards the ceiling of the room Jahrys was in. There had been palms, like the ones on top of Pastor Allen's church, except these palms had been holding a sphere. Jahrys studied it, fascinated. He had never seen anything like it. He wondered where this temple was—it was definitely not in Astenpoole.

When Jahrys had returned to Elyara and Kevrin, Kevrin had asked, "Did you find anything upstairs?"

Jahrys had decided to keep the temple he found to himself. He didn't want to worry his teammates. "Nope, everything is clear. Let's make camp down here."

Thoughts of their journey and the mysterious temple in the room above made Jahrys forget his bad dream. He looked at his friends—

Elyara was there next to him, still sleeping, but Kevrin was no where to be seen. Kevrin had taken watch last night.

Jahrys tossed Lily's necklace into his bag and jumped to his feet, feeling the tightness in his ankles from the traveling they had done the previous day. He looked over at Elyara, who was still sleeping.

"Elyara, wake up," he whispered, nudging her.

"What?" Elyara murmured, her eyes half open.

"Kevrin is gone."

That got her attention. She shot up. "Gone? What do you mean *gone?*" Her eyes searched the room for Kevrin. "Where is he?"

"After you went to bed, we stayed up a bit to talk. He told me he would take the first watch." Jahrys noticed Kevrin's bag was also gone. "He must have gone out into the Junkland."

"Let's go find him," Elyara was up and moving.

They both put on their helmets and helped each other clip on their Captor Packs. As soon as Jahrys's Captor Pack clipped in, the blue lights on his suit and the light on his Captor Pack illuminated. They both grabbed their Captors and attached them to the long tubes.

Jahrys noticed the blue light on his Captor was fading.

"I'm running low. How's your Captor?" Jahrys asked Elyara. He knew he would have to recharge his soon. The lights on their helmets used up a lot of their energy.

"I have enough for now. We can recharge them later." Elyara turned towards the door. "Follow me," she ordered.

They walked out the back door, which brought them out to another porch at the back of the house. The air was musty and thick. It was also dark and hard to see, but Jahrys didn't want to risk using his light. It was probably close to early morning anyway.

"Maybe we should stay here just in case he comes back. We don't want him to have to come look for us," Jahrys suggested. He was worried they would get lost and not be able to find their way back in the darkness.

Elyara didn't stop. She walked down the uneven steps and said, "I'm going out there to look for Kevrin. He would have told us if he was going out alone. He wouldn't go out there without us. He doesn't even have a Captor."

She was right. He was out there with just his knife. Jahrys didn't have a choice. He stumbled after Elyara, staying close behind her. He raised his Captor and his finger rested lightly on the top trigger. He walked down the slanted steps of the porch.

What could have been a courtyard before the Hoarding was spread out before them. A thick fog hovered over the ground. A fountain was toppled over in the center, and a bench to the side was split in two. A few yards past the courtyard, Jahrys could see the start of a junk wall, but its top was lost to the darkness of the sky.

Through the fog, Jahrys made out a path that separated the junk wall. Jahrys motioned to the opening with his Captor, and him and Elyara headed towards it.

They crossed the courtyard. There was no grass, only hard dirt. Junk blocks had fallen from the walls around them and were scattered across the yard. Some of the blocks had shattered and had broken into pieces of metal, glass, and wood. Visibility was low, and it was difficult to dodge the loose debris on the fog covered ground.

Jahrys's foot caught on something hard, and he fell face forward. His hands went flying out in front of him to break his fall, causing his Captor to go spinning to the ground.

"Are you okay?" Elyara spun around. Jahrys couldn't see her face through her helmet, but he could tell by her voice she was concerned.

"Yea, I'm fine. I just got my foot caught on something." Jahrys rolled over to see what had caused him to fall. Even through the fog, he was able to make out the outline of a body.

Elyara gasped. With fear in her voice, she asked, "Who is that?"

Jahrys found his Captor and turned to bend over the person.

"It's a Retriever," Jahrys said, analyzing the body that was lying face down. The lights were still illuminated, giving the suit a blue glow.

"Is it someone we know?" Elyara bent down next to Jahrys.

"Let's find out." Jahrys clipped his Captor back to his hip.

He unclipped the Captor Pack from the person's back and placed it on the ground next to him along with the Captor. Jahrys then rolled the body over and reached his gloved hands out towards the person's helmet. He unclipped it and wiggled it off to reveal a man's face. His eyes were swollen, bulging out of his skull. His face was ghost-like and waxy, and his lips were purple. He had been dead for several days.

"It's Havrick," Jahrys could tell from the dark hair and crooked nose.

"Why haven't the Hoarders taken his body?" Elyara inquired.

Jahrys looked down Havrick's body.

"Look." He pointed towards Havrick's foot. A metal trap was digging into his suit, down to the flesh of his foot. Dried up blood stained his suit and the ground around his leg.

"The Hoarders must be setting traps. They must not have discovered his body yet," Jahrys proposed, trying to fit the pieces together.

A blast suddenly whipped past the left side of Jahrys's head, exploding into the fountain in the center of the courtyard several yards behind them. He could feel the heat even through his helmet.

Jahrys scrambled for his Captor and spun around.

"Run!" A voice yelled out across the courtyard.

Jahrys recognized Kevrin's voice. Kevrin was running through the fog, towards them. His left arm was covered in blood.

"Kevrin what—" but his words were cut short when he saw what also came into view across the courtyard.

Five Hoarders exploded out of the entrance between the junk walls. Their yellow suits glowed bright in the darkness. They had their Captors raised and were shooting at Kevrin.

Captor blasts filled the courtyard.

Chapter 17
Jahrys

ELYARA FIRED, BUT Jahrys grabbed her arm and pulled her back.

"We can cover him from the porch," Jahrys yelled over the blasts.

Elyara agreed.

They left Havrick and sprinted back towards the porch. They passed the fountain, dodging the loose debris on the ground. They were only a few yards away from the porch now.

Kevrin was a hundred feet behind them when he made it past the fountain. Captor blasts were exploding into the ground and off the scattered junk blocks.

Heart pounding, Jahrys followed Elyara up the crooked porch steps, towards the back door. He reached for the doorknob, twisted it, and pushed it open for Elyara.

"Grab what you can. I'll cover Kevrin," Jahrys yelled.

Elyara nodded and ducked through the door.

Now on the porch, Jahrys turned back towards the courtyard.

He saw a Hoarder standing over Havrick in the distance, pointing a Captor at his dead body. The other four Hoarders were now between the fountain and the porch, firing at Kevrin.

Jahrys bent down on one knee and lifted his Captor to the right side of his face, leaning against the railing. He took a deep breath in, trying to focus, but the railing began to shake and Jahrys lost his concentration.

There was a deep, low hum.

VHRUUUUMMMM.

A yellow beam shot out from the Hoarder's Captor. The beam filled the courtyard with a blinding light.

When the light cleared and Jahrys's eyesight returned, Havrick's body was gone.

The Hoarder took off after the others.

The shaking had stopped and Jahrys regained his focus. He aimed and shot at the Hoarder closest to Kevrin. He missed. He shot again. Missed. Then a third time. The third shot hit the Hoarder's tube. There was a loud hiss as the tube broke, sending yellow smoke into the air, blinding the Hoarders as Kevrin ran safely up the steps.

Jahrys grabbed Kevrin and pushed him through the door. Jahrys kicked the door shut and locked it, knowing it wouldn't give them much time. They ran through the hall.

"Kevrin!" Elyara shouted when she saw him. She threw her arms around him.

Jahrys wasn't happy, however. He grabbed Kevrin's shoulder and twisted him around.

Kevrin winced. "My arm—"

"Again? You disappeared again!" Jahrys was furious. "We talked about this."

Kevrin held up the diary in his hands.

Jahrys couldn't believe it. "How did you—"

There was shouting as they heard the Hoarders marching up the porch steps.

"I'll explain later. We need to go." Kevrin motioned for the front door.

Elyara handed Kevrin their bags. He tied them all together and hoisted them over his shoulder.

The house began to shake. The three Retrievers tried to balance themselves as the floor shook beneath their boots.

There was a deep, low hum outside the back door.

VHRUUUUMMMM.

A loud crack sent the door flying off its hinges, disappearing. The five Hoarders piled into the room—Captors raised.

The teammates exchanged quick glances and bolted for the front door, Captor blasts exploded around them. Kevrin and Elyara pushed through the front door. Jahrys followed, but one of the shots grazed his left shoulder. He cried out in agony as he felt the heat burning through his suit.

"Come on, Jahrys. Let's go!" Kevrin yelled out. They were already down the porch steps.

Elyara was pointing her Captor at the door, giving Jahrys cover. Jahrys leaped over the steps, landing hard on the ground. He clipped his Captor onto his hip and regrouped with his teammates. They ran down the path they had come from the previous night, back towards the lake.

Captor blasts exploded around them, sending debris flying dangerously in the air. The Hoarders were close behind. The junk walls around them were getting narrow. They had to form a single line as they twisted and turned through the maze. Jahrys was hit numerous times in the helmet by something hard, probably stray pieces of metal from a junk block, but he ignored it; his helmet protected him. His shoulder was burning, a searing pain was spreading from his shoulder to his arm. He kept running.

The fog was beginning to clear and the darkness was beginning to lessen. It was getting easier to see all the obstacles in their path.

Jahrys jumped over a statue that was jutting out of the ground. He felt the heat of a Captor blast burst against the statue beneath his feet. His heart was pounding in his chest. He could feel the sweat soaking his suit. His sweaty hair was stinging his eyes under his helmet. His ears were ringing from the blasts from the Captors, yells from Elyara and Kevrin up ahead, and the shouts from the Hoarders behind him. His legs were wobbling beneath him; he was afraid they would give out any second. He had to keep moving, though. He didn't want his fate to be like Havrick's, sucked up inside a Captor Pack, being crushed into a junk block.

The path parted up ahead into Ocean Lake. They would soon be out in the open of the shoreline. If the Hoarders made it through, they would be easy targets.

When Jahrys stumbled through the opening, Elyara turned and fired her Captor at the junk wall above Jahrys's head. The blast exploded and junk blocks came crashing down behind him. There was a cloud of smoke covering the opening, but when the smoke cleared, the path was blocked by numerous junk blocks that had fallen.

They all let out a quick sigh of relief. They were saved—for now. The Hoarders would find a way around eventually, or simply break through. They needed to keep moving.

Junkland

"Don't move," a deep, muffled voice ordered behind him.

Jahrys felt something hard jab into his side. He turned his head slightly to see three people in blue suits pointing Captors at them.

He couldn't believe it. "Rallick, what the—"

"I said don't move, Jahrhead. All we want is the diary."

Stade was pointing his Captor at Kevrin, and Taygar had his pointed at Elyara.

Rallick turned his head. "Stade, grab it."

Stade kept his Captor pointed at Kevrin as he marched over to him. He snatched Kevrin's bags from his hands and fumbled through them.

"Get out of there." Kevrin tried to grab his bag from Stade, but Stade slammed his Captor across Kevrin's bleeding arm. He let out a scream as he fell to his knees.

"Kevrin!" Elyara yelled.

Stade pulled out the diary and handed it over to Rallick.

Rallick grabbed it with his free hand.

"Rallick, please," Elyara pleaded. "We must keep moving. The Hoarders. They will—"

"Keep your mouth shut, you stupid forester," Rallick snapped at her through his helmet. He held the diary out in front of him.

"You've been following us?" Jahrys asked through gritted teeth.

"Let's just say you all have been helpful guides," Rallick said.

Jahrys knew Rallick was grinning under his helmet.

"You can't do this," Jahrys yelled. "It's *our* job." He wouldn't let Rallick get away with this. They couldn't go back to The Arcalane with another failed job—not this time.

"It's the Junkland, O'Jahrys. We can do whatever we want," Rallick sniggered.

Stade and Taygar laughed through their helmets.

"No hard feelings, really. Come on guys, let's get out of here." Rallick motioned for Stade and Taygar to follow.

Kevrin reached out towards Stade, a knife at his neck.

"No one's going anywhere until we get that diary back." Kevrin's hand was shaking, but he held the knife firmly below Stade's helmet, right on top of his Adam's apple.

The pressure was released from Jahrys's side as Rallick swung his Captor towards Kevrin. "Don't be doing anything stupid now. We weren't going to hurt anyone—really. We just wanted the diary." Rallick said, but he sounded worried.

Stade was whimpering and Taygar was moaning.

"No one will get hurt as long as you hand Jahrys the diary." Kevrin's body was shaking.

Jahrys watched the knife begin to dig into Stade's suit; blood was seeping out.

"Kevrin," Jahrys said, concerned. "Stop!"

But the knife dug a little deeper. Stade moaned.

Everyone held their breath.

Suddenly Captor blasts exploded around them. The Retrievers turned and saw the five Hoarders piling through a newly opened path.

"Run!" Jahrys yelled.

The Retrievers ran south along the shore, bumping into each other, trying desperately to get ahead of one another, as they searched for another path to take them out of the open. They needed cover—fast.

Blasts zipped past their heads, feet, and arms as the Hoarders closed the distance behind them.

Junkland

"Where do we go?" Elyara yelled from up ahead.

"Over there! Go left!" Jahrys ordered, pointing to an opening fifty yards ahead. They picked up their pace, but it was difficult running on the sand. Jahrys felt his ankles give out beneath him a few times. Blasts exploded around him, sending clouds of sand into the air. The sand clouds blinded Jahrys, but he kept running. Jahrys winced as sand dug into his wound.

They reached the opening and Elyara, Kevrin, and Jahrys piled into it.

"Where're you going?" Jahrys turned to see Rallick, Stade, and Taygar running past them.

"Sorry Jahrhead, but we have another path to take. Good luck!" Rallick gave him a salute as he took off after Stade and Taygar.

Jahrys ducked from a blast that almost took his head off. He crouched down on one knee, whipping out his Captor. He clenched his finger down on the top trigger and fired a shot out towards the five Hoarders. He hit the Hoarder farthest to the left in the chest and the Hoarder stumbled to the ground. Jahrys fired another—missed. The four remaining Hoarders were thirty yards from the opening now. Jahrys fired again, but when he pressed down on the trigger, his Captor hissed.

He was out. His Captor needed to be recharged.

Jahrys clipped his Captor to his hip and sprinted after Elyara and Kevrin.

When Jahrys caught up to his two friends, the path curved to the right and then back to the left, giving them some cover from the Hoarders. The path straightened out and they ran and ran and ran until Jahrys slammed hard into Kevrin.

Jahrys groaned. "What's going on? We need to keep moving."

"It's a dead end," Elyara said flatly.

Jahrys looked over Kevrin's shoulder and saw Elyara pointing down to the Farrest Sea. They were at the edge of High Point—at the edge of the cliffs.

Images of the cliffs popped into Jahrys's head when he had visited the Sandy Shore years before. They were at least a hundred and fifty feet high, with sharp rocks protruding out like fingers at the base of the cliff. He never thought he would ever be on the other side, looking down at the Sandy Shore. If they jumped, they could easily hit the rocks. And if they miraculously avoided them, the rough water would throw them into the rocks, or suck them down into the darkness, drowning them.

"What do we do?" Elyara asked desperately.

"Do we fight?" Kevrin asked.

"We only have one Captor. Mine is out and we don't have time to recharge it. They'll kill us if we fight." Jahrys didn't know what to do. His head was pounding. The Hoarders would be around the bend any second now.

"What do we do?" Kevrin asked.

There was only one thing they could do.

"We have to jump." Jahrys knew he sounded crazy saying it.

"Jump? Are you mad?" Kevrin shouted, throwing his hands up in the air in disbelief.

"He's right," Elyara agreed. "We'll die if we try fighting. But there might be a chance if we jump." Elyara was trying to be brave. She knew the chances were slim.

"Does anyone else see how far that drop is?" Kevrin pointed towards the rough water below.

"We have to," Jahrys placed a hand on his friend's shoulder.

Junkland

"Jump out far and stay clear of the rocks. Make sure to hit the water feet first and swim up as soon as you can." He turned to Elyara. "We should take our Captor Packs off. We don't want the extra weight pulling us down."

Kevrin helped Elyara and Jahrys unclip their Captor Packs and helmets.

"What about the bags?" Kevrin asked.

"I'll carry mine," Jahrys said. He couldn't lose Lily's necklace.

"You can let go of mine," Elyara said. "I don't need it."

Kevrin handed Jahrys his bag and threw Elyara's to the side. They both tied their bags around their waist, making sure they were secure.

Jahrys saw Kevrin shaking. "It will be o—"

"Look out!" Kevrin spun Jahrys around and pinned him against the junk wall.

A blast zipped past them and exploded at Elyara's feet, sending her off the cliff.

"NO!" Kevrin yelled.

"Come on." Jahrys pushed Kevrin towards the cliff. "Jump!"

Kevrin sprinted and jumped.

Jahrys didn't hesitate. He ran into the cloud of debris and leaped, feeling his legs leave the earth and his stomach drop as he fell into the cold darkness below.

Chapter 18
Jahrys

IT WAS DARK. He searched for a sign of light. But there was nothing. *Am I dead?* He very well could be. But he never thought death would be like this. Wasn't there supposed to be light? Wasn't it supposed to be warm and happy? He could have sworn he would be in a land far past the Western Mountains, where there was no humidity, no stormy season, and the grass was green for miles on end. He would see his parents smiling and waving at him as they greeted him.

But there was no one here and this place was not green, nor was it warm and happy. It was dark and cold. A cold Jahrys had never felt in his life.

Feeling came to his fingers as he realized he was lying on a floor. He traced the outline of the flooring. *Is this tile?* he wondered as his index finger traced around a square.

He stood up. His body was shivering; he realized he was naked. He wrapped his arms around himself as he took a cautious step forward in the darkness and then another.

Something hit his waist. He reached his hands out and felt something smooth. *A table? Where am I?*

A blinding light suddenly overcame the darkness.

When it began to fade, he realized where he was. *I'm in a kitchen— my kitchen.*

Thump.

Something hit the floor in the darkness.

Thump.

Jahrys heard it again. He crawled underneath the table, hiding. He hugged his knees into his chest and kept silent underneath the table. He was too scared to move.

He suddenly heard something sliding along the floor. It sounded like a heavy bag being dragged. He felt his heart thumping in his chest. Heavy breathing echoed around him. He thought it was from him, but he realized the breathing was coming from the darkness ahead.

The sound of something scraping the marble tile sent shivers down his spine.

Screeeeeeech.

Screeeeeech, Screeeeeech.

Something was crawling towards him. And it sounded like there was more than one. His eyes still hadn't adjusted and it was still too dark to see in front of him.

Screeeeeech.

It was getting closer. Jahrys didn't know what to do or where to go; he was frozen.

A streak of moonlight filled the room.

Then he saw them.

Two bodies were crawling across the kitchen floor toward him, their fingernails scraping the tile floor. The left body had long hair: a woman. The other he made out to be a man. They were naked. Their skin was white, and their eyes were bottomless pits. He could not make out their faces, but deep down he had a sickening feeling he knew them—his parents. A crow sat on top of the woman, ripping at the flesh of her neck, but she didn't seem to feel it.

Then, he heard a voice. "She is coming for you, O'Jahrys Grent." It was a high, chilling voice. It seemed to be coming from the woman, but her lips did not move. The sound of tearing flesh grew louder as the crow and the woman came closer.

"Who?" he yelled out into the darkness. "Who is coming for me?"

"The Dark One has a plan for you, O'Jahrys Grent." The voice echoed throughout the room, high and scratchy, cold, lifeless.

They were almost upon him now. Their cold, white lips moved as they both repeated in unison. "The Dark One has a plan for you, O'Jahrys Grent."

The voices were getting louder and louder. He tried to close his eyes. To shut it all out. But it only made it worse. The room began to shake. The tile shifted beneath him and a chair that was tucked underneath the table banged against his head. He heard knives clattering against the tabletop and plates shattering on the floor.

"She will not rest until she has you, O'Jahrys Grent!" They screamed it this time, their cold voices urgent. They kept repeating their warning as the world around him shook.

Suddenly the room was filled with complete darkness, and Jahrys saw nothing. All he heard was the sound of screeching fingernails, the voices of the two lifeless bodies, the crow ripping at his mother's flesh, and the sound of a Captor. It was all bouncing around the kitchen. Jahrys tried to cover his ears, but it was no use. It was as if the sound was coming from inside his head. He closed his eyes.

Screeeeeeech.

VHRUUUUMMMM.

Screeeeeech.

VHRUUUUMMMM.

When he opened his eyes, the bodies were gone. In place of the bodies was a person dressed in a black robe standing over him, holding a black staff. The person's face was a dark shadow. The figure raised the staff, pointing a sphere towards Jahrys. A dark smoke swam inside the glass.

Jahrys was petrified. There was nowhere to run; he was trapped, frozen. All he could do was watch as the dark smoke shot out from the sphere towards his body, and the world around Jahrys disappeared as he fell back into darkness.

His eyes shot open. Jahrys leaned over and threw up the water that congested his lungs. His blurred vision began to focus. He was on a shore bank. The golden sand was hard beneath his body. His helmet was gone. All he heard was the sound of waves, crashing like thunder around him. He could feel his legs still in the water as a wave crashed over him. His chest was on fire. When the water receded back, he crawled forward, getting as far away as possible from the shore break. He collapsed onto the sand.

He felt the pain return to his left shoulder as the salt water bit into the wound. Jahrys looked over and saw a graze in his suit where the blast had hit him.

He tried to recall what happened.

All he remembered was running and jumping off High Point. After the jump, all Jahrys remembered was the dream. Who was the

Dark One that was coming for him? He must have hit his head on a rock.

His hands suddenly shot down to his waist in panic. Relief flooded his body as his hands found the bag still tied around his waist. He dug his hand into the bag, fumbling around the soggy food, and Riago's knife, until his hand wrapped around the necklace. Jahrys let out a deep breathe. *I didn't lose it.* He pulled it out and clutched it to his chest. *By Zalus, thank you.*

He placed the necklace back in the bag and looked around. *Kevrin…Elyara…*his friends had been with him. *Where are they?*

When Jahrys's hearing returned, he heard someone yelling to his right.

"No. NO!"

Jahrys turned his head to see Kevrin hunching over Elyara; his helmet was also missing, but his bag was still tied around his waist. Jahrys struggled to his feet, coughing up seawater as he rose. His knees shook beneath him as he stumbled over to his friends. He placed a hand on Kevrin's hunched back.

"Elyara!" Kevrin yelled. "Come back to me. Please come back to me." He had her rolled over to her side with her mouth open as he desperately patted her back, trying to get the water out of her lungs

Elyara's once dark skin was pale and lifeless. Her wet hair was coated in yellow-crusted sand, and there was a deep gash on the back of her head.

"NO, ELYARA!" Kevrin screamed in pain. "BREATHE! Just…just breathe!" Tears were falling down his face. He pulled her close to his body, cradling her as his body shook.

Jahrys began to cry. He squeezed Kevrin's shoulder, trying to comfort him. "I'm sorry, Kevrin. But…she's gone. She was probably gone before she even hit the water." He said, indicating the wound on her head.

"I'm going to kill him." The veins in Kevrin's neck were bulging. "We could have been far away from those Hoarders if it wasn't for Rallick."

"I know. But there's nothing we can do now. We have to get back to The Arcalane." Jahrys knew the Hoarders would find them soon enough.

"Help me bury her, Jahrys. Like the old way. I don't want to burn her body." Kevrin stared at him hopelessly.

"I'll help you." Jahrys gave Kevrin a rub on his shoulder.

It took several hours to dig a grave with their bare hands. They had picked a spot under a tree by the shoreline. They lifted her body and lowered her down into the grave. Tears fell down both their cheeks as they covered their fallen teammate.

They stood together, reminiscing about old times from before the Hoarding and their times as Retrievers.

Jahrys wiped a tear from his eye. "If only we took the diary from Rallick, then her death wouldn't have been for nothing."

Kevrin grabbed his damp bag and fumbled through it. He took out the diary, presenting it to Jahrys.

Jahrys's eyes lit up. "How—how did you…?"

"I took it right out of Rallick's hand as we were running," Kevrin gave a small smile. "I'm still going to give him a piece of my mind next time I see him. Here…" Kevrin handed Jahrys the diary. "I don't want to look at it anymore."

Jahrys held the diary out in front of him as if it was a delicacy. It was white with golden hinges, just like the picture Riago had given them.

Jahrys flipped through the pages. It was soaked. The writing was smudged and unreadable. *Riago is not going to like this*, thought Jahrys.

"How?" was all Jahrys managed to say.

Kevrin let out a long, deep sigh. Jahrys could tell that this was painful for him. But he needed to know how it happened.

"Well," Kevrin began, "when I took the watch last night, I went outside on the back porch to get a little air. I heard some yelling coming from the other side of the wall, past the courtyard." He paused to take a sip out of his waterskin. "I followed the voices. I took the path between the walls that brought me around the corner into an opening. That's where I saw them: Hoarders.

"They were just sitting around in a circle, talking to each other and laughing, having a good time. So I crept in, silently. I hid behind a broken cart.

"There were five of them. I was pretty close, maybe twenty feet away. I could see their Captor Packs lined up behind their circle. One of the packs began to shake and beep; the yellow light on the back spiraled in a circle. The Hoarder closest to it said, 'Ah, finally done. I'll take care of this one.' He left the circle and clipped on his pack as he walked over to the wall of debris close to my right. He raised his Captor up to the sky and yelled, 'Hey! Let's see how high I can get this one.' The other Hoarders all turned around to watch. He pressed down on the top and bottom triggers on the handle and a junk block flew out of the Captor. He pressed the triggers again and another block popped out.

"The blocks arched up into the sky. The first junk block must have landed on top of the wall. But the second block didn't quite make it, and it came crashing down, shattering into pieces. I had to duck to avoid being hit as debris landed all around me. I suddenly heard a thump to my left. When I looked over, I saw it—the diary! It must have been compacted in that second block that shattered on the way down.

"I looked back to see if anyone was watching. The Hoarders were all busy applauding the Hoarder in front of me for shooting the first block all the way up to the top of the wall. 'Let's see you all beat that,' the Hoarder said as he walked back to the circle. While they all were distracted, I reached over and grabbed the book. It matched the description Riago had given us, so I put it in my bag and crept my way back towards the path. I only made it two feet when I stepped on a piece of wood that snapped in half. I didn't stop to look back to see if they had heard. I just ran."

Jahrys flipped through a few more of the soggy pages. "This is going to be worthless. Riago will not like this."

"I don't give a damn what Riago thinks about the diary. He better accept it after what it has cost us." Kevrin said angrily, giving Jahrys a stern look.

"We won't let this go to waste, don't worry." Jahrys handed the diary back to Kevrin.

But Kevrin refused. "You take it. I don't want it around me."

Jahrys placed the diary into his bag and then took out some cloth to wrap their wounds.

"We better wrap ourselves up tightly so we don't get our cuts infected on our journey back." Jahrys handed Kevrin the cloth. Kevrin took it and began to wrap up Jahrys's shoulder. Once he was done, Jahrys wrapped up Kevrin's arm.

As he was wrapping Kevrin's arm, Jahrys said, "Remember my parents used to take us just south of here? Before the Hoarding?"

That brought a smile to Kevrin's face. "Your father cramped up in the water and we had to go out and save him." He laughed.

Jahrys laughed, too. "He kept shouting and shouting for help, and when we got out there, the water was only three feet deep."

They both laughed for what seemed like a long time. But that happiness faded when Jahrys looked around again. Junk walls rose up high around the cliffs of High Point. There were even junk walls protruding off shore into the Farrest Sea. The trees around the Sandy Shore were dead, the sand was hard and crusty, and the air was heavy and stale.

Jahrys let out a disappointed sigh as he finished wrapping Kevrin's arm. Nothing was the same.

"If we walk to Seaport, I'm sure we can find a boat to take us upstream. We should make it there in four days if we hurry," Kevrin said.

Jahrys agreed. They gathered their things, said their final goodbyes to Elyara, and headed south towards Seaport.

They would have made it back to the Retrieval Stations in four days, but another storm rolled through. Jahrys and Kevrin had to deal with high winds and decided to pass the storm on land, which added an extra night to their journey. Overall, the journey had left both Jahrys and Kevrin sore and tired. The boat ride had been mostly silent. Kevrin didn't want to talk about Elyara.

Jahrys couldn't wait to get back to The Arcalane. He could taste the ale in his mouth and the feel of dry, clean clothes. He desperately needed a shower and a good night's sleep.

After they had docked the boat at the boathouse, they had continued the rest of their journey by foot, heading back into Palor. They had walked by the closed Western Gate—which mocked

Junkland

Jahrys and Kevrin—and headed north to Riago's Retrieval Station.

They walked up the creaking steps, and stepped inside the dark cramped room. Jahrys rang the bell.

"Hey Riago. We're back with the diary. Hey? Riago!" Jahrys continued to ring the bell.

"Will you stop ringing that damn bell? You woke old Riago up from his nap." The window shot open and Riago came into view. "Who goes there?" His bald head shined in the candle light. He smiled when he saw their faces. "Hargh, hargh. Old Riago thought you all were dead by now." He chuckled to himself and then paused. "Where's the pretty girl?"

"Elyara didn't make it back," Kevrin said, a tear escaping his eye. "She's dead."

Jahrys hung his head in silence.

"Ah. Riago's sorry to hear that. She was a fine lady, she was. May Zalus show her peace beyond the Western Mountains." Riago hung his head while he mumbled a little prayer.

Jahrys took out the diary, which was still damp from the water. "Here you go, the diary that was requested." He handed it to Riago.

Riago took the diary from Jahrys's hands. He flipped through the pages, taking quick glances. His face turned sullen. "Aye what is this? It's soggy straight through! And the words are all smudged!"

"We got you the diary, Riago," Kevrin said. "That's what you asked for."

"Yea, but a readable diary. Not a soggy one!" He looked at Kevrin and Jahrys and sighed. "Tell ya what, I'll give you five loafs of bread for this. Riago feels for your loss of the pretty girl and the trouble you guys have gone through."

"Five loafs of bread?" Jahrys was aghast. "You told us we would be rewarded highly for this job!"

"Aye that I did. That I did. But this is not even worth one loaf of bread. I'm sorry, boys. Riago has a reputation to keep. This is what I'm offering." Riago crossed his large arms across his chest.

Kevrin put his hand on Jahrys's undamaged shoulder. "Come on, let's go," he said. "Elyara's life is worth more than five loaves of bread. We'll dry off the diary and find someone else tomorrow that will pay us more for this."

"So be it. Don't be coming back to old Riago with anymore job requests." He slammed the window shut and left Kevrin and Jahrys in the silent, darkness of the small room.

Jahrys was speechless. He couldn't believe it. Would they ever not be the laughing stock of The Arcalane?

They walked out of the dark Retrieval Station into the road. They followed a junk wall until they reached a clear opening that took them two streets over. The Arcalane appeared, half embedded into a junk wall, which helped to keep it hidden. The inn looked like it was about to fall apart with the slightest touch. The marble stone covered as much as the roof as it could, but it looked weak.

One more bad storm will take it down, Jahrys thought.

As they approached the unstable steps to the inn, Jahrys caught a glimpse of something black sitting on top of the overhang above the steps. A crow was sitting calmly, staring at both Kevrin and Jahrys as they walked inside.

Chapter 19
Jahrys

IT WAS NIGHTTIME when Jahrys and Kevrin returned to The Arcalane, and most of the Retrievers had already returned from their jobs. They were both shocked at the amount of noise that hit them when they walked through the door. The room was lively and loud with celebration. There was a large group of Retrievers in the corner at a booth playing Pooles and Palms. In the other corner, a band was playing and people were dancing to the music. The bar was packed with people trying to get a drink. Miller was weaving in and out of people's stomping feet, pecking at loose crumbs on the floor.

"Boys! Welcome back," yelled Innkeeper Willem over the loud talking and music that filled the air. He was shouting from behind the bar. He motioned to the serving girl, Ebanie, to take over while he walked over to them.

However, Kevrin pushed right past Willem towards Rallick standing at the bar.

Oh no, Jahrys thought, watching Kevrin's hands ball up into fists as he approached Rallick.

Kevrin tapped Rallick on the shoulder while he was laughing up a storm with two ladies.

Rallick turned.

Kevrin swung his fist and hit Rallick in the mouth so hard that Rallick went spinning into the bar. The two ladies gaped in horror.

Stade and Taygar, who had been at a table close by, rushed over and grabbed Kevrin to constrain him.

Rallick stood up, wiping blood from his mouth.

"YOU KILLED HER!" Kevrin yelled, struggling to get free from Stade and Taygar's grasp. The whole bar was watching; the band stopped playing—everyone was silent.

Rallick spat blood on the floor. "I didn't kill anyone. But I wouldn't mind killing you right now."

Rallick raised his fist and swung it towards Kevrin's face.

Willem stepped forward and caught Rallick's fist midair. "I will *not* be having this fighting inside my inn. How many times do I have to tell you both?" He looked angrily at Rallick and then at Kevrin. "Today is the Coming of Zalus and I demand respect inside my inn. Let go of him." He yelled, looking at Stade and Taygar.

Stade and Taygar freed Kevrin from their grasp.

"Now, standard procedures. You three—" Willem stopped when he noticed Elyara wasn't there. "Where's Elyara?" he asked, caressing his large mustache. "She didn't make it back," Jahrys said, as he met Willem and Kevrin by the bar.

Willem hung his head, understanding dawning. After a pause, he murmured, "May Zalus find her peace and clarity. She was one of a kind, that one." He placed an arm around Kevrin's shoulder as they walked around the bar to the back of the inn. "Let's get you washed up and get you a drink."

Junkland

The tension died, and the music started up again. People returned to their conversations, drinks, and games.

Willem guided them to the back room. Jahrys and Kevrin stripped down and hopped into the bathing area, rinsing the Junkland off themselves. Willem tossed their suits into a tub and scrubbed them down.

After the rinsing, and after they were scolded by Willem for losing their equipment, Willem rubbed some herbs on their wounds and wrapped them up. "You guys are lucky you weren't out there so long with these wounds," he told them. "These should heal up just fine."

He handed them both sand colored tunics and a pair of light pants. "Now how many times do I have to tell you guys there will be no fighting in The Arcalane? Especially with Rallick and his gang."

"I'm sorry, Willem," Kevrin hung his head in shame. "I won't do it again. I promise."

"It's okay, son. I know you're hurting over your loss. Elyara was one of a kind: tough, funny, smart, and beautiful. She'll always be remembered.

"But let us not hang our heads. She wouldn't have wanted that. We need to celebrate as a family and enjoy the time we have with each other. It's not every day that it's the Coming of Zalus." Willem gave them both a pat on the back.

Jahrys had forgotten about the Coming of Zalus. The day Zalus came down from the Western Mountains nine hundred and sixteen years ago. When he raised his hands high towards the sky and life poured out of his palms. He created life…or so people like to believe.

The Coming of Zalus always took place on the single full moon of the year, and the day before Jahrys's birthday. But these days, it was impossible to see the moon and Jahrys had lost track of the days. *I can't believe I'll be eighteen tomorrow.* He always hated how anticlimactic his birthday was, following the most sacred day of the year.

"I think I'm going to go upstairs," Kevrin said. "I just want to go to bed."

Jahrys didn't blame him. Kevrin was pale and looked worn out. Jahrys had not seen Kevrin like this since the day they were supposed to practice sword fighting before the Hoarding.

"Aye, let me give a toast to Elyara before you go up. I would like you to hear it," Willem pleaded.

Kevrin nodded.

"Willem, we found the whereabouts of Havrick," Jahrys had forgot to mention it.

Willem's ears perked up. "You found him? He's alive?"

"No. He didn't make it," Jahrys said. "We found him out by the Manor. His leg was caught in a trap set by the Hoarders. When we were attacked, a Hoarder took his body. I'm sorry."

Willem's eyes started to water, and a single tear leaked out. "Thank you, Jahrys, Kevrin. You two are brave boys." He wiped the tear from his eye. "Let's get back to the celebrations so I can make a toast."

Before they left the room, Jahrys dug the blue-gemmed necklace out from his bag and slipped it into the pocket of his tunic. He then followed Willem and Kevrin out of the room. Willem returned behind the bar and Jahrys and Kevrin hung out at the end of the counter. Willem picked up a glass and a knife, hitting them together over his head.

Junkland

Cling, Cling, Cling.

The music and talking stopped immediately.

"Happy Coming of Zalus, everyone," Willem's head rotated around the room, locking eyes with all the surprised faces. "Today is a special day, but also a sad one. Today we lost two members of our family. Elyara M'ava, a smart and beautiful girl from Kaluk, and Havrick Overhill, a hard worker and a great friend. Both have been with us before the start of the Hoarding. They were family. Just like everyone here is family. Elyara was brave, adventurous, and tried her hardest to provide for us at The Arcalane. She helped us survive out here in the Junkland. Havrick worked hard inside this inn with me for nearly twenty years. He was a good man, a great friend."

Willem poured himself a drink and raised it towards the ceiling. The whole bar was silent, staring at Willem with sad, wet eyes. "Tonight we celebrate Zalus! The birth of life! And the memory of Elyara and Havrick. They will never be forgotten and will always have a place inside our hearts and this inn." He raised his glass and drank.

The crowd followed.

Willem wasn't done speaking, however. He slammed his glass onto the table. He hoisted himself on top of the bar and stared out at all the curious eyes. "But the time has come, my brothers and sisters. We've been here long enough, serving King Leoné behind his closed wall. He has yet to open the gates and save his people. Instead, he's leaving us to rot out here with these damn Hoarders."

The crowd murmured in agreement, as they stared up at Willem with hopeful eyes.

Willem continued. "We need to get through this next year, collecting as many supplies, food, and weapons as we can. Then we can leave Astenpoole behind forever."

Heads turned in confusion.

"Leave?" a woman shouted out from the crowd. "But where'll we go?"

Willem smiled down at the woman. "Wherever we want." He shot out a hand to the ceiling. "We'll travel north along the farmlands of Danor to grow as many crops as our hearts desire. We'll travel south to build our homes high up in the forests of Kaluk, where we'll be safe from anyone on foot. We'll travel east across the Farrest Sea, living out on the water with the sea breeze runnin' through our hair. Or we'll travel west, across the Western Mountains, to discover what no man, knight, or King of Astenpoole has yet to do.

"But wherever we end up, we'll start a new home, a new life, and a new beginning. It's just like the stories of how the Four Cities formed back in the days of King Gabriel. When there was no room left inside the castle, King Gabriel closed the gates and abanonded his people, forcing them to live outside the castle walls. But our ancestors came together, and formed the Four Cities. We learned to live together and to fight for ourselves without the help of any king. Times are no different, because now this king will not help us. We'll come together as Retrievers, as a family, and survive together, just like our ancestors have done before us! Because when the darkness rises, my friends, the ones who matter will be there next to you in the end."

With that, the whole bar erupted in applause. The band started back up and people clinked their glasses and mugs together in celebration. The group in the corner continued their card game. And Miller happily squawked around the room.

"Wow. What a spee—" Jahrys turned to Kevrin, but he was

gone. *He must have gone upstairs,* thought Jahrys, feeling his friend's pain of losing a loved one.

Jahrys bent down to pick up Miller who had just skittered by. "How're you doing, Mill? Keeping The Arcalane safe, I hope?"

"BUCUUUUUCK!" The chicken replied, his big, round eyes twitching in all directions.

Jahrys laughed, petting his little, round head. He set him back down on the floor and watched Miller run away, looking for crumbs.

Jahrys walked up to the bar and asked Willem for a drink. Willem slid Jahrys a mug across the table.

"Did Kevrin go up?" Willem asked.

"Yea, he wasn't feeling well." Jahrys took a sip from the mug. The warm ale tingled his throat.

"Ah, poor lad. He loved that girl. He would have died for her." Willem said, as he returned from helping another Retriever on the other side of the counter.

And he almost did, thought Jahrys.

Old Lan stumbled up to the bar next to Jahrys, putting an arm around him.

"Sorry...bout your loss, laddy." His breath reeked of alcohol and his graying beard was wet with foam.

"Thanks Lan. I appreciate it." Jahrys raised his mug. Lan attempted to raise his, but as he moved his mug forward towards Jahrys's, he fell backwards onto the floor, bringing down a chair with him. Jahrys shook his head as he bent down to help him up, but Old Lan was lying peacefully on the floor, already snoring, so Jahrys left him there.

Jahrys walked over to a table towards the center of The Arcalane. "Tarl, Kat, Gabe," he nodded and smiled to all three.

"Jahrys!" they all yelled in unison, welcoming him to their table. Kat moved herself over so Jahrys could grab a chair and squeeze in.

"Sorry to hear about Elyara. We all loved her, too." Tarl said, as he gave Jahrys his condolences.

"I can't believe she's gone," Kat wiped the tears from her eyes. "She was one of my best friends."

They all hung their heads, sadness creeping over them.

"To Elyara." Gabe raised his mug with his good hand.

"To Elyara!" They all said, raising their mugs together and drinking.

"Thanks guys," Jahrys said as he lowered his mug. He turned to Gabe, looking at his wrapped arm. "How's your hand doing?"

"What hand?" Gabe laughed, holding his wrapped arm up to show him his nub. "Willem has me rubbing some herbs on it every night. The skin is healing up, but my hand obviously won't grow back." He looked down at his nub and then back up at Jahrys. "But I should be back out there with my team in about a week or so. I can't hold a Captor, but I can still help out."

"Not like we'll miss carrying around your ass," Tarl said, hiding his face behind his mug.

"You mean me carrying around both of your asses!" Kat chimed in.

"I saved the two of you from that ambush half a year past," Tarl argued.

"Yea, but who was the one who pulled both of you out of the Seaport River and saved you from drowning?" Kat retorted, giving them both a sassy look.

"Fair enough. Fair enough," said Tarl, nodding in agreement. "To Kat! For saving both our asses." They all clinked their beers together. Jahrys joined them again.

Foam spilled down the sides of the mugs when they brought them back down to the table.

"Ah, you got my wrapping wet! Now I'm going to have to ask Willem to re-do it," Gabe moaned.

"A little alcohol will be good for it," Tarl chuckled.

"Can I get you all anything else?" Ebanie, the same serving girl from before, asked. She was holding a round plate above her shoulder with empty glasses. Ebanie had skin as white as her teeth and beautiful, straight blonde hair. Her Danorian accent only added to her beauty.

"No, I think we're all good here," Kat replied sharply, giving her an irritable glance.

"I'll take another, actually," Jahrys said, handing her his empty mug. He shuffled his feet up and down to ward off Miller, who had started to peck continuously at him under the table.

"Going a little hard tonight are we, Jahrys?" Ebanie gave him a flirty smile; her teeth were the brightest thing in the room.

"The Coming of Zalus happens only once a year. I might as well enjoy myself a bit," he said, trying to hide his blush.

"Well if you want to enjoy yourself a little more"—Ebanie gave his arm a little squeeze—"you know where to find me." She gave him a dangerous smile as she walked away.

"Woah!" Gabe leaned excitedly. "That Ebanie has always had a thing for you. Have you kissed her yet?"

Kat rolled her eyes and took a sip from her mug.

Jahrys looked away, embarrassed. "I—uh—only one time. And *she* kissed me."

"Don't tell me you're still holding on to that Lily girl?" Gabe shook his head in disappointment.

Jahrys instantly took his hand away from the necklace in his pocket. "I saw her being taken into the castle. She's still—"

Gabe flung his hands up in disgust. "Come on, Jahrys. It's been three years." He held up three fingers in front of Jahrys's face. "Three years!"

Jahrys brushed his fingers away.

"And for some reason"—Gabe threw his hands in Ebanie's direction—"*this* girl's obsessed with you. Every guy in this inn would give their left hand to be in your position."

"By every guy, do you mean yourself?" Kat spat, shooting him a dirty look.

"You know what I mean," Gabe spat back.

"He's right, Jahrys," Tarl said. "You have to move on. Lily's gone. And even if she did make it inside the castle, there's no way for you to get to her. Give Ebanie a chance. She likes you! And, she's *here*."

Jahrys glanced over at the bar and saw Ebanie looking over, smiling. But as much as her smile was enchanting, her hair enticing, and her accent exotic, his heart was still with Lily Bellsworth. Ebanie's kiss would never replace Lily's, and he wasn't even remotely interested in checking.

Jahrys shook his head. "You guys don't know what you're talking about. Lily is still alive and I'll find her!"

Gabe shook his head in disgust, but gave up.

"Well, I think it's cute," Kat smiled at Jahrys.

Ebanie returned with his drink. "Here ya go. Drink slow, I don't want you to pass out and miss the night!" She gave Jahrys a wet kiss on his cheek before she walked away.

"I'll keep my mouth shut," Gabe said, taking a sip from his mug. They all laughed.

Jahrys felt another pain in his foot and bent down to see Miller staring up at him, clearly looking for attention.

"Guys, I think Miller's jealous," Jahrys pointed out.

They all looked under the table. Miller turned his head in every direction, frantically looking at all the faces. Eventually he got scared and scurried away.

They laughed even harder.

The band, which was made up of recovered instruments from the Junkland, was preparing for their next tune. The drummer was setting up the beat while the singer prepared the band for the upcoming song. The guitarist, bassist, and horn players all waited for their cue.

"So, to get the night moving and to honor Zalus, as well as the memory of Elyara and Havrick, how about 'Drunken Day at the Arcalane'?" the singer, Felix, asked the crowd.

The crowd answered with applause. The people *loved* 'Drunken Day at the Arcalane'.

"Start it up!" he yelled back to the band.

The band began the song. The horn player blasted the introduction while the guitarist strummed away. The bassist bobbed his head back and forth, keeping in time with the fast beat of the drummer. The singer smiled at the crowd as he snapped his fingers to the rhythm.

Tarl grabbed Kat and they both climbed on top of the table, kicking and dancing. A young woman named Fallon took Gabe by his good hand.

"Ah! Watch the nub, watch the nub!" Gabe yelled as he was

dragged to the dance floor.

"Care to dance?" it was Ebanie. She was leaning on the table, staring at Jahrys with innocent eyes.

"Don't you need to work?" Jahrys asked her nervously.

"I won't tell if you don't." Her eyes looked dangerous. "Besides, you owe me for that kiss…"

"I—" but before he could say no, she grabbed his hands and brought him out towards the dance floor.

The singer started to sing. Everyone in The Arcalane joined Felix, drowning out the singer's voice.

> *Cheers, cheers to all the girls in here,*
> *We toast to you with all our beer,*
> *We chug and chug until we're done,*
> *Now fill us up again, my dear.*

The band played while everyone danced and sang along. Innkeeper Willem was even up on the bar dancing and kicking his legs.

> *Cheers, cheers to all the girls in here,*
> *We hope you stay so close and near,*
> *We chug and chug with you for fun,*
> *Now fill us up again, my dear.*

The song repeated again and again, growing louder and faster each time. The rhythm of the band got faster and faster, and people were getting drunker and drunker. As the song repeated for the tenth time, the lyrics had completely fallen apart.

> *Cheers, cheers…girls here,*
> *We toast you…with our beer,*

Junkland

> *We chug...chug...til...we're done,*
> *Another...dear!*

Old Lan was on his feet and singing the loudest. "Girls! Here! Cheers and beer! Done! DEAR!" He was stumbling all over the dance floor, waving his mug sporadically in the air, raining beer.

People pointed and laughed at the drunken old knight. *I guess he got a good sleep,* thought Jahrys as he watched Old Lan stumble all the way over to the center table where Tarl and Kat were dancing. Old Lan got his foot caught on a fallen stool and fell face first into their table. The music stopped along with everyone's hearts. Tarl fell backwards and Kat went flying into the air. She must have went at least ten feet high before she landed safely into Rallick's arms. The entire room exploded with applause and cheers. The music and dancing instantly started up. Kat smiled up at Rallick, and he carried her straight up the stairs, to the right of the bar, and disappeared.

Jahrys scowled. *It's like everything the guy wants falls directly into his arms,* thought Jahrys, as Ebanie swung her curvy hips into his, trying to refocus his attention.

Tarl got up and brushed himself off, looking around for Kat. Not seeing her, he scratched his head in confusion. Old Lan laid motionless on the floor, his legs tangled awkwardly in a knot as he snored, asleep once again. People ignored him as they stepped over his sleeping body and continued to dance.

Jahrys eventually broke away from Ebanie. He left her with her hands on her hips, pouting. He walked back over to the bar and sat down, waving down Willem for another round. As he waited, he overheard Stade and Taygar bragging about Rallick. "...You should see the guy out there. He's a legend. He knows exactly where to find things in the Junkland..."

Jahrys turned back around and found his new ale waiting for him. He took a sip. He spat it back out when he felt a hand land on his hurt shoulder. He winced at the sudden sting from the wound. Stade took a seat next to Jahrys. He was nothing like Rallick. Stade was as thin as a stick, short, and looked young for his age of nineteen. Taygar was breathing heavily behind him.

"Saw you looking over at us, Jahrhead," said Stade. "Are you lonely since you lost your little friend?"

"Don't talk about Elyara." Jahrys felt the heat growing inside of his chest. He just wanted to be alone.

"How about we talk about another failed job by the great O'Jahrys Grent and his sidekick Kevrin?" Stade was getting close to Jahrys's face...*too close.*

"Huh," yelled Taygar.

"We wouldn't have failed if it wasn't for you and wheezy behind you."

Taygar narrowed his large eyes.

"Are you guys wishing you fell into Rallick's arms and he carried you upstairs instead of Kat?" Jahrys smirked.

Taygar pushed past Stade and grabbed Jahrys by his tunic. Jahrys's mug splattered to the floor as the big oaf lifted Jahrys up out of his seat, his feet dangling in midair. Taygar was grimacing up at him, and Jahrys could see where Taygar's tongue had been cut out.

"Boys! Please. Take this outside. We don't need that in here. It's the Coming of Zalus," yelled Willem from behind the bar.

Taygar dropped Jahrys back on his seat.

Stade leaned towards Jahrys's right ear and whispered, "You

watch yourself O'Jahrys. You watch yourself out there in the Junkland. One day you might just *accidentally* disappear."

Taygar grunted.

They both walked away, back into the crowd.

"You okay, O'Jahrys?" Willem asked, looking over at him in concern.

"Fine, just fine," he answered, wincing at the sound of his name.

Willem poured Jahrys a new mug of beer. Jahrys grabbed it and took it through the crowd to the other side of the room to sit down by himself at a booth. Miller hurried over and jumped up next to him on the bench. Jahrys petted him.

The band was finally finishing their song—*What number was this? The thirteenth time through?* Jahrys wondered. The singing was louder than ever.

Just a drunken day at The Arcalane,
A drunken daaaaaay at The Arcalaaaaane.

After the singing broke off and the band stopped, the crowd started to simmer down as they retired to their beds upstairs. Jahrys sat staring at his mug recalling the sailing trip he took up the river to Zalus's Tears with Lily. How they were so close to each other, shoulders touching, as they pointed up at the stars, asking which one they would want to travel to. *'It looks like a place I could run away to and no one would ever find me.'* Jahrys recalled her words.

He would find her. He was sure of it.

Jahrys wondered if this was how Palor A'kal had felt when he was torn away from Princess Melaine. Did he think about her every single night of his banishment while he was lying on the cold ground of the mountains? Did he wish he could hold her? Or did his heart move on to someone new? Jahrys refused to believe that their story simply ended.

He took a sip from his mug, trying to escape his thoughts.

A cat suddenly leapt onto the table.

Jahrys's hand twitched, and his face was splashed with ale.

Miller hopped onto the table, squawking at the black cat.

"Miller—"

The cat hissed and bared its teeth at the chicken.

"Mr. Squibbles! Mr. Squibbles, get down from there this instant. Get down!" A wooden staff smacked the table and swept the cat away. The black cat screeched and jumped onto the opposite bench. The cat glared at Miller with menacing eyes, continuing to hiss.

Jahrys placed his half-emptied mug on the table and wiped his face with his tunic. "Is this your cat?" Jahrys was grumpy. The last thing he wanted was to be covered in ale.

"I am sorry, my dear. So sorry. Sometimes my cat can forget his manners."

Jahrys finished wiping his face and looked up. He was startled when he saw a hunched old lady standing at the end of the table. She was covered in a gray, wool cloak and was wearing a hood that covered most of her face. Jahrys could tell the features underneath were not pleasant. She held a wooden cane she used to hold her weight, even though there wasn't much weight to her.

The old lady inched her way towards the opposite side of the table and sat down. She tucked her staff onto her lap and began to stroke the head of her cat, making him purr.

Miller took a few steps forward across the table and cocked a curious eye towards her.

"Don't mind him. He won't hurt you. He's just curious." Jahrys assured the old lady, who was staring at Miller suspiciously.

"Curiousity is the key to many doors." The old lady took her hand from her cat and began to pet Miller's tiny head lightly with her fingers.

The cat hissed in the corner.

Miller squawked in terror and backed away until he fell into Jahrys's arms.

The old lady smacked the cat on the head. "Pipe down! You are frightening our new friends."

The cat gave the old lady an angry look, but he stopped hissing.

Jahrys placed Miller on the bench next to him. "Who are you? I haven't seen you around here before." Jahrys glanced over at the black cat. "And I haven't seen him around here either."

The old lady looked at him. "I am just an old lady who has lost her youth along the way. But, I think the real question here is...who are you?"

Jahrys hesitated. "Erh. I'm Jahrys Grent."

The old lady chuckled. The wrinkles on her face were pulled in all directions. "Are you sure? You don't seem so confident."

"I am Jahrys Grent!"

"Meow."

The old lady glanced at her cat and nodded in agreement. "Yes, Mr. Squibbers. Yes. It seems we have found the right person."

What is this lady talking about? "Right person?" Jahrys was confused. "For what?"

"The right person for a job." The old lady smiled, her teeth were yellow and crooked.

"A job? From the castle? I thought all jobs had to come through the Retrieval Stations?"

"Yes, yes. But this isn't any ordinary job. No! This job came from King Leoné himself."

"The king? You came from the castle?" Jahrys could feel his head spinning. He couldn't tell if it was from the alcohol or from the confusion. "How did you get outside the walls?"

"There are always ways in, and there are always ways out," the old lady said in a scratchy voice.

"But how did you survive out in the Junkland in just…*that*." Jahrys motioned his hands towards the old lady's outfit.

"Meow."

The old lady cleared her throat. "Rude indeed, Mr. Squibbers." The old lady shook her head.

"Sorry. I didn't mean to affend you. It's just—it's dangerous out there."

The old lady pulled the sleeve of her cloak back up to her shoulder and stretched down a flab of skin at her triceps. "This skin may look old and wrinkly, but it's as thick as armor, I tell you! Isn't that right, Mr. Squibbers?"

"Meow," the cat agreed.

This lady is crazy. Jahrys looked around to see if anyone was noticing their conversation. The bar was mostly dead, except for Tarl and Gabe who were talking by a table, Willem who was cleaning some glasses, Ebanie who was rubbing down the tables, and Old Lan who was still passed out on the floor. Jahrys turned his attention back to the old lady. "What's this *job* the king is offering?"

The old lady reached a wrinkly hand into the deep pocket of her cloak and pulled out a piece of crumpled paper. She stretched it out and held it up in front of her face.

Both Jahrys and Miller raised their heads to get a better look.

"It looks like a bottle of wine," Jahrys said, after examining the picture.

"Yes, a bottle of red, a bottle of white. But not just any bottle. No—look closer." The old lady shoved the parchment into Jahrys's face.

Jahrys backed away in annoyance and focused his eyes on the description at the bottom. Jahrys read it: *Palor Red. The wine of Astenpoole. Grapes harvested fresh from the backyard of the Grent family.*

"Grent Wine," Jahrys repeated aloud.

"Meow."

"Yes, Mr. Squibbers. The boy can read." The old lady nodded in agreement.

Jahrys tried to snatch the parchment from the old lady, but she pulled it back as if she had predicted his move. Jahrys sighed. "Why does the king want this wine?"

"There has been a shortage of wine in the castle ever since the Hoarding."

"Meow."

"Yes, yes. The king does love Grent Wine. And he's offering a hefty reward for this job."

"What kind of reward?" he asked curiously.

"The person that completes this job will be granted access to the castle." The old lady gave a smile, showing her yellow teeth. He noticed many were missing.

Jahrys's mouth dropped. "Inside the castle?"

"Those without ears will never hear," the old lady recited.

"I have both my ears." Jahrys touched both of them to prove his point.

"Then you can hear."

"Meow."

The old lady nodded to her cat. "Yes, Mr. Squibbers. He is a stupid boy."

Jahrys couldn't take these mind games much longer.

"So…do you accept this job?" asked the old lady.

Jahrys thought it over. This could be his chance to finally get into the castle and find Lily Bellsworth. But none of this made any sense. Why would the king go through all this trouble just for a bottle of wine? And why is he granting this person into the castle?

"How did you find me?" asked Jahrys.

"All I had to do was look."

Jahrys shook his head, not wanting to be bothered with her ridiculous mind games. He took a sip of his half-filled beer. His head was starting to spin. He eventually shook his head and said, "Screw this job and screw the king. He left us out here to die and rot while he is camped in his castle, worrying about his thirst for wine. No, I do not accept this job." Jahrys stood up and Miller flew off the side, squawking.

Jahrys would find his own way inside the castle.

"So be it," the old lady showed no sign of disappointment or frustration. "But if fate changes your mind, bring the bottle of wine back to The Arcalane, a day from this hour, and I will be here."

Jahrys left the old lady and stumbled his way towards the stairs. Miller followed.

"Goodnight, Jahrys. Happy Coming of Zalus," said Willem, as he waved to Jahrys from behind the bar.

"Goodnight, Jahrys." Ebanie gave him a bright smile as he walked by her.

He staggered his way up the staircase to the second floor, Miller hopping up behind him. He turned right and stumbled down the hall to his room at the end. Jahrys was furious now thinking about the king. How he had left them all to die and be constantly attacked by the Hoarders.

"He wants wine. I'll give him wine." Jahrys was talking to himself while zig-zagging down the hallway with Miller.

Jahrys flung open the door to his room and fell in. Miller sprinted across the hardwood floor and flew up to the bed, getting cozy into a pillow.

"Dammit, Miller. That's where I sleep," he yelled. But Miller didn't move.

Jahrys noticed that his bag and belongings were lying on his nightstand. Kevrin must have put them there.

He went into the bathroom on the far right of the room. He went over to the bucket filled with water and splashed some water on his face. He looked up in the mirror. He saw red scratches covering both sides of his cheeks and forehead. There was a nasty cut on his chin. His brown hair was a mess. He dunked his head forward into the bucket of cool water. When he rose for air, he pushed his wet hair back over his head. He realized his tunic was still on and was now soaking wet. He took it off and saw his hurt shoulder in the mirror. The burnt skin was oozing through the wrapping. He took a cloth from the rack on the side of the barrel and started to wash out the wound. He finished by wrapping it up with a thin layer of cloth. Jahrys looked at himself again in the mirror. His body looked worn down and scarred.

He stumbled back into the room and fell on his bed. He reached over to his nightstand and picked up the necklace. He twirled the gem around in his fingers, thinking of Lily. He placed the necklace back on his nightstand and his eyes were caught by something else: the diary. He reached over again and picked it up.

Drunken anger filled his body. The diary was the reason Elyara was dead. If they didn't get this stupid job from Riago…if they hadn't woken up earlier than everyone else had…

He yelled and threw the diary across the room. It landed with a thump by the door.

Miller cocked his head up at the sudden noise.

Jahrys laid back, staring at the ceiling. He let his head roll to the side, facing the door. He found himself looking at the diary again. It was open to a random page. Something on the page caught his attention. Was he imagining it? He rubbed his eyes to be sure.

Jahrys raised his head to get a better look. The page had writing on it, and it was legible. Jahrys jumped out of bed and walked over to the diary. *Riago must have missed this page*, he thought, as he picked it up and brought it over to his desk across from his bed. He lit a candle, laid the diary down, and began to read.

Chapter 20
Alana

THE SPACE AROUND her was dark, tight, and cramped. She could barely see her hands in front of her as she crawled. Clouds of dust surrounded her. Her throat was scratchy, making it hard to breathe. She stopped every couple of minutes to let out a cough, trying to clear her lungs. No matter how many times she crawled through the tunnels, she never got used to it.

She had discovered the secret passageway when she was ten years old. It had been a tough time for her. It was shortly after her mother's death, after they had burned her body. Her father had permanently shut the Eastern Gate and limited access to the Western Gate. He had stopped her sword lessons with Sir Mazo Dapher and told her she was to remain inside the Castle Keep—that was what had sent her over the edge.

Alana had been furious and had pouted all day inside her room after her father had told her the news. There was a painting on a bookshelf of her, her mother, and her father, all happy and smiling. She had let out a scream and ran over to the bookcase clumsily. She was going to destroy that painting of her broken family. In her fury, she had tripped over her rug. Her body had gone flying forward towards the bookcase. She had thrown out her arms in desperation to protect her fall and the bookcase caught her. For a second she thought it was going to topple over, but there was a loud click and the bookcase moved.

Alana had regained herself, taking her weight off of it. She had watched the bookcase swing away from the wall, revealing a small door behind it, just big enough for a person to crawl through. That was how she had discovered the first of many secret passageways.

She had spent most of that year exploring parts of the castle she had never been to before. Alana had kept track of all the secret passageways, mapping them out in the back of her diary. It gave her freedom to roam wherever she wanted without having Mother Claraine and her handmaids following her around. When they thought she was by herself in her room, she was really out exploring Astenpoole.

She found it marvelous that no one else knew about the secret passageways except for her. The only conclusion she could think of was that King Alas Danoi had built the secret passageways back when he had constructed his plans for the castle. He must have been a secretive man, and the secrets must have died with him. Alana would have thanked him if he were still alive today. She was able to use them as she pleased—except for the one now boarded up in her room.

When her father's men had found her outside the castle wall the night of the Hoarding, her father had been furious. She had never seen him so angry before. In his fury, he ordered his men to strip every inch of her room until they found something. Eventually, they found the secret passageway behind her bookcase. They had boarded it up so she could no longer leave without permission.

But that didn't stop her. There was another secret passageway a few floors below her room in the library.

Alana would never leave the castle again; it was too dangerous and her father checked up on her too frequently. However, she did use the passageway to continue her sword lessons with Sir Benjamin in Riverside. She also used it to check the Retrieval Stations to see if her job had been fulfilled.

That was where she was going now. It was a month before the Coming of Zalus and the castle was already busy planning and setting up for the sacred holiday. Alana thought this would be a perfect opportunity to check if anyone had found her diary without anyone noticing her disappearance.

She had been so foolish, dropping her diary three years ago. She had been planning to tell Jahrys the truth that night. She didn't want to keep it from him, he deserved to know. She had brought her diary with her as proof that she really was the princess and not Lily Bellsworth from the Manor. But it had slipped from her pocket when Jahrys pushed her away from the falling debris of the building during the Hoarding.

As each day passed, Alana feared more and more for Jahrys's life and for the lives of his friends. Who knew if they were still out there, but she had hope. She had to have hope. What else did she have to live for?

Every month Alana would crawl through the tunnels in the Castle Keep, out to the abandoned house a few streets away from Pooles Road, and down towards the Western Gate—where the Retrieval Stations were located. She had to be discrete about it. No one could know she was putting out a job. If anyone found out she was looking for a diary, all of Astenpoole would be out looking for it. And if it fell into the wrong hands...

Alana didn't want to think about that scenario. It couldn't fall into the wrong hands. She had to get it back. The diary she wrote was putting her life, her father's life, and the lives of everyone inside the castle at risk.

If the Hoarders found it, they could easily discover how to enter the castle. Alana had mapped out everything.

It was roughly a two-hour trip to get to the Retrieval Stations from her tower inside the Castle Keep. So she had to move fast. The tunnel wasn't smooth. Her knees were starting to sting from scraping the stone beneath her. But she kept crawling, her hands moving along the cold surface as she twisted and turned through the tight tunnels. She had them memorized at this point. She could do it with her eyes closed, but it was so dark, it was like they were closed anyway.

Mice occasionally skittered over her hands and brushed her legs. She felt their little paws and bodies against her skin and shuttered. She never made a sound, however. She didn't want anyone to hear her through the walls.

She was still crawling out of the Castle Keep when a sudden noise through the wall made her stop. Her sudden halt made the dust in the tunnel rise. A deep voice echoed around her in the tunnel. She held her breath, afraid to make any noise. She felt a little scratch in her throat that she had to hold. She listened closely.

"When she assigns the job to the boy, *he* will die," a voice said.

Die? Who will die? thought Alana as she placed her head closer against the hard wall. She didn't recognize the voice, but it sounded like a man.

"But it will work? You are sure it will work?" it was a woman's voice, but Alana couldn't make out who it was. The voices were muffled through the wall.

"I am sure of it," the deep voice assured her.

"We have waited too long already. We cannot afford to waste any more time." The woman sounded anxious.

"Yes, my love. You'll soon have *him*. And then we'll have what we need and we can be together again."

Dust crept into Alana's throat. She didn't realize she was breathing so heavily. She tried to hold it in, but she didn't think she could contain her cough. She turned her head and tried to muffle her cough inside her arm.

"Did you hear that?" the woman sounded alarmed.

"Stay here. I'll go have a look," the man with the deep voice said.

Alana froze. She was too scared to move. Her heart was pounding in her chest. It was beating so loud she thought they would hear it through the wall. Sweat was rolling down her brow and her arms were shaking uncontrollably. Her body felt as if it weighed twice as much as it usually did.

She waited for the footsteps, for the door to open and slam, but all she heard was silence. She decided to keep moving. She needed to see if someone found her diary. *Who were those people and who were they talking about? Who is going to die?* She wondered as she crawled.

After what felt like hours, the tight passageway opened up, and Alana was able to rise to her feet. She found the ladder and climbed to the top. Her hands searched the wall, looking for the switch. She found it and pushed it inwards. There was a click and the door swung open. She stepped up onto the floor and dusted herself off.

She finally arrived at the abandoned house two blocks from Pooles Road. She closed the door behind her and swung the painting that was covering it back towards the wall until it popped back into place. The painting was dusty, but Alana loved it. It was a painting of a beautiful sunset falling behind the Western Mountains, a sight that hadn't been seen since the Hoarding.

Alana put her hood up and crept her way outside into the chilly night. She made sure to stay away from Pooles Road. She didn't want to be seen as she walked through twists and turns, towards the Western Gate. Houses lined the streets with balconies hanging over her. She was reminded of that night sailing up the river with Jahrys.

She took a path that led her just north of the Western Gate. She did not want to be seen by one of Sir Krist or Sir Martellus's men on the wall. They had been heavily managing the castle walls since the Hoarding.

She walked up the steps to a wooden door. It creaked as she pulled it open and walked inside. She entered a large room that had been built inside the wall. She noticed a foul smell in the air as she weaved through pieces of paper lying on the floor. There was an overweight man passed out on the couch in the corner to her right, his stomach hanging out past his shirt. She walked past him and passed two desks that were covered in stacks of papers and folders. Alana had to constantly kick pieces of paper off of her shoes that had glued themselves to the bottom.

Past the two desks was a hallway that branched off to the left and right, following the length of the wall. She took the left hallway, passing a bunch of tiny rooms with people either reading under a candle light, or leaning far back in their chairs, snoring loudly. No one seemed to pay her any attention. She kept walking until she found the man she was looking for.

She entered the room. She rolled her eyes when she saw him with his head flat on his desk, snoring. She walked over to him, shaking him lightly.

"Riago? Psst. Riago? Wake up." She finally gave him a hard slap on the head.

"What? What's this?" Riago's head spun left and right as he tried to get a hold of reality.

"It's me. It's Alana." She smiled at him as she pulled her hood back to reveal her face. She must have looked disgusting after crawling inside those dusty tunnels. She probably looked like a ghost.

"Ah, Princess. You startled old Riago," he ran a hand over his balding head. "I thought you might be one of those Hoarding things from the Junkland." He wiped drool from his mouth. "What can old Riago do for my fair lady at this hour of the night?"

"You know I can't come here during the day," she reminded him. "Any luck on my job from last month?" she asked anxiously.

"Job? What job?" he was still trying to wake up. He poured himself a cup of coffee. "Would you like some?" Riago offered a cup to her.

"No thanks," she declined, feeling agitated from his poor memory. "The job I've been giving you every month for almost three years now, Riago," she put a hand on her hip.

"Oh! Right, *that* job." Riago rubbed his bald head again.

His excitement was too much for Alana. "So did someone find it?"

"No. Sorry Princess…not this time." Riago took a sip from his cup. "Ah!" he spit the coffee back into his cup and placed it aside on his desk. "By Zalus, that's hot."

Alana let out a long breath of disappointment, watching the steam rise to the ceiling. "Ah, well I thought I'd come visit you with another request." She reached down to her bag that hung from her right shoulder to her left hip. She pulled out a folder.

"Here it is again," she said, handing it to Riago.

"Ah, yes, another request. You really want this book, huh?" Riago began to straighten up. "Do you have another payment for Riago?" Riago smiled innocently.

"Yes," she fumbled around her bag again for the coin. "I'll give you another hundred pooles for the hassle, plus another fifty pooles for you to keep your mouth shut, and the reward for the job will be anonymous. Just tell them they'll be paid highly if it's brought back." She handed him the coin.

Riago leaned back in his chair and looked at it. "Ah, my sweet princess, surely you can afford to give good old Riago a little more for the hassle. It's not easy offering out the same job with no outcome. It looks bad on Riago. I've a reputation to keep."

Alana grabbed another hundred poole coin from her bag. "How does another hundred pooles sound?" She held out the extra coin to him.

Riago stared at it greedily. "Ah my sweet princess, that will make Riago a very happy man." He reached out for the money, but Alana pulled it away.

"Now Riago. I need you to give this job out to trustful Retrievers. Give it to a team you know will get this job *done*." She hoped she made herself clear.

"As you command, my princess. Riago will do his best." He sounded serious.

"Thank you." Alana handed him the money. "I will check back

one month from now."

"Goodbye sweet princess. Riago will get on this first thing in the morning."

Alana saw him lean back in his chair and begin to snore again. *What kind of man am I trusting?*

She left the Retrieval Stations and walked down the wooden steps. As she was walking back towards the path, a shiver went down her spine. *Someone is behind me.* She turned, but no one was there. Only the empty steps she had just descended. She was about to turn back around when her eyes caught something black sitting on the entrance sign of the stations. It was a crow, and it was staring directly at her.

Chapter 21
Jahrys

HE STUFFED THE diary into his bag: the one Lily had dropped before she disappeared three years ago. *Or is it Princess Alana.* Jahrys didn't know what to think anymore. *Why did she lie to me? Why didn't she tell me she was the princess?* Jahrys shook his head in disbelief. *By Zalus, I kissed the princess…*

Jahrys's head had been spinning in circles since he had finished reading the legible pages of the diary. The truth about Lily, along with the drinks he had earlier, made Jahrys very confused. *She was going to tell me that night. She was going to tell me she was the princess.* The legible pages also told Jahrys how her father had her trapped inside the castle. She was a prisoner inside the Castle Keep. *That's why she ran that night when the horn blew. She must have been afraid of being caught outside.*

He was packing his bag now, forgetting sleep.

"She's alive, Mill!" Jahrys couldn't control his excitement. Miller scurried around in happy circles around Jahrys's legs. "By Zalus, she's alive!"

He knew it had been Alana requesting the job from Riago. It all made sense now. He was going to take up this new job and get into the castle. He would save Alana from her imprisonment.

But the problem was…where to find the wine?

Jahrys had an idea. He could check the cellar outside his house to see if there was any wine still there that the Retrievers hadn't recovered yet. If not, his father had always talked about a secret storage he kept inside their home. He had to go back and look, maybe he could find it? He was afraid, though; he hadn't been back since his parents died. Would his house even still be standing?

Jahrys added a few more things to his bag: bread, some berries, a new waterskin, and the necklace. He walked to the door and Miller followed.

He quietly walked downstairs, not wanting to wake anyone up. The place was still a mess. Bottles were scattered sporadically on the floor, along with crumbs, pieces of clothing, and puddles of beer. Old Lan was still passed out in between the tables, snoring. The entire place reeked of alcohol.

There was no sign of the old lady. *'Bring the bottle of wine back to The Arcalane, a day from this hour,'* the old lady had said. Jahrys had less than a day to find his father's wine before his chance to enter the castle was gone.

Jahrys almost slipped on a puddle of beer as he walked around the bar to the back room. He unhooked a suit and pushed his legs through. He pulled the suit up his body, sliding his hands through the armholes until his fingers reached the tips of the gloves at the end. He snapped a Captor Pack to his back and the suit lit up. He then attached the tube to a charged Captor. Jahrys finished with his helmet. He tried to hold his bag on one shoulder, but his Captor

Pack made it slide off.

"You need help with that?"

Jahrys turned around, alarmed. He didn't notice anyone enter the room.

It was Kevrin. He walked over and grabbed Jahrys's bag from his shoulder. He then unhooked a suit hanging from the sidewall.

"What are you doing?" Jahrys asked him.

"I'm coming with you," he said, as if it weren't a question. He pushed his legs into the suit.

"You don't have to do this. I don't want you to risk your life." Jahrys didn't need any more of his friends dying.

Kevrin hoisted the bags onto his back and placed a hand on Jahrys's shoulder. "We're a team, Jahrys. You're not going out there without me." He gave Jahrys a smile. "Now, hand me a helmet."

Jahrys grabbed a helmet and gave it to his friend.

"Thanks," Jahrys said.

"You don't have to thank me. We're family."

Family. That word felt strange to Jahrys. His family was dead. The Hoarders murdered them three years ago.

But Kevrin had been there for him as long as he could remember. He had been there through all of the harassment from Rallick, Stade, and Taygar. He was there those times with his family at the Sandy Shore. He was there when they would travel south into Kaluk and go fishing in the Two Branch River. He was there when they would practice their sword fighting, hoping to one day become Knights of the Poolesguard. And he was there during the Hoarding. Kevrin *was* his family. He was a brother.

They walked out of the back room, towards the door of The Arcalane. Miller tried to follow them out.

"You stay here, Miller." Jahrys pointed a finger at the chicken. Miller cocked a large eye up at Jahrys.

"The Junkland is no place for a chicken." Miller turned and skittered away from the door. Whether he actually listened to Jahrys or something else had caught the chicken's attention, Jahrys hadn't the faintest idea.

It was dark and foggy outside. It was still nighttime, possibly closer to early morning. Since Kevrin didn't wear a Captor Pack, the light on his helmet didn't work. So Jahrys had to use the light on his helmet to guide both of them.

"So," Kevrin said to Jahrys as they turned left outside The Arcalane. They headed down what remained of Zalus Road. "Are you going to tell me why you're so eager to get back out here?"

On their walk, Jahrys explained everything that had happened in The Arcalane after Kevrin had gone to bed. Jahrys told him about the old lady, the job she had offered him, and how he had discovered the diary entry. He explained to Kevrin how Lily Bellsworth had been Princess Alana the entire time and how he had to get into the castle to save her from her father's imprisonment.

"So the girl you've had a crush on this whole time turned out to be the princess in disguise?" Kevrin shook his head, he couldn't believe it. "You kissed the princess?"

Jahrys nodded.

"That's my boy! Kissing royalty. I always knew you had it in you." He gave Jahrys a slap on his shoulder.

"I didn't know she was a princess. I wouldn't have been so forward if I knew!" Jahrys was glad Kevrin couldn't see how red his face was through his helmet.

"Maybe that's the reason she lied to you. I can't believe you had a date with the princess and didn't even know it!" Kevrin was still shaking his head in disbelief. "Just don't mention this to Ebanie. If she found out you kissed the princess, she will have a meltdown."

"Ebanie's the last thing on my mind right now. I need to find that bottle of wine before I miss my chance of entering the castle."

"Oh, right. The job the old lady gave you. You really think she's telling the truth? I mean, how does an old lady have a way of getting into the castle when we don't even have a clue?" Kevrin asked. "It just doesn't add up to me."

"I guess there's only one way to find out. And I really have nothing to lose. If I fail, I'll just carry on my legacy of being the worst Retriever in the Junkland."

"I think you mean *we* will carry on our legacy of being the worst Retrievers in the Junkland."

Jahrys laughed. "Hopefully since we're a team, we can enter the castle together."

"Yea, that would be nice. I wouldn't mind becoming a real knight. Sir Kevrin Danell. I like the sound of that!" He said while ducking underneath a rotten tree. "What would you go by? Sir Jahrys Grent? No. What about—Sir O'Jahrys Grent? Now that's a name for a true knight. People will remember you as Sir O'Jahrys Grent, the Princess Kisser."

Jahrys didn't like it. He hated O'Jahrys. "I'll just stick with Jahrys."

Kevrin shrugged. There was a pause before he asked, "So, where are we going exactly?"

"I was going to check my old house down Zalus Road. We can check to see if the Retrievers missed any bottles of wine in my father's old cellar in our backyard. If there's nothing left, my father used to always talk about a hidden stash of wine hidden somewhere inside the house."

"Yea, that sounds like a good idea," Kevrin said in agreement.

They continued down the road. The junk walls on either side of them gradually grew higher and higher the farther they walked. They had to dodge scattered junk blocks that had toppled down from the walls.

They passed Pastor Allen's old church. Surprisingly, it was not crumpled down to pieces from the weight of the wall on top of it. The golden hands of Zalus were hanging at an awkward angle and the windows were shattered to pieces, however.

Jahrys almost expected to see Pastor Allen, preaching to the world from his steps about his insane beliefs. *I guess he wasn't insane after all*, he thought, thinking back to the day Pastor Allen passed out on the steps.

Jahrys still remembered his words.

> *With dusk comes the dreadful night,*
> *When giant walls block out the light.*
> *Yellow rain will fall. A storm of eternity!*
> *Taking it all as the innocents lose energy.*
> *Oh Zalus!*
> *Come down from the Western Mountains*
> *With your palms of light.*
> *And save us from the darkness*
> *That will bring us all an endless night.*

And where are you now, Zalus? Jahrys thought, as they continued walking, stepping over broken, cracked steps that covered the road.

It took him and Kevrin most of the night to walk down the road. While keeping an eye out for Hoarders, they reminisced about the old times they had had together before the Hoarding. All the times they used to mess with Hugo's short temper. The times they had failed to meet girls and all of the fights they had gotten into with Rallick and his gang. But those times were long gone and it was strange seeing the road this deserted and quiet.

While the fog had cleared, it was still dark. The light on Jahrys's helmet guided them down the road. They made sure to stick close to the side so if they were seen, they could escape down a side path.

Jahrys had been worried his house wouldn't be there anymore. But there it was. Still standing tall and proud. Well, maybe not tall and proud, but it was still standing. A junk wall had piled onto the far side of his home and spread into the backyard. It looked like his bedroom was crushed on the second floor. But the rest of the house was still in good shape.

They walked around the left side of Jahrys's house, towards the remaining part of the backyard.

"Let's check the cellar first." Jahrys pointed to the cellar to the right of the back door.

Jahrys and Kevrin had to lift junk blocks to clear the hatch to the cellar. Some were more heavy than others, but they were still manageable. It reminded Jahrys of all the boxes of wine he had to lift for his father.

After they were done clearing the blocks and the loose debris, Jahrys pulled on the cellar door handle. It took him a few tries to open the cellar door since it was caved in. He eventually ripped it open and walked down the steps, using the light on his helmet to guide him.

"Damn. Nothing," Jahrys said in disappointment.

"What do we do now?" Kevrin asked, gazing down at the empty cellar.

"Let's go into the house and find where my father kept the hidden stash."

They stepped up to the doorless back entrance and entered Jahrys's home. They had to keep their heads low to avoid banging them on the ceiling that was caving in. They walked through the kitchen and into the living room.

Memories flooded through Jahrys's mind. Memories of all those awkward dinners with his family in the kitchen. Memories of his father always examining his woodwork and his mother yelling at him to put it away. Memories of Miller scurrying around the living room, pecking at his and his parent's feet.

Everything was gone now. There was no kitchen table or chairs, no dishes, no cabinet doors, and no living room furniture. His father was not analyzing his woodwork and his mother was not cleaning the dishes, yelling at his father to help. Jahrys never thought he would miss those things. He would give anything in the world to have it all back.

"Look over here," Kevrin kept his voice low. He was pointing at the wooden floor in the corner of the room.

Jahrys went to look. "What is it?" he asked.

"Look at the wood. It looks like it has been lifted a few times," said Kevrin, looking over at Jahrys.

"This is where we used to keep the couch," Jahrys pointed out. "He must have hid his stash under here."

Jahrys reached his hand out to the loose wood, his gloves gripping into the fold. He lifted the panel. There were a couple of snaps as the nails broke off one by one. Once the panel of wood was free, Jahrys threw it to the side and started on the next one.

He continued until it was large enough for a person to squeeze in.

Jahrys stepped forward but Kevrin placed an arm across his chest.

"Let me go," Kevrin insisted, handing Jahrys his bag but keeping his own.

Jahrys wasn't about to argue; he didn't like cramped spaces. He took his bag, placing it on the side, and watched as Kevrin squeezed through the opening, disappearing into the darkness. Jahrys heard the clanking of glass—his bag must have knocked something over—and the echoes from Kevrin's footsteps.

After a few minutes of waiting, Jahrys yelled down. "Did you find anything?" His voice echoed back up at him.

A bottle popped up through the opening. "Is this what you were looking for?" Kevrin yelled up from below.

"By Zalus...my father's wine. We found it!" Jahrys grabbed the bottle and held it in front of his helmet. The label on it read: *Palor Red. The wine of Astenpoole. Grapes harvested fresh from the backyard of the Grent family.*

This brought a tear to Jahrys's eye. He could see his father now, smiling in the garden as he looked over every single vine and grape with pleasure. All of his hard work...

"And this one's for us." Kevrin hoisted himself out of the hole.

"For us?" Jahrys turned back to Kevrin after placing the first bottle into his bag.

Kevrin was holding a second bottle. He took out the knife Riago had given him and popped the cork.

"You first," he handed the bottle to Jahrys.

Jahrys hesitated. "Shouldn't we be getting back to The Arcalane?"

"I'm not traveling back out there until it gets lighter out. So we might as well enjoy ourselves. Besides..." Kevrin pushed the bottle closer to Jahrys's face. "It's your birthday! Your eighteenth birthday! And we need to celebrate."

Jahrys had forgotten. His mind had been too busy focusing on finding his father's wine and on Lil—on the princess.

"Damn, am I old..." Jahrys took off his helmet and set it down. He grabbed the bottle from Kevrin, sat down against the wall, and took a long pleasant swig.

"Now that's the spirit!" Kevrin laughed, taking his bag off his shoulder and sitting down next to Jahrys.

The wine was hot, but the flavor was great. It was fruity and a little sour, but not too sour. Just enough to give the cheeks a little sting. It was refreshing. Jahrys had not tasted anything this good in a long time. No wonder people were obsessed over this wine. He could understand why the king wanted it.

"You know I was saving my first taste of this wine for my father. He never let me try it because he was afraid mother would have a fit," Jahrys mentioned as he passed the bottle to Kevrin. Kevrin unclipped his helmet and grabbed the bottle.

"Well, I'm honored to be your father's replacement for this moment. I'm sure he would have highly valued your opinion on his wine." Kevrin tilted his head back and took a sip. He passed it to Jahrys. "You're mother thought you weren't drinking by the age of fifteen?" Kevrin shook his head in amazement.

"Yep."

Kevrin chuckled.

Jahrys laughed too as he took a sip. The wine brought back memories of Frayel. "Frayel would always talk up a storm about my father's wine. He would always say how he was getting it for him and his loving Astonia," Jahrys chuckled, taking another sip. "What a strange man. Who would've thought I would miss him." He passed the bottle to Kevrin.

"He would always talk about his loving Astonia," Kevrin laughed and drank a few gulps from the bottle. "It's a shame, really. He would have made a great Retriever."

Jahrys nodded in agreement, wondering if his loving Astonia was still alive.

"Remember when we used to dream of being Knights of the Poolesguard?" Kevrin asked Jahrys as he hiccuped, passing the bottle back to Jahrys.

"I think about it every day. I haven't touched a sword in years."

"Maybe this is your shot."

Jahrys gave Kevrin a look of disbelief. "What are you talking about?"

"You're about to barge into the castle to save a princess from her father! It sounds a lot like the tale of Palor A'kal when he saved Princess Melaine from her father. It will be a tale people will talk about for years to come. Just like all the tales about Palor A'kal, Galagar Poole, and all the true knights in the Poolesguard," Kevrin said.

Jahrys thought about that. *Is this really my shot at becoming a knight?*

He took a sip from the bottle and said, "Knights are fearless, wise, and strong. I'm none of those."

"Knights are human. And all humans fear and have a weakness.

Junkland

It's what we choose to do in those moments of fear and weakness that define us."

"Since when did you become so philosophical?" Jahrys teased.

"In my spare time." Kevrin snatched the bottle from Jahrys. "I think you would make a great knight." Kevrin took a sip.

Jahrys smiled at that.

Kevrin and Jahrys sat against the wall, passing the bottle back and forth, until the bottle emptied and the walls started to spin around them.

"You know, w-we are going to be m-more famous than Rallick after this. All f-for a bottle of wine. Why's this happening for just a bottle of wine?" Jahrys was slurring his words now. "W-why would that old hag pick me over anyone else? We haven' done anyfin' Kev, ha!"

"Who—" Kevrin hiccuped, "who knows Jahr. Maybe she saw s-something in you. And—you know th-there is a shortage of w-wine these days. Willem can' even—can' even get wine in his own bar."

"A king needs wine. Ha!" Jahrys let out a burp, "he mus' be under—too much stress—ruling this fallen hole of a kingdom." He took another drink. "Look at this place, Kev. I mean, *look* at it. By Zalus. N-now if Princess Alana were here. That would be a s-sight. She was beautiful, Kev."

"Yea? I bet she w-was a good kisser. She must have had lots of practice with all them lordlin' boys. I bet—I bet she's had her fair share of experience by now," Kevrin said jokingly and hiccuping.

Jahrys got defensive. "She's not like that! I honestly d-don' think she even kissed a guy before—before me. She was nervous. It was the best n-night of my life."

"Well—don't flatter yourself," Kevrin rolled his drunken eyes.

"Was she—was she better than Ebanie?"

"A million and five times better than—than Ebanie."

"Wooo!" Kevrin sank into the wall.

"Am I ever going to fi—to find her?" Jahrys's head fell to the side and landed on Kevrin's shoulder.

Kevrin laughed, putting his arm around his friend.

"Yes—you'll find her. If it was meant to be…you will find her."

Jahrys's eyes started to feel heavy as they slowly drooped down. He tried to resist a few times, but eventually the wine sent his world spinning into darkness.

Chapter 22
Piller

A GIANT PAINTING hung on the wall of King Leoné's chamber. It showed Leoné, standing tall, proud, and confident with his family. Queen Asha was smiling next to him, her white teeth glistening. Her blue eyes were striking against her pink skin and blonde hair. Princess Alana was a little girl in the painting. She had her father's brown hair, which fell down to her shoulders, and her blue eyes matched perfectly with her mother's. She had a smile as big as the Western Mountains. Her parents both had a loving hand on Alana's tiny shoulders.

Times were simpler back then, before the stormy season, before The Sickness, before the Hoarding, thought Piller, as he admired the painting and happiness of the once complete family. *Before all this chaos.*

Arnold and Hollow waited anxiously on either side of Piller as they waited for Leoné to enter. It was early morning, and they had come to give Leoné their weekly report.

Leoné appeared from his bedchamber, grumbling to himself as he struggled with a crumpled up sleeve on his green tunic. He walked over to a large desk. He realized the sleeve was a lost cause and gave up. He looked up and gave the knights a faulty smile.

"Piller, Hollow, Arnold," he nodded to each of them in turn.

"Your Grace," the three knights said as they took a knee and rose back up.

"Before I hear the report, I wanted to thank the three of you for your hard work. I know times have been difficult and the circumstances unreasonable, but you three have managed to get your work done. The construction of the Retrieval Stations have been very beneficial to Astenpoole and the Retrievers. We have suficient communication with the survivors and things are running smoothly because of you three. Astenpoole is forever in your debt."

Leoné turned to Hollow and Arnold. "I know you boys are still young and these are hard times, but I honor the hard work you boys have put in. Keep up the good work! I expect a bright future for the both of you."

"Thank you, Your Grace," the two young knights said in unison.

Leoné nodded and turned to Piller. "So tell me, how are things going along the wall? What are the reports?" Leoné asked anxiously, his fingers tapping rhythmically on the table.

"Not good, Your Grace," Piller admitted, not breaking his gaze from Leoné's hazel eyes.

Hollow and Arnold turned nervously to Piller.

Leoné's face hardened. "What do you mean, not good? I thought things were running smoothly between us and the Retrievers? Has there been an attack?"

Piller shook his head. "No, Your Grace. Things *were* running smoothly." He was trying to figure out the best way to say this without angering him. Leoné had to see reason, he had to understand the situation they were facing.

"Tell me what's happening, Piller," Leoné demanded, slamming his giant fists on the table.

Hollow and Arnold jumped, alarmed at Leoné's reaction.

Piller decided to lay it on the table. "Astenpoole will not survive another year if we keep proceeding this way, Your Grace."

Leoné turned away. Piller knew he did not want to hear this, but he had to. He had to see reason.

Piller continued. "The number of jobs have been diminishing. The number of recorded Retrievers in the Junkland are dropping. There have been sightings of Hoarders getting closer and closer to the castle walls each day, killing the Retrievers. While we stay put inside these walls. The land outside is getting more and more corrupt. Soon there will be no more food to gather, no more water, no more anything as long as these Hoarders are still knocking at our door. We *must* open the gates. We have to fight for the kingdom. For Astenpoole. For *our* people. We have to open the—"

Leoné held up a hand, signaling Piller to stop speaking. "I will not hear any more of this. Opening the gates is *not* an option. We must find another way around this."

"There is no other way, Your Grace," Hollow spoke up.

"He's right, Your Grace," said Arnold. "Opening the gates is the only way."

Leoné let out a grunt of annoyance. "I cannot do that. You know I cannot open the gates. Asha died because—"

Piller had had enough of the king's fears about The Sickness. "We all miss Asha, Your Grace. We all know how she died, but you can't keep blaming people for her death. We all have to move forward and assess the situation at hand. The Sickness has long been over now...and the illness is the least of our worries..."

"My daughter..." Leoné lowered his head.

"We all want to see your daughter safe, Your Grace," Piller assured him. "Benjamin has been doing a fine job of that. But you *can't* keep her locked inside the Castle Keep forever. Look at how that is working out! We all know she escapes to go practice sword fighting with Benjamin. She needs to be free, just like the people of Astenpoole. Nothing good will happen when you constrain someone down."

"I don't need parenting advice from you, Sir Piller," Leoné snapped. "I know how to handle my own daughter."

Piller saw the veins bulging in Leoné's neck. He decided to speak no more on the subject.

"The gates will remain closed and I expect the three of you to carry out that order to Krist and Martellus upon the wall." He pointed a finger at the three of them. "Do I make myself clear?" Leoné stared at them through slanted eyes as if trying to see if they would disobey.

"Yes, Your Grace," the three said in unison.

"Good. Now go pass the word along the wall and at the Retrieval Stations. Tell them we need to find another way around this. We *must* find another way."

"Yes, Your Grace," the three knights said.

They all turned towards the door and left Leoné hanging his head over his table.

"How'd he take it?" Devan asked, as they walked out of Leoné's chamber. Devan had been standing guard outside the door.

"Not well," Piller said.

Junkland

"By Zalus. What are we to do, Piller?" Devan bit his lip in frustration.

"I don't know," Piller admitted. "I just don't know."

Piller, Arnold, and Hollow left Devan and the King's Tower. It was early morning, but the sky was dark and there seemed to be no attempt from the sun to push out through the thick layer of clouds. They walked under the Village Gate and headed towards the stables to ready their horses.

When they arrived at the stables, Piller hopped onto his black horse, the largest horse in the stable. Arnold and Hollow mounted their own horses and followed Piller under the King's Gate to leave the Castle Keep. They headed towards the Western Gate to spread the news.

Piller admired the two young knights. They had both grown so much since they joined the Poolesguard. They had worked hard to help Piller design the plan for the Retrieval Stations after the Hoarding. Piller had learned a lot about them during that time.

Arnold had lived in Northside in a small house with his parents and two brothers. He had lost all of them from The Sickness when he was only a boy of ten. He had joined the King's Army and had dreamed of becoming a Knight of the Poolesguard.

Hollow was from Riverside. His parents died when he was a baby and his sister had taken care of him his entire life. But after she had died from The Sickness, Hollow saw no other choice but to join the King's Army in hopes of becoming a Knight of the Poolesguard.

After The Sickness took the life of Sir Mazo Dapher, and when Sir Landerin Raneir was asked to step down from Captain of the Poolesguard, King Leoné held a tournament in the gardens of Riverside to decide which two knights would fill these spots. The tournament lasted for over a week. Brave men of Astenpoole fought for their chance to become the chosen knights of the kingdom. The end of the tournament resulted in Arnold Beck and Hollow Tryant, both quite young, becoming the two new Knights of the Poolesguard.

Piller wondered if the Poolesguard was everything Arnold and Hollow had dreamed it was. Piller had definitely been disappointed. When he was their age, he had dreamed of being in the Poolesguard, as well. He had always wanted to become a protector of the kingdom. But now, he wasn't sure what it meant to be a Knight of the Poolesguard. Two knights were guarding a gate, another knight was babysitting a princess, and he was in charge of building Retrieval Stations. How were these knightly duties? Piller certainly did not feel like a protector of the kingdom. If anything, he felt like he was helping to destroy it.

"Hey, Captain."

Hollow kicked his horse faster to move alongside Piller.

Piller smiled down at the young knight. "What is it, Hollow?"

"Do you think the king will come to his senses?" Hollow looked concerned.

"In opening the gates?"

Hollow nodded.

Piller turned to face the Western Gate that they were approaching. The giant wooden doors were bolted together.

Piller let out a deep sigh. "I hope so."

"What do we do?" Arnold spoke to him on his other side.

"All we can do is follow our orders," Piller lectured. "That is our duty of being a Knight of the Poolesguard. We must follow out the king's orders."

Junkland

"Even if we don't believe in the king's orders?" asked Hollow.

They really are growing up fast, thought Piller. "It's our job to advise the king to make the right decisions, but in the end, we must carry out his orders...whatever they may be."

Piller could see Hollow and Arnold were frustrated by this answer. "I know these are hard times for the both of you, and things might not make sense sometimes. It's a learning process and you both are learning fast."

Piller could tell Hollow and Arnold were still not satisfied, but they did not argue.

They tied their horses up to a post on the side of the road and walked up the steps of the gatehouse until they reached a small wooden door at the top of the tower.

Knock. Knock. Knock.

Piller heard yelling from the other side.

"Are you getting the door?" a voice that sounded like Krist asked.

"I thought you were getting it?" another voice that sounded like Martellus questioned.

"Why do I have to do every thing my damn self?" Piller heard shuffling and then footsteps heading towards the door. "Next time I see Piller, I'm going to have a—"

The door opened.

"Ah! Piller! Just the person I was looking for." Krist smiled and stepped aside, motioning the three of them inside. "Arnold, Hollow, how're you boys doing?" He slapped the three of them on the back as they entered the room.

"Are you two getting along?" Piller stepped into the small room. There was a round table in the center piled with papers, books, and mugs. There were two beds bunked on top of each other to the side. A large wheel was facing towards the Western Gate.

"Barely," Krist admitted.

"He can't get enough of me," Martellus said, placing down the book he was reading. His legs were on the round table as he leaned back in his chair.

Krist rolled his eyes. "So, what brings you lot this far west of Astenpoole?"

"We just met with King Leoné," Piller said.

Martellus's chair fell forward. "What did he say? Did you tell him?"

"I did," Piller assured him.

"How did he take it?" Krist asked curiously.

Piller rubbed the back of his neck with his hand trying to figure out how to phrase it.

"Not good," Arnold stepped in.

Krist hung his head in disappointment.

"He's aware we won't survive another year?" Martellus asked.

"He knows," Piller answered.

"By Zalus," Krist looked up at Piller. His eyes were clouded in fear. "What are we to do?"

"We need to keep following our orders and pray to Zalus we find enough food to last us a lifetime."

"A lifetime won't be very long if we keep these gates shut," Martellus pointed out.

"I know. But we don't have a choice," said Piller.

"We can take control," Krist recommended.

"Take control?" Piller couldn't believe what he was hearing. "You mean disobey Leoné's orders? You're talking about treason!"

Junkland

"Look," Krist was getting frustrated. "Everyone in this castle, hell, everyone who survived the Hoarding knows that Leoné has gone mad. He can't get over the loss of Asha and he doesn't want to lose his daughter. That's all he cares about. He doesn't care about us, or the people outside the wall or inside it. By Zalus, he doesn't even care about his own wife, Nadia. Do you know how many people we hear dying every night from on top of these walls? The screams keep me up at night!"

"He's right, Piller," Martellus agreed. "I lie wide awake at night listening to the screams of dying men and women and the blasts from the Hoarders."

"We can't keep living like this," Krist finished.

Everyone turned to face Piller, all eyes were on him. What was he to do? He wasn't about to commit an act of treason. They were still Knights of the Poolesguard.

"I—"

Before he could finish speaking, the sound of blasts poured in through the open window across the room. All heads turned to it.

Krist ran over to the door and flung it open. Piller, Arnold, Hollow, and Martellus followed Krist outside on the wall.

"Over there!" Krist shouted over the blasts.

Piller placed his hands on the wall and followed Krist's finger through the darkness with his eyes. Not too far off from the wall was an inn called The Arcalane, where most of the Retrievers stayed hidden. Piller could make out the inn through gaps in the junk walls. The windows were glowing yellow from the blasts. Piller could hear screams and cries for help.

"What do we do, Captain?" Hollow yelled over the screams.

What could they do? They couldn't open the gates. Nor could

they magically jump over the wall to help them. There was nothing they could do.

"Captain?" Arnold yelled out.

Piller turned to his men, looking over their nervous faces. "There's nothing we can do for them. King Leoné has given us his orders. The gates will remain shut."

Krist growled in anger. "King Alexander Poole formed the Poolesguard to create knights who were worthy to protect the kingdom. He would have been ashamed of us."

Piller had no words for Krist or the rest of the knights. He couldn't stand there any longer looking at his men's disappointed faces. Nor could he stand listening to the suffering of the people inside The Arcalane.

"The gates *will* remain shut." Piller turned and walked away from the screams and blasts that hung in the air.

Chapter 23
Jahrys

THERE WAS FIRE in his head when Jahrys woke. He placed a hand on his forehead as he lifted himself from the floor. It felt like a knife was splitting his head open. *I really need to stop drinking,* he thought as he looked around, trying to remember where he was. He was in a large room, but there was no furniture. An empty bottle of wine lay next to his legs. A few red drops had dripped out onto the floor, staining the wood dark red. Light was seeping in through the window. *How long did I sleep for?* It was all blurry to him. All he remembered was Kevrin—

Jahrys jumped to his feet. "Kevrin?" he shouted. But there was no answer.

He ran into the kitchen, keeping his head low because of the collapsing ceiling. Kevrin wasn't there. He searched the wreckage of his old home, every inch, but found no sign of his friend.

He went back to the living room, pacing in circles, unable to make a decision. He didn't know if he should wait here for him to show up or head back to The Arcalane. Where could he have gone?

Suddenly, there was a voice from outside.

"Over here!"

Jahrys leaned against the front window in the living room, staying out of view of the road. He peaked through. There were two Hoarders, and one had black stripes on his helmet. *It's him*, thought Jahrys.

"Are you sure it's this one?" the other Hoarder asked.

"I'm positive," the black-striped Hoarder replied.

Sweat began to soak Jahrys's suit. He clipped on his helmet and attached his Captor Pack to his back and his Captor to the tube. He then tied his bag around his waist.

Should he stay and fight or turn and run? If he ran now, he could make it through the back door and head to The Arcalane. But he couldn't just leave Kevrin. However, he had no clue where he had gone. And this could be the only chance he had to get his revenge on the black-striped Hoarder; the one who had killed his parents.

Feet crunched on loose debris as the Hoaders walked up to the doorless frame.

Jahrys's breathing echoed inside his helmet. He could feel his heart pounding under his suit. He clenched his Captor tightly with both hands as he watched the Hoarder's Captors poke through the doorway.

He couldn't do it.

He ran.

"There he is!" A Hoarder yelled out behind him.

Captor blasts suddenly filled the room. A blast exploded into the wall to his right as he flung himself forward. He ducked. A second blast exploded by his feet, sending him flying into the empty kitchen. He hit the broken tile floor hard. His Captor slipped from his grasp and slid across the tile.

Jahrys reached a hand out and grabbed the tube, yanking it towards him. The Captor slid back. He grabbed it, turned, and pressed hard on the top trigger.

There was a moan as his blue blast hit the right Hoarder in the shoulder. The Hoarders ducked behind the wall, taking cover as Jahrys continued to fire, keeping them pinned behind the wall.

Still firing, Jahrys used his free hand and legs to push his way towards the back door. He was inching closer and closer to the door. He kept firing his Captor, because he knew once he stopped, they would be upon him again.

Jahrys pressed down on the trigger again and a low hiss sounded from the tip of his Captor. *Dammit, I thought it was fully charged!* He didn't hesitate. Jahrys jumped to his feet, clipping the Captor to his hip. He sprinted and flung himself through the back door. Captor blasts exploded against the doorframe as the Hoarders followed him.

Jahrys zig-zagged across the destroyed yard, praying to Zalus the Hoarders continued to miss. He dodged junk blocks and loose debris as he ran.

"He's getting away," one of the Hoarders yelled behind him.

There was a sound of marching footsteps behind him. When he cleared the back fence, heading away from his home and Zalus Road, he took a quick glance over his shoulder. There were now dozens of Hoarders piling around the house, shooting at him.

Jahrys sprinted up a side road where junk walls towered over him. Captor blasts flew past his head, exploding into the walls and sending clouds of debris and junk blocks into the air. His vision was limited. His heart was pounding in his chest as he continued to twist and turn through the maze of walls, trying to lose them. He ran faster than he had ever run before. His legs felt like they were flying beneath him. His only thought was to make it back to The Arcalane to warn the others and hopefully find Kevrin.

The path opened to the Seaport River, but that didn't slow him down. He leapt out over the river and landed on a broken boat. He jumped again, towards the other side. He fell into the cold water but was able to grab onto the ledge of the dock on the side of a road. He felt the current swing his legs towards the castle. Captor blasts exploded inches from his hands and he decided to let go, letting the current take him back towards The Arcalane.

Jahrys crashed through the door to the inn, soaking wet. "Willem! Help! Kevrin—Hoarders—"

He stopped.

He took off his helmet to rub his eyes and make sure they weren't playing tricks on him. He couldn't believe what he saw. The Arcalane was destroyed. One of the pillars in the center of the room had collapsed. The tables were scattered and broken. Shards of glass were on the floor. There was blood everywhere. It covered the walls, the floor, the bar, *everything*.

"Willem?" Jahrys shouted. "Gabe? Tarl? Kat? Miller? Ebanie?" There was no answer, only an eerie silence.

They're all gone.

Jahrys heard a groan coming from the other side of the bar. He sprinted to the noise, jumping over the counter and looked down.

It was Willem. He was covered in blood.

"Willem!" Hope returned to Jahrys. "What happened? Are you all right?" Jahrys felt the hope fade when he looked down at the wound in Willem's stomach. He tried to lift Willem's large body from the floor, but couldn't. Instead, he let Willem's head rest on his arm.

"They came, Jahrys." Willem's voice was hoarse and lifeless.

"Who came? The Hoarders?"

Willem nodded his head. "I tried—to protect—our—family…" A bloody tear rolled down his cheek.

Jahrys wiped it away with his glove. "Did anyone survive?"

The whiteness in Willem's eyes began to show as his eyes rolled up. He started to lose sense of his surroundings. He was fading.

"I tried—to protect—family…"

With the last word, Willem's head fell gently back onto Jahrys's arm as he faded from the world.

"Willem!" Jahrys cried out. "Willem! Don't leave me! Please don't leave me too!"

Jahrys's lips began to tremble. *Everyone's gone. I'm all alone.*

He let the tears roll down his face. He brought Willem's forehead up to meet his as he cried over him. *My family,* thought Jahrys. *My family is gone.*

Jahrys sprinted upstairs to his room. He fell to the floor while the tears poured out of his eyes.

The diary was still on his desk, undisturbed. Jahrys stomped over to the book angrily. "It's all your fault!" He felt crazy talking to a diary—but he didn't care. "If I didn't find this damn book, if I didn't learn the truth about Lily—Alana—whatever her name is…maybe Kevrin would still be here. And Elyara would still be alive! I could've been here to protect The Arcalane." He threw the book hard across the room, yelling, "All for a bottle of wine!"

The diary hit the bathroom door with a smack. The door crashed hard against the wall. Paper went flying in the air. A few sheets floated down to his feet.

What's this? He bent down to pick one up.

Jahrys examined the paper closely: it was a map.

He felt the anger rising in his chest as he studied it. His eyes glared at the King's Tower. He was finally able to see clearly and finally understand where his anger stemmed. It wasn't the diary, nor Alana, it wasn't the wine, nor the old lady.

It was King Leoné Poole—the king who had abandoned them.

Chapter 24
Alana

DUST STUCK TO her sweaty body as she crawled through the tunnels—back towards her room. Alana had just finished her sword fighting lesson with Sir Benjamin. They had been meeting up in Riverside ever since he followed her there before the wedding.

Every day she felt her body getting stronger. She noticed a change in her physique, along with new calluses on her palms. Three years ago, Benjamin could easily beat her in one fell swoop. Now, Alana was able to have a long rally with the knight. She was faster, her movements were smooth, and she was much more confident.

Alana considered going to check on her job down at the Retrieval Stations. She had just put out another job a few weeks ago, and she was anxious to find out if there was any success. She had to get her diary back before it fell into the wrong hands. But she had already been gone too long, it was almost the afternoon. She didn't want her father to catch her outside the Castle Keep. Alana hated sneaking around like this, but what choice did she have? She did not want to disobey him, but she couldn't stay cooped up inside the Castle Keep for the rest of her life. She needed freedom! To practice her sword fighting and to escape Mother Claraine and her annoying handmaids. If only her father could understand.

The tunnel ended, and Alana flicked the switch. There was a click, and the small door opened slightly—she had made it to the library. Alana opened it a bit more and peaked through to check if anyone was around. When she saw the coast was clear, she stepped down to the library floor. She gently shut the giant, swinging painting until it clicked back into place. She turned and quickly walked out of the library and took the stairs up to her room.

Alana opened the door to her bedroom. Quiet as a mouse, and with her body facing the door, she shut it.

"Practicing your sword fighting with Sir Benjamin again?" a heavy voice asked behind her.

Alana's heart jumped. She swung around, flinging herself up innocently against her door. She placed a hand on her racing heart. "Father...I—"

"It's okay, Alana. No need to explain yourself." Her father was sitting on her bed, smiling at her. He had something laying across his lap. "Please...come sit." He patted his hand down next to him.

Alana hesitated. *Is this a trap?* She thought. Her father had just caught her red-handed and he was...being nice? She cautiously walked over to her bed and sat down next to her father. *He's probably going to board my bedroom door up next and never let me out again.*

She heard her father let out a long, deep breath, his thick beard expanding with his chest.

Her father turned and smiled down at her. "Have I ever told you how I met your mother?"

Alana shook her head. She had always wondered, but was always too shy to ask.

"Ah, what a story." Her father shook his head as if he couldn't believe the story himself. "During my first year as king, I had to pay respect to the unfortunate who had fallen ill at the start of The Sickness. Gala had had me wrapped up in some crazy contraption to prevent me from catching anything. I walked up and down the aisles of beds, looking at all those poor children, mothers, fathers, and elderly folk. All the poor Kalukians, Danorians, Palorians, and Sibleman looked the same as the wealthy. All different and yet, so similar. None of them would make it past that year.

"On my walk, I came across one woman whose beauty made me stop. Even being as sick as she was, she was more beautiful than any sunrise over the Farrest Sea. Even when her hair was a tangled mess, she looked stunning.

"I asked Gala about her, trying to discover her story. Gala told me she was brought in by a young man who had found her lying unconscious on the road. She was alive, but hadn't woken up ever since they had found her. She had no family that visited her. No loved ones that cared for her—she was alone. So do you know what I did?"

"You married her?" Alana guessed.

Her father chuckled. "Well, yes, but before that?"

Alana shrugged.

"I visited her every chance I had. I slipped away from my mentors and advisors just to sit with her, to brush her hair behind her ears, to hold her hand. I loved her, even before I knew her, even before we spoke. Being with her took the burden of being king away from me, the burden I never asked for. It took away the pain from my dead parents, and my brother, Timmon, who had sailed off into the Farrest Sea, abandoning me, abandoning his birthright! My father, my mother, and my older brother, who were supposed to be there for me, were gone. They left me their burdens and this woman was my only freedom from them. I wouldn't let her suffer the same fate as I did. I wouldn't let her suffer alone. And when she woke...I was there for her. She smiled up at me as if she knew I had been there with her the entire time.

"But she didn't remember anything. She didn't know her name, where she had come from, or anything about her life before The Sickness."

Alana watched a tear fall down her father's cheek. He wiped it away with a large hand.

"She didn't remember anything?" Alana asked in wonder.

"Not a single thing."

"I never knew..."

Her father continued. "I told her I would take care of her, that I would help her restore her memory, that I would never abandon her like my brother had abandoned me. She was a strong woman. She made a miraculous recovery from The Sickness and was able to leave the Clinic. I showed her everything that Astenpoole had to offer and we fell in love and had you." Her father smiled at her, placing a hand on her back.

"Your mother is the bravest woman I have ever met. I see so much of her in you. By Zalus! You are so much like her, Alana! You have her eyes, her face, her guts, her commitment. You are one of the bravest woman I know."

Alana's eyes began to tear up.

"Your mother would have been ashamed of me for keeping you locked away inside this castle. I'm ashamed of myself. It was wrong and I see that now. I was just so afraid of losing you. I didn't know what I would do without you and your mother."

Her father wrapped his hands on the sword lying on his lap. "I wanted you to have this for your lessons with Benjamin. I had it made specifically for you." He handed her the sword still inside the scabbard.

Alana held it out in front of her with both hands. "You had this made...for me?" She couldn't believe it. She was so happy she began to cry. The tears were flowing down her face.

"The grip is smaller for your hands and is lighter and swifter than any sword you have held. It will be perfect for you." Her father watched her examine it.

"Father—I—thank you." She wrapped a free arm around his neck and dug her face into his chest and beard.

"Anything for you, Alana. I just want you to be happy." Her father patted her back. "I know how hard things have been, especially with Nadia."

"I am happy, Father." She was smiling through her tears.

"Just promise me you'll be careful."

"I will, Father. I promise."

They broke apart, and her father gave her a kiss on her forehead. "Don't be too hard on Benjamin. He won't know what hit him when you use that sword against him." Her father chuckled.

Alana giggled. "I'll be nice."

Her father gave her a wink and walked over to her bedroom door. Before he left he looked back at her. "You know I will never abandon you."

"I know." Alana smiled at him.

"Your mother would have been proud." Her father smiled and

closed the door behind him, leaving Alana to examine her new sword and freedom.

Chapter 25
Jahrys

HIS BODY SHOT up as he gasped for air. He looked around, trying to figure out where he was. *It was a dream, just a dream.* A hand grasped his chest. He took a few deep breaths. *It was just a dream.* Jahrys's head was spinning. All he remembered was a woman, a baby, and a flash of blue.

When he finally settled down, he looked around. He was in a cave, and he was alone. He half-expected Elyara and Kevrin to be next to him when he woke. But then he remembered Elyara was dead and Kevrin was gone, probably dead as well.

The cave was cold, something he wasn't used to. He was following a dried up stream that once branched off from the Seaport River in Kaluk. He found it using the maps Alana had drawn in her diary. He was so close to entering the castle walls. He was so close to confronting the king.

Jahrys didn't stay at The Arcalane for long. He didn't want to wait around for the old lady after discovering the maps and his newly directed anger. He didn't know if he could trust her.

He had quickly gathered his things. He had packed as much as he could fit into his bag: the bottle of wine, bread, water, berries, Riago's knife, the diary, an extra shirt, and of course, Alana's necklace.

He didn't leave without recharging his Captor. He had pointed the weapon at his desk, knowing he would never need it again. He pressed down on the bottom trigger, and the floor began to shake beneath him.

There was a deep, low hum.

VHRUUUUMMMM.

A blue beam had shot out, encompassing the desk. When the blue light disappeared, the desk was gone. The light on Jahrys's Captor had flashed blue again, and Jahrys felt his Captor Pack vibrating on his back.

He had clipped his Captor to his hip, secured his bag around his shoulder, and grabbed his helmet. He left his room after taking one last look at it. He had sprinted down the steps of The Arcalane. The smell of death lingered in the air, even through his helmet. Jahrys had quickly said his goodbyes to Willem and to The Arcalane as he walked out the doors, back into the Junkland.

Thunder had boomed above his head and the wind had swirled around him. Debris had been blowing violently around, and he had to be careful. Jahrys did not want to be stuck out in the Junkland during the storm, but he had to find the cave. He couldn't wait.

He had looked at the first map that showed the path that would lead into the castle. It had brought him close to the castle wall, which he had followed towards Kaluk. The populated buildings of Palor had faded away as the forest of Kaluk took its place. Or what used to be a forest. The bark on the trees had dried up and broken off in many places, and none of the trees had any leaves.

The map had then showed a cave a few miles away from the southernmost part of the wall. Jahrys had traveled through Kaluk, keeping a sharp eye out for Hoarders, as he followed the map deeper into the forest. The thunder had continued to roar over his head, the rain pounded against his suit, and the branches of the dead trees whipped in the wind, almost touching the forest floor.

He had picked up his pace. It had taken him most of the day to find the cave and the dried-up stream that fed into it. It had been hard to find at first, being hidden behind a rock crevice.

Jahrys had followed the stream bed inside the cave for a few hours before he had decided to rest; he was exhausted. Now awake, he didn't know how long he had been asleep. He didn't know what time of the day it was. It was too dark in the cave to tell.

Now, after he had calmed down from the dream, Jahrys realized he was clutching Alana's necklace in his hand. He placed it back into his bag and stood up, stretching his legs. His body was stiff from sleeping on the hard rocky floor. He flung his bag over his shoulder, strapped his Captor to his hip, and continued his way down the stream bed.

He was eager to enter the castle and confront King Leoné. Jahrys was going to demand that the king open the gates and save his people and the kingdom he had abandoned, including Princess Alana. It was time for the king to stop cowering behind walls while Hoarders slaughtered his people. It was time for him to stand up and face his mistakes.

The words sounded perfect in Jahrys's head. He would tell the king exactly that and he *would* listen. He had to listen.

After a few more hours of walking, he came to a dead end. There were bars submerged into the dirt with light peaking through; it almost looked like a cage. *This is the way out,* thought Jahrys. His heart was filled with excitement. A few of the bars were rusted away and left a gap just big enough for a small person to squeeze under. *This must be how Alana escaped the castle that night.*

Jahrys studied the gap. He wouldn't be able to fit underneath, but he had an idea. He pointed the Captor at the rusted bars, pressed the top trigger, and fired two shots. When the smoke cleared, the gap was now large enough for Jahrys to crawl under.

He stripped down to his pants, placing his suit, helmet, Captor Pack, and Captor under a crevice of a large rock. He thought it would be best to not stand out inside the castle. He dug his hands into his bag and pulled out a loose shirt that he flung over his head. When he was ready, he made sure everything was secure inside his bag. He pushed the bag through the gap of the bars first, and then slid in himself.

He crawled for a few yards before the ground started to rise. He picked up his bag and smiled as he walked into the light of Astenpoole.

After spending his whole life on the other side of the wall, he had finally made it inside the castle. It was daytime now, and the city was alive. The architecture of the stone buildings was beautiful, nothing like Palor. Every building had a balcony. Some houses had thick, spiral columns with grand steps that led up to the front doors. The buildings were three, sometimes four stories high.

People walked busily in the streets carrying things Jahrys had never seen before. The women were beautiful and the men were well-dressed. Jahrys hadn't seen this many people in one place in nearly three years.

Junkland

He couldn't walk straight to the Castle Keep because the guards would just turn him away, thinking he was crazy or a drunken fool. He had to find a different way in. The map showed a house a few streets away from Pooles Road that had a secret passageway that led into the Castle Keep.

People were eyeing him oddly as he followed the map towards Pooles Road. Jahrys walked across the most beautiful bridge he had ever seen. It arched high over Seaport River. The stonework was flawless and had flowers carved into the stone. The river glistened and sparkled, a rich blue. Jahrys couldn't believe that the Junkland did not touch anything inside the castle.

The Castle Keep stood proud on top of its hill not too far off in the distance. The towers rose high into the sky, the stone twisting around in a spiral. Jahrys recalled his father's words about where the king's chambers were: the southeast tower in the center of the Castle Keep. Jahrys looked up at the massive tower, which looked over Astenpoole from its hilltop. King Leoné was probably in there now.

A sign appeared in the center of the bridge. The left arrow pointed to Western Village and the right arrow pointed to Riverside. Jahrys must have just come from Riverside so he followed the path towards the Western Village, eventually finding his way to Pooles Road.

He was blown away as he looked at the famous road, which led to the Castle Keep. Tall buildings lined the road. Taller than any building in Palor, including Pastor Allen's church. People hung outside their windows, waving to people in the streets, slapping towels or rugs against the side wall, or just enjoying the sights while having a smoke. Carts, led by horses and mules, clicked and clacked as they traveled in all directions on the cobblestone road. They were carrying fruit, sacks of rice, heavy lumber, and even passengers. There were little shops and tents lined up on every inch of the road. People were selling jewelry and pearls, homemade pies, and fruits and vegetables. Pigs were being herded across, reeking of mud and ammonia. Music was playing in the background.

Jahrys continued walking as he admired the scenery around him.

"Sir, sir? A gem for your dearly beloved?" asked a rather large man off to Jahrys's right. He shoved a green gem into Jahrys's face.

Jahrys shook his head. "No, thank you."

The man continued to walk with Jahrys. He put away the gem and quickly took out a necklace. "A necklace for her then? No? Earrings? What woman doesn't love earrings?"

Jahrys just shook his head again and kept walking. It took the man three blocks to finally leave him alone.

"A delicious pie for your mother, sir?" asked another man with a funny looking mustache.

"A pig to bring home to your family?" asked a fat lady.

"A love potion for your secret love?" asked a tall, bald man.

Jahrys shook his head for what seemed like the hundredth time.

"No? Is it a secret manly love you seek? We sell those, too," he said with a wink.

Jahrys was bombarded with people from all directions. Even though he shook his head *no* to everything, he enjoyed the attention. The only excitement Jahrys had since the Hoarding were the crazy nights in The Arcalane with Kevrin, Elyara, and the rest of his friends. But he had no time to stop and enjoy the excitement. He had a mission: to confront King Leoné and save the kingdom.

He walked past a stage where a band was playing. People were gathering around to watch as they started their next song.

"I want to see everyone singing and dancing to this next song," the singer shouted out to the crowd.

It reminded him of Felix's band at The Arcalane.

There was a mixed arrangement of horns—Jahrys had never seen some of them before. There was a guitarist, bassist, drummer, and a bunch of singers.

They began to play.

> *A little feast to win your fair,*
> *Or something nice for her to wear.*
> *There are pearly whites and diamonds, too,*
> *When you roam the streets of Astenpoole.*
>
> *A crazy celebration to last the day,*
> *And a place for you to get away.*
> *Come see a circus bear or dancing fool,*
> *When you roam the streets of Astenpoole.*

People danced and sang along. The crowd was growing larger and larger, girls were twirled into the air. People lined up and synchronized their dancing. It seemed as if this was a daily routine. The song continued.

> *A crusted pie or homemade cake,*
> *A million things were freshly baked,*
> *To cast a scent that will make you drool,*
> *When you roam the streets of Astenpoole.*

A woman approached Jahrys. She couldn't have been more than ten years older than him, but she was at least three times his size.

She smiled at him and grabbed his hand. He tried to resist and pull away, but it was no use—her grip was much too strong.

She pulled Jahrys into her and squeezed him tight against her large bosom. The woman laughed hysterically, almost insanely, as she twirled Jahrys round and round. He felt like he was going to be sick. He felt more hands grab him as he was flung high up into the air. He felt his stomach drop as he fell. *I'm going to die.* But the hands caught him. They flung him up again. *What is happening?*

The music kept playing.

If you're new, no need to fear,
Everyone is willing to help you here.
Take their hand, don't be a fool,
When you roam the streets of Astenpoole.

When you roam the streets of Astenpoole,
When you roam the streets of ASTENPOOOOOOLE.

The singer held the last note for what seemed like a minute. The audience around Jahrys had grown tremendously. After he was done holding the note, Jahrys thought the band was finished. But they only grew louder. The instruments carried the song on while the singer danced around the stage. He picked people out from the crowd, brought them on stage, and twirled them in circles.

Jahrys finally escaped his dancing partner, but he still had trouble escaping the crowd. Everyone was pushing towards the stage, dancing and twirling. It was chaotic. It was an endless progression of music and dancing.

He found an opening. He dove for it. He was almost through the crowd until he saw the woman at the end.

Oh no, he thought.

She smiled when she saw him. Jahrys had no choice but to go back the other way. He pushed and shoved until he finally found his way out.

He ran over to a large trough and knelt beside it. He dunked his head into the warm water. As he was sipping the water, a horse's head plopped down next to him. The horse started slurping.

"Boy, what're you doing?" A man with a funny hat was looking down at him from his horse.

Jahrys put two-and-two together.

"Just thirsty, sir. Lots of dancing." He wiped the slimy water from his mouth.

The man turned his horse away from the water, shaking his head. "Kids these days," he mumbled as he left.

Jahrys wiped his mouth again. He took out the map and examined it. The house looked like it was two streets up and two streets to the right. He hurried towards his destination. Excitement flowed through him as he was getting closer to the king—closer to Alana.

He arrived at the house. It was a small, two story shack, which was snuggled between two taller houses. It looked like it was about to fall apart. The windows were shattered, and the paint on the house was chipping away.

Jahrys looked back down at his map. The notes pointed to the dinky house. *Well, I guess this is it,* he thought, as he walked inside.

The door creaked open. The place was filled with dust. The furniture in the house was toppled over, ripped, and falling apart. A leg from the couch was missing. The glass table in front of it was shattered. *I wonder what happened here.*

There was a large painting hanging on the wall across the room.

Jahrys examined it. It was a beautiful painting of the sun setting behind the Western Mountains. Jahrys teared up a little. It reminded him of home before the Hoarding.

Jahrys looked down at the map. The notes pointed to the painting hanging on the wall in front of him. Jahrys noticed that there was no dust covering the frame on the left side. *It seems someone has moved it recently. The entryway must be behind that painting!*

Jahrys walked over to the painting. He tried to pull it off. It didn't budge. He looked back down at the map. He saw a note that mentioned a switch. He ran his fingers along the edge of the painting. As his fingers moved towards the bottom-left corner, he came across a switch. He flicked it.

Click.

The painting swung away from the wall, revealing a tiny door behind it. Jahrys turned the handle and opened it, revealing a ladder.

He gazed at the second map that would lead him to the king's chambers. He wanted to memorize as much as possible just in case there wasn't any light where he was going. He traced his finger along the path. *Okay, no big deal. Just go down the ladder and then take the tunnel as it rises towards the Castle Keep. Then I need to go right, another right, a left, a straight away, two more lefts, and I should finally be there.* He looked at the ladder before him. *Well, here goes nothing.*

He climbed down—He was ready.

Chapter 26
Jahrys

THE AIR WAS filled with dust and dirt. Jahrys had to stop numerous times to cough. He hoped no one would hear him through the walls. A couple of times he felt vibrations from footsteps stomping above his head, encompassing him in a cloud of dust and dirt. Mice skittered past his hands and legs. He was down on his hands and knees for what felt like hours. The tunnels were more cramped in certain areas to the point that he had to squeeze through. Sometimes he considered turning back, he *hated* cramped spaces.

He was trying to remember the steps he had to take when the tunnel branched off into multiple directions. *Was it two lefts and then a right or two rights and then a left?* Jahrys was having a hard time remembering. His eyes failed to adjust to the darkness so Jahrys had to stick one hand out in front of him to feel where the turns were.

After two hours of crawling, Jahrys heard a voice. He put his ear up against the cold wall, listening closely.

"…yes, Piller, I know they finally have a secure hold by the castle wall. I'm aware of the deaths of all those Retrievers. Tell Krist and

Martellus to keep people away from the Retrieval Stations and away from that wall. Things have not changed. We *must* keep the gates shut."

"Yes, Your Grace. I will give the order out right away."

Jahrys heard footsteps fading away. A door opened and closed shut.

"What has this kingdom become?" he heard a man say through the wall, letting out a long sigh.

This is my chance, thought Jahrys, as he searched the wall for a switch. He found the switch on the side of the door. He flicked it down. There was a click and a pop.

"What? Who's there?" the man demanded.

Jahrys cleared his throat. "Don't be alarmed. I am a Retriever who was left outside of the wall during the Hoarding."

"Well, then why are you in my wall talking to me? You're making me think I'm going crazy. Show yourself, Retriever. Let me have a look at you," he commanded.

Jahrys pushed on the handle of the door as he crawled through and stepped down. He was standing in a large chamber with a giant desk in the center. Paintings of Galagar Poole and other past kings hung on the walls. When Jahrys closed the secret passageway door, he noticed the other wall had a painting of King Leoné, Queen Asha, and Princess Alana. Jahrys's heart skipped a beat when he saw Alana in the painting.

Jahrys turned and saw the largest man he had ever seen standing before him. Jahrys's father had been right: King Leoné was a giant. His beard was bushy and thick, but his hair was graying. He was wearing a golden crown on his head and wore a dark-green tunic. The sigil of Astenpoole was pinned above his heart. And he had a sword that was pointed directly at Jahrys's throat.

"How did you find out about this entrance, Retriever? I didn't even know it existed." The tip of the sword was piercing Jahrys's skin.

"I—" Jahrys stuttered, afraid to clear his throat. He had to be confident. He had to be a knight. "Your daughter helped me, Your Grace."

"My daughter? What are you talking about?" the king asked, frustrated.

Jahrys slowly reached around his back for his bag, being cautious as the sword followed him. King Leoné kept his eyes glued to Jahrys's hand.

Jahrys reached into his bag and brought out the diary. He handed it to the king.

Leoné examined it with his free hand, still pointing the sword at Jahrys as he read.

"By Zalus...Alana wrote this?" the king asked. "She drew these maps?"

"She did, Your Grace."

"How did you come across this diary?" Leoné sheathed his sword and began to flip through the legible pages.

Jahrys told Leoné the entire story. How he had met Alana three years ago before the Hoarding. How he had saved her from a man who was accusing her of stealing. How they had become close and were planning to meet again. That she must have dropped the diary during the Hoarding. Jahrys explained how his team of Retrievers had recovered it.

"By Zalus. I never even knew..." Leoné said more to himself, shaking his head in shame. Leoné looked at Jahrys. "Why have you come to me?"

"I have come to bring you the wine you've requested, Your Grace." Jahrys puffed out his chest. This was his moment to save his people, to make the king listen to him. "I have come to fulfill my job as a Retriever and as payment, demand you open the castle gates and save the people you abandoned outside those walls." Jahrys pointed to the window behind the king's desk. He was sweating after he had said it. He hoped Leoné didn't notice. He tried to stay strong and confident, but his finger was shaking.

Leoné eyed him up and down suspiciously. He put the diary down on the table. "Job you say? What job?" He ignored everything else Jahrys had said.

Jahrys quickly went into his bag and pulled out the wine bottle. "This job, Your Grace."

Leoné's hazel eyes grew wide at the sight of the bottle. "Is that Grent Wine?" He walked over and snatched it from Jahrys's hand.

"Uh—yes, it is, Your Grace," answered Jahrys, suddenly confused at Leoné's reaction. "My father made it in his garden."

"You're telling me that your father is Alvys Grent?" Leoné sounded astonished.

"Yes, Your Grace." Jahrys was still confused.

"By Zalus," Leoné reached for Jahrys's hand and shook it. "I met your father years ago. How is he?"

"My father is dead."

"Oh," Leoné's eyes softened. He let go of Jahrys's hand. "I'm sorry to hear that, son. What's your name?"

"My name is Jahrys, Your Grace. I have come to d—"

"Well…Jahrys. Let us toast to your father with his own wine. He was a great man." Leoné walked behind his desk and fumbled through the drawers while he talked. "I haven't had Grent Wine in years. There has been a shortage ever since the Hoarding."

"Your Grace, I—"

"Ah! Here it is." Leoné pulled out a wine opener. He popped the cork and grabbed two wine glasses from a cabinet behind his desk. He placed them on the desk and poured them both glasses.

"Please, Your Grace—" Jahrys couldn't get a word out.

Leoné shoved the glass into Jahrys's hands. Jahrys accepted it begrudgingly.

Leoné twirled the wine inside the glass and bent down to smell it. "Ah! That's the best damn thing I've smelled in a long time." Leoné held his glass out in front of him.

Jahrys did the same.

"To your father, Alvys Grent, may he find peace beyond the Western Mountains." Leoné clinked his glass against Jahrys's and took a hefty swig of his wine.

Jahrys studied his glass. The wine only brought back memories of his father and of Kevrin.

King Leoné wiped his mouth with the back of his hand. "Well, drink up, Jahrys. It's not every day that you get to share wine with the King of—"

King Leoné let out a cough. He placed a hand to his mouth. "My apologies. I must have—"

The wine glass fell from his hands. A red stain spread slowly on the white carpet as Leoné gagged. His hands shot up to his throat, clutching it. His face turned as red as the wine. Thick-blue veins protruded from his neck.

He tumbled to the floor. The king's crown rolled under the desk. He was clawing at the skin of his throat. He raised one trembling hand up at Jahrys, begging for help.

Jahrys dropped to his knees beside him. What was he to do? All he could think of was yell, "Breathe, Your Grace! Just breathe! It will be okay!" But Jahrys felt like an idiot for how useless he was. He watched Leoné struggle. His legs twisted and turned in odd angles.

The king managed to get a few words out, "Pro—tect—Alana…" After he spoke these words, King Leoné laid motionless on the carpet of his own chamber.

What just happened? Jahrys stared at the wine bottle sitting innocently on the table.

Jahrys didn't have much time to think. The door slammed open behind him. Two Knights of the Poolesguard marched in. Their eyes instantly went to the dead king lying on the floor, surrounded in red wine. The taller one, with a scar across his face, unsheathed his sword.

"Don't move!" the knight yelled.

Jahrys didn't resist. He didn't know what to do. He let the knights take him. Jahrys just stared at the king's body as the two knights dragged him out of the room.

But before he was taken out the door, something caught his eye in the window above King Leoné's desk. Hovering in the window was a crow, and it was watching Jahrys being dragged away.

Part Three
The Fight

# Chapter 27
Nadia

THE GREAT HALL sat in the southwest corner of the Castle Keep. It had a unique architecture compared to the other buildings in Astenpoole. The roof towered high into the sky, the size of it extraordinary. Painted glass windows covered the perimeter of the first floor and balcony. The sun stained the flooring with the colors from the windows. There were doors that led out to many courtyards and gardens that surrounded the hall on the outside.

At the entrance by King's Way, there was a massive marble staircase, which led up to a beautiful courtyard with giant white pillars that populated the perimeter of the building. In the center of the courtyard, towards the entrance door, was a fountain—not as large as the Fountain of Zalus, but still large. It had a statue in the center of it. It was a memorial for King Galagar Poole, who had reshaped the kingdom after King Alas Danor had destroyed it. The entrance to the Great Hall was a pair of large red oak doors, which stood high and proud at the end of the courtyard.

The first room inside was the Hall of Heroes. Paintings of each king and famous knight of Astenpoole hung in this room. King Leoné Poole hung on a marble showcase in the center, as he was the current king—but soon to be deceased.

Nadia sat inside the throne room, high upon the Wave. The large marble chair was shaped to its name. A giant wave formed the backrest that flowed upwards towards the ceiling and arched over Nadia's head, as if it would suddenly all come crashing down upon her. The armrests were both carved into smaller waves that flowed outwards.

She waited anxiously, her fingers massaging the sphere on top of her staff. Her chin rested in her left palm as she leaned her elbow on the armrest. She felt lonely in the large open room, it was so massive. Pillars lined the sides of the throne room, holding up a balcony that wrapped around the room. There was a spiral staircase to either side of her that led up to the next floor. But there was no one occupying it at the moment. She was alone—waiting.

Her eyes studied the engravings on all the pillars. They were covered in artwork from the years of the first king, when the throne room was first built. Each one told a different story. There was the story of King Alas Danor's voyage over the Farrest Sea, when he first set foot in Astenpoole, at the time known only as Kaluk. Everything had been covered in forest from the north to the south all those years ago. There was the story of his conquering the land during the War of Two Worlds, when the Kalukians rose against him. There was the story of his banishment of the worship of Zalus—the Western God.

After her eyes were tired of examining the pillars and recalling the stories, she stared past the grand marble staircase to the black and white marble floor that lay before her like an ocean. The design of the floor was a mixture of squares and circles, either in black or white. It could send the head spinning if one stared at it for a long period. The center of the floor was colored white. It formed a path that continued all the way from the marble staircase to the entrance door across the throne room.

She got bored of that quickly and glanced up at the high ceiling. There was a painting of Zalus on his knees before the Western Mountains. His palms were raised to the sky, light shining out of them.

Nadia laughed to herself. She found the belief in the Wetsern God rather humorous.

The silence was starting to disturb her. She let her left hand fall onto the armrest. She started tapping her fingers against the small wave.

Tap, Tap, Tap.

The sunlight from the windows around the room was making her sweat through her long, silky black dress.

When she assigns the job to the boy, he will die. Carthel's words rang through her head; it was supposed to happen today. And she was to wait patiently in the throne room so no one would accuse her.

Once Leoné was out of the picture, she would finally be able to open the gates. She would finally be able to collect the energy she needed to save Carthel and together, take over Astenpoole to prepare themselves for Emilia.

She glanced over at the sphere. It was glowing a bright yellow. Nadia couldn't remember the last time it glowed that bright; it must have been before Emilia destroyed the temple.

It still wasn't enough energy, however. She needed more for her plan to work. She had never tried anything like this before, and she had waited far too long for this to fail.

Nadia let her mind wander back in time as she waited. She couldn't believe how long it had been. Eighteen years. Eighteen years since the battle at Bellow Hill, when Emilia had attacked the castle and ruined everything. She remembered it perfectly, as if it had happened yesterday. Nadia had been waiting patiently in the throne room during the battle. Just like she was doing right now. Except she hadn't been alone then. No. She had had her son with her, her beautiful boy who was only a few months old. She remembered comforting him, rubbing his thin, black hair on his little head. He smiled up at her with gums as pink as lilies.

Her mother had been there with her, too.

Far off explosions from the battle shook the throne room. She could tell they were losing as the explosions grew louder and louder as the night carried on. She remembered crying. She had been afraid of losing Carthel, of losing her only child, of losing her life and family.

They were fighting Emilia and her army. Emilia was too dangerous—she couldn't control her powers. But Carthel believed he could help her.

As the battle continued and the hours flew by, Nadia had seen something glowing in the corner of her eye. She had lifted her head from her smiling baby and looked over at her staff, which was leaning against the armrest of the chair. The glass sphere on top of her staff had been glowing, but it wasn't glowing yellow like it normally did—no, it was glowing black. Nadia had never seen it glow black before.

Giving her baby to her mother, Nadia had reached over for her staff and held it in front of her. She had looked deep into the glass.

She remembered the energy she had felt. It was nothing she had ever felt before. She saw images inside the glass. A baby's face covered the sphere. He was smiling up towards the ceiling. But as the image inside the glass zoomed out, she saw a man and a woman staring down happily at the baby in the woman's arms. *Partha*. She remembered how far her heart had dropped when she realized who they were. The image had faded. A crow had appeared in the glass now, lying helplessly on the ground. The crow had faded into darkness and words had suddenly appeared across the glass—a prophecy. She remembered the words perfectly as if they were engraved inside her—

CRASH.

The door to the throne room slammed open. Nadia came back to reality. Her head shot up. Four knights walked towards her. Their footsteps tapped against the marble flooring. Their armor glistened off the sunlight from the window. They knelt before her.

"Sir Piller, Sir Hollow, Sir Arnold, and Sir Devan. What do I owe this pleasant acquaintance?" Nadia asked, trying to sound surprised. But she already knew why they had come.

"Your Grace," Piller stood up. The others followed him. "I have grave news." The scar across his face moved like a wave as he talked.

"What is it, Sir Piller? Tell me."

"The king, your husband, is dead, Your Grace." Piller was looking up into her eyes. "He was murdered."

The other three knights hung their heads in sadness.

Dead, thought Nadia. *He's dead! Leoné is finally dead!*

As these joyous words rang through her head, she kept her composure. She had to use these knights as her pawns. She needed them to trust her.

"My husband? Murdered? Is this some sick joke?" She jumped out of the Wave. She grabbed her staff that she had placed against the armrest of the chair. She walked down the grand steps, her staff echoing against the marble floor. She stood before Piller and the knights.

"I'm sorry to inform you of this treacherous news, Your Grace. But it is *not* a joke. We have captured the one responsible. A boy, Your Grace. It was just a boy." Piller lowered his head. "He poisoned the king's wine," he handed a bottle to her. "We've placed him in a cell, but have not begun to question him yet. We wanted to speak with you first, Your Grace."

Nadia already knew who the boy was. She took the bottle and examined it. The label on it read: *Palor Red. The wine of Astenpoole. Grapes harvested fresh from the backyard of the Grent family.*

"Who was supposed to be guarding him?" She was proud at how angry she sounded. She thrust the bottle back to Piller.

"It was me, Your Grace." Devan stepped forward. "I have failed you. I have failed my king." He hung his head in shame. "The boy found a secret passageway into the king's chamber, Your Grace."

"A secret passageway?" she tried her best to sound confused. But she already knew about the passageways. Carthel had informed her of it previously.

"Yes, Your Grace," Piller spoke now. "We have men searching them as we speak. We've gone through his bag, and it seems that the boy had a map of the castle."

She pretended to think this over for a few seconds. "A map, you say?" She already knew about the map. "This was beyond you, Sir Devan. I do not hold you accountable for this." She put a hand on his shoulder.

"Thank you, Your Grace. You are most kind." He smiled, but it looked foolish against his sad, red eyes.

She looked at the knights. She needed them dispersed for what was about to happen. "Sir Devan."

"Yes, Your Grace?"

"I need you to stand guard outside the boy's cell. No one speaks to him unless I know about it first. Is that clear?" *That should keep him busy.*

Devan smiled at this. He seemed to find honor in this job. "Yes, Your Grace. As you command."

"Good," She turned to Piller and his squires. "I need you three to go find Alana. She needs to be sent to her bedchamber at once, and remain there. Her life could be in danger, and she will be miserable once she finds out about her father. She won't be fit to rule—especially with what's going on. I will act as queen until all this chaos has passed and Alana is older."

The knights looked at each other, surprise showing on their faces.

Nadia continued. "Tell Sir Benjamin I want him outside of Alana's door day and night. No one enters or leaves her room without informing me. She speaks to no one. Is that clear?"

The princess was her only threat. She couldn't have Alana ruin her plans. "Make sure she does not escape this time."

"Yes, Your Grace." They all said.

"Please leave me so I can mourn my husband in peace. Now." She looked at each of the knights, her gaze steady.

The knights turned to walk out of the throne room.

"Sir Piller," she called out. "One moment please."

Piller told his knights he would catch up with them outside. He walked back up to her. "Yes, Your Grace?"

"I need a favor from you," she stated.

"Of course, Your Grace. I am yours to command." He took honor in that. Nadia respected him.

She walked back up to the Wave and took a seat. She rubbed her hand on the sphere as if petting it. She wanted to feel the energy within it. "There will come a time, not too far from now, when we'll need to open the gates."

"The gates, Your Grace?" he repeated, sounding idiotic.

"Yes, the gates. We have to investigate the attack outside the Western Gate. If there are any survivors, we need to save them. To help them."

"But, the Hoarders—"

"Isn't this what you've wanted?" she smiled at him. "King Leoné has trapped us inside here for far too long. It's time to take action and help the survivors outside the wall, along with the people trapped inside!"

Piller hesitated for a second, as if there was actually something to consider. He then looked up at her. "Yes. I agree. We must save the kingdom."

"We *will* save the kingdom, Sir Piller. But we'll first need to open the gates to investigate the attack that occurred just outside the wall." She knew Piller would like that plan.

"As you say, Your Grace." He continued to look at her. "But what about the Hoarders?" he asked again.

"I'll take care of the Hoarders," she responded, giving him a trusting smile.

"As you say, Your Grace."

"That is all." She waved him away.

After he left, she let out a long, happy sigh. She sat back onto the large wave of the chair, relaxing. It was all happening perfectly. Soon the gate would be opened, she would get enough energy to save Carthel, and finally find a use for the boy. She had been waiting for him to come of age all these years. Just as part of the prophecy had said...*the energy will flow within his palms of light, when his eighteenth moon rises full in the night.* She and Carthel would rule Astenpoole, and when Emilia came for them again, there would be nothing she could do to stop them.

A yellow light caught her attention; her sphere was glowing again. She smiled as new energy flowed within the glass.

Suddenly, she heard a gust of wind from a window to her far right. Something landed on the armchair next to her.

"It's done, Nadia. The king is dead and the boy has been captured. We'll soon have enough energy so we can be together again."

"It's been too long, Carthel. Too many years have passed where I've not felt the touch of your lips." She stroked Carthel's feathery head as he looked up at her with those black, beady eyes. "I will have my king back soon."

Chapter 28
Alana

ALANA WAS IN the courtyard, sitting at her favorite spot near the fountain. The water was roaring out of Zalus's palms, crashing down like a waterfall. The mist felt nice against her face. She watched the fish nibbling at the surface. She was alone with her thoughts about her mother, and the night with Jahrys under the stars.

She wasn't completely alone, though. Benjamin was not far off in the distance, watching her. She would have much rather been left alone, but she didn't mind Benjamin. He was handsome and pleasant to talk with. Sometimes she even pitied him. While his brothers were doing knightly tasks, he was stuck babysitting a girl of seventeen.

She knew Benjamin found enjoyment teaching her how to fight. Ever since her father had given her her new sword, her skills had improved tremendously.

She was excited to practice with Benjamin again later that day.

Alana rolled up the sleeves of her silk dress and twirled her right index finger in the glass-like water. The fish swam up to her finger with curious mouths, but they kept their distance. She wondered what they were thinking. If they suffered from pain like she did.

"Princess Alana," it was Sir Piller who crossed the yard towards her. He would have been a good-looking man if it wasn't for the terrible scar that stared Alana in the face every time she looked at him. He was only thirty-seven, but the scar made him look much older. The young knights, Hollow and Arnold, followed close behind him as they approached her by the fountain. Benjamin walked over to join them. Piller's face looked like he had just heard terrible news.

Piller bent down on one knee. The two young knights followed like two school boys. "Princess Alana, we have some…" he paused and looked at his other two companions and then at Benjamin. "We have some rather upsetting news to inform you of."

Alana took her finger out of the water. She looked over at Piller, Hollow, Arnold, and Benjamin. Her heart was sinking deep into her stomach. She knew this couldn't be good.

"Sir Piller, Sir Hollow, Sir Arnold, what a pleasant surprise. What grave news have you brought me?" Alana did not like the look in their eyes. She saw sadness and pity, and, perhaps fear? *What has happened?*

Piller took a step towards her. His armor glistened as he placed a hand on her shoulder. He didn't smile. His eyes looked glassy. "My princess. Your father, is…" he was struggling to finish. He turned his head away from her.

"My father is what, Sir Piller?" Alana could feel her stomach sink lower, but she did not let her eyes leave his face.

Piller turned back to her. "Your father is dead, Alana." Piller's eyes broke as they fell to the ground. "He has been murdered."

Junkland

Alana felt like she was going to throw up. She placed a hand on her mouth and a hand over her chest. Her head spun as tears poured down her face. She couldn't believe what she had just heard. *No. Father cannot be dead. It isn't possible. He's the king and kings are strong and immortal! Just like all the stories.* She could feel her hands start to tremble. *I have no one now. My family is gone.* She let her head fall into her hands as she sobbed.

Piller got up from his knee and sat next to her on the fountain. He leaned her head onto his armor, trying to comfort her.

"I'm sorry, Alana. Your father was a great man, and he loved you and your mother very much." He took a deep breath. "We have caught the boy who did it."

Alana raised her head. Her eyes were red. She choked. "Who?" It was all she could manage to say through the pain of losing her father.

"Devan and I are planning to question the boy once you are safe within your bedchamber. We *will* find out everything we need to know about him—I promise."

She stood up. "I must see him at once, Sir Piller," she demanded. She had to see for herself who her father's murderer was.

"I'm sorry, but it's my orders to take you straight to your bedchamber for your protection. We believe your life is in danger, as well."

"Orders? Whose orders are you following?"

"Your mother's orders, my lady."

"My mother? My mother is dead!"

"Queen Nadia, my princess."

"SHE IS NOT MY MOTHER." Alana screamed. Her voice echoed throughout the courtyard. "If my father is truly dead, then I am now Queen of Astenpoole. Nadia has no power over me—or you. She's nothing but a dowager queen."

"That is true, my princess—I mean, Your Grace, but Nadia's still your guardian, at least until your next birthday, and she does not seem to think you are ready to rule in this state of mind. You need rest. We're unsure if the boy was working alone, or if there's another murderer roaming around the castle. We must take precautions."

"I am not a baby, Sir Piller," Alana had snapped. "I'm the Queen of Astenpoole. There have been younger rulers before! Isabella Danor was only sixteen when she became queen!" She never thought she would hear herself say those words. She never wanted to be queen. But she would not let Nadia keep a title that didn't belong to her.

The knights glanced at each other. They weren't sure what to do.

"I didn't mean to offend you," Sir Piller said quietly. "But Nadia is right. She will act as the regent while you rest in your bedchamber."

"As a prisoner? For how long!"

"Please, Alana, don't make this harder than it must. Your life is in danger. I need to bring you to your bedchamber to know you're safe. Please..." Piller stood up and had offered his hand to her.

She looked to Benjamin for help, but he was speechless. She was furious. *I'm the true Queen of Astenpoole!* But she didn't see any other choice. They were not going to listen to her. Alana let her head fall, but before taking Sir Piller's hand, said, "The people will not like this. I'm the true heir to the throne." She grabbed Sir Piller's hand tightly, but there was a dark look in her eyes.

"You're making the right choice," Piller assured her, helping her to her feet. But there was doubt in his eyes. "Benjamin, see that

Alana gets back to her bedchamber safely. Guard her door and do not let anyone in or out without running it by me first. Is that clear?"

"Yes, Captain." Benjamin had turned to Alana. "Come with me, my princess. I will keep you safe." Benjamin had offered his right arm to Alana.

"You mean queen." She muttered before taking his arm.

Benjamin guided her across the courtyard, through the Village, and up the spiral staircase to her bedchamber at the top of the tower. He opened the door for her and laid out his arm for her to walk inside.

Alana turned to face Benjamin. "We'll sneak away like we always do, right Benjamin? We'll still continue to practice?" She just wanted to forget the pain.

Benjamin shook his head in disappointment. "I'm sorry, my lady, but not this time. Things are serious now."

Alana tried to hold back angry tears as her lips trembled. She began to sob. "Nadia is keeping me a prisoner! Can't you see that? Please...I don't want to be left alone."

Benjamin walked into her room and placed a muscular arm around her. "I won't let anything happen to you. I promise. I'll be right outside your door. You need to get some rest."

Alana nodded. She did not feel well. Her head was spinning. She wanted to lie down and forget the world, forget the fact that she was now an orphan.

Benjamin guided her to her bed, and once she was settled, he walked back towards the door.

Alana watched him close it and heard a loud click as he locked the door from the outside.

She was locked inside her room with no way to escape.

Chapter 29
Jahrys

HE WAS BACK at the Sandy Shore, swimming below the tall, rocky walls of the cliff. It was sunny—a beautiful day. The water was a refreshing escape from the humidity and blaring sun.

He was racing Kevrin. They wanted to see who could swim to the large rock out beyond the waves and back to the shore the fastest. Jahrys crashed through the waves, extending both arms and kicking as hard as he could. He was getting tired, and quickly fell far behind Kevrin, who was already on his way back to the beach. Jahrys tried to quicken his pace. He was never the best swimmer. He finally reached the large rock, touched it, and turned back to shore. He was aided by the waves, but it was too late. Kevrin had already won.

When their race ended, they sat on the beach next to Jahrys's mother. She looked beautiful lying in the sun. Her hair was blowing behind her in the gentle wind. Her pale skin glistened in the sunlight.

They were all watching Jahrys's father, who was fighting with his fishing pole by the water. He looked like he was having a spasm in his lower back.

Junkland

"Darn fish!" his father yelled. "Zalus give me strength..." The fishing pole was bent in a large arc in the air. The fish gave a giant tug, and his father flew face first into the water. He came up empty handed, spitting out the salt water he swallowed.

Jahrys, his mother, and Kevrin couldn't help but laugh.

After they recovered, Jahrys noticed someone walking in the distance to his right. It was a woman. He could make out her shapely hips and her shiny, brown hair, which glistened in the sunlight. Her skin was lightly tanned, and Jahrys could see her smile from a mile away. It was her: Alana Poole.

He jumped to his feet, wiping the sand off his hands, and began walking towards her. It was like a fairy tale when two lovers run towards each other on the beach, with waves crashing on the shore, running over their toes and splashing their ankles. When they finally met in each other's arms they would fall into the sand together. Just like the stories about Galagar Poole and Isabella Danor.

This was kind of like that. His heart was pounding in his chest. He began to pick up the pace. He had to have her, to hold her, to be with her, to tell her how he felt.

Alana began to run towards him. The distance, which had felt endless, was starting to close between them. They were so close.

But when they were only feet away, the earth began to shake. It felt like an earthquake. There was a loud rumbling sound. The ground beneath Jahrys's feet began to break away. He stopped short at the edge of the crack that divided him from Alana. The shaking made him lose his balance and fall backwards. Alana was on the other side, calling out to him.

The earth had come alive all around them. The world went dark as the beautiful day turned into a nightmare. Cracks sprang from the ocean, causing the water to fall into them—filling the darkness.

He turned back towards his mother, father, and Kevrin. They were all hanging onto the edge of a crevice that went deep within the earth, their legs dangling down. He watched them fall one by one into the darkness.

"Jahrys!" Jahrys turned back to Alana. "Jahrys, help me!"

Alana was hanging onto the edge of another deep crack within the earth. Something dark had climbed out of the darkness and grabbed her leg, pulling her downwards. It looked like a man, but it was if he was made of ash.

Jahrys had to do something. He studied the distance to the other side. Jahrys got his footing down, and ran towards the crack. When he got to the edge, he leapt forward. He was inches away—but fell short.

And fell into darkness.

When he woke, he found himself hanging against a hard wall. His back was stiff and aching. His arms were chained above his head. The metal was digging deep into his wrists, cutting him, causing blood to trickle down his forearms. He could feel his fingertips tingling as the blood flowed out of his hands, down towards the ground. His feet were barely touching the cold, wet stone. His breaths were short and raspy. He let out a frightening cough; it sounded like his insides were trying to force their way out. But it was only bile he threw up onto the dark stone floor beneath him. His stomach was growling.

How long have I been hanging here? Jahrys thought. He tried to remember all he could, but his head hurt and his memory was vague. He remembered the king's last words, the wine-stained carpet, being dragged out of the room, and the crow in the window—the same crow he had seen after his parents had died. He was sure of it.

The dripping water in the corner of his cell was slow and repetitive. He occasionally heard footsteps. It was the only thing giving him hope—that there were people out there.

Drip, Drip, Drip.

The sound continued.

It was cold, but Jahrys was covered in sweat, making him shiver. The air smelled of urine, sweat, and fear. He heard moans and yells of terror from outside his cell. There must be other prisoners out there.

He heard the footsteps again. They were getting closer. Hope returned to Jahrys—maybe it was Alana!

But when the door opened, it wasn't Alana. A knight with a long-jagged scar appeared. Jahrys knew who it was immediately. He raised his head to get a better look at the knight he so admired: Sir Piller Lorne.

An older knight with brown-graying hair and a thick beard followed him in. Jahrys knew him to be Sir Devan Lark. He was holding Jahrys's bag; they had taken it from him.

They stared at him as if he was a creature they had never seen before.

"What is your name?" Piller asked him, his voice echoing off the walls of the small cell.

"My name's Jahrys Grent. I'm a Retriever from outside the wall," Jahrys replied. His voice sounded hoarse and drier than his skin felt.

"Grent…Grent…where have I heard that name before?" Piller thought out loud as he looked over at Devan while rubbing his chin with his thumb and index finger.

"Ah!" Piller snapped his fingers. "Your father must be Alvys

Grent, the inventor of Grent Wine?"

Jahrys nodded. He no longer knew if he was proud of that or not.

"So that explains where he got the wine bottle," Devan grunted.

"I didn't poison the king!" Jahrys defended himself.

"No?" Devan's dark eyes studied him. "Then who did?"

"I don't know," he admitted. "I was set up."

Devan grunted.

"Tell us everything," Piller demanded.

Jahrys told the two knights everything about the job the old lady had given him. He told them about his trip into the Junkland with his friend Kevrin. He told them about the wine bottles and what he had found when he arrived back at The Arcalane—Piller's face twitched when Jahrys mentioned The Arcalane and his dead friends—Jahrys told them about his trip into Astenpoole, how he had used the maps to get in. He finished with his conversation with the king before he had died.

"That's an interesting story," Piller said, thinking it over.

"It's the truth," Jahrys said, defending himself again. "Check my bag. You'll find the maps inside there."

Piller nodded towards Devan, who was still holding Jahrys's bag. Devan fumbled through it until he pulled out the diary, filled with loose pieces of paper. Devan opened it and shuffled through the papers until he found the maps. Piller and Devan analyzed them.

"How did you come across this?" Piller asked in concern.

"It's Princess Alana's."

"You mean to tell me that the princess drew all of these maps?" Devan was in disbelief.

"Yes."

"That's utterly ridiculous," Devan grunted.

"It's true. You need to go and ask her. She knows who I am." Jahrys tried to explain.

"Unfortunately, Alana is locked away in her tower," Piller sighed.

"Locked away?" Jahrys didn't know what to make of that.

"We're afraid her life is in danger, and didn't know if you were working alone or not. But if what you say is true, then her life could very well still be in danger." Piller replied.

"Please! I must speak with her."

"That is out of the question for now. We'll get to the bottom of this, Jahrys. If all you said is true, we will get you out of here. We'll figure out who has plotted against the king." Piller gave him a reassuring smile.

Devan only rolled his eyes.

"Can you get me out of here? Now?" Jahrys pleaded. He didn't want to spend more time down in this cell. He had to get to Alana.

"I'm afraid I can't do that just yet," Piller admitted. "You are to remain here until this matter's settled."

Jahrys hung his head in disappointment. *This isn't right!*

Piller unhooked a key from his belt and undid the chains that held Jahrys's hands. He helped Jahrys back down to his feet.

"Thank you," Jahrys said, as he rubbed his raw wrists.

Piller nodded. "I'll return when I figure this out."

Jahrys looked over at the bag that Devan was holding. "There's a necklace in the bag. Please, can I have it?"

Piller looked back at Devan. Devan did not move a muscle.

"So you can use it to escape?" Devan spat.

"No. I promise. It's just a necklace! It reminds me of my mother," Jahrys lied. "I was with her as she was dying during the

Hoarding, and she had given me that necklace right before she died." Jahrys teared up.

Piller nodded at Devan. Devan groaned and dug his hand back into the bag, pulling out the blue necklace. He handed it over.

Jahrys grabbed it with a trembling hand and held it close to his heart. "Thank you."

Piller gave him another pat on the shoulder and turned to leave the room.

Devan studied him one more time before he turned and followed Piller out the cell door.

The door shut, and Jahrys was left alone in the darkness with the necklace in his hand.

Chapter 30
Piller

THE DESOLATE STREETS sent a chill down Piller's spine. Five days had passed since the king's death. Nadia had ordered everyone to clear the streets and to stay inside. There was no music, no laughter, no haggling; just silence as they walked down Pooles Road.

They had locked Alana inside her tower for her protection, but the princess had not been pleased. Piller was doing it for her own good; her life could still be in danger. Though, he did not feel good about it.

They had finally figured out the boy's name. Jahrys Grent, the son of Alvys Grent, had claimed he did not kill the king, that he was supposedly set up.

Piller believed the boy was telling the truth, but he couldn't fit any of the pieces together. He couldn't figure out who wanted Leoné dead. He needed to figure it out soon, before the boy rotted in his cell for a crime he possibly did not commit.

Nadia walked in front of him, a crow sitting on her left shoulder, her staff in her right hand. She had on a black dress with a black shawl draped around her shoulders. Her hips swayed with purpose as Piller, Arnold, and Hollow followed closely behind. They were dressed in their blue armor, the crest of Astenpoole on their breastplates, swords ready at the hip. They all walked towards the closed Western Gate.

"What are we doing here?" whispered Arnold. "This doesn't feel right."

"I agree, Cap'," Hollow kept his voice down so Nadia couldn't hear.

Piller didn't take his eyes off Nadia's back when he spoke. "The other day you guys were talking about over throwing my orders about keeping the gates closed."

"But that was different," Arnold said. "This isn't what the king wanted and it's disrespectful so soon after his death. We should have talked about this. And something doesn't feel right about *her*." Arnold nodded towards Nadia.

"I feel the same as you, but we must do our duty as Knights of the Poolesguard," Piller said. "Nadia is the queen for now, until we're certain Alana's life isn't in danger."

Hollow and Arnold exchanged worried looks.

"We're with you no matter what, Captain," said Arnold.

"Just be on your guard and follow my commands," Piller nodded to the two young knights.

"As always, Captain," Hollow said.

They are good lads, thought Piller, as he continued to march down the cobblestone road. *They've been through more than I ever have in my years of service. May Zalus watch over us today.*

A heavy fog hung low in the air. There was a cold breeze that carried the stench from the Junkland, along with paper and other light objects. The shops around them were deserted. Piller noticed eyes watching them curiously from the windows above their heads. Whenever he made eye contact, the eyes would disappear.

They were nearing the Western Gate now. The king had commanded them to shut the gates three years ago and now they were to be re-opened. *But what had been right about closing the gates?* thought Piller, as his thoughts traveled back in time to the Hoarding.

He remembered the screams, the pleas for help. They were yelling out to him, to his brothers, to the men who were supposed to protect them, begging for help. He remembered Landerin Raneir, banging on the gates as they closed upon him, trapping him outside. He remembered the look Landerin gave him—a look of pure hatred. But what did he do? Nothing. He had shut them all out and left them to die.

But now they were going to open the gates. *Will this make up for all of those deaths?* Piller tried to find clarity, but there was a cold shiver running through his bones.

As they marched in silence, Piller's thoughts drifted towards Jahrys. The boy said he knew Alana, but the princess—the true queen—was locked away, and no one was allowed to speak to her. *After the survivors are taken care of, I'll go speak to Alana. I must find out the truth.*

They arrived at the Western Gate. The giant oak doors stood before them, at least twenty feet high. Ten people could stand arm's length away from each other and still fit between them. That is, when they were open.

Piller's head began to spin. Was this the right thing to do? Wasn't there a reason King Leoné had closed the gates in the first place? Was Arnold right? Was this disrespectful to the memory of their king?

But isn't this what he wanted? To re-open the gates and save the people left outside the walls? All his training, all his years of experience, did not prepare him for this. He started to doubt his knighthood. Wasn't knowing right from wrong part of being a good knight? Why was he stuck in between? He felt his clothes underneath his armor start to dampen. Sweat rolled into his eyes, but he couldn't wipe it through his helmet. What would the previous Captains of the Poolesguard do? Would Letholdus Quinn know what to do in this situation? Would he be doubting himself?

Nadia turned, facing the knights. Her staff popped as it hit the cobblestone. The crow cawed on her shoulder. It stared at them with its small, beady, black eyes. Nadia had a strange look on her face—a dark look.

"Sir Piller." Her voice was sweet. She called him like a puppy.

"Yes, Your Grace?" he stepped forward. He could feel the tension between his two brothers behind him. They were scared. So was he.

"Sir Piller...command your guards on the wall to open these gates." She pointed her staff to the guards looking down at them.

Piller looked up to see Krist and Martellus peering down. They were far away, but he could tell from their posture that they were scared.

Nadia noticed this as well.

"It's normal to be scared, Sir Piller. I, too, am afraid. But we need to do what must be done. We need to save our people. Do you not trust me?" she cocked her head.

Is she testing me? thought Piller. "It's not that we don't trust you, Your—"

"Then what is it?" she snapped at him.

"This is wrong!" yelled Arnold from behind. "I know we wanted these gates opened for the longest time, but we should respect King Leoné's wishes. It's too soon after his death. We should take time to discuss this."

Nadia glared at the young knight. "Well at least you're honest. But you're not fit to make commands here. Do you boys want to one day command the Poolesguard?"

Arnold and Hollow stared blankly at each other.

"Yes," said Arnold.

"Yes, we do," Hollow agreed.

"Well then step forward. Kneel before me." She waved a hand before her feet.

The two brothers awkwardly approached her and slowly kneeled.

"Your little Princess Alana is not fit to rule, so I am in command. So tell me, who do you take orders from?" she asked them, leaning against her staff.

"You," they replied in unison.

"Yes. Good. And what happens when I give an order?"

"We obey."

"Very good! You guys are fast learners," she smiled, both hands gripping the staff. The crow cawed on her shoulder. "Now here is an easy command. Let's see if you boys have learned something today. You will stay on your knees until I say you can rise." Her voice was light and harmless.

"As you command, Your Grace," Arnold and Hollow said. The knights lowered their heads in shame as they continued to kneel.

Piller did not like how she was treating his knights.

"You can't—"

"I am in command here, Sir Piller, and you are a knight who takes orders. Now why haven't you ordered your men to open this gate? You don't want anything to happen to your boys now, do you?" Nadia gave him a dark smile as she pushed the sphere against Arnold's chest. The yellow light inside the sphere began to glow brighter, illuminating Arnold's armor.

Arnold began to shake.

A chill ran down Piller's spine. "Don't!"

His hand went to his sword hilt. Piller never liked that sphere on top of Nadia's staff. He had always tried to believe it was just some strange fashion used in Farrest, but here was proof it was something more. Something magical.

"Then do as I command," she said, keeping her staff pointed at Arnold.

Piller let out a long breathe. He looked up at Krist and Martellus, who were still peering down at them.

"OPEN THE GATES!" he yelled up to them.

Krist and Martellus both exchanged a worried look. They looked back down.

"AS YOU COMMAND CAPTAIN!" Krist yelled back down.

The last word didn't sit well with Piller.

Krist and Martellus disappeared behind the wall. Moments later, there was a loud thump.

The gate doors rotated inwards. The metal bars across them broke, and there was screeching from the rust that had eaten away at the metal for the past three years. It sounded like thunder and lightning. Inch by inch the doors opened.

Piller's heart sank lower as the doors widened until—

BANG.

The two doors came to a halt. The opening was cloudy from the dust and fog that had accumulated in the air. Piller could not see past the gates.

Nadia stared happily into the opening. They waited for her reaction. She was still pointing her staff at Arnold's chest.

After the minutes ticked away, Piller heard something through the fog.

Crunch, Crunch, Crunch.

Piller tightened his grip on his hilt.

Crunch, Crunch, Crunch.

He thought he glimpsed something yellow.

"Captain! Look out!" Hollow cried out, but he remained on his knees alongside his brother.

Crunch, Crunch, Crunch.

Piller unsheathed his sword.

A Hoarder appeared through the fog. Not one, but two. Then another and another until Piller lost count. Dozens of Hoarders were coming through the gates.

"Your Grace?" Piller was waiting for her command. The Hoarders were marching towards them. Nadia's expression did not change. She did not move the sphere.

The yellow army stopped. One of the Hoarders stepped forward, standing directly in front of Piller.

"Put him in the dungeon," she commanded.

"Yes, Your Grace," said Piller, relieved she was finally acting.

Piller walked over to the Hoarder. But before he could act, the Hoarder stepped behind Piller and thrust a boot hard into his back. Piller went face first into the cobblestone.

Arnold and Hollow started to rise to help their captain.

"Stay where you are!" Nadia yelled at them, keeping her staff pointed in their direction.

"Your Grace?" Piller's helmet had popped off. He coughed up blood. He turned to look up at her. He spat. "What..."

Nadia stared down at him. The crow on her shoulder flapped its wings and cawed. The Hoarder lifted Piller to his knees. He was now facing his two brothers. They looked at each other with frightened eyes.

Nadia gave a nod to the Hoarders behind Piller. They walked around to stand behind Arnold and Hollow. The young knights were afraid, as was Piller.

The Hoarders raised their Captors. They pointed them at Arnold and Hollow.

"No!" Piller pleaded. "You said you would take care of the Hoarders?"

"I *am* taking care of the Hoarders, Sir Piller." She smiled as she looked at the yellow cloud floating in her sphere. "I needed the gates opened, and you know how cautious Leoné was. I needed him out of the picture."

"*You* killed the king?" Piller's head was spinning.

"I didn't kill him, but I did have something to do with it," she smiled again.

"Why? What are you trying to do?" Piller didn't understand any of it.

Nadia walked over to Piller and crouched low, so she was face-to-face with him. "My life, Sir Piller. I'm trying to get back my life." She rose back up and walked over to Arnold and Hollow, petting their heads. She nodded to the Hoarders next to her.

Arnold was shaking uncontrollably and Hollow had tears rolling down his face.

Piller reached a hand out towards his two brothers. "NO! PLEASE! LEAVE THEM AL—"

Two yellow blasts shot out before he could finish begging for their lives. Both Arnold and Hollow screamed in terror as they fell forward. Their screams echoed throughout Astenpoole. They landed with a chilling thump on the cobblestone. Blood filled the cracks of the road.

"No." Piller's voice was lifeless as he looked at his two brothers, now lying motionless in front of him.

The Hoarders kept their Captors raised. A deep, low hum gradually filled the air. The ground began to shake under Piller. A yellow beam shot out from each weapon.

VHRUUUUMMMM.

The light blinded Piller's eyes. He looked away. When the light disappeared and he regained his vision, he turned back to find the bodies of his two brothers were gone.

Nadia stood over him, her crow cawing.

Piller's eyes were frozen on the spot where his two friends had just been.

"I'm sorry, Sir Piller, but their lives were needed." She turned to the Hoarders behind her. "Take him to the dungeon along with the rest of the Poolesguard."

"Yes, Mother," the Hoarder in front replied.

Piller was dragged away as he watched Nadia's sphere glow even brighter.

Chapter 31
Alana

THE STONEWORK SPIRALED above her head. Alana was lying on her bed, following the pattern with her eyes. They swirled up to a single point at the tip of the tower. She started to count the stones as she lay there, twirling a piece of her hair in her fingers. But the counting didn't take her away from her racing thoughts about the death of her father, and about her mother—her real mother. It also didn't take her anger away from Nadia, who had her locked away in her bedchamber. *I need to take my rightful spot as queen before she corrupts everyone.* But she was trapped, no different than the prisoners in the dungeons below.

Her room was located in the High Tower, just north of the King's Tower. The window across from her bed overlooked the courtyard below her room. It provided a pleasant view of the large Fountain of Zalus. Her bed was next to another window that looked out over the armory and the training grounds. On some days, when there wasn't a cloud in the sky, she could see the highest peak of the Western Mountains. But ever since the Hoarding, that sight had been destroyed by the endless gray sky.

A round white rug filled the center of the room. There was a dresser next to the door that had her jewelry box sitting on top. The bookcase sat next to her bed, across from the large walk-in-closet. The closet was filled with all of her clothes and shoes, along with a secret box she kept hidden under the floorboard.

Paintings hung all around her room. Paintings of legendary knights that little girls dreamed and giggled about, like Galagar Poole, saving Princess Isabella from menacing outlaws. There was Letholdus Quinn, the first Captain of the Poolesguard, and the romantic Palor A'kal, saying goodbye to his stepsister, Melaine Danor, below the Western Mountains. But Alana was no longer a little girl and didn't fantasize about those knights anymore.

She contemplated escaping, but she didn't know how. Her father had boarded up the secret passageway behind her bookcase years ago. And Nadia had ordered her to be locked inside her bedchamber, so she couldn't even get down to the library beneath her room where the other secret passageway was.

Just when her father had acknowledged he was wrong for keeping her locked away, Nadia had her locked up. And she hadn't even come to see her since her father had died.

She was trapped. All she could do was pass the time on her bed, staring at the ceiling and thinking.

She lost count of the days she had been confined to her bedchamber. No one came to visit her except for Benjamin. Mother Claraine wasn't even allowed to visit her anymore. Alana was beginning to miss her and her handmaids. For some reason, she missed their snarky comments about how unkempt her body was.

Knock. Knock. Knock.

Alana's heart jumped at the sudden noise. She jumped out of her bed and hurried to the door, waiting for him to unlock it. The door flew open.

"Sir Benjamin!" She was excited to see him. She needed someone to talk to.

"My princess. I've brought you something to eat." Benjamin walked into her room with a plate of chicken, roasted vegetables, and some bread. He had been bringing food to her, but he didn't speak much. He had been ordered to keep his conversations quick and simple.

"What happened to the boy?" she asked him once again. "Have you found out his name?"

"I'm sorry, Princess. I'm not allowed to tell you. I would if I could." Benjamin placed the plate down on a table against the wall.

"You're not allowed to tell me? What are you talking about! I am the true Queen of Astenpoole!" Alana still felt weird saying those words. "You *must* tell me! Nadia has no right to such commands!"

Benjamin only gave her a pitiful look. "I'm sorry, Alana."

"Please, I *must* see him for myself. I want to know who killed my father."

Benjamin sighed. "I'll tell you his name, but nothing more. I cannot disobey my orders."

"You disobeyed your orders every time you snuck away to practice sword fighting with me." Alana was frustrated. "How's this any different?"

"This is different because your life is in danger!" Benjamin raised his voice.

Alana sighed. She didn't feel like arguing anymore. "What's his name?"

Junkland

"His name's Jahrys Grent. Now please, eat and get some rest." Benjamin marched out of the room, shutting the door behind him. There was a snap as Bejamin locked the door.

"Wait! Benjamin! You must tell me more!" Alana ran to the door and banged her fists against the wood. "Benjamin! Come back!" Alana screamed.

She moved back to her bed, her hunger forgotten. *Jahrys?* A wave of confusion washed over her. Was it her fault her father was dead? She couldn't find herself believing that Jahrys killed her father. It didn't make any sense. *How could he have done such a thing? And why?*

Days past, but the time felt endless inside her bedchamber; the minutes felt like hours, the hours felt like days, and the days felt like weeks.

Benjamin had never returned to her with more food and water; it had been days since she had eaten. She had taken to drinking from the basin, what was meant for hand washing. Without it, she probably would have died already, but she couldn't live off only water for much longer.

Alana's stomach was a hollow pit. *Where is Sir Benjamin?* She thought. She was getting worried. She was going to starve to death if he didn't return soon. She needed to find a way out, to save herself and to find out the truth about Jahrys.

Ding, Ding, Ding.

Alana sat up on her bed. She listened to the bells ringing outside her window, forgetting her empty stomach.

Ding, Ding, Ding.

There's going to be a city gathering which means—No! I need to get to him!

Alana jumped out of bed. She ran to the door, pounding it with her fists. She banged on the door violently. "Let me out! You must let me out!" She yelled, but no one replied.

After her fists were bright red and stinging, she stopped. She turned her back to the door and let her weight fall against it as she slid to the floor. She needed to get to the library. She needed a distraction. She needed to get out, but how?

Suddenly, she had an idea. Her gaze went to her closet across the room. She ran inside and pushed a dresser hidden in the back away from the wall. She got down on her knees, plunging her fingernails into the floorboard that was beneath it. She lifted it, and several dozen different knives and pieces of armor stared back at her. She slipped on her light elastic pants, her leather gauntlets and faded green vest, and her boots. She clipped on her belt and picked out two knives, one short, but very sharp, and the other a little longer, and just as sharp. She placed them in her belt.

She walked out of her closet and picked up her long sword that was leaning against the wall next to her bed inside its scabbard. Tears flowed down Alana's cheeks as she looked at the sword. *I will make you proud, Father.* She strapped the scabbard around her waist so the sword was on her left hip.

Alana threw a dark cloak over her shoulders and walked towards the locked door. She took one last look around her room before letting in a deep, deep breath.

"Helppppppp! Please! Someone helpppp!" she screamed at the top of her lungs.

She placed her ear against the door, but she didn't hear anything. No one was coming to her aid. She was about to scream one more time, but only tears came to her eyes; it was hopeless. Alana fell against the door, crying. She would never get to Jahrys in time. She would never find out the truth about her father's death. She would never be able to stop Nadia from stealing her title.

But then she heard a man's voice.

"...I know we aren't supposed to open her door! We'll just take a quick look inside to make sure everything's all right."

Alana pressed her back against the wall, inches from the door, waiting. She didn't expect there to be two people. Was Benjamin with someone? Regardless, if she kept them in the doorframe, she could take them one at a time.

It felt like an eternity as she waited for the slightest movement from the handle. She wasn't going to hurt Benjamin. She was just going to knock him out for a bit, long enough for her to escape through the tunnels. She was confident she could take him after spending so much time with him sword fighting.

As the door flung open, a man came flying in. Alana stuck out her foot and tripped him. He stumbled forward, but before he hit the floor, she flung her elbow straight into his back. The man slammed hard into the floor.

"Don't move!" another man yelled behind her.

Alana turned. A second man entered. She was face-to-face with him. He was pointing something at Alana's chest.

Alana recalled her lessons. *Breathe. Swing. Don't miss. Breathe. Swing. Don't miss.* She quickly reached out to grab his weapon and yanked it forward. The man stumbled into her room. She stiffened her leg behind the man, wrapped her arm around his chest, and rotated her body. The man went flying down on top of the first man.

She looked at both of them. They were wearing suits that glowed yellow with black belts and boots. They had helmets on also. *Where was Benjamin?* She thought.

She found keys hanging from the second man's belt. She grabbed them. Alana ran out the door, slammed it behind her and locked it. She ran for the stairs and made her way to the library beneath her room.

She had to get to Jahrys before it was too late.

Chapter 32
Jahrys

THERE WAS A woman. She was barefoot. Her feet looked torn up and bloody. She walked with a limp in her right leg. Blood was soaked through her ripped clothes, which hung in rags off of her body as if they were two times her size. She was skinny, too—terribly skinny. It looked like she hadn't eaten in days, weeks maybe. Her cheekbones were poking out of her skin. Her blonde hair was dirty, thin, and dry. She was carrying something. It was wrapped up in a blue blanket. She clutched it close to her chest. It looked like a baby. She was leaning on a staff she held with her right hand as she struggled to walk. A glass sphere glowed a faint blue at the top of her staff.

It was a silent night. Trees surrounded her. The woman limped down a steep slope, her feet crunching on fallen leaves. The path was not smooth; the ground was scattered with large, sharp rocks that looked like knives protruding from the earth.

She stumbled on a rock. She lost her balance and the baby went flying from her hands. The silent night was broken by the baby's cry.

The woman yelled as she crawled towards him. She dug her staff into the hard ground, trying to balance.

A howl echoed in the distance, bouncing off the mountain around her. The woman's face shot up. She looked frightened. She mustered her strength together and managed to half-limp, half-sprint towards her baby. She let out a yell from the pain as she scooped up her baby in her arm. She leaned all of her weight into her staff to rise up.

The howling grew louder. It was hard to tell which direction it was coming from—it seemed to be everywhere.

Another howl called back in the distance. Panic struck the woman's face. She looked left and right, searching. The baby continued to cry. The woman whispered, trying to comfort him.

HOWWWW. HOW, HOW, HOWOOOOO.

The crunching of leaves behind the woman startled her. She spun around. She was face-to-face with a large gray wolf, almost the size of a horse. She took a step back. There was another crunch behind her. She turned again. A second wolf appeared from the darkness of the trees. This one was even larger than the first wolf. A third wolf appeared, and another. She lost count. Dozens of glowing eyes surrounded her. There was nowhere to run. She clenched her baby close to her body with her left arm. Her right hand tightened around her staff.

The largest wolf stepped out from the circle, towards her. It bared its teeth, drool leaking from its mouth. The wolf was challenging her to make the first move, but she waited patiently. The sweat dripped down the woman's face. Her baby continued to cry.

The wolf sprung forward. The others followed, breaking the circle around her and her baby. The woman raised her staff high above her head and a flash of blue illuminated the night.

Jahrys shot up from the cold hard floor. He had had the dream again. Usually he could only remember screaming, but this time the dream was as vivid in his mind as his hands in front of him. Who was this woman he always dreamed about? And who was the baby she was carrying?

Jahrys grabbed the necklace that was lying on the stone floor next to where he was sleeping. He must have fallen asleep, and it fell from his hands. Jahrys traced the smooth edges of the gem. It was almost as blue as the light in his dream.

He didn't know how long he had been in the cell for. All he knew was that Sir Piller had abandoned him. He did not keep his word that he would return; if he had, he would have come already. They must suspect him of being the murderer and that his story was false. His life was over—they were going to kill him.

The only person that came to visit him was an old lady. She would enter with her hunched back, carrying a hot bowl of soup. There would be a few pieces of chicken, but other than that, it was mostly broth. Jahrys was always too hungry to care, though.

Countless times Jahrys would try to communicate with the old lady, asking where Piller was and if Alana was safe. But the old lady would never speak, nor would she even look at him.

She reminded Jahrys of the old lady from The Arcalane. The old lady who had given Jahrys the job. The old lady who had lied to him. But that night had been a blur to Jahrys, and he couldn't remember her features. Jahrys had tried to confront her about it, but she simply ignored him.

Jahrys wished he could erase it all. That he could be back in The Arcalane with Kevrin, Elyara, Willem, Miller, Gabe, Kat, and Tarl.

He even wished Rallick, Stade, and Tayger were there. But better yet, he wished he could go back to before the Hoarding, when all he and Kevrin would talk about was becoming Knights of the Poolesguard. Back when he believed knights were fearless and wise. Now he didn't know what to think. Sir Piller just seemed like a normal man: confused and scared.

Jahrys hung his head and thought about his parents. He missed his father talking about Grent Wine and Woodwork. He missed his mother giving him kisses on the forehead. He missed their bickering across the kitchen table. He missed Miller scurrying by his feet, pecking at him. He missed all the times they had shared in Palor, by the Sandy Shore, and together as a family. He couldn't ask for better, stronger parents.

Jahrys hung his head even lower. His father had never gotten a chance to live out his dream of being a sailor. He would never build his boat and sail across the Farrest Sea to distant lands, searching for adventure. *'Keep dreaming.'* His father's words rang through his head. *'The world needs people like you now more than ever. People who believe in themselves. Because when the world goes dark, the dreamers will be the ones who find the light.'*

But what do I believe in? thought Jahrys.

The cell door began to rattle across the room; someone was coming. Jahrys quickly slid the necklace into the pocket of his pants. The door flew open and there was the old lady, holding another bowl of steaming soup. But Jahrys didn't care about the food.

"I must speak with Alana." Jahrys pleaded as the old lady shuffled across the stone floor. The muscles in his throat clenched from hunger and pain. "Please!"

The old lady still didn't answer. She twirled the spoon in the soup, trying to cool it off. She slid the bowl towards him.

"Are you the one from The Arcalane? Are you the one who assigned me that job? Why did you lie to me?" Jahrys tried to make eye contact with her. But the old lady stood up, not even glancing at him.

"The king's dead because of you!" he yelled.

The old lady turned and walked towards the cell door.

"Please! I need answers! Where is Sir Piller Lorne?" Jahrys tried to rise to his feet, to run after the old lady, to shake the answers out of her. But when he tried to move, his legs were frozen. He could barely move. He must have been sleeping on them for too long. He could only watch as the old lady disappeared out of the room and slammed the door behind her.

Jahrys stumbled forward, his hands landing in the bowl of soup as it toppled over, spilling onto the stone floor. Steam rose into the air. Jahrys cursed. His stomach was rumbling as he sipped the remaining broth and ate the pieces of chicken off the floor. He let out a cough as the heat stung his dried throat.

Jahrys sat back, gripping the necklace, and continued with his thoughts about his dream in the darkness.

Drip, Drip, Drip.

The water continued to drip.

The door remained shut for the rest of the day. Jahrys's stomach felt like it was constricted in a tight knot; he was so hungry. His lips were dry and cracking and his throat was raw.

After Jahrys woke from another long sleep, the door opened again. Jahrys shot up, looking forward to the warm soup.

But it wasn't the old lady that came.

Three men marched across the stone floor over to Jahrys. The yellow glow of their suits reflected in the puddles of his cell. They were holding Captors that were attached by a tube to their Captor Packs.

Hoarders.

Chapter 33
Jahrys

BROKEN. *WHAT WAS* it like to be broken? To have a rope tied tightly around his neck? The rough edges biting deep into his skin? Was it the death of all his friends and family? Kevrin, Elyara, his mother and father. Was it the thought that he would never see Alana again? The fact that he had been so close to finally being with her. Yet, he felt further away from her than ever. Was it the fact that he had failed to save the kingdom? Or the thought of being betrayed and accused of something he did not do? Was that what it felt like to be broken?

Jahrys Grent contemplated this while he stood barefoot on the stage. The wood pressed hard against the balls of his feet. The rope around his neck pulled tightly against his Adam's apple. The Hoarder behind him held the end of the rope as if he was an animal. His clothes were glued to his body from the sweat. His hands were tied together in front of him.

The world felt like a daze around him, almost unreal and dreamlike. Maybe he was still dreaming, and he would wake up back in his cell. Or maybe he would wake up in his bed in Palor, covered in a puddle of sweat from another bad dream.

Every muscle ached in his body. His back screamed with pain. His legs wobbled beneath him. But he fought it all as he attempted to stand straight and be strong.

The crowd was growing in front of him. Jahrys couldn't tell what the people were thinking from their expressionless faces as they stared up at him, whispering to their neighbor and pointing at him.

Jahrys felt a raindrop hit his right cheek. He looked up. The sky was gray and growing darker. The rain felt nice against his dehydrated skin.

He had been able to catch one of the signs on the road as they dragged him here with the rope tied around his neck. He was in a courtyard in Western Village. There were shops lining the perimeter. They were empty, however. Inside the courtyard, there were fountains, benches, other stages for theater acts, bushes, trees, and flowers.

An eerie silence hung over the crowd as the bells faintly rang from the Castle Keep.

Ding, Ding, Ding.

Jahrys felt the weight of the necklace inside his pant's pocket. He was lucky the Hoarders didn't bother to check his pockets for anything. He needed to give it back to Alana, but he didn't know if Alana was even out there. Was she watching him standing broken on the stage? Would she see him die? Would she even recognize him?

Jahrys was scared as the bells continued to ring. He wasn't sure what they were going to do with him. He assumed the gallows.

Ding, Ding, Ding.

Junkland

Where was Sir Piller Lorne? He had promised he would return. But Jahrys didn't even see him in the crowd. Had the Hoarders captured him, too? Was he now rotting in a cell? If so, Jahrys saw no hope for himself. No one would know the truth. No one would believe him.

Jahrys recalled Willem's words. *'Because when the darkness rises, my friends, the ones who matter will be there next to you in the end.'* But the end was here, and there was no one next to Jahrys, only the Hoarder behind him, and the speechless crowd in front of him.

The rain began to fall harder onto Jahrys's face. He heard the pitter-patter of rain drops hitting the wooden stage by his feet.

Pit, Pat, Pit, Pat.

The dry dirt in the courtyard was slowly turning into muddy puddles. The bells continued to toll in the background, counting down the seconds to his death.

Ding, Ding, Ding.
Pit, Pat, Pit, Pat.

The bells suddenly stopped. Anxious murmuring began to spread throughout the crowd.

Nadia appeared across the courtyard, walking purposely across the open path towards the stage. Three Hoarders marched directly behind her. A crow sat on top of her left shoulder, and she carried her staff in her right hand. There was a glass sphere at the top, glowing a bright yellow.

It's just like the one from my dream, thought Jahrys, as Nadia ascended the steps of the stage. His eyes were glued on the swirling yellow of the sphere. *What is that?*

The three Hoarders marched behind Jahrys and stood next to the Hoarder who held his rope. They were armed with Captors and wore their Captor Packs.

Jahrys didn't see any place they could hang a rope for his death. He grew anxious at this—*will I die by the Captors?*

Nadia crossed the stage to Jahrys. She studied him. As she passed, she rubbed the top of his head as if he were a child. The crow cawed and flapped its wings on her shoulder. Jahrys kept his eyes on the glowing yellow sphere.

Nadia turned to the anxious crowd. "People of Astenpoole! This is the start of a new beginning." Her head turned as she looked over every breathless face.

"You are all about to witness something marvelous, something grand, something that will change Astenpoole forever."

The murmuring grew louder, more restless.

"I know many of you are frightened by our new knights in yellow. I ask you not to be alarmed. They're here to protect us from what is to come. Dark times are coming over those mountains, and we need to be prepared."

"If they're here to protect us, why are they taking our things?" a woman yelled out from the crowd. "They're destroying our homes. They're turnin' Astenpoole into —into—the Junkland!"

Murmuring spread throughout the crowd in agreement with the woman.

"She's right," another man joined her. "There are junk walls already starting to form in the city. How does this help us? These yellow men are taking our belongings! They're ruining our land!"

"You'll all be repaid for your losses. I promise you!" Nadia said, patiently. "I also promise that it will all stop today, right now. After I bring forth our new king."

More murmuring spread throughout the courtyard, the people

were even more confused now than before.

"New king? What new king?" a man spat. "King Leoné was murdered."

"That he was," Nadia admitted. "But a new king is about to rise. A king that will not be afraid to open the gates and fight when the darkness comes over those mountains."

Another man stepped forward and said, "Aye, and what's comin' over those mountains we should be fearful of? We should close the gates again. Nothin' will get us in here."

The crowd cried out in agreement.

"The Red Sorceress is coming with her army. She will—"

"Ha! A sorceress? Are you mad?" It was the same man who had just spoken. "You're the one we should be 'fraid of. You're the one we need to fight. You're a murderer! We know you killed the king! Release this poor boy, and give us back our Princess Alana, the true Queen of Astenpoole. Face your crimes! Admit you murdered the king, and send your yellow men away. It's those weapons that're magic! You're the sorceress!"

"Murderer! Murderer! Murderer!" The crowd yelled together, throwing their fists into the air.

Nadia gave a light nod to the three Hoarders standing behind her. The Hoarders descended the steps, pushing and shoving people out of the way. The crowd parted to reveal the man who was yelling at her.

"She's the witch we should be 'fraid of!" he was waving his arms. "Do not listen to her. She has murdered our king and is brainwashin' all of you. What has happened to the Knights of the Poolesguard? What has happened to Queen Alana? Where are all the people who were left outside those walls? What'll happen to—"

Thump.

The back of one of the Hoarder's Captors hit the man across the jaw. Bloody teeth went flying from his mouth. His head twisted awkwardly and he fell face first into the muddy grass. Blood spilled from his mouth.

"The Knights of the Poolesguard were traitors. As are you. A traitor to your new king—but I am generous." Nadia's voice echoed across the yard. "Kneel before me and accept your new king and me as your queen. Accept the new king who will lead us into battle when the Red Sorceress comes to claim this castle, for our new king will save this kingdom." She turned to the man. "Kneel now, so all can see your obedience." Her eyes were dark as she glared down at him. "And I will spare your life."

The man crawled around in the mud to face her. He spat out blood and another broken tooth. He stared deep into Nadia's eyes. "King Leoné was the true king, and his daughter Alana is now the queen! I shall never serve a false one."

Nadia gave another nod. The second Hoarder pulled out a knife and slid it across the man's throat. The man fell, making a gurgling sound as he clutched at his throat. Blood spilled out over his hands and through the cracks between his fingers. The heavy rain washed the blood into the muddy ground. The man twisted and squirmed as he died. After a minute of struggling, the man was motionless in the mud.

There was utter silence in the courtyard.

Pit, Pat, Pit, Pat.

The first Hoarder pointed his Captor at the dead man. He pressed down on the bottom trigger on the handle. There was a deep, low hum that shook the courtyard.

Junkland

VHRUUUUMMMM.

A yellow beam shot out, blinding the crowd and Jahrys as it encompassed the dead body. When the light cleared, only a bloody puddle of mud remained.

"And now you have seen how generous I can be. I gave him a chance and he refused. This is what will happen to traitors," Nadia explained. Jahrys noticed that the sphere on her staff glowed a deeper yellow. She turned to it and smiled. She brought her gaze back to the crowd. "So I ask all of you now, are you a traitor or will you join me to save Astenpoole and welcome our new king?"

No one spoke.

She finally turned to Jahrys. Her eyes were yellow. She smiled at him. It was a dark smile, calculating. She walked over and stroked his wet hair, her smile spreading.

"Astenpoole!" she yelled out to the crowd again. "Here is my gift to you. I give you the boy who will bring back the lost king."

She pulled Jahrys's head back and whispered to him. "So long I have waited for this moment. It's you I need to bring back Carthel. And now I have you. I finally have you. It's time to show the world your power—a power unlike any other Asten."

Jahrys had no clue what she was talking about. *Asten? What's an Asten? And who's Carthel? How can I bring him back? And back from where!*

Nadia took out a knife.

Jahrys's heart dropped as Nadia held the sharp blade in front of his face. The knife inched closer, but away from his throat. Instead, she sliced the bonds that tied his hands.

Jahrys rubbed the soreness from his wrists.

Nadia then lowered her staff, placing the sphere directly in front of Jahrys. The rain was rolling down the glass, dripping off the bottom.

Jahrys looked at her, confused. *What does she want me to do?*

The crow flapped down from her shoulder, landing on the stage beneath the sphere.

"Grab the sphere. Hold it. Feel the energy within," Nadia guided him. "This is what you were born to do. Bring him back."

Jahrys eyed the sphere. There was a yellow cloud swirling inside of the sphere. Jahrys had to squint his eyes. What was going to happen if he placed his palms on that glass? Jahrys recalled the explosion he had seen in his dream.

He slowly reached his hands out.

Nadia was growing impatient. "Grab it!" she yelled.

Jahrys was inches away from it. He could feel the warm heat building in his palms; it felt as if there was water flowing into his skin.

"My queen, look out!" One of the Hoarders jumped in front of Nadia. An arrow pierced the Hoarder through the neck, just above the line of his suit, and he fell off the stage to the muddy ground below.

Nadia pulled her staff away and looked past the stage. The crowd was rioting. The Hoarders surrounding the courtyard had turned away from the stage, firing their Captors. People ran at the Hoarders with knives, rocks, sticks, and bare hands. People had appeared with swords and bow and arrows outside the courtyard, surprising the Hoarders.

Jahrys couldn't believe it. Astenpoole was fighting back!

"Get him out of here," Nadia yelled to the Hoarders behind Jahrys.

Jahrys felt a hard tug on his neck as the Hoarder holding the rope dragged him towards the steps. Jahrys tried to struggle with the rope with his free hands, but it was no use. They dragged him through the chaos of yells and screams. Captor fire and arrows flew over Jahrys's head. The clashing of swords against suits and flesh rang through the courtyard.

The Hoarders tried to push through to exit the courtyard. Nadia was protecting Jahrys with her staff from anyone who tried to touch him. She butted them away or sent a yellow blast flying. But there were too many for her and her Hoarders.

They were almost out of the courtyard when Jahrys felt the tension of the rope disappear. Someone had sliced it.

Suddenly a small hand grabbed his. The touch felt familiar.

There was a voice in his ear. "Trust me," the voice ordered; it was music to his ears.

Alana.

Jahrys felt a pull. He held on to her hand as they sprinted out of the courtyard together.

Nadia screamed. "After him! Don't let him escape!"

Jahrys never looked back. He just kept running and running and running.

Chapter 34
Jahrys

COME ON! THEY'RE right behind us!" Alana yelled out. Her voice sounded distant, but Jahrys kept pushing towards it. She was wearing a dark cloak and a hood that covered her face, but he would bet his life it was her.

They had run out of the courtyard and into the city. The rain had lightened up, but their clothes were still wet. They zig-zagged down deserted roads and alleyways as the sound of fighting faded behind them.

Hoarders were following close behind, though. Jahrys could hear their heavy footsteps against the cobblestone road. Captor blasts flew past their heads as they twisted and turned through the streets. Jahrys didn't know where they were going. He was struggling to keep up. But he kept moving. He didn't want to go back to the dungeon. He didn't want to go back to that stage. He didn't want to die.

"This way! They went this way!" A Hoarder yelled out behind them when they ducked behind a corner to avoid more Captor blasts.

Junkland

It was difficult running in the streets; Junk blocks were scattered sporadically throughout the road. It reminded him of being back in the Junkland. Except now, he was running barefoot instead of wearing boots.

His legs, already weak, were beginning to falter. He didn't know how much farther he could run. He was lightheaded; he couldn't remember the last time he had eaten. His breathing began to shorten, and his vision felt distant—almost cloudy.

"Stop. I must stop," he said with a low, hoarse voice.

"We're almost there, Jahrys. Stay with me!" Alana yelled back to him as she pulled his hand tighter.

They finally lost the Hoarders around a sharp bend. Alana took him down another side street and burst into a house with the door barely on its hinges. She slammed the door shut behind them. Dust encompassed them inside the house.

"Jahrys?" Alana called out. Her voice sounded like an angel's, but it was so distant. "JAHRYS?"

Jahrys felt his vision fade away and his legs give out beneath him as he fell to the floor.

His eyes shot open. He was lying on the floor staring at a dark ceiling. His clothes were still damp, but drier than before. He slowly lifted his head. The entire room was dark, dusty, and worn down. The room had overturned furniture. The fabric was ripped on nearly all the couches and chairs. The glass on the table was shattered. The bannister of the staircase at the far end of the room was shattered, broken wood was on the floor. The place looked like it had been abandoned for years. He saw a large painting hanging on the wall across the room. It looked oddly familiar. *I know this place*, he thought as his eyes swept around the room.

Jahrys shot a hand up to his chafed neck. The rope was gone. He looked over at what remained of it, now tangled in a mess on the floor.

"Jahrys?" A woman spoke from the corner of the room. There was something peaceful about her voice. She walked out of the darkness, towards him. She was still wearing the dark cloak, and the hood still covered her face. "I was so—" she choked up. "I was so worried about you. I thought—They said terrible things. They told me *you* murdered my father…"

"Alana…" he reached out to her. His voice raspy. "I was there when your father died. But I did not kill him. I was set up."

Alana pulled her hood back to reveal her face and bent down to grab Jahrys's hand. She was tearing up. "I believe you, Jahrys. It was Nadia. Nadia set you up. I always knew."

"Thanks for believing." Jahrys smiled. He still couldn't believe it was her; it had been so long. "Am I dreaming?"

Alana laughed and smiled through her tears. "No. I promise you, you aren't dreaming. I'm really here." She handed him a water skin with her other hand.

Jahrys stared at her while he accepted the water. He took a long drink—nearly finishing the water skin. Her smile was the brightest thing Jahrys had seen since that night under the stars—before the Hoarding. Her long, brown hair glistened, even in the darkness. Her eyes were as blue as the Farrest Sea. He scanned her as if it was the first time he ever laid eyes upon her. She was beautiful.

Jahrys didn't know what to say.

She grabbed his other hand and brought his hands close to her face. She began to softly sing.

> *Trust me as I take your hands.*
> *And I will bring you to distant lands.*
> *Far beyond the lined horizon,*
> *Past the wall your mind's in.*

"You remembered…" Jahrys gasped in surprise.

Alana smiled, turning red.

Jahrys smiled back. "It's been so long. That night of the Hoarding—I shouldn't have let you go—I should have held on."

Alana brushed the hair back from Jahrys's forehead. "Forget the past. I'm here now, and I'm not going anywhere this time."

Jahrys smiled. He dug his hand deep into the pocket of his pants and pulled out the necklace.

"I think you dropped this." Jahrys handed her the necklace.

Alana took it and looked down at her hand, studying it. Her mouth fell open. "You held onto it all this time?" She stared at the blue gem in wonder.

"It was the only thing I had that reminded me of you," Jahrys admitted.

Alana began to cry and tightened her grip around the gem and his other hand. She looked at Jahrys with happy, tearful eyes. She bent over him, and suddenly her lips were on his. It felt like a spark hitting his lips and sent a shiver running down his spine, which quickly spread throughout his body. He forgot about his blistering feet, his aching stomach, and his painful cuts from the rope. It felt like every pain and ache in his body was suddenly healed. He wrapped his arms around her, pulling her closer. He never wanted to break away. He would be happy if he stayed in this moment for the rest of his life.

Alana broke away. "I'm sorry I lied to you. I thought—I thought if you knew, you would have treated me differently." She hung her head in disappointment. "I was going to tell you that night. I tried, but—"

Jahrys lifted her chin. "I will always treat you like Lily Bellsworth."

Alana couldn't help but smile. She kissed him again.

When they broke apart, Jahrys stared deep into her eyes. She smiled back at him. He knew this was the moment to say it, what he had been wanting to say to her for three years. He opened his mouth.

"Alana, I—"

There were voices outside. Alana quickly broke her gaze and turned towards the door. She stood up and helped Jahrys to his feet.

"We have to leave. We can't stay here." She whispered.

Jahrys felt embarrassed, hoping Alana didn't realize what he was about to say. "But where do we go? The whole castle is out looking for us. Nadia will find us both eventually." Jahrys was lost without a plan.

"We must stop her." Alana said, seriously.

"Stop Nadia? Are you out of your mind?" he waved his hands in disbelief. "Have you seen what she did with that staff of hers? She has some crazy plan that involves me bringing a king back…And what's up with that crow…she's mad!"

"I don't know what she's up to. But if we don't stop her, more innocent people will be killed. The castle will become exactly like the Junkland." She stared back at Jahrys with glassy eyes. "We *must* stop her!"

Jahrys sighed. "But we have no army, no weapons, and no leader."

Alana smiled. "Luckily, I know where to find all three."

"Where—"

"Don't move!"

Jahrys's heart fell. He *knew* that voice. A Hoarder appeared from around the staircase at the far corner of the room. He was pointing his Captor at the back of Alana's head. *How did he get in? Was he hiding upstairs this entire time?*

"Jahrys, who is it?" asked Alana nervously. She began to shake.

"Stay still," Jahrys said, trying to comfort her. "It will be all right."

"You"—the Hoarder motioned to Alana—"turn around and face me. Both of you put your hands behind your head. Down on your knees. Now!" He kept his Captor pointed at Alana.

They did as he commanded. Jahrys looked at the Hoarder. He was alone. He had a sword hanging in a scabbard on his left hip. His Captor was attached to his Captor Pack on his back. It glowed yellow.

"Who are you?" Jahrys asked, keeping his hands raised.

The Hoarder took a few steps closer to Jahrys and Alana, now only a few feet away. He used his other hand to unclip his helmet and took it off, his other hand still pointing his Captor at them.

Jahrys couldn't believe what he was seeing.

"Kevrin?" Jahrys's mind was racing.

"You know him?" asked Alana, her hands still above her head.

"Yes, he is—was my friend." Jahrys began to lower his hands.

Kevrin dropped his helmet. He placed both hands on his Captor and pointed it at Jahrys's chest. "Keep your hands raised!"

Jahrys put his hands back in the air. "You disappeared...What happened?"

Kevrin's hair was thinner and his eyes were yellow. He looked like he had aged thirty years.

"She came to me that night," Kevrin began.

"Who came to you?" Jahrys was confused.

"Nadia."

"Nadia? How did she get out of the castle?"

"She has powers, Jahrys. Powers beyond any of us. Powers beyond *you*."

"Me?" Jahrys shook his head. "I don't understand. I don't have any powers!"

Kevrin stepped closer to them. "She told me *you* have the power to bring Elyara back."

"That's ridiculous," Jahrys couldn't help but laugh. He stopped when he noticed Kevrin's stern face. "You know that's ridiculous, right?"

"That's what I thought…until she showed me the prophecy."

"The prophecy? What prophecy?"

"The prophecy that involves *you*. That's why Nadia is here. She has been using her army to collect enough energy so she can finally use your powers. The powers that formed inside of you when your eighteenth full moon passed over the sky. Powers that can bring back my father and bring back Elyara."

"Your father?" Jahrys said, shocked. "What happened to your father?"

Kevrin said nothing.

"I don't believe this," Jahrys continued to shake his head in disbelief.

"I know you believe it, Jahrys. I know you felt it on top of that stage; the energy within Nadia's sphere. Your parents, all our friends at The Arcalane, King Leoné"—Jahrys felt Alana tense up next to him—"They've done their part in helping bring back my father and soon, Elyara."

Jahrys's face hardened. "You killed King Leoné." It wasn't a question.

"You're a murderer!" Alana yelled, tears filling her eyes.

"No. That was *you*, Jahrys. I only helped. Nadia gave me the wine bottle that night with the poison. She told me to hand it to you during our job—that *you* would give it to the king. And once he was finally out of the picture, and the gates were open, she would be able to gather enough energy to bring back my father and Elyara."

"Who is your father?" Jahrys was growing impatient. His head was on fire.

"Carthel Danell. The King Beyond the Mountains. The rightful King of Bellow Hill. He will return to stop the Red Sorceress, who has destroyed his—*our* home. She'll come again to claim this castle and to use your powers. But my father will save Astenpoole and protect the people when she comes. We need him."

"So Nadia is…is…"

"My mother."

Jahrys couldn't believe this. He had known Kevrin his entire life, but now it felt like he didn't know him at all.

Alana was trembling, afraid of what she was hearing.

"Please, Kevrin. Don't do this." Jahrys had to make him see reason.

"I have to," he said. "I need Elyara back. I need my father. You know what it's like to lose the ones you love."

Jahrys couldn't disagree with that.

"On your feet, both of you." Kevrin signaled with his Captor for both of them to rise. "I have to take you to her."

Jahrys shook his head in disbelief, but he listened. He rose to his feet. Alana followed as she tried to hold back tears.

"She won't kill you, Jahrys," Kevrin said. "She needs you. And if you cooperate…she will let Alana li—"

There was an explosion outside, distracting Kevrin. Jahrys didn't hesitate. He dove forward, pushing the Captor to the side, and tackled Kevrin to the ground, causing him to accidentally pull the top trigger. A yellow blast shot out from the Captor. It exploded into the painting across the room, sending smoke and debris into the air. Jahrys coughed, but kept his focus on Kevrin. They rolled around on the floor, scrambling at each other. Jahrys punched him hard in the face, his knuckles screaming with pain. Kevrin went limp.

Jahrys grabbed the Captor and pointed it at Kevrin. He rolled Kevrin onto his stomach and unclipped his Captor Pack.

"Keep this pointed at him. If he moves…shoot him with the top trigger." Jahrys handed the Captor over to Alana, placing her hand around the handle and two fingers over the trigger.

Jahrys began to strip Kevrin's suit.

"What are you doing?" Kevrin moaned.

"I'm taking this." Jahrys couldn't look Kevrin in the eye as he took the suit off his old friend. Jahrys then grabbed the rope lying on the floor and cut it in two with Alana's knife. He tied Kevrin's wrists together and then his ankles.

"You're making a mistake!" Kevrin yelled.

"I think you're the one who made a mistake. You betrayed your family." Jahrys began putting Kevrin's suit on his own body.

"Can you help me with the Captor Pack?" Jahrys asked Alana, who had lowered her Captor since Kevrin was tied up.

Junkland

"The what?" Alana looked at him as if he had two heads.

"That…" Jahrys pointed to the pack the Captor was attached to. "Just clip it on to the back of my suit." Jahrys turned to show her.

Alana lifted the Captor Pack and lined it up with the clips on the back of Jahrys's suit. There was a click and a pop. The lights on his suit and Captor lit up. The suit now glowed blue. Jahrys turned around to take the Captor from Alana.

"Thank y—"

The voices outside cut him off. They were getting louder and closer.

"We have to go," Alana urged Jahrys to hurry.

Jahrys grabbed Kevrin's helmet and followed Alana over to the secret passageway that was now exposed. The painting had been blown off.

"I'm sorry! Jahrys, I'm sorry…" Kevrin's voice grew fainter and fainter as Jahrys and Alana climbed down the ladder to the secret passageways below.

Chapter 35
Nadia

PLEASE, YOUR GRACE. Mercy!" The man was on his knees, pleading to Nadia. His head was hanging down. His lips trembled like a baby. He tried repeatedly to look up, but he was too afraid.

And so he should be, thought Nadia. She sat high above the man on the Wave. She clutched her staff tightly in her right hand, her veins clearly visible. She had used too much energy during the riots. How could she have been so ignorant? She thought the people would listen. She thought they would understand.

But none of that mattered now that the boy escaped. After all these years of waiting and finally having the boy in her grasp, he had gotten away from her. It was that damn Princess's fault. Nadia had known Alana would give her trouble.

Now she needed to regain the energy she had lost, and fast, before they recaptured the boy. She was going through all of the prisoners from the dungeons. The ones that were disloyal to her, the ones that didn't see her cause, they were the ones she had to sacrifice. She was questioning them, seeing who would serve her and who was trustworthy. She *was* a generous queen.

She repeated the words she had been reciting all afternoon. "Do you pledge to serve under me and cause no treasonous acts against your queen?"

"I d-do, Your Grace," the man stuttered. "Anything f-for you." The man was shaking from head to toe. He looked as if he was going to wet himself.

Nadia motioned to her guards. They had been standing behind the man with their Captors raised towards the back of his head. "Take him away," she ordered.

"Thank you, Your Grace. Thank you!" The man said, as the two Hoarders dragged him back down to the dungeon.

After they left, two more guards entered, carrying yet another prisoner.

As she waited for them to cross the room, Nadia turned her eyes to a window above the balcony. She noticed the sunlight fading and night gradually taking its place. *Where are they?* She thought. *Carthel or Kevrin has to have found him by now. It's been too long!*

Her son, Kevrin, had been out with her men searching for the boy and the princess ever since they had escaped that morning. Carthel was flying around the city. But Nadia was getting worried, since neither of them had updated her since the search began.

The guards forced the next prisoner down to his knees in front of her. This one was much larger than the last. He was old and bald, but there was no fear behind his eyes.

This one will give me trouble. "Do you pledge to serve under me and cause no treasonous acts against your queen?" Nadia asked, projecting her voice over the empty hall.

"Aye, good old Riago prefers to serve on top of you, Your

Grace." He gave a sly, mocking grin.

"You dare mock the queen in the presence of death?" The guard to the right of Riago yelled. He butted the man across the face with his Captor.

"Agh!" Riago fell to the marble floor. He slowly rose back up to his knees, wiping the blood from his cracked bottom lip with the back of his hand.

Nadia walked down the steps, carefully, so not to trip over her trailing black gown. Her shoes and staff made a tip-tap sound as Nadia made her descent down the stairs.

Tip-Tap, Tip-Tap, Tip-Tap.

The old man eyed her cautiously as she descended.

She stood over the man kneeling on the floor. He was smirking at her. She didn't like that. The key to control was fear. "Would you rather die than serve me?" she asked calmly.

She wanted to kick him in the face, to wipe that stupid smile away. How could he sit there and not take the situation at hand seriously? He hadn't the faintest idea of what she had gone through to get here—what she had sacrificed. He had no idea what was coming for him. Nadia kept her composure.

"Riago'd rather feel the touch of those royal breasts in my hands, Your—"

Thump.

The guard hit Riago again, this time hard in the center of his back. He went down to the floor a second time. Riago rose back to his knees, more slowly this time. His body was trembling, a bloody cough exploded from his chest.

He spat at her feet. "Is this how you treat your prisoners? This is not justice. Riago will never serve a murderous queen."

He stared coldly into Nadia's eyes. "You raided our land, you murdered our king, and you treated our princess—our *queen*—as if she was a prisoner. The poor girl's mother died and instead of being the motherly figure she deserves, you went ahead and killed her father, and blamed some boy for your actions. Where's the honor in that, Riago asks you? Killing prisoners if they refuse to serve you? Where's your honor? Riago serves the real Queen of Astenpoole. Queen Alana Poole! You're a disgrace to the kingdom."

"A disgrace?" her muscles tensed. "Do you have any idea what I've sacrificed to get here? The pain I've been through? King Leoné was weak and would never have been able to survive what's to come. Astenpoole needs a king that will fight and win. Astenpoole needs Carthel! He'll save your kingdom from what's coming over those mountains! Which you fools falsely worship."

"Aye? And what God do you serve? False god or not, at least ours doesn't believe in murdering innocent people!" Riago coughed. "You call this saving? This is destruction!" Riago coughed again. This time more blood sprayed the floor. "Good old Riago would rather face whatever comes over those mountains than you, your sorcery, and your false king. Leave this place. You're no help to Astenpoole!"

Nadia glared at him. Her blood was boiling. He did not respect her. How could they not appreciate what she was doing? They were selfish. Just like Emilia.

"Very well," she said. "Because of your defiance, I'll give you one last chance, with a more drastic consequence. Serve me, or suffer."

Riago stared at her, defiantly. "No." He spat at her, shaking his head.

"I see." Nadia gave a slight nod to the two guards standing behind him. The guard on his left raised his Captor, pointing it at Riago. Riago's eyes widened, panic clear across his face.

"I have been kind," Nadia said softly, "killing your people first before I take their energy, but for you…"

Riago gasped.

"For you there'll be no mercy." Nadia nodded again at her guard.

He pressed down on the bottom trigger. There was a deep, low hum as the floor began to shake under Nadia's feet.

VHRUUUUMMMM.

A yellow beam shot out and encompassed Riago's body. There was a blinding light and a sharp scream.

Nadia didn't even blink.

When the light cleared, Riago's body was gone. His shrieks could be heard inside the Captor.

The sphere at the top of her staff began to glow a brighter yellow—the brightest it had been in ages. Nadia stared deeply into it—smiling. She clutched her staff tighter, closing her eyes and taking in a deep, satisfying breath.

She opened her eyes and looked at the blood in front of her; the red reminded her of Emilia. Her dark red hair…and her blood red eyes. "Clean this up at once!" she ordered the two guards. "This is a mess."

She started walking towards the council room at the back of the hall. She wanted to wait in peace. But she turned and glanced at her two guards.

They saw her looking. "Yes, Your Grace?" they asked.

"Bring me Sir Piller Lorne," she commanded. She turned and entered the council room, slamming the door behind her.

She let out a long sigh as her eyes looked around. There was an oval shaped table in the center of the room where Leoné had once held his council meetings. But now, he was dead, and the council room was hers.

Nadia took a seat at the opposite end of the room, beneath the large painting of the Western Mountains. She leaned her staff against the chair next to her.

Her head was spinning in an endless circle. If only she had used the boy while she had had the chance. Instead, she wasted time on that man in the courtyard. How could she be so stupid? She had had him in her hands! He had even placed his hands over her sphere!

She found tears escaping her eyes. She wiped them away in disgust, but more only followed. She let her head fall into her arms on the table as she broke down.

It had been a stressful eighteen years since Emilia drove them out of Bellow Hill. Carthel thought he could help Emilia, but he had been wrong. He had failed to protect his kingdom. Nadia wouldn't let that happen again.

There had been a time when Nadia admired Carthel, loved him. When he was a strong and powerful king, she had adored him. When he had been a man—a real man. When he wasn't just a helpless crow. Her love and respect for him had faded over the years—and those beady, black eyes didn't make it any better.

Nadia didn't know if she could handle this life any longer if this plan didn't work. She didn't want to—no, couldn't—live with a crow as a husband. Not anymore. The plan *must* work.

She lifted her head and massaged her temples with her fingertips. *Is Carthel going to disappoint me again?* The minutes ticked by as she waited. But the minutes quickly crept into hours. Nadia was half-asleep when she heard a tapping at the door.

The sound had frightened her and had made her jump. She shot up and sprinted around the table, towards the door. She swung it open. Carthel flew in, landing on the table. He turned to look up at his beloved wife.

"Well?" Nadia asked impatiently, as she closed the door behind her. She stood over the black crow with one hand on her hip, glaring.

"There has been no sign of them," the crow answered. His voice was deep, hinting at the man he once was. "But we're still look—"

"AH!" Nadia felt the blood boil in her skin. This was not the news she wanted to hear. She turned away from Carthel.

"Nadia?" Carthel said behind her, softly. "How much more must die?"

Is that sorrow in his voice? Nadia whipped around to face him. "You knew exactly what the price would be, Carthel. Don't act like you were unaware this would happen."

"Yes, but we had the boy. We had the energy to turn me back! This could've been over. I thought this would end when Leoné was dead. Why are we still killing people?" Carthel stared up at her with those beady, black eyes.

Nadia couldn't believe what he was saying. "Don't act like you are the innocent one. You were all for this plan after you knew it would turn you back. You knew the sacrifices."

She pointed a trembling finger at his beak as she continued. "I've given up eighteen years of my life for you, Carthel. I've crossed the entire world—through rough seas and terrain! I've married two men who treated me as if I was nothing, a peasant! I've taken over a castle and I captured the boy who will change you back to the man you were and help us stop Emilia. But now I'm beginning to think you aren't the man I once knew."

"What are you saying?" Carthel flapped his wings in frustration.

She slammed her fists down on the table. She was beginning to frighten herself, but she had to stand her ground. She couldn't waste anymore time. "I can't do this anymore! I've sacrificed too much of my life to be defeated by Emilia again and again. I can use all this energy to stop her. I can save our people. I can save our family and our son."

"Our son? Our son is dead..." Carthel cocked his head, confused. "You told me Ren had killed him while—"

"Our son is *not* dead, Carthel."

"Our son is alive? But how?"

"I sent him away—to Palor with my mother, to protect him. To—"

"YOU LIED ABOUT OUR SON?" Carthel was furious. "WHY? WHY DID YOU HIDE HIM FROM ME?"

"It wasn't safe to tell you. To tell anyone," Nadia felt warm tears sliding down her cheeks. "I didn't want Emilia to get to him. She has spies—"

Carthel had heard enough. He flapped his wings and rose into the air. He flew into Nadia's face and started pecking at her eyes with his black beak and talons.

Nadia screamed. "GET OFF OF ME!" She swatted the air with her hands. After a few tries, she hit Carthel with the back of her hand.

Carthel went flying into the wall. He sank slowly to the floor, his feathers out of place.

Nadia grabbed her staff from the other side of the room and

stood over Carthel. "I try to protect this family and all you do is disappoint me!" She wiped the blood off her cheek. He hadn't pierced her eyes, but her cheeks had been badly scratched.

Carthel was out of breath. "You...did not try...to protect...this...family," Carthel wheezed, trying to regain himself. "You turned against Partha and Ren, and now they're dead. You're attacking their boy! And you hid Kevrin from me. *You* destroyed this family. At least Emilia has a heart..."

Nadia thrust her sphere into Carthel's body, ruffling his feathers even more.

Carthel let out a groan.

"Oh, you're so pathetic. The mighty King Carthel, just a tiny black crow." Nadia was smiling now. "You are *useless*.

"Partha is dead and her sphere's still out there. I will find it and I can use it. And instead of wasting the energy on you, I'll use the boy's power for myself, just like how Kala Karuge used Zalus's powers all those years ago. I'll be the most powerful sorceress—stronger than Emilia. I'll bring peace to Astenpoole and the world. And after I'm done, I'll make a cage just for you and keep you as my pet." She laughed, pointing the sphere just under Carthel's head.

Carthel used his wings to push himself up. He lifted his head away from the sphere. "Nadia you're out of control—"

"No, Carthel. I am *in* control now. You do not speak unless I tell you to speak. You do not act unless I tell you to act. You will not talk to our son unless I let you." She glared at him as her staff crushed him against the wall.

Carthel looked up at her with his eyes. "Nadia, please—" he said weakly.

"You'll spend the rest of your life as a crow. You better get used to those wings of yours."

The sorceress gave a high laugh. She felt the energy flowing through her veins. She had never felt so alive. Taking Riago's energy had made her feel something she hadn't felt in years. "Now get back out there and find me that boy!"

Chapter 36
Piller

THE CELL SMELLED of piss and sweat. The air was thick and humid, making breathing difficult. The lack of windows made the room a dark, claustrophobic box. The cries of babies could be heard, along with the soft comforts coming from their mothers. Piller had no choice but to listen as the sounds flowed through the bars of his cell.

The cells were located in a dungeon deep below the northeastern tower in the Castle Keep. The only source of light came from two dim lanterns on both sides of the door at the end of the hall.

The only door to freedom, thought Piller. *But why do I want freedom when all I've done with it is fail? I've failed to protect my city, my king, my people, my family, my brothers—that little girl. I deserve to be locked away.*

He sat with his head between his knees. He had failed Hollow and Arnold. They had been so young. They had looked up to him as a leader, almost a fatherly figure. But he was no knight. A true knight would have been able to save them, like Galagar Poole, who had defeated three outlaws single-handedly. Piller couldn't even defeat one. He just watched his brothers die. The frightened looks they had on their faces right before death had given Piller nightmares.

His sympathy went out to the poor boy who Devan and he had dragged into the dungeon. Piller should have believed him. He should have went straight to Alana. He should have known it was Nadia who murdered Leoné. How could he have been so naïve? He was blinded by his duty, by *orders*. And now the boy was probably dead, hung by a rope.

He wasn't entirely sure how long he had been locked away. It could have been a couple of days, maybe a week. Piller let his head sink even lower. He rubbed his fingers through his sweaty hair.

He let his thoughts drift back fourteen years to his first night on the Poolesguard. He had been so young, only twenty-three; barely older than Arnold and Hollow were. He remembered how brave and powerful he had felt roaming the busy streets of Astenpoole. His sword proudly at his side. Young boys stared at his shiny armor and looked up to him as if he was already a hero. Young women would give him looks he had never witnessed before, just for wearing the armor. He felt as if he had meaning and purpose in his life.

His boots had tapped loudly on the cobblestone, making his presence known. He had felt taller than the Western Mountains.

But it must not have been tall enough, he thought in reflection.

"AHHH! HELP!" The little girl's high-pitched screams were still fresh in his head after all these years. The screams had come from a dark alleyway off of Pooles Road in the Western Village. Piller sprinted towards the source.

When Piller turned down the dark alleyway, towards the yelling, he found two rather large men surrounding a little girl.

"Please! Leave me be! I just want to find my mother!" The girl screamed.

A third man was constraining her arms behind her back. She must have been no more than seven. The little girl had long, black hair and chubby red cheeks. She was crying hysterically. When she saw the knight in shining armor come around the corner, she yelled for him. "Please, Sir Knight! Help me! Save me from these—"

"Shut it, girl," the man behind shook her violently to shut her up.

The two men in front of the girl had turned around. All eyes were on Piller.

The largest one, the one on the left, had been the first to speak. "Well look what we have here. A knight in shining armor. You're a pretty boy, now aren't you?" The man had dark brown hair on the sides and was balding on top. There was a crazy look in his eye. A look that Piller didn't want to dig deep into. "Be gone with ya, pretty knight. This business is none of yours. Just us and this little girl here." He turned to reach out towards the girl and rubbed her head as if she was his daughter. "We don't be wantin' any trouble."

The other two men smirked at this.

Piller didn't realize how much his legs were wobbling. He tried to control it, but it was no use. His heart was beating so loud he was sure the three men could hear it. He remembered how scared he had been. He easily could have walked away and turned his back. But he was a Knight of the Poolesguard now. Therefore, he drew his sword.

The blade had made a pleasant sound as it left his scabbard on his left hip. He held the sword in front of his face. The steel was brand new, forged specifically for him at his initiation into the Poolesguard. Piller remembered it was like looking into a mirror. He remembered being able to see his reflection, his jagged scar staring back at him. His thoughts had drifted to his mother and father. *This is for you*, he remembered thinking.

The three men had only laughed.

"You think a lil' bit of steel will scare us off?" The man on the left had said, still petting the girl's head as he turned to his men. "A pretty knight, but a dumb one, too."

The other two men laughed.

Piller had taken a step closer to the three men. "Step away from the girl!"

"Ooo, not so pretty are you. Who gave you that scar, ugly?" The same man asked.

"I said…step *away*!" Piller felt the blood rushing to his face.

"Walk away. I already warned ya once." The man's hand tightened on the girl's hair. "Don't make it twice."

The girl screamed.

"By the name of King Leoné, you three are under arrest." Piller's voice was shaky. It was not as powerful as he imagined it would be.

"Ha! Arrest? For what crimes? We be just havin' a little word with our niece here. Isn't that right?" The man on the left said.

"Yea Chitt, that's right. Just a word with our niece," the man on the right replied.

"Yep. Just a word with our niece, is all." The man holding the girl's arms from behind nodded with a stupid grin sewn across his face.

"It seems this knight thinks we're going to rape this poor girl," the one named Chitt pointed out.

"I think this be the dumbest knight I've seen. Raping a girl this age? By Zalus!" The man on the right spat at Piller's boots. He took out a knife. "I say, Chitt, I think we should be teachin' this knight some manners to mind his own business. What d'ya think?" He took a step towards Piller.

"I think for once you be talkin' some sense, Ky." Chitt unsheathed a sword at his hip.

"Don't come any closer!" Piller's voice bounced off the walls of the alleyway.

But they didn't listen. The two men stepped towards Piller.

"Please! Sir Knight! Help—"

"I said shut it!" the third man yelled at the screaming girl, tightening his bind around her.

"Keep that girl quiet, Hem!" Chitt yelled back.

Piller had taken this chance to charge. He collided into Chitt, knocking him to the ground. Piller rose to his feet to finish him off, raising his sword.

"AH!" Piller had screamed out in pain. A knife dug deep into the gap of his back plate, behind his shoulder. He had spun around violently, swinging his sword, but Ky ducked underneath the deadly blow. Something smashed against the top of Piller's head as he spun face first to the cobblestone road. His world went black.

When he woke, several hours later, the back of his head was throbbing. He sat up on one elbow, placing a hand on the spot and felt a lump crusted in dried blood. The bump was so large it could be a second head. He couldn't remember what had happened. His eyes glanced around. He was in a dark alleyway. It must have been close to early morning. He glanced over, noticing the body of a girl. He crawled towards her. There had been a puddle of blood surrounding her dead body. It looked like she had been stabbed in the stomach numerous times. Piller remembered looking at her fragile body. She looked so innocent and pure. She was ghostly white with blue, cold lips. Piller saw his sword by her side. He rose to his feet and picked it up. His new steel had been soaked red with blood.

No, he remembered thinking. Piller's eyes went back to the wounds in the little girl's stomach. He felt sick. Piller had fallen to his knees and threw up on the cobblestone road.

When he had regained himself, he took the young girl over his shoulder. He had carried her to the graveyard and buried her right next to his own mother and father.

I didn't even know your name, he remembered thinking, as he went to his knees before her grave. He had begun to cry. *I'm sorry I failed you all. All of you! I promise I'll be a better knight. I promise all of you.* He had glanced at his mother and father's graves. *I promise.*

When Piller had returned to the Poolesguard chambers, all his brothers were there. There was Edmond Gifford, Raulin Clere, Wymon Kitt, Mazo Dapfer, Devan Lark, and their captain, Landerin Raneir.

"I see you got yourself into a little trouble, Piller," Landerin had confronted him.

Piller had tensed up. "Wh-what?"

"There's blood all over you. What happened?" Landerin asked.

All eyes were upon him.

Piller had bowed his head and told them the story of how he had saved the little girl from those men.

To this day, Piller regretted lying. But he had been scared of ruining his reputation, of destroying everything he had worked for.

Back in his cell, Piller covered his face between his knees so the rest of his brothers could not see. He didn't want them to see their captain crying. He didn't want them to know the truth, that he was a fraud, that he had always been a fraud.

His thoughts drifted towards the sea of screams. The screams of all the innocent men, women, and children pleading for help. He had wanted to help them. But he had been following the king's orders and had been blinded by his duty—or what he thought was his duty.

He thought he was fixing his wrongdoing by opening the gate. Nadia had told them they would save the Retrievers who had been attacked at the inn. But was there anyone even left out there?

I wonder what happened to all those people, Piller thought, as he took in a deep breath. He had a feeling they suffered a similar fate as Hollow and Arnold: a cold heartless fate, sucked into one of those packs that the Hoarders carried.

Piller finally lifted his head. He tried to force himself out of his mind. He needed to escape his thoughts; they were eating him away. He tried to adjust his back to a more comfortable position, but there was nothing comfortable about sitting against steel bars.

He saw his last remaining brothers: Devan, Krist, Martellus, and Benjamin. They were all tightly packed inside the cell. Krist and Martellus were sitting back-to-back, sleeping upright. Devan was carving something on the wall with a small rock he had found lying on the stone floor. Benjamin was sitting against the back wall, staring out into space. Piller wondered what they were all thinking.

Other cells lined the dungeon walls. Piller had taken many prisoners down to the dungeon before, so he was familiar with the layout. There were a hundred and forty-seven cells. The first hundred were lined from the entrance door to the back wall. There was a turn halfway between that branched off with the other forty-seven cells.

Each cell had a mixture of men, women, and children who were all huddled together, trying to comfort each other. There was fear in all of their eyes. None of them knew what was to come. Even Piller couldn't answer that question.

Two guards, in their yellow suits, would consistently enter through the door, taking yet another victim out of the dungeon. Sometimes the prisoner would return and other times...

Piller shuddered. He didn't want to think about the other times. They had taken Riago last. The guards had walked down the hall, past Piller's cell. It was weird seeing them up close. The weapons they carried were nothing of what he had ever seen before. He wouldn't even know what to do with it if he tried to steal one.

The guards had turned right and out of sight. Piller heard the clinking and clanging of keys as they swung on the guard's belt.

Then there was screaming.

"No! Get your bloody hands off! No! Don't—"

There was a loud thud and—silence. They dragged Riago back down the hall, back past Piller's cell again. Riago had a bruise on his forehead and was unconscious as they dragged him by his feet.

He had yet to return. And frankly, Piller didn't think he would.

His thoughts ran off again. He wondered about what his mother and father would think if they saw him right now. If they saw him behind these bars...would they be proud of him? Or would they shake their heads in shame of his mistakes?

Piller rubbed the scar that ran across his face. That was another dark memory. Too dark to even think about...it was the last time he had seen his father...*Father. Please guide me. I don't know what to do anymore.*

He let his head fall deep into the palms of his hard-callused hands. He tried to shut out all the noise, but the sound of people coughing, moaning, and praying continued to surround him. They were all waiting anxiously for the door to open again, to see who would be chosen next to be taken to Nadia.

"What's the plan, Captain?"

Piller raised his head from his sweaty palms to see Martellus looking at him with his hard face and curly black hair. He looked so much like his older brother, Krist. He was usually upbeat and happy. However, today he was broken, just like the rest of them.

"Plan? There's no plan. As you can see, we're trapped behind these bars waiting to be plucked out like pigs ready for slaughter by Nadia." Piller looked away from him. "No, Martellus, there's no plan this time."

"Come on, Cap'. There must be a way to escape." Krist spoke now. "We can't just give up. We need to avenge our king and save Astenpoole!"

"Alana's still out there somewhere," Benjamin had joined the conversation. "She needs us, Piller. King Leoné told me to protect her. I can't do that stuck rotting in this cell."

"They're right." Devan stopped his carving on the wall and looked over. "These are hard times. But I'd be dead before I see Nadia destroy our home. As long as I'm alive, I'll fight! And I'll fight beside you, my captain."

"Aye, my captain!" They all yelled together.

Piller let out a long, deep breath. "I'm sorry I've failed you all. Every decision I've made has brought failure upon myself and the ones I care about. Look at Hollow and Arnold. How can I not be blamed for their deaths? I don't know what's right and wrong anymore. I'm blinded. Our best bet is to pray to Zalus that a hero emerges and—"

"AHHH!"

A shout came from outside the door. All eyes turned towards the two lanterns. People tried to stick their heads through the gaps of the bars to get a better look.

The shouts grew louder. They heard the sound of Captor blasts. *Thump. Thump. Thump.*

Something had fallen down the steps outside the door—and then something else. *A body? The guards?* Piller wondered.

There was the sound of struggling, yelling, and screaming.

Then—silence.

Everyone waited patiently to see what would come through that door. The entire room held its breath.

There were footsteps approaching the door. There was a shadow as the light in the cracks went dark. They heard keys rattling and then the door flew open.

Chapter 37
Piller

A HOARDER STEPPED into the torch light. Everyone in the dungeon gasped in fear. Who were they going to take next?

However, there was something different about this Hoarder. The suit he was wearing was glowing blue instead of yellow. Piller watched as the Hoarder stepped into the dungeon. A girl followed closely behind.

"Princess Alana?" Piller stuck his face in between the bars to try and get a better look. "Alana? Is that you?"

Benjamin shot up and hurried over next to Piller. "Alana?" he yelled through the bars.

Alana walked into the torch light, and Piller could finally see her features. She didn't look well. Her brown hair was tangled, her face was almost black, and she had cuts and scrapes running up and down her body. She was also thin, very thin.

She ran over to the knights. "Benjamin! Piller!" she turned to the rest of the knights in the cell. "My Knights of the Poolesguard! How happy I am to see—" her expression turned from happiness to confusion. "Where are Sir Hollow and Sir Arnold?" She turned her gaze back on Piller.

"My lady, they are—Nadia murdered them." Piller hung his head in sadness.

"No..." Alana's hand clutched her chest.

"It's true." Krist broke in behind Piller and Benjamin. "They were shot and sucked up by those damn weapons the Hoarders have." Krist nodded towards the Hoarder behind Alana.

Alana turned and realized the cause of their tension. "Don't worry. He's not one of them. He's a Retriever!"

The Retriever stepped towards the cell and unclipped his helmet, sliding it off his head to reveal long, brown hair, sweaty and tangled.

Piller gasped. It was the boy: Jahrys. Piller's stomach dropped. *By Zalus, he's still alive!* He clung to the bars of his cell, looking out.

"By Zalus," Devan gasped behind him.

"Jahrys...I'm sorry. I didn't come back." Piller hung his head in disappointment. *Just another thing I've failed.*

"It's not your fault. Nadia has betrayed us all." Jahrys held his helmet at his side. He looked so young. He couldn't be older than eighteen. His face was hard, and the suit he wore gripped around his muscular body, though he looked tired and malnourished.

"We have to stop her," Alana said. She made it sound so simple.

"Aye. But how can we stop her when we're all stuck behind these dreadful bars?" asked Devan.

Alana turned to Jahrys. "Let's get them out."

Jahrys stepped towards their cell. He took out a ring of keys from his belt. He jiggled key after key inside the lock, testing to see which one would work.

Click.

Benjamin slid the cell door open with a rusty creak.

"Well, I'll be damned," said Devan.

Benjamin was the first to exit, followed by Piller, Krist, Martellus, and finally Devan. They all stood before the boy and Alana.

Devan stepped forward. "I...apologize for my actions. For not believing you," said Devan, ashamed. "I was blinded by my judgement and my assumed duty. But that's no excuse. I should've listened to you." He bent down on one knee. "I thank you for saving us, and I'm forever in your service."

"My name's Jahrys Grent." Jahrys held out a hand towards Devan.

"Jahrys," Devan repeated his name like it was a foreign language. He studied the boy's hand. "I'm Devan Lark." He stood up, still staring at the simple gesture. "And I apologize for not believing in you."

"It's in the past now," said Jahrys, still holding out his hand.

"Erh, yes." Devan finally reached out and shook the boy's hand. "It's in the past." He smiled.

Piller took a step towards the boy. "I, too, apologize for my actions. I should've seen Nadia for what she really is. I, along with the rest of the Poolesguard, are at your service." He took a knee before the boy. His brothers followed him.

Jahrys looked down at the knights. "These are hard times for all of us, and we've all been betrayed by Nadia. It's time to put an end to her evil and save Astenpoole from her destruction!"

"I couldn't have said it better myself." Piller stood up and shook Jahrys's hand. "My name's Piller Lorne. I'm Captain of the Poolesguard." He turned to the rest of his brothers. "This is Benjamin

Burrow, and Krist and Martellus Perriwill."

They all stepped forward to shake Jahrys's hand.

"It's a pleasure to meet you all," Jahrys said. "I've looked up to all of you my entire life."

Piller's heart dropped. *He wouldn't look up to me if he knew the truth.*

Jahrys continued. "...I'm forever grateful for your honor and commitment. We're going to need all the help we can get to stop Nadia. Which reminds me..." he pushed past the knights with the keys in his hand. "Excuse me while I free the rest of the prisoners."

Jahrys continued down the long hall, freeing the people from their cells. There were sounds of joy and happiness, of thankfulness and laughter as the cell doors creaked open.

Piller turned to Alana. "My lady," he said lightly, "are you hurt?" He lifted her arm. "These cuts—"

"I'm fine." She took her arm back. "All is well, save my heart, Sir Piller."

"I'm sorry about your father." Piller looked at her with pure sympathy.

"As am I," she said.

Benjamin approached her. "Alana. I'm sorry for not being there. For not being by your side."

"Even when you're not there Sir Benjamin, you're always by my side in my heart." She gave him a kiss on the cheek.

Benjamin blushed. "I will protect you through what is to come, my lady." But Benjamin suddenly looked ashamed. "But I don't have a sword to protect you with..."

"That's okay." She laid a hand gently on his left shoulder. "Jahrys and I have come up with a plan."

"A plan?" Piller repeated. *The boy may not have killed the king but I still know nothing about him.* "Please forgive me for asking"—he lowered his voice, leaning closer to Alana—"but do you trust this boy?"

Alana turned to Piller and looked at him with serious eyes. She looked like a lady, almost like her mother.

When did she get to be so old? thought Piller.

"I trust Jahrys with my life," she said. "He's my Retriever, and my knight who has traveled so far to find me. He is our hope. Our hope for saving Astenpoole and the Four Cities."

"If you say you trust him, I shall follow behind you. You are the true Queen of Astenpoole, our queen!" Piller said.

"But my lady," Krist spoke up, "please forgive me for questioning you, but we don't have weapons. Nor do we have an army. What is your plan?"

"Oh, but we do have an army. Look around you…" She waved a hand across the hall. Piller didn't notice the crowd that had grown in size behind them.

"Well, I'll be damned," said Devan, again.

"Alana is right!" Martellus stepped forward. "We have at least a hundred men and women down here and many more still out there on the streets. If we start a rebellion, the others will surely come to our aid."

"For once, Martellus is talking some sense." Krist slapped his brother on the back.

"He's right," Alana said. "The people of Astenpoole have all ready begun to fight back against the Hoarders outside the Castle Keep. I've seen it with my own eyes."

"By Zalus…" Devan said.

"Okay. So we have an army," Piller agreed. "But we still need weapons. We cannot fight the Hoarders with our bare hands. We've all seen what they can do." Piller thought back to his two brothers who had fallen at the Hoarder's foreign weapons. "Who knows what sorcery is inside those weapons."

"Sir Piller," Jahrys said, returning to them. "You said you are the Captain of the Poolesguard?"

"That's correct." He nodded. He hoped no one heard the hesitation in his voice.

"We need one of your knights to stay behind and bar down the dungeon door in order to protect the women and children who choose not to fight. Alana has a sword she can leave for him to carry out this task in case things go…wrong."

Piller looked at his four remaining brothers. "Benjamin."

"Yes, Captain?" Benjamin stepped in front of Piller, waiting for his command.

"You will stay here and protect the women and children. Protect them as you would protect Alana," Piller said with a strong voice.

"Yes, Captain. But…Alana," Benjamin turned to her. "Are you not staying?"

"I cannot stay here," Alana said. "I need to guide us through the secret passageway to the armory." She put a hand on Benjamin's cheek. "I'll be okay. I promise you." She looked at him with sweet eyes. "I'm asking you to stay here with the women and children. They need you most." She smiled at him. "A true ruler leads her people into battle. Not stay behind. And besides, I have your training to protect me."

Benjamin was worried. But he let out a long breath and said, "As you wish, my lady."

Alana unsheathed her long sword and handed it to Benjamin.

He looked at the sword and then back at her. "The sword your father gave to you?"

"I trust you with it," Alana smiled at him.

"I didn't know my lady had skill with a sword," Krist scratched his head.

"One should never underestimate the skills of a lady." She stole a quick glance over at Jahrys and gave him a wink, which Krist saw. His face turned red.

"Thank you, my lady," Benjamin said, taking the sword.

"Okay," Jahrys continued his commands to Piller, "the rest of you will come with me and Alana to the armory. We'll collect as many weapons as we can and bring them back here to disperse among those able to fight. Then we'll stop Nadia and take back our home!"

A loud cheer bounced off the dungeon walls.

There's hope after all, thought Piller, as he admired the boy. *This boy has the blood of a knight running through him.*

"Are you ready?" Jahrys looked at each Knight of the Poolesguard.

They all nodded in agreement.

Jahrys turned to Alana, pausing before saying, "You should stay here with Benjamin. I can find the armory. I don't want you to get hurt."

"I'm coming with you, Jahrys."

"But you will be safe here with the other women and—"

"O'Jahrys Grent," Alana crossed her arms and cocked her hip, "who was it that saved you from Nadia? And besides, you need me. You won't find the armory without my help and you know it!"

Jahrys was about to argue, but Alana placed a finger on his lips. "Don't worry. I'll be by your side, *always.*"

Jahrys sighed, giving in.

"Okay, let's get moving!" he yelled, as he put his helmet back on.

How did the boy get to be so brave? Perhaps I should learn from him, Piller thought, as he gazed at Jahrys before following him out.

Jahrys and Alana marched out the door, with Piller and his brothers close behind them.

Chapter 38
Jahrys

A HOARDER WAS on his back, a pool of blood surrounding him on the stone floor. A knife was protruding from his neck.

"What happened here?" asked Krist, as they all walked past the body.

"Alana and I ran into a bit of trouble," answered Jahrys. He began to tell the story.

After Jahrys and Alana had left Kevrin tied up, helpless, and had taken his gear, Jahrys and Alana had taken the passageway all the way to the Castle Keep, crawling through cramped corners and other twists and turns that seemed to be a maze for Jahrys but second nature to Alana. The passageway had spat them out behind an old bookcase in the Dungeon Keeper's quarters, where all the records of criminals and of dungeon maintenance was kept.

When Jahrys and Alana found their feet on the rough wooden floor, they had dropped in on two Hoarders who had been caught off guard.

One Hoarder had been sitting down behind a desk, reading a

book. "What the—" He had stumbled with his Captor, which had been stuck on his hip.

Alana, without hesitation, had leaped across the room with her sword. She swung it upwards, slicing the Hoarder's hand off before he could fire.

"AHHH!" Blood had sprayed out as the hand flew in the air, along with the Captor. Alana had finished the Hoarder off by shoving her sword into his stomach.

The other Hoarder, who had been sleeping on a couch on the opposite side of the room, had woken and raised his Captor, pointing it at Alana. Jahrys had rushed forward, colliding with the Hoarder. The Hoarder had shot his Captor, but the blast had missed Alana and exploded into a bookcase on the far wall.

Jahrys and the Hoarder were struggling on the ground. Jahrys had kept trying to peel the Captor from the Hoarder's grip, but he was too strong. They rolled across the floor, not noticing the staircase. The struggling ceased as they toppled over each other, falling down the stairs. Jahrys had landed hard on the cold, stone floor at the bottom.

When he had regained himself, the Hoarder was already on top of him, raising his Captor high above his head.

The Captor had come swooshing down.

Jahrys grabbed the knife from the Hoarder's belt, and dug it deep into the Hoarder's neck. The Hoarder let out a scream as Jahrys twisted the knife deeper and deeper until the Hoarder dropped his Captor and fell to the floor.

Jahrys had found the keys to the dungeon door hanging from the dead Hoarder's belt.

"Well done, I say!" Devan acknowledged, slapping Jahrys on the back after he had recalled the story.

Jahrys walked over to the Hoarder and ripped out the knife that was still in his neck. He wiped it clean on the Hoarder's suit and handed it to Krist. He then picked up the Captor lying on the floor. He detached the tube that connected to the back of the weapon.

"Piller, you can take this one." Jahrys handed it to him.

Piller took it and looked down at it curiously. "How do you use one of these…?"

"Captors," Jahrys finished.

"Ah, right. These Captors."

Jahrys looked around at the curious faces. He never thought he would be teaching Knights of the Poolesguard how to fight.

Jahrys held up his own Captor, the one he had stolen from Kevrin. Devan, Martellus, Krist, Piller, and Alana all gathered around to get a better look. "It's pretty simple to use. You just point and shoot. Look here…" Jahrys first pointed to the top trigger on the handle. "When you press this, it fires a blast, so be mindful of where you're aiming it." He then pointed at the bottom trigger. "When you press this, it absorbs whatever it is you're pointing it at. This is how you recharge the Captor. But in order to use this function, you need to attach it to the Captor Pack with that tube." Jahrys pointed to the tube that ran from his Captor Pack to the back of his Captor.

He continued. "It's possible to use a Captor without the tube attached, but once the energy from the Captor is drained, you will *not* be able to fire it anymore. You can check how much energy is left in the Captor by this light." Jahrys pointed to a glass tube that was glowing blue in the center of the Captor.

"And what about both triggers?" Martellus asked. "What would happen if you press both at the same time?"

"We aren't quite sure yet, to be honest," Jahrys admitted. "All we know is that when both are pressed, it shoots objects back out of the Captor Pack. It processes some kind of energy in there. We call the objects that come out junk blocks. Junk blocks are what form the junk walls in the Junkland."

"It's sorcery," Martellus exclaimed in wonder.

They all nodded in agreement.

"Anymore questions?" Jahrys asked.

When there were no more questions, they headed upstairs.

Jahrys walked over to the other dead Hoarder and grabbed his Captor, detaching it from the tube.

"Who wants this one?" he asked, holding it out. "Devan?"

"Me?" Devan pointed a finger at his chest. "I think I'll stick with a sword for this battle, young Retriever."

"Martellus? You seem to be interested." Jahrys held it out to the black-haired knight.

Martellus held out his hands and grabbed it. "I wonder where this came from," Martellus said curiously, as he examined it with wide eyes.

"I don't think I want to find out," Piller replied.

"We really must be moving," Alana insisted. "They'll be coming to the dungeon any moment!"

"Alana's right," Jahrys said. "Let's get moving."

Alana walked over to the bookcase and found the latch, opening the entrance to the dark tunnel. They all climbed in and started to crawl towards the armory, Alana leading the way.

After what seemed like hours of crawling through the dark, dusty tunnels, they finally arrived at a dead end. Alana placed a finger up to her lips, signaling for Piller, Devan, Krist, Martellus, and Jahrys to be quiet. They didn't know what was on the other side.

Alana placed one hand gently on the switch to the door. She flicked it.

Click.

Alana carefully pushed it open with one hand. A wave of light seeped in, blinding them. When their eyes adjusted to the light, they took turns stepping down into a large room.

Large cupboards lined the room, along with tables, chairs, and dressers. There was a giant chandelier hanging from the ceiling in the center. Swords and axes hung on the walls. Bows, arrows, and quivers were piled in the left corner. In the center of the room were racks of spears and dozens of swords.

There were voices that echoed from behind a closed door to the right of the room.

They stayed silent, walking around the room as they examined the weapons.

Jahrys found a dozen sword belts piled on a table in the center of the room. He picked one up, counting how many pockets it held.

"Look. Over here," he whispered. He gestured everyone to look at what he had found.

They all gathered around the table.

"Yes. This should be more than enough," Piller approved. "Let's start filling these with long swords from the racks." He glanced at his brothers. "Devan and Krist, start collecting the swords over there," he pointed to the swords on a rack across the room. "Those look to be newly sharpened. I'll have a look at the shields and armor inside the cupboards."

The two knights nodded in confirmation.

"Martellus, start collecting all those bows, arrows, and quivers in the corner," Piller pointed his finger to the corner. "We'll be needing all the projectile weapons we can get to win this fight."

Martellus nodded in agreement.

"Alana and I will gather everything into the tunnel," said Jahrys. He looked around the room. His gaze stopped at a red rug lying on the stone floor. He walked over to it and picked up one end. "I'll lay this down inside the tunnel so it will muffle out the sound of the weapons scraping against the floor when we drag them back to the dungeon. We can lay down the shields on top of the rugs and fill them with weapons."

"That's a good idea," Piller agreed.

After Piller and Martellus placed their Captors on a table, they all went to work, taking as many weapons as they could. Krist and Devan gathered as many swords and axes as they could carry, placing the swords into sword belts and then handing them off to Jahrys, who place them onto the shields. Piller gathered as many pieces of armor his hands could hold and carried them over to the tunnel. Martellus worked quickly with the bows, arrows, and quivers.

Alana made a neat pile on the rug inside the tunnel. She had found a long rope coiled up on a table that she had cut into pieces. She first tied pieces to the shields so they would be able to pull them as they crawled. She then wrapped the remaining pieces of rope around the rug and shields to hold it all together.

They continued working while the voices resumed echoing behind the closed door.

Martellus had decided to make his trip easier by picking up a few extra quivers on his way over to the tunnel. His hands were full but his vision was now blocked.

"Watch out," Piller whispered as loudly as he could without his voice carrying through the door.

Martellus stumbled forward into a rack of swords. The quivers went flying into the air. The rack leaned over and hung for a split second—

Clang.

Everyone turned to look. Jahrys's heart dropped. The rack had toppled over and all the swords fell to the floor. The sound bounced off all the walls.

Jahrys turned to Martellus with a deafening look. *What a fool. He's going to get us all killed.*

"Did ya hear somethin'?" asked a muffled voice through the closed door.

They all turned their gaze to the door.

"Perhaps it be the ghost of King Leoné," another replied, laughing to himself.

"That ain't funny. I heard somethin' in the other room," the first voice said.

"All righ' let's check it out."

Shuffling feet and the scraping of chairs hung in the air.

Jahrys acted fast. "Martellus, Piller, grab your Captors. Devan, Krist, finish helping Alana gather the weapons into the tunnel." Jahrys tried to keep his voice as low as possible.

They acted immediately. Devan and Krist ran over to help Alana with the weapons while Martellus and Piller picked up their Captors from the table.

"Remember what I told you," Jahrys said to the two knights as they approached his side, waiting for direction. Jahrys couldn't believe he was commanding the Knights of the Poolesguard. "Keep a steady aim on that door at all times. Do not hesitate to fire when they barge through. They will not show you any mercy. Cover me."

They raised their Captors, aiming them at the approaching voices.

Jahrys had an idea. He quickly pushed a table in front of the door and took a few steps back, pointing his Captor. He waited with his finger against the bottom trigger.

The doorknob turned, and the door was pushed forward. But the table held it in place.

"It's stuck," he heard a Hoarder say through the door.

"Stand back," another Hoarder yelled.

Jahrys waited. He held his breath. His heart was racing in his chest. He had to time this perfectly.

There was a deep, low hum. The floor began to shake under Jahrys's feet.

VHRUUUUMMMM.

A yellow light surrounded the door. There was a crack as the door began to snap off its hinges.

Jahrys didn't hesitate. He slammed his finger on the bottom trigger of his Captor. His Captor came to life. The blue light in the center lit up. His Captor Pack vibrated behind him. There was another deep, low hum that shook his entire body. But he kept his aim.

VHRUUUUMMMM.

A blue beam shot out from Jahrys's own Captor. His beam encompassed the door. A green bubble now surrounded the door.

The plan had worked.

The door was held in place as it pushed back and forth between the two Captors.

"What's going on?" One of the Hoarders on the other side yelled in confusion.

Suddenly, another deep, low hum echoed from the other side of the door.

VHRUUUUMMMM.

A third light now surrounded the door, making the bubble more yellow again.

The door inched away from Jahrys—he was losing it.

"Hurry! I can't hold it much longer!" Jahrys yelled out to Krist, Devan, and Alana.

He turned to the two knights next to him. "Get ready!"

Martellus and Piller readied their aim.

There was yet another deep, low hum.

VHRUUUUMMMM.

A fourth light now encompassed the door and Jahrys watched as it flew away from him.

"FIRE!" he yelled to Martellus and Piller.

The two knights fired their Captors through the space where the door had been. Jahrys joined them. The three of them started stepping back towards their exit, still firing.

"Into the passageway!" Jahrys yelled over the Captor blasts.

The Hoarders pushed the table into the room, while taking cover behind it.

Jahrys knocked over a table and hid behind it with Piller and Martellus. He looked back towards the passageway and saw that Alana, Krist, and Devan had made it through safely.

"Jahrys, run! We'll cover you!" Piller shouted over the chaos.

Jahrys didn't hesitate. He kept his head low and sprinted towards the passageway. Captor blasts zipped past his head and exploded into the back walls. The heat was excruciating.

He dove into the passageway after Krist, Devan, and Alana. He helped them push the pile of rugs and shields forward in order to make room for Piller and Martellus.

"Come on!" Jahrys yelled out to the two knights still in the armory.

A yell of pain echoed into the passageway.

Jahrys turned back. He looked down to see Martellus bleeding from his shoulder.

"Jahrys!" Alana yelled behind him. "We have to go!"

"Keep going! I'll catch up with you!"

Jahrys jumped out of the passageway. He stayed low and crouched behind the table that Piller and Martellus were taking cover behind.

Martellus was clutching his wound as Piller fired Captor blasts across the room.

Suddenly, there was a hissing sound that came from Piller's Captor. He pressed down on the trigger again and the hiss continued. "I'm out!"

Krist jumped down from the passageway and joined them behind the table.

"Krist, help Piller lift Martellus," Jahrys ordered. "I'll distract them. Take Martellus's Captor."

Krist nodded, grabbing the Captor.

Krist and Piller picked up Martellus and dragged him towards safety.

Jahrys covered them. When there was a clearing between the enemy's blasts, he would jump up and shoot across the room. He hit one Hoarder in the head. But there were still too many of them—at least five. He couldn't fight them alone.

His heart was pounding in his chest. He had to give Piller and

Krist cover while they helped Martellus. He leaned around the table and fired from the side.

"Jahrys! Get out of there!" Piller yelled from the passageway.

Jahrys knew if he stood up, he would be dead. He needed a distraction. He gazed around the room, looking for anything. His eyes locked on to the chandelier hanging from the ceiling.

Jahrys aimed his Captor up and fired three shots. All three missed. He fired another. The blast caught the chandelier and Jahrys watched as it broke free from the ceiling and fell to the floor. Jahrys didn't stay to watch the result. He ran for the passageway.

An ear-splitting crash filled the room. Shards of glass exploded in every direction. Jahrys yelled in pain as he felt a large shard of glass pierce his suit through his right calf—he stumbled to the floor.

He felt an arm wrap around his body, holding him up. He looked up. Piller was there helping him towards the passageway before the Hoarders could begin firing again. When they were both inside, Piller turned around, and using Martellus's Captor, blasted the entrance of the passageway so the Hoarders couldn't follow them.

Piller and Jahrys caught up with the others. They disappeared into the darkness, dragging the weapons behind them.

When they arrived back at the dungeon, they assessed their wounds. Martellus had a gash on his right shoulder, while Jahrys had a large shard of glass stuck in his calf. Gala the Healer, who had been taken prisoner at the same time as the Knights of the Poolesguard, plucked the glass from Jahrys's leg and found some water to clean the cuts. She then took care of Martellus's wound as best she could—she had little experience with blast wounds.

Alana, Devan, Krist, and Piller all helped gather the weapons into the dungeon. The men, women, and children who were old enough, lined up to pick up swords, axes, bows, quivers filled with arrows, shields, and armor.

After they were done, Benjamin regrouped with them.

"What happened?" Benjamin asked Piller.

"We were attacked in the armory. Martellus took a wound to the shoulder, but he'll survive. And Jahrys took a large shard of glass in the leg. Nothing life threatening. Any problems down here?"

"No. We didn't run into any trouble." Benjamin turned to Alana. "Are you okay?"

"Never better, Sir Benjamin."

"Your sword." Benjamin handed the sword back to Alana.

"Thank you." Alana placed the sword back into her scabbard.

She then walked over to Jahrys, who had been resting against one of the cell walls. His suit was off. His clothing stuck to his skin, hinting at the strength of his muscles when he was stronger, not malnourished. She sat down next to him. "How's your leg?"

"It's okay. Gala did the best she could with what she had. But I'll live," he assured her, turning his leg to show her the bandage.

Alana traced her fingers over it. Her touch seemed to heal him instantly.

"We need to stop these Hoarders before they hurt more innocent people," Jahrys said. "We need to stop Nadia."

"Together?" Alana stared at him with serious eyes.

"Together," he said, and wrapped his arm around her body, closing the distance between their faces.

"Jahrys." Piller was standing in the cell door, looking down at them. "I'm sorry to interrupt, but we need to be moving."

"Of course," Jahrys said, disappointed.

Alana stood up first and offered her hands down to Jahrys. He took them with a smile as she helped him up.

Jahrys and Alana walked over to the knights who were all huddled together.

"Are you sure you are okay to fight, Martellus?" Jahrys asked, concern on his face.

"I wouldn't miss a chance to get back at Nadia even if it killed me," Martellus stood up, proud. "What about you? How's your leg?"

"It will hurt, but I'll be able to fight," Jahrys assured him.

"Join us Jahrys…Alana," Piller motioned a hand towards them, bringing them into their group. "We have formed a plan"—he pointed a finger at the two of them—"and you two have an important part to play."

Chapter 39
Jahrys

THE PLAN WAS a simple one. Alana and Krist would take a quarter of the army through the passageways. She and her men would surround the Hoarders from the other side of the Village by the Village Gate, while Jahrys, Martellus, and the remaining prisoners attacked the Hoarders out in the courtyard. They would then regroup in the center of the Village—hopefully.

This plan would not be enough to completely stop the Hoarders, however. They were outnumbered and needed more people.

There had been fighting outside of the Castle Keep and Piller had told Jahrys his plan of getting those people to help: the King's Horn. It was located on top of the King's Gate and if blown three times, it would summon a warning throughout the city that the Castle Keep was under attack. Jahrys only prayed that the people of Astenpoole would come to their aid.

But this plan was useless unless Piller, Devan, and Benjamin were able to open the two gates of the Castle Keep that Nadia had shut after the riots.

Jahrys stood frozen at the door that opened into the Village, staring at it as if he had never seen a door in his entire life. *This is it*, he thought. He turned around to look at the men and women who were waiting nervously behind him. Their swords, bows, and axes were shaking in the air and their armor clattered with nervousness.

All eyes were on him, including Martellus's, who stood next to him. They were all waiting for him to say something. But what could he say? He thought of his mother and his father, how they sacrificed their lives to protect him. He thought about The Arcalane and all of his friends who had died to protect his home. He thought about Kevrin. How his former best friend had protected him from Nadia for so long. Until he had betrayed Jahrys. He thought about Alana, how she had saved him, more than once. It was his turn to make his mark. It was his turn to make a difference. It was his turn to save the people he loved.

But he knew nothing of battle or of leading an army. How could he be responsible for all of these lives? Jahrys thought back to all of the stories he had read when he was younger, about Galagar Poole, Palor A'kal, and Letholdus Quinn. What would they do? What would they say? But better yet, what would *he* do?

His father's words rang in his head. *'Heroes don't have to always wear armor and carry swords, O'Jahrys. Heroes can be anyone who simply makes a king's day by a taste of his wine.'* Jahrys clenched his jaw and raised his Captor proudly over his head so the men could see.

"I always believed there were such things as true knights and fearless heroes," he began. "But I finally realized that no such thing exists in this world. No. True knights and heroes only exist in fairy tales."

The army stared at him as if he had given up all hope.

"Everyone is afraid of something. Everyone feels fear." Jahrys made eye contact with everyone in the front row before continuing his speech. "I know all of you are probably scared right now. I know I am. I've never felt this scared in my life—and I watched my parents die before my eyes in the Hoarding, I felt the girl of my dreams slip through my fingers, I've been betrayed by a friend I thought I could trust, and I've lost all my friends during the attack at the inn. I've watched my childhood dreams of becoming a knight disappear. No. There are no such things as true knights. But do you know what's real? Do you know what's true?"

The men murmured and shook their heads.

"*Us.* Everyone here!" Jahrys waved a hand over the crowd. "We are the ones who believe. We are the ones who hope. We are the ones who love. We are the ones that stand up and make a difference. And we are the ones who *dream*! And we need to keep dreaming. The world needs people like us now more than ever. People who believe in themselves." He pointed his finger out towards the crowd. "Because when the world goes dark, the dreamers will be the ones who find the light!"

Murmuring bounced off the walls. Everyone nodded their heads in belief of his words.

Jahrys continued. "We are *all* Retrievers and it's time to retrieve our home back from these Hoarders, back from Nadia, and back from her false king!" Jahrys yelled at the top of his lungs.

The stairwell echoed with yells from his army—the yells from his Retrievers.

"FOR ASTENPOOLE!" Jahrys yelled.

"FOR ASTENPOOLE!" the crowd repeated.

"FOR THE FOUR CITIES!" Jahrys yelled again.

"FOR THE FOUR CITIES!" the crowd repeated.

Jahrys tapped his helmet and turned to throw open the door. A dim light stung his eyes. It felt like weeks had gone by since he had last seen any kind of light. There was a foul stench in the air that reminded Jahrys of being back in the Junkland. When his eyes adjusted, Jahrys stepped out onto the road. The men followed, pouring out of the dungeon.

"That was an inspiring speech for someone so young," Martellus said, as they walked through the Village. "I was about your age when I joined the Poolesguard…I am honored to fight by your side."

"And I'm honored to fight next to a Knight of the Poolesguard," Jahrys admitted.

They walked down the road of the Village, towards the courtyard; junk blocks were scattered everywhere. Houses and shops lined the road, but there was no sign of life inside them. In the distance, behind the Fountain of Zalus, there was a long, yellow line. The Hoarders extended from end to end of the courtyard, blocking their way to the Village Gate.

Jahrys continued to speak to those behind him. "Do not be afraid! Remember my words. Use trees, bushes, and the fountain for cover. Those in the back without swords and axes, follow those in front and pick up as many Captors and weapons as you can from the fallen. Remember that Captors will not work as well in short range. Archers, give us cover! We *will* push forward to the Village Gate to meet with Alana. We need to fight long enough to give our knights enough time to open those gates!"

His army yelled in agreement.

Let's just hope Piller and his men can get those gates open, or we'll be stuck like a mouse in a trap, thought Jahrys.

Jahrys and his army marched up the road towards the open courtyard where the army of Hoarders waited. The streets were quiet as they passed all the empty houses and shops.

Jahrys's heart was pounding when they entered the courtyard. Not even the beautiful scenery of benches, trees, bushes, gardens, and paths could relax him.

A Hoarder in the center walked out in front of his men. He stepped up onto the base of the fountain. The Hoarder had black stripes running down his helmet.

It's him, thought Jahrys, his fist tightening.

"Stop where you are and drop your weapons with your hands in the air!" The Hoarder pointed his Captor towards Jahrys and his army. "This does not need to end in bloodshed. Put down your weapons. This is your only warning."

Jahrys couldn't lie to himself. He was scared. Scared like everyone else—but he couldn't let it show. He needed to be brave. He needed to be the Retriever he was meant to be. He turned to look back at his men. He raised his Captor high into the air.

"FOR ASTENPOOLE!" he yelled at the top of his lungs. His heart was beating in his chest, but he didn't know if it was from fear, excitement, revenge, hatred, or a mix of all those emotions. All he knew was he was ready. He took a step towards the Hoarders and then another and another until he was running.

He didn't look back to see if his people were following. He wouldn't blame them if they all turned and ran. He did hear the stomping of feet as the ground shook around him and that was what kept him moving forward. It was as if his legs were moving on their own accord.

Arrows zipped past his head, breaking the line of Hoarders.

The Hoarders took aim. "Fire! Do not let them pass! Fire!" the black-striped Hoarder yelled. The blasts from the Captors flew past Jahrys's head with lightning speed, missing him, but hitting several others. There were screams. He heard men and women falling, their bodies hitting the hard ground. But he continued forward, one foot after another. Martellus was right by his side, firing his own Captor.

Jahrys ran and fired, ran and fired. When they were closing in on the Hoarders, Jahrys clipped his Captor to his hip and took out his sword.

The two armies collided with a mix of metal: Captors and swords, suits and armor.

Jahrys dodged a blast and swung his sword around, aiming for any yellow he could find. There was a mist of red as blood constantly sprayed into the air. He had to keep wiping his helmet in order to see.

The Captors didn't work as well in short range. This was an advantage for the Retrievers. The Hoarders soon realized this as well, and they picked up swords from the ground and began to attack the Retrievers.

"Pick up the swords of the fallen! Grab a Captor! Get your hands on anything!" Jahrys yelled, reassuring his army that he was still there with them, fighting to the death. He blocked a blow from a sword. He swung his sword around and took off the Hoarder's arm. One less Captor to be shot.

The courtyard became a pit of chaotic noise. There were blasts from the Captors, the clanging of swords and axes, and yells and screams from the dying as the two armies fought on.

Jahrys began to push his way to the fountain. His sword was heavy, and he was starting to feel fatigued. The air was also starting to smell worse—those who had fallen were releasing noxious smells. There was also pain in his calf, but he continued to run, locking eyes with the black-striped Hoarder. He knew he could not stop, no matter how tired he was.

He is mine, Jahrys thought, as he kept fighting his way to the fountain.

Chapter 40
Piller

PILLER WAS CLIMBING the tower steps of the dungeon with Devan and Benjamin close behind him. They carried swords and shields and wore the armor they had found from the armory. It wasn't the shiny armor they wore in the Poolesguard, but it would suffice.

The door to the outer wall was heavy. When Piller opened it, he had to shield his eyes from the haze as he walked out. The two knights followed out behind him.

The air was thick and heavy, and it smelled foul. The sound of blasts, metal, screams, and explosions stung their ears.

The three knights looked over the wall at the battle below; it was chaos. Jahrys's blue suit was barely visible in the mix of the yellow Hoarders, and the brown, black, and gray of the prisoners. Arrows zipped through the air like a flock of birds; yellow light from the Captor blasts was flying in all directions; swords were gray blurs swinging heavy in the air. Trees, bushes, and buildings caught on fire, along with one unfortunate soul who got too close to a collapsing tree.

"By Zalus," said Devan, his mouth gaping as he looked down at the battle. "In all my years as a knight, I've never seen anything like this."

"It's a slaughter down there," yelled Benjamin over the chaotic noise.

"Yes. We need to keep moving or else they'll all be slaughtered like pigs." Piller motioned them to gather around him.

"How're we splitting up, Cap'?" asked Devan, turning his gaze from the battle and walking over to Piller.

Piller pointed to Benjamin. "Benjamin, you need to open the King's Gate as quickly as possible and blow the King's Horn three times. No more, no less," commanded Piller, looking at his knight. "There are more people out there that can help us fight. They will come." *By Zalus, I hope they come.*

"Aye, Captain," Benjamin nodded. "And what about you and Devan?"

"There will be Hoarders guarding the gatehouse and I'll need Devan's help to kill them so we can open the Village Gate," Piller said, glancing at Devan. "This will allow Jahrys and Alana an escape route if they need it. And if more people do come to our aid, they'll be able to join the battle. Benjamin, you command the army when they gather at the King's Gate. Devan and I will return to the battle below."

"I like the plan already. Let's not be wasting time!" Devan slammed his fist against his shield sending out a loud bang.

"I'll have the King's Gate open in no time." Benjamin yelled, as he turned to start running along the wall, towards the gate.

"Ben."

Benjamin turned back to face his captain.

"If you fail…this could be the end for Astenpoole. We need all the help we can get from outside. We *need* that gate open."

"I won't let you down." Benjamin nodded. Then he turned and was off down the wall.

Chapter 41
Alana

THE PITTER-PATTER of hands and knees crawling on the cold, wet, stone echoed behind Alana. Her sword was heavy at her hip. She was leading her army through the hidden tunnel beneath the courtyard. Krist was right behind her. They were crawling as fast as they could in order to get to the other side of the battle. If they didn't get there in time—*I don't want to think about what would happen. Jahrys is counting on me. I won't lose him again!* She trekked forward even faster, her hands and knees cut and bruised from the impact with the stone.

The air in the narrow passageway was foul. Alana had to cringe her nose and hold her breath to avoid passing out from the smell. The noise from the battle could be heard above their heads. Clouds of dust engulfed them every time someone stepped down hard on the ground above. It sounded like thunder clapping. They were trapped inside a dark, raging storm. But Alana continued and so did her army.

When they finally came to a dead end, Alana placed her hands on the wall in front of her. She was searching for the switch in the darkness. When she felt the smooth, cold handle, she pulled it down and a small door swung open in front of her. The light blinded her eyes.

There were startled voices in the light. "Behind! They're coming from—"

Alana dove hard onto the floor inside the room, remembering everything she had learned from her training. She grabbed her sword from her scabbard. Her eyes regained focus in the bright light. She saw a yellow glow and slashed out towards it, making contact with a Hoarder.

She felt something hard hit her back, and she went flying to the floor. She turned to find a second Hoarder pointing his Captor at her head. She raised her sword, ready to swing up—

Suddenly, blood splattered her face. Alana saw the Hoarder's head falling to the floor. The body collapsed and Krist stood standing in front of her with a bloody sword.

Krist extended his hand to her.

"Thank you," Alana said.

"I knew my lady was sneaking away to practice sword fighting, but I didn't know you were this good," Krist said, as he helped her to her feet.

"I know it's not going to be that easy out on the field. We need to be ready," Alana said, as she helped her army out of the tunnel. They had finally reached the bottom floor of the gatehouse next to the Village Gate.

After they grouped together, Alana looked into the eyes of her small army and locked eyes with Krist. "Are you ready?"

The fighting rang through the windows from the courtyard outside.

Junkland

"Ready as I'll ever be," Krist said.

"For Astenpoole!" Alana yelled at the top of her lungs.

"For Astenpoole!" her army replied behind her.

Her heart was beating heavy in her chest. Alana put her hand on the door handle, spun it, and ran out into the courtyard.

Chaos hit immediately. She ducked from a swinging sword, not knowing if it was from friend or foe. She tried to focus in on the yellow. She raised her sword and went to work, turning yellow to red. Captor blasts and the sound of steel rang in her ears. Screams of the dying surrounded her.

Their army was still too small. The gate behind them was still closed, but she caught sight of Piller and Devan out of the corner of her eye, running on top of the wall towards the Village Gate. *They must get it open...we need help!*

She saw a Hoarder aiming up at the two knights a few yards away. Alana dove for a Captor lying on the ground, the ripped tube dangling. She brushed it aside, taking aim.

She took a deep breath and fired.

She hit the Hoarder, who went soaring through the air, but it was not in time to stop him from firing his own Captor. She looked up at the castle wall and saw only one knight now, instead of two. *No. I was too—*

A sharp pain blinded Alana's vision as something smashed against the back of her head. She went crashing into the ground. Hands grabbed her around her chest, lifting her into the air. She was dazed. She tried to kick and free her arms, but it was no use. The person that grabbed her was significantly stronger than her; he was dragging her away.

Chapter 42
Piller

HE COULD FEEL Devan's arm starting to loosen and slip. Piller dug his fingers deeper into Devan's wrist.

"I got you! Hang on!" Piller yelled over the noise of the battle behind them.

"I hope that wasn't your attempt of a joke." Devan yelled up at Piller, while his feet dangled in the air above the ground.

"Captain, behind you!"

Four Hoarders, two on either side of Piller, were making their way down the length of the wall towards them.

"Quick, give me your other hand!" Piller yelled.

Devan reached up with his injured left arm; he had been hit by a Captor blast from below. He barely got it half-way into the air when it collapsed back down to his side. "I can't reach you. Save yourself and get that gate open!"

"I'm not letting you go." *I will not let you go. I'm not losing another brother.* Piller gripped him tighter, but his hand was sweaty. He could feel Devan slipping.

"I'm ready to go beyond the Western Mountains. I'm ready to see my family again. It's okay. Open the gate and save Astenpoole, my captain." He winked at him and smiled.

Devan released his hand from Piller's. Piller tried to tighten it again, but it was no use. Devan fell to the ground below, never taking his eyes off his captain, his smile never faltered.

"No!" Piller yelled, as he watched Devan fall.

The Hoarders were almost upon him. Filled with rage, he picked up his shield and took out his sword. He charged at the two Hoarders closest to the Village Gate. He raised his shield to cover himself. The heat from their blasts burned his arm, but they hadn't hit him yet. He kept running. Piller collided into the Hoarder on the right, knocking him off his feet. He turned and swung his sword, slicing the second Hoarder's stomach. His insides spilled out onto the stone floor. Piller then spun around, plunging his sword into the first Hoarder's throat.

He quickly turned around and ducked behind his shield to protect himself from more Captor blasts.

"Ah!" he yelled as a blast grazed his shoulder. His shield lowered, but he did not let it go.

Piller dropped his sword and reached out for the Captor that was lying on the ground by his side, but it was just out of reach. His shield was shaking from the Captor blasts that were hitting it. His shoulder stung, but he kept reaching.

The other two Hoarders were getting closer. Piller stretched again and tried to tug the Captor with a single finger, but it was no use. His shield continued to vibrate. His arm felt like it was on fire now. Piller decided to dive forward, grabbing the Captor and holding his shield up. He raised the Captor and pressed down on the top trigger and fired. He fired again and again and again. But missed each time. He took a second to breathe. *You can do this Piller. You can do this.* He focused his aim, concentrating on his target. He fired again at the Hoarder on the right, hitting him in the stomach, causing him to fall to the ground. He then turned to the final Hoarder and fired. The blast hit the Hoarder in the head and he collapsed backwards.

Piller dropped his shield. He released the Captor from the tube and continued to run to the gatehouse.

Chapter 43
Jahrys

ALANA'S ARMY HAD piled out of the gatehouse. The plan was working. They had caught the Hoarders off guard. It looked like the battle was going their way, even though they were outnumbered five to one.

Jahrys continued to dodge swords and blasts as he pushed his way towards the fountain. He had to get to their leader, he had to avenge his mother and father.

He ducked from a sword that almost took his head off. He turned and swung his sword at the Hoarder. There was a loud clang as the Hoarder caught Jahrys's blow with his own sword. Jahrys pushed forward. His calf was stinging even more, but he ignored it. He suddenly stepped back, releasing his weight. The Hoarder stumbled forward. Jahrys took the butt of his sword and smashed it into the Hoarder's helmet. The Hoarder fell and Jahrys continued to run to the fountain.

He was almost at the black-striped Hoarder.

When he arrived at the fountain, he sheathed his sword. He

hoisted himself onto the marble platform, struggling with the weight of his Captor Pack on his back.

He circled over to the Village Gate side, approaching their leader. He unclipped his Captor from his hip and held it firmly with both hands.

As he ran towards the Hoarder with black stripes, Jahrys raised his Captor and fired. The Hoarder ducked as the blasts soared over his head. Jahrys continued to shoot, but the Hoarder predicted his every move. When Jahrys fired again, there was a hiss from his Captor. *No! I can't be out.* Jahrys checked the light on his Captor; the color had disappeared.

Jahrys looked up to see a yellow blast flying right at his chest.

Jahrys dove into the water just in time to avoid the blast. He heard it explode against the marble of the platform before he hit the water.

It felt like a wall had hit him. The water was cold and deep. He tried to swim, but his Captor Pack was weighing him down. He couldn't unclip it, though; he needed it to recharge his Captor. Struggling, he eventually swam towards the statue in the center.

Jahrys found the surface and lifted himself up onto the platform of the statue, wrapping his arm around Zalus's left leg as he regained himself. His balance was off with the pack heavy on his back. His sword was still in its scabbard, and his Captor was hanging at his feet by its tube. Jahrys picked up his Captor.

Jahrys searched for the black-striped Hoarder. He found him, but he could barely see him through the misty cloud that had formed from the waterfall. Jahrys unclipped his helmet to get a better look.

The mist suddenly glowed yellow. Jahrys, with an ill feeling, ducked behind Zalus's marble leg. The blast collided into it, shattering the leg into pieces. The statue managed to stay upright, however.

The mist glowed yellow once again as a second blast was fired. Jahrys dove behind the other leg. The blast missed and disappeared into the water. Jahrys breathed heavily as he tried to collect himself. He raised his Captor, aiming it at the debris of what remained of Zalus's shattered leg. He pressed down on the lower trigger. His Captor Pack began to shake and the loose stone around him clattered against the marble platform.

There was a deep, low hum.

VHRUUUUMMMM.

A blue beam shot out and encompassed the debris of the statue. It disappeared and flowed through the tube, into the Captor Pack. Energy flowed back into Jahrys's Captor.

He stepped around the still standing leg and raised his Captor to eye level. He saw the yellow suit through the misty cloud. He fired. But missed the Hoarder.

CRACKKK.

The fighting in the courtyard stopped for a split second. Everyone turned to the noise. The Village Gate was being lifted. *By Zalus, they did it!*

Jahrys ran around the platform of the statue, trying to find a clearing from the mist. He found it and saw the black-striped Hoarder was distracted by the gate. He aimed his Captor at the Hoarder's chest and fired. The blast shot out and flew across the water, colliding into the black-striped Hoarder. He flew away from the fountain and was lost in the sea of yellow Hoarders.

Jahrys let out a long breathe.

He looked around for his helmet, but it was gone.

He swam back to the edge of the fountain. He had difficulty lifting himself up and over the platform because his suit was soaked and heavy. Jahrys detached the Captor from the tube and unclipped his Captor Pack; he felt much lighter now. He threw his Captor onto the platform and hoisted himself up and out of the fountain.

He picked up his Captor and gazed across the battlefield towards the Village Gate. *Now we just need Benjamin to blow the King's Horn and open the King's Gate. We need more help.* As he was looking at the open gate, something else caught his eye. Two Hoarders were dragging someone through it: Alana.

Chapter 44
Piller

THE KING'S HORN echoed throughout Astenpoole: once, twice, thrice.

AHWOOO. AHWOOO. AHWOOO.

Yes, he did it! We're almost there! Piller thought as he gazed out of the window of the gatehouse tower. The Village Gate was open, the King's Horn was blown, and now it was up to Benjamin to get the King's Gate open.

Piller saw the horn, lying out in the open above the King's Gate on the wall. But there was no one there now.

Benjamin was running back towards the gatehouse. Five Hoarders were also running towards it on the opposite side of Benjamin. *If he doesn't get that gate open, we're done for.*

He saw Benjamin fly through the door. There was yelling and the sound of struggling—then silence. *Come on Ben!* The seconds ticked by. Piller's heart was racing. His eyes never left the gate. The five Hoarders were about to enter the gatehouse from the opposite side.

CRACKKK.

The gate opened. The two large oak doors swung inward. *Yes! Good work B—*

"AHHH!" A scream came from the gatehouse.

Piller heard shouts and the sound of struggling.

Benjamin limped out of the door he had entered. He was wounded, and three Hoarders were right behind him.

Piller saw the middle Hoarder raise his Captor, finger ready on the bottom trigger.

There was a deep, low hum.

VHRUUUUMMMM.

A yellow beam shot out and encompassed Benjamin.

"No!" Piller cried, shielding his eyes.

Benjamin's shrieks could be heard after he disappeared.

Piller was stunned; he had lost another brother. *Why had that Hoarder not killed him first like all the others? I must put an end to this.*

The sound of marching feet brought Piller back to reality. He looked back towards the now open King's Gate.

They have come, thought Piller. *The people have heard the horn.*

But it wasn't people of Astenpoole entering the Castle Keep. It was more Hoarders.

Piller's heart dropped. *No. This cannot be. Where are the people of Astenpoole? The ones fighting outside the Castle Keep?*

Piller heard screaming from below the Village Gate. He looked out towards the Great Hall. He saw two Hoarders dragging Alana up the grand staircase towards the giant double doors.

Piller didn't hesitate. He dropped his shield and ran down the steps of the tower. At the bottom floor, he took out the Captor from his belt and flung himself out into the courtyard. He ran towards the Great Hall.

"Alana!" he yelled over the noise from the battle. He dodged Captor blasts from the approaching army of Hoarders that were marching through the King's Gate.

Piller lifted his heavy legs as he climbed the great steps—Captor still in hand. He ran past the small courtyard and the fountain. He was out of breathe when he reached the double doors. But he didn't stop. He wrapped two hands around the large handles, thrusting them open.

"AH!" Piller groaned, as a pain spread in his lower back. He felt something warm sliding into his stomach. He looked down.

A sword was protruding out. He watched it as it slowly disappeared. He placed a hand where the steel had just been, taking a step back. Blood seeped through the cracks between his fingers.

Chapter 45
Jahrys

THE OAK DOORS slammed shut behind Jahrys. The sound of the battle faded instantly. No more screams, clashing of swords, or blasts from Captors—just silence.

Jahrys took a few steps forward. His feet echoed off the black and white marble floor. He was in the Hall of Heroes. Paintings of all the past kings lined the walls around him, along with paintings of the bravest knights. All the knights Jahrys had so admired and looked up to were now looking down on him. Would he, one day, be placed on that wall? Did he even *want* to be placed on that wall anymore?

King Leoné's portrait hung on a stone pillar in the center of the room. The king's hard face looked straight at him. His last words rang through Jahrys's head. 'Protect Alana,' he had said. *I will not let you down, King Leoné!*

Jahrys held his Captor firmly in his hands as he looked down the hall, his sword ready at his hip. There was a trail of blood leading to the throne room. He followed it.

All his life, Jahrys had just been a boy from Palor, who helped in his father's shop. He then became a mediocre Retriever. But today, he wasn't those things—today he was O'Jahrys Grent, and he was ready to face whatever fate had in store for him at the end of the hall.

As he got closer and closer to the door, he felt his heart racing inside his chest. He tried to tighten his grip on his Captor to stop it from shaking, but it only made it worse. He wiped his sweaty brow and pushed his hair out of his eyes. His muscles felt tight underneath his suit.

There was an echo from behind him. It sounded like the door was opening. He snapped around, but couldn't see who had entered. He kept moving, running down the hall.

He pushed open the door and ran into the throne room. A beautifully designed balcony wrapped around the room, complementing the high ceiling with archways. Pillars raised the balcony, each intricately carved. Archways were underneath the balcony and a black and white marble floor glistened like the sea in the center of the room. Jahrys's eyes followed the trail of blood on the white marble path that led to the grand staircase before him.

He heard shuffling. Hoarders appeared from doors off to the side, and stood under the archways, raising their Captors and pointing them directly at him. Jahrys stopped in the center of the room—he was surrounded.

"Jahrys! Get out of here!" Alana was standing on top of the stairs, next to a giant throne that resembled a wave.

"Alana—" Jahrys took a step forward.

"Not another step." A blade appeared at Alana's throat. Nadia's white face came into view behind Alana's left shoulder. Nadia was holding her staff in her left hand, across Alana's body—constraining her.

Tears were rolling down Alana's cheeks. "Please Jahrys! Run! Before—"

"Silence!" Nadia pressed the knife deeper into her throat.

"Ahhh!" Alana screamed, as a thin line of blood started to drip from her throat.

Jahrys raised his Captor, pointing it at Nadia. *I don't have a clear shot. I can't hit Alana!* He held his fire.

"Love…what a beautiful thing…," Nadia pressed the blade deeper into Alana's flesh.

Alana let out another scream.

Jahrys's insides turned. His finger was trembling over the trigger.

Nadia smiled, "…until it betrays you."

Jahrys watched as the blade slid across Alana's throat. Blood spilled out, covering her neck.

"NO!" Jahrys cried.

Alana gagged and fell to the floor, clutching her throat. Blood seeped through her fingers as she struggled.

Nadia only laughed. The knife in her hand was dripping blood as she kicked Alana down the steps.

Alana rolled down the stairs until she landed on the white marble path. Alana was clutching her neck, choking. Blood was spilling rapidly from her throat.

Jahrys clipped his Captor to his hip and ran to her. He fell to his knees in the puddle of blood and lifted her up. He rested her head in his arm, trying to stop the blood with his other hand.

"Don't worry! I got you, Alana. Everything will be all right. Everything—"

But Alana was gagging on the blood, her eyes unfocused.

Jahrys watched helplessly as the blood continued to pour out of her neck. He watched as she struggled, looking up with frightened, dull eyes. The veins around her face looked like they were about to burst.

Jahrys felt helpless. "Don't leave me, Alana! Don't leave…" His tears fell on her neck. "I won't let you go."

The gagging ceased. Jahrys felt Alana's body go limp and still. Her eyes were now lifeless. Her head lolled to the side, into his chest.

"No!" Jahrys screamed. He could feel the insides of his stomach creeping towards his throat. Everything wanted to come out.

He groaned as he placed Alana down. He rose to his feet, grabbing his Captor and raising it. He clenched the handle in anger, aiming it at Nadia. He began to squeeze his finger down on the top trigger—

Nadia raised her staff.

Jahrys's finger froze, along with his entire body. He tried to pull the trigger, but he couldn't move. He felt like a statue.

Jahrys felt wet tears pooling in his eyes, but they refused to move, to fall down his cheeks.

He watched Nadia descend the steps. Her black cloak trailed behind her. Her face and hands were stained in blood. She stopped at the very last step—in front of Alana's dead body.

"I have sacrificed myself for love, Jahrys." Nadia looked directly at him with her yellow eyes. "I sacrificed eighteen years of my life and did things I will regret. And I did it all for love. And you know what happened?"

Jahrys couldn't speak.

"Love betrayed me." A tear ran down Nadia's cheek.

Nadia looked down at Alana's body. "You don't need her, Jahrys. She would only have blinded you from what you truly are. You need to face your destiny. Because when you do, we can make peace in this world together. We can stop the Red Sorceress when she comes over those mountains!"

Nadia turned to the Hoarders. "Kevrin," she called.

A Hoarder walked over, taking off his helmet.

"Yes, Mother?" Kevrin bowed down to her.

"Finish her." Nadia waved a hand over Alana's body.

Kevrin hesitated.

"Do it for Elyara."

Kevrin nodded. He lifted his Captor and pointed it at Alana's body.

NO! Jahrys screamed but he couldn't move his lips. He felt the ground shake beneath him as he stayed frozen in place. He couldn't let Kevrin do this to Alana, even if she was gone. He had to break free.

Jahrys concentrated hard. He tried to relax. He could feel something inside of him, something that was trying to break free. He felt his breath begin to deepen. He pulled himself out of his mind and took his focus down to every muscle in his body, every fiber. He felt his toes and then his legs. He traveled up to his stomach, his chest, and his arms. He felt life return to his body. He felt himself regaining control.

Jahrys stepped forward, stumbling. He had broken free. He regained himself and lunged at Kevrin.

"No!" Nadia yelled.

He collided into Kevrin, pushing the Captor away from Alana. There was a deep, low hum.

Junkland

VHRUUUUMMMM.

A yellow beam shot out towards Nadia. She deflected it with her staff and the beam was sent flying towards a pillar that was holding up an archway on the second floor. The beam hit the pillar with a loud crash, and absorbed a large chunk.

Kevrin butted Jahrys across the face with his Captor.

Jahrys's head spun as he fell to the floor. His Captor went flying from his hands. He regained himself and unsheathed his sword, wiping blood from his face with his other hand. He dove forward and sliced the tube that connected Kevrin's Captor. Yellow smoke formed a cloud around Kevrin, blinding him as he coughed. Jahrys kicked the Captor from his hands.

Nadia raised her staff and wind blew around the room, clearing the smoke.

"Kevrin," she yelled out to him as she continued to raise her staff. "Take this!"

A sword began to form in midair in front of Kevrin. He grabbed it and leaped forward. His sword flew down on Jahrys. Jahrys raised his sword to meet Kevrin's. Sparks sprayed as the two blades met. The vibration from the sword handle stung Jahrys's hands. His legs wobbled beneath him as he tried to stand his ground. He was already so tired...Briefly his mind went back to their last sword fight. So long ago...

Hoarder and Retriever swung their swords back and forth, back and forth, as they danced around the throne room. They were both panting and sweating, their muscles straining, their hearts were hurting, but the two old friends, now foes, continued to fight.

Kevrin swung his sword at Jahrys's head. Jahrys ducked and dove his body into Kevrin's stomach. They both crashed to the floor.

Jahrys's calf was on fire, the cut seemed to have open. He could feel the blood oozing out, but he ignored it as he rolled on top of Kevrin, pinning his old friend down. *If she can manipulate him, I can bring him back,* he thought.

Kevrin let out a groan.

"Listen to me," Jahrys yelled. "Elyara cannot come back. She's gone. You must accept that!"

Kevrin shook his head in denial.

"She wouldn't want to see you like this!" Jahrys tried to make him see reason. "Nadia is using you for herself. Do not listen to her. There was a reason you saved me the night of the Hoarding. There was a reason you kept me hidden from her all those years. You are my—"

Kevrin head butted Jahrys and pushed him off. He was back on his feet. He lashed out at Jahrys with his sword, but Jahrys rose to one knee and blocked it.

"Kevrin—you must listen to me!" Jahrys pushed all his weight into his sword as he rose to both feet, his calf screaming in pain. "Nadia has manipulated you. This isn't who you are! You are my friend…my brother!"

Kevrin let out a yell as he released his weight, swinging his sword at Jahrys's head. Jahrys ducked and kicked Kevrin's legs out from underneath him. Kevrin flipped back to the floor.

Jahrys pointed his sword at Kevrin's throat. He heard the clicks from the Hoarders readying their Captors around him.

"Don't shoot!" Nadia yelled to her Hoarders. "We need him alive."

"You see? She doesn't care what happens to you," Jahrys said. "She only cares about herself."

"Don't listen to him!" Nadia yelled out. "We *will* bring back Elyara, I promise you."

"She isn't coming back," Jahrys said honestly. "You need to—"

CRACK.

Jahrys turned, eyes wide. The pillar that had been hit by the beam had been wobbling all this time, and was now falling upon him.

Something hard collided into Jahrys's side, taking his breath away as he was flung to the floor.

The pillar collapsed with a thunderous roar as it shook the throne room, sending a large cloud of dust and stone into the air.

Jahrys coughed. His lungs were filled with dust from the pillar and his eyes stung.

"Are you okay?" It was Kevrin who had saved him.

"Kevrin…what—"

"I cannot see another friend die." Kevrin stood up, holding out a hand, his eyes asking for forgiveness and understanding.

Jahrys hesitated, but then smiled and reached up for his friend's outstretched hand. Kevrin began to lift him to his feet.

"AH!" Kevrin screamed.

Jahrys fell backwards. Kevrin had let go of his hand. The floor came up hard against his back. Something hot flew past his face. He heard Nadia screaming from the side.

Jahrys looked up.

Kevrin was clutching a hole the size of a fist in the center of his stomach. He let out a low groan.

"Jahr…" His eyes glistened for forgiveness as his life ended. He collapsed to the floor.

Behind where Kevrin had stood, Sir Piller was on his knees, holding a steaming Captor with his right hand. He was clutching a bleeding wound at his stomach with the other.

Jahrys was too shocked for words. He could only look at the wounded knight, who smiled painfully as his hand slowly dropped the Captor, and his body collapsed to the floor.

"MY SON!" Nadia charged forward through the fading smoke, raising her staff. "YOU KILLED MY SON! I WILL—"

The oak doors suddenly slammed open down the hall. The sound of marching echoed into the throne room. Jahrys was afraid to see what was to come through that hall. Had the Hoarders defeated his army? Was he the last to stand against the sorceress?

He slowly rose to his feet and grabbed his sword while Nadia was distracted.

The throne room door slammed open and men piled into the hall. "FOR ASTENPOOLE!" They screamed.

They were led by Krist and Martellus.

The men opened fire at the army of Hoarders with their own Captors.

"No…" Nadia took a step back. "This cannot be."

The Hoarders reciprocated against the oncoming army. The throne room came to life as blasts exploded into pillars and walls, people screamed and yelled, and swords and arrows met flesh.

Nadia whipped around to face Jahrys. "You will *not* take this from me." She raised her staff straight up to the high ceiling and brought the end of it down hard onto the floor—cracking the marble. The floor around Nadia rippled like a wave. The wave sent Jahrys flying backwards, his sword leaving his hand.

Nadia pointed her staff at Jahrys and a yellow blast fired out. Jahrys rolled to the side as the blast hit the floor and exploded. Pieces of marble scattered the air, bruising his skin.

Nadia was quickly on him. She shoved the glass sphere into his chest, pinning him down. "I have waited years for this and you will not take it from me. You're the key. I'll be far more powerful than *her*. I—

"Ahhh!" Nadia screamed. The pressure lightened against Jahrys's chest. "Get off of me!"

Jahrys looked up. Nadia was swatting the air.

"What are you doing?" Her hands were protecting her face.

A crow was flapping its black wings repetitively as it dug its talons into Nadia's face.

Jahrys reached for his Captor, but his hands only gripped the air. Jahrys looked around and saw his sword lying behind him. He crawled towards it. After dodging two sporadic blasts, he gripped the hilt and rose to his feet, his injured leg aching.

He turned to face Nadia, who was still fighting off the crow. She lifted her staff into the air, swinging it dangerously around and around. She finally made contact with the crow. The crow was sent flying, hitting a pillar on top of the balcony on the floor above. The crow fell hard to the floor.

Jahrys drowned out the sound of the battle as he focused on the wounded sorceress. Her face was unrecognizable from all of the scratches and blood that covered it.

She turned to face him. "You don't understand what you're doing! You need me. Emilia will come for you! For the same reason I came for you. It will never end! But I'll be generous. I will not hurt you. We can bring back Alana. I—"

Jahrys closed the distance, raising his sword and swinging it down on Nadia. But Nadia blocked him with her staff. Jahrys swung again, this time on her left, but she was too fast. Again and again

Jahrys swung. He swung for his mother, for his father, for all of his friends who had died in the Hoarding. He swung for Alana. But Jahrys could not make contact with Nadia's flesh.

Nadia ducked under his sword and jammed the butt of her staff into Jahrys's chest.

He fell to the floor, his sword flying out of his hands again. He was panting. When he looked up, he was face-to-face with Nadia's glowing sphere; the light was growing brighter and brighter. Jahrys rolled to the side just in time as part of the marble flooring exploded next to him. He jumped up and ran for his sword, panting hard.

Nadia continued to fire at him.

Blasts rained around him. He was closing in on his sword, it was only a few feet away.

"AHHH!" he yelled as he collapsed to the floor. There was a sharp pain in his already injured leg. He looked and saw that several inches of his calf were burnt and oozing.

He didn't make it to his sword.

Nadia stood several feet away, her staff pointed at him.

Jahrys struggled to one knee as he stared deeply into the glowing sphere at the end of her staff. The yellow cloud was swirling around in the glass.

He was panting. His heart was racing faster than ever. His calf was on fire, and he could feel his world spinning from the pain of his wound.

He watched as the sphere continued to grow brighter and brighter.

"You chose unwisely, Jahrys." Nadia said, firing once again.

Jahrys raised his palms to shield his face—his last hope of survival.

He felt the force of the blast as it dove into his hands. He felt the material of the suit melt away as the heat dug deeper down his arms, into his skin.

But there was no pain.

The blast subsided, and Jahrys stood standing—unharmed.

Nadia was confused. She fired again and again.

Jahrys engulfed each blast with his palms. He felt the blasts running through the veins of his arm and flowing through the rest of his body. The warmth flooded his heart and then subsided.

The fighting had stopped. All eyes were upon them.

Nadia stared at him in awe. She fired again.

Jahrys rose to his feet and caught the blast with both of his palms. It was like sticking his hands out during a rush of wind during the stormy season. It felt like running his hands under Zalus's Tears with the water thundering into his palms. He felt the energy flowing in every muscle in his body. He felt his mind focusing in on it. There was a faint blue, glowing deep in the center of his palms. He pushed it all out—all towards Nadia.

A blue light fired out of both his palms, blinding everyone in the throne room. Jahrys was yelling. His voice echoed off the walls, powerful and strong.

The blue light encompassed Nadia. She let out a high-pitched scream as her body slowly disintegrated into nothing.

Jahrys's arms collapsed to his sides, his palms scorching. He fell to his knees. The blue light was no longer visible in his palms, and his hands were now searing in pain.

Nadia's body was gone. All that remained of her presence was her staff, and the yellow sphere that glowed at the top.

Chapter 46
Jahrys

THE FIGHTING HAD stopped. There was silence in the throne room. All eyes turned to Jahrys.

He was on his knees, his suit dented and frayed. He was wheezing, trying to gasp for breath. His hands were numb; the skin on his palms was red and burning like he had just held a hot coal. What had he just done? Nadia was dead, and he had no idea how it had happened.

"Is she dead?" a hoarse voice said behind him. It sounded like a man.

Jahrys turned to see the crow crawling towards him. The crow's beak was bent and bleeding, his stomach looked to be caved in, he was missing a few feathers, and one of his legs looked to be broken. He couldn't believe the crow just spoke to him.

"Yes..." Jahrys replied, not sure if he was going crazy answering a crow.

"Good." What seemed like a smile passed over the crow's beak. Jahrys stood over the crow. "You're Carthel? The King Beyond the Mountains? Kevrin's father?"

The crow nodded.

"I saw you the night my parents died," Jahrys said. "And the night of the Coming of Zalus, and the morning King Leoné was murdered." Jahrys felt the anger running through his body as he remembered it all. He raised his voice. "I saw you on Nadia's shoulder when I was standing helpless on that stage! Have you been watching me? Betraying me to Nadia all these years?"

"I…I'm sorry…I didn't—I was…blinded…selfish…" the crow wheezed. "Where…is…my son?"

"Kevrin is dead."

It was as if a knife went through the crow's heart, sadness filled his eyes.

"You could have saved so many lives…my parents, Alana, Kevrin…" Jahrys turned away in disgust.

"I…I'm sorry…" the crow said in disappointment. "I…didn't mean—Jahrys…"

Jahrys bent down over the crow and lifted him up. Jahrys looked into his beady, black eyes.

"There's…not much time," the crow said. "Emilia…"

"The Red Sorceress? Did she do this to you?" Jahrys asked. "Is she the one who changed you into a crow?"

The crow let out a frightening cough. "She has—a good heart. She means…well. But—she is—*dangerous*."

"Dangerous?" Jahrys's head was spinning. "More dangerous than Nadia?"

The crow nodded and then tilted his head to the side. "The staff…"

Jahrys followed the crow's gaze to the staff lying on the floor where Nadia had once stood. Jahrys walked over and picked it up with his free hand, examining it. The yellow cloud swirled inside the glass.

"Protect—" The crow's beady eyes began to fade. "Protect—"

"Protect what? What must I protect?" Jahrys asked, desperate for an answer.

"…the sphere…"

The life was slowly fading from the crow; he was gasping for air now. His eyes were lost in Jahrys's face, spinning in all directions. The crow seemed to lose sense of his surroundings.

"Please!" Jahrys yelled, knowing he was losing time. "Please, tell me what I am? What I did?"

"Jahrys…" the crow whispered.

Jahrys bent his head down to hear.

"Your father…," the crow's head began to fall. His voice was distant, "…was a good man."

"You knew my father?" Jahrys couldn't believe it. "You knew Alvys Grent?"

The crow stopped breathing.

"No…No! Please, I need to know!" Jahrys begged.

But the life had faded from Carthel.

Jahrys was left with a million questions running through his head. *What do I protect the sphere from? What kind of sorcery is in it? What kind of sorcery is inside me? Why did Father never mention Carthel?*

"We did it, Jahrys! We won!" Krist slapped Jahrys hard on the back.

"I don't know what kind of tricks you've been hiding from us, but it worked. You put on quite a show." Martellus placed a hand on Jahrys's shoulder.

Junkland

The Retrievers had forced the Hoarders to their knees with their hands behind their heads. They had taken control of the throne room and had won the battle. But it didn't feel like a victory to Jahrys. He looked at Sir Piller and Kevrin. They were both motionless on the floor. He looked at Alana lying beneath the steps.

"Take him," Jahrys handed the crow over to Krist. Krist took him without question, though uncertainty was in his eyes.

Jahrys handed the staff to Martellus. "Keep this safe."

Martellus looked at it with curious eyes as he grabbed it.

Jahrys limped across the room to Alana, ignoring the pain in his calf. He collapsed to his knees before her dead body. Even in death, she was still beautiful.

Jahrys recalled Alana's words the night they sailed underneath the stars, when she gave him her reason for which star she would travel to. *It looks like a place I could run away to and no one would ever find me.*

"I'll find you," Jahrys whispered as tears fell down his cheeks. "I *will* find you." He kissed her cold lips. He reached down to hold Alana's hand in his.

As he did, something hard fell into Jahrys's hand. It was the necklace—with the full moon shaped gem.

Epilogue

BLOOD DRIPPED FROM the wound in Partha's right leg. But still she continued, half-limping, half-crawling. There was a light in the distance; it kept her moving, knowing her baby might be safe there. She held the baby safe in her left arm, cradled close to her body. It was so dark she could barely see, but she kept moving towards the light. Her right hand guided her and supported her. Her knees were cut up and bleeding, along with her forearms. Her entire body ached.

One of the wolves had gotten too close and had torn deep into the flesh of her left leg. She had cried out, but, of course, no one had heard her. She was far away from home, so far past the mountains. Her leg wouldn't stop bleeding. Every minute she could feel herself fading away from the world around her. But she had to keep moving. She had to make sure her baby was safe.

She had found a cloth and a rope in her bag, which she had used to tie around her wounds. The whiteness of the cloth didn't last long, as the cloth turned a dark red, almost brown, shortly after. It did help with the pain, however.

'*Run. To the mountains.*' Partha recalled her husband's last words. She was well beyond the mountains now and had not reconnected

Junkland

with Ren. She only hoped he had escaped. She refused to believe he was dead.

Her staff was gone. She had dismantled the sphere from the staff and had buried it after she used the last bit of her energy to escape the wolves. She had buried it deep into the earth so no one could ever find it. There was no more energy left, and it was just another thing to carry. She needed all of her strength to carry her baby. Her brave baby boy.

Partha was wheezing. The thick air around her made it hard to breathe, and it made her head dizzy. She was fading rapidly. But she had to keep going.

Her baby began to cry.

"Shhh, my darling. Shhh. Mamma's got you. Everything will be okay. Shhh." She held him tighter.

HOWWWW. HOW, HOW, HOWOOOOO.

The wolves were still in the distance. They were tracking the trail of blood from her leg. She had tried to clean her wound in the river, but it had been no use.

HOWWWW. HOW, HOW, HOWOOOOO.

The howling grew louder. She quickened her pace as she struggled to keep going.

Her right leg collapsed and she fell hard to the ground. Her baby rolled out of her arms.

"No!" she reached out for her boy.

His crying grew louder.

"I'm coming! Hold on. I'm coming!" she couldn't tell if she was actually speaking—her mind was a fog. She dug her fingertips into the soil, pulling herself forward as she pushed with her good leg.

She was a hundred yards from the light in the distance. Her vision was blurring. She crawled. The cloth was tearing around her wound. But she didn't care. None of it mattered. She just needed to get to her boy, to get him to safety.

HOWWWW. HOW, HOW, HOWOOOOO.

Partha crawled faster. Her leg was screaming with pain. Her stomach was torn by a sharp rock, but still she kept moving—she had to. She reached for her baby, grabbing him and pulling him close to her body. She wrapped him in his blue blanket and rocked him back and forth.

"Shhh. It's okay. Everything will be okay." She broke down crying. She looked up at the light ahead. It was now fifty yards away. She had no more energy to fight the wolves. She had to make it to the light before they tore the rest of her apart.

It took the rest of her strength to lift herself up. She held her baby in her right arm as her left arm supported her weight on the ground. She kept crawling. She was now twenty-five yards away—so close. She would make it. She had to—for Ren, for their son.

HOWWWW. HOW, HOW, HOWOOOOO.

The wolves would not get to her again. Not while she was still alive. She crawled forward. She kept moving for the sacrifice Ren had made for her and their boy. She would be as brave as him. She would not let Nadia have their son.

Partha crawled to the front door of the house where the candle light was glowing, welcoming her. She reached out a trembling hand towards the wooden door.

Bang, Bang, Bang.

Her hand collapsed. She pushed her baby forward. Partha took one last heartwarming look at her baby boy, smiling at him.

As her world faded around her, she was able to say one final thing. "I love you—my son."

The door opened and a couple stood at the door, looking down at the baby boy. He was crying and wrapped in a blue blanket. The woman picked him up and cradled him into her chest. The couple then looked around the dark road, searching for the parents, but saw no one.

Note From the Author: If you enjoyed this book and look forward to the rest of Jahrys's adventure, please write a review on Amazon and Goodreads! Every review matters!

Patrick Johns is a wordsmith who grew up in Ramsey, New Jersey, where he would play for hours in his basement with his dinosaurs, and out back in the woods with his imaginary friends in imaginary worlds. He has been writing since he was young—creating worlds and drawing the made-up characters within them, but his imagination was put on hold while in college.

Patrick is a graduate from Virginia Tech (Go Hokies!), with a degree in Industrial and Systems Engineering and a second degree in Mathematics. While he is doing very well, he never forgot his imaginary friends, and always imagined bringing their world to life in a novel.

Upon graduation, Patrick's wonderful parents took him to see *Aladdin* on Broadway, one of his favorite childhood stories. And yes, it is his dream to one day soar high into a diamond sky on a magic carpet, singing a beautiful duet with someone he just met and fell madly in love with! After the play, Patrick's creativity sparked and he started writing again to make this dream come true—as well as his childhood dreams of imaginary worlds.

Junkland is his first novel, now available on Amazon. The second novel in *The Hoarding* series is underway, with the third soon to follow.

To see what Patrick Johns is up to, follow him on Instagram ([@patrickjohnswrites](#)), Facebook ([@patrickjohnswrites](#)), and Twitter ([@patjohnswrites](#)).

For more information about *The Hoarding* series, subscribe to his website (http://patrickjohnswrites.com/).

Made in the USA
Middletown, DE
05 March 2018